Getting It Right

Also by Elizabeth Jane Howard

The Beautiful Visit
The Long View
The Sea Change
After Julius
Odd Girl Out
Something in Disguise
Mr Wrong
The Light Years
Marking Time
Confusion
Casting Off

ELIZABETH JANE HOWARD

Getting It Right

WITH AN INTRODUCTION BY

Peter Vansittart

MACMILLAN

First published 1982 by Hamish Hamilton Ltd

This edition published 1996 with an
introduction by Peter Vansittart by Macmillan
an imprint of Macmillan Publishers Ltd
25 Eccleston Place, London SW1W 9NF
and Basingstoke

Associated companies throughout the world

ISBN 0 333 66452 3

1 3 5 7 9 8 6 4 2

A CIP catalogue record for this book is available from
the British Library.

Typeset by CentraCet Limited, Cambridge
Printed by Mackays of Chatham PLC, Chatham, Kent

For Ursula Vaughan Williams
with love from Jane

Getting It Right

INTRODUCTION

ELIZABETH JANE HOWARD has described herself as being in the straight tradition of English novelists. 'I simply write about other people, by themselves or in relation one to another. The first aim of a novel should be readability.'

True, she does not offer the tractarian, the gothick, the prophetic, the mythic; not faction, or the experimental preliminaries of a screen script set in concrete verse, or computerized documentation of a junkie paradise, for an audience dedicated, even fanatical, but scanty. She writes novels, of personal conflict, scheming, dismay, resolution against odds. Social issues are implicit, but subtly realized through discussion, reflection, group-codes. They are never flourished like war cries or lecture headings masquerading as imagination: they are a reminder of Rebecca West remarking that there is very little in Shakespeare which can be used as propaganda for adult suffrage.

'Straight tradition' may suggest stodginess, at best pellucid imitation of classical models. Here, it is very misleading. Original perceptions and inventive narrative transcend form. This author can transform the familiar – a dinner, a walk in a park, a garden vista – into the strange, the enticing, the extraordinary. Simultaneously, she conveys the desirability of life, by demonstrating that appearances, however ominous, may deceive, little can be taken for granted. Life is no disease or trauma to be partly cured by worldly success, romantic coincidence, perfect love or a word in the right quarter. It is a gift not to be squandered or lost: both sexes must work at it, with imagination and intelligence, as they grapple with each other or with themselves; they must keep at concert pitch, in friendship, love, marriage, and the apparently normal.

Humour helps. Elizabeth Jane Howard's is not rollicking; the false nose and battered hat are not among her props. Like E. M. Forster she relishes the sly, the oblique, the deft exchanges of minds civilized if not always genteel. She can use satire, shrewdly, but not to hate or pettily despise and is quick to spot sudden incongruities. In this novel, she casually mentions a retired, one-legged prostitute residing in a Home 'with what she described as a not very nice class of person', and observes 'various salads fainting gaily in their bowls'.

Her career began with the considerable advantage of omitting school, thus saving her from her convictions and standardized thought, reinforcing some ingrained independence. She has been model, actress, secretary, dramatist, worked for the BBC, tirelessly served authors on platform and committee, has travelled widely, married distinguished but difficult men, been a mother and step-mother; splendid qualifications for writing humane novels. Her independence does not falter; she will never be fooled by some Post-Literature claque into accepting the impossibility of making value judgements between *King Lear* and *The Song the Old Cow Died Of.* An authority on cooking and gardening, she knows how things work. Theatrical experiences may have helped her ease with scenic effects, time-changes, dialogue, small clues to an eventual climax, the depiction of both the private and public self in a single incident.

Her gaze is cool, sympathetic yet gently tempered by irony. None knows better the traps threatening freedom or happiness, however well fortified the home, thickly padded the conscience, heavily stocked the bank balance. Most people are vulnerble to guilt, self-doubts, nagging suspicions, sometimes torment. Fine manners, witty rejoinders, stylish routines barely disguise the brute struggle to survive, if possible with dignity. Irresponsibility, wilful blindness, invite retribution. Always, freedom is important. Sybille Bedford, a leading contemporary writer, praising Elizabeth Jane Howard's 'complex and original talent', mentions the theme of choice, of limited free will, inherent in any novel of stature. Throughout her work, Howard allows her characters the dignity of choice; none are ciphers, digits, pretentious symbols fulfilling some lifeless pattern. Fate may exist but it is more useful, more entertaining to behave as if it does not.

In *Getting it Right*, Gavin Lamb does at first seem to exemplify our northern ancestors' apprehension of *wyrd*, inexorable Destiny. He is a London hairdresser, skilled but scarcely fashionable, at thirty-one still a virgin, living with his suburban parents, perhaps fated to wither on the bough or be fatally pecked. He is spotty, dandruffy, and perforce diplomatic, at times obsequious. He is also decent, doggedly fair-minded, reticent. Virtually self-educated, he listens to Mozart, Brahms, Richard Strauss, discriminates between Curzon, Gieseking, Serkin; he reads Anthony Powell, Aldous Huxley, can quote Tolstoy; a client's stutter reminds him of Demosthenes, George VI, Somerset Maugham. Yet he has only one real friend, feels himself 'not up to real life', is complete only in dreams and day-dreams where he is free to utter real thoughts, behave as he wishes, not as others command. An art catalogue, or a mere closing of eyes, can provide impossible girls against vivid southern décors but, awaking, he finds movement in any direction actually perilous. He has sex on the brain yet hopelessly confines it to the head, and his friend recommends him to find a boy and leave home. Familiar with a Berthe Morisot or Vuillard painting, he shrinks from real people outside his professional range, particularly those who 'are up to it', and must content himself with acute though suppressed observation, noting a face under the dryer 'suffused to the matt apoplectic bloom of unpeeled beetroot'. He resembles an early

H. G. Wells young hopeful, though his creator has sustained a belief in the Novel as a self-sufficient art-form, which Wells did not. Wells wanted to change the world by lecturing it; Howard knows that the novelist and poet are already changing the world by giving new coatings, new imageries, to make the familiar altogether unfamiliar, and revealing the hitherto unperceived.

Gavin realizes that drifting can be as dangerous as lingering. He needs some shock, some catalyst, to propel him into 'getting it right' with those who really are up to it. Unwillingly, he goes to an expensive party. Elizabeth Jane Howard is finely tuned to parties, their nuances, brief encounters, chasms, blocked escape routes, ambiguous promises, the undercurrents, pockets of boredom, hope, menace. Arriving, Gavin is immediately closeted with his hostess, Joan, wealthy, fifteen stone, in an orange wig, who at once starts a truth game, and he unexpectedly finds himself talking freely to a stranger.

He finished his drink. Then, with a final effort, he said, 'I invent girls who are in love with me. Girls who'll do anything I want. You're the kind of person that, in a different way, I'm afraid I am.'

(She said:) 'I'm grotesque. I underline it, so that everybody else will know that I know I'm grotesque. I make the most of a bad job. I love men – particularly beautiful men – and I'm sorry for myself. When I saw you, I wondered what you'd cost.'

There was a silence between them during which Gavin became conscious of his total absence of fear. He could look at the figure before him – at the orange hair and orange mouth painted on to a dead white face, the plate-glass diamanté spectacles, the corseted bulk of the silver lamé – simply as part of the pieces of declared truth about her which neither of them felt the need to judge or disclaim. It was as though she had made herself transparent; as though what ordinarily constituted the brick walls of personality had become like glass – or even clear water. Had he become like that for her? Had she accepted those fragments of truth about him, and if she had, what might happen next? Some of his exhilaration ebbed and he felt a familiar spasm of fear.

Very soon, in stark contrast, he meets Minerva, waifish, unstable, clinging, and surely a liar. If his relation with Joan resembles an operatic duet, that with Minerva seems a duel, at first clumsy and tentative, then points are scored, feints accomplished, a swipe dodged. A direct hit might settle everything. There emerges, however, a third girl, hitherto barely noticed though continually present and unobstrusively waiting. To disclose more would spoil things. Suffice that rosebuds are swiftly gathered, a tree of knowledge is partially ransacked, and Gavin realizes that set-backs can be transformed to assets, that glittering prizes can tomahawk the receipients, and that chance can be as fruitful as design. Joan's party presents him with a maze, with intricate twists and illusions, perhaps leading to a challenging centre, or perhaps only to an escape-hatch no longer wholly desired.

There ensue comedy, pathos, suspense. A visit to Weybridge, visiting self-made rich at their nastiest, introduces Sir Gordon, who 'held out his hand with a gesture just short of warding him off that turned into a handshake', and whose face drains from plum 'to the mauve, twilit dusk of far-off hills'. Gavin's mother is a memorably comic compression of aggrieved self-contradictions and scathing non-sequiturs, the perpetual small explosions 'of an excitable person who was short of excitement'.

Mum kept the rest of the house so nice that it was in a perpetual state of suspended animation – there was no sign that anyone ever read, sewed, talked, left things about, or even dropped or broke them – whatever they did, she cleared it up almost before they had finished doing it. Even meals were cleared off the table the moment their mouths – or possibly only plates – were empty. The garden was rather like that as well. It was so tidy and symmetrical that putting even one deck chair in it made it look lop-sided. Largely on the strength of these things, Mrs Lamb had the reputation for being a wonderful wife and mother.

Getting it Right is an excellent story, yet some very good stories have made very bad books. The matter of style is crucial, the author's individual slant on life, thus on language. Vision, though this word is too often followed by the pompous or vague. Yet vision, style, ensures the survival of such writers as dissimilar as Henry Green, L. H. Myers, Patrick Hamilton, and extinguishes a long gallery of best-sellers ennobled by Hollywood, gossip columnists, and indeed the Crown. Some styles are so instantly recognizable that to name the author is unnecessary –

The woman's a whore, and there's an end on't.

With the single exception of Homer, there is no eminent writer, not even Sir Walter Scott, whom I can despise so entirely as I despise Shakespeare when I measure my mind against his.

The station master's whiskers are of a Victorian bushiness and give the impression of having been grown under glass.

Evelyn Waugh is unlikely to be mistaken for Charles Lamb, Virginia Woolf for Pepys. Several facets of Graham Greene entwine in a single sentence:

A man like Titus Oates occurs like a slip of the tongue, discharging the unconscious, the night-side of an age we might otherwise have thought of in terms of Dryden discussing the art of dramatic poesy, while his Thames boatmen rested on their oars and the thunder of an indeterminate sea-battle came up from the Medway no louder than the noise of swallows in a chimney.

Elizabeth Jane Howard has assured literary personality, a style not declamatory or grandiose, but fresh, flowing – one cannot strain for originality – and very visual. She presents notable set-pieces but it is often the small observation slipped in almost as an aside that can illuminate the page:

> Her mouth, as moist and pink as an uncooked chipolata, curled into its miniature smile.

> She must have looked extraordinary when pregnant – like a young tree with one enormous pear.

> Her profile was almost beautiful if her skin hadn't been so stretched over her bones, like silk on a model aeroplane.

Inexperienced writers give us too much explanation, too many details, not trusting their readers' imagination, so that the work sags. *Getting it Right* is brisk in pace and leaves fruitful gaps, because its author well knows that, however substantial the evidence, answers are seldom final, that truth, like love, is usually provisional, neat verdicts can be unreal. Some areas of life will, and should, remain mysterious. Mystery, of course, is one thing, jargon and obscurity quite another; the former quickens the imagination, the latter suffocates it. A re-reading of this novel will prove what a heap of pleasure remains long after the outcome is known. Indeed, for some readers the deepening, more leisurely pleasures, will then actually begin, the co-ordination of craft, characterization and language.

Peter Vansittart

CHAPTER ONE

'**M**R GAVIN! Mrs Whittington's ready to come out.'

He glanced across the salon to the table at which a large middle-aged woman sat, under a hair-dryer, her face suffused to the matt apoplectic bloom of unpeeled beetroot.

'Take her out then, Mandy, and get her ready for me. Tell her I'll be over in two ticks.'

He was combing out Lady Blackwater, who had remarkably little hair the colour, but not the consistency, of steel wool. A blue rinse idealized this effect, and having brushed the sparse, curly tufts he was now engaged upon a good deal of ingenious backcombing to give the illusion of body. Lady Blackwater's eyes – round, pink-rimmed, and the shade of well-used washing-up water, watched him trustfully. Gavin was most reliable. Now he was folding the surface hair over the puffed sub-strata – merging the tufts into three, main diagonal sweeps; Lady Blackwater evolved from looking like a very old negro child, to someone amusingly surprised in bed in an eighteenth-century print, and then – and this was what Lady Blackwater paid for – to some distinguished old dyke – a Fellow of the Royal Society – famous for some esoteric service to the Arts or Sciences.

He stepped back from his work, and handed her a looking glass.

She looked at herself carefully. The sculptured effect emphasized the fleshy folds and cracks between what had always been the anonymous features of her face.

'Very nice, Gavin.'

1

'A little spray?'

She shook her head, nearly blushing. Spray seemed wickedly theatrical to her.

A receptionist came into the salon.

'Gavin, would you be able to see Mrs Buckmaster about her daughter?'

He put his comb back in his pocket and glanced again at Mrs Whittington. She was not reading her magazine, and was patently awaiting him. He observed that Mandy had simply removed the dryer, but had done nothing about the rollers.

'Mandy!'

Mandy trailed over to him. She walked as though her feet hurt.

'I told you to get Mrs Whittington ready. Take the curlers out and put everything back on the tray.'

'She's outside at reception now. Shall I tell her you can spare a moment?'

'Right. Perhaps you would take Lady Blackwater through for me.'

As he turned to say good-bye to her, Lady Blackwater clutched his jacket and made a futile attempt to slip some coins into the lower pocket. A 5 and a 2p coin rolled across the black and white checkered linoleum. The mean old bitch exposed for once, he thought, as he retrieved the money, thanked her, and popped over to Mrs Whittington to tell her how soon he would be with her. Mrs Whittington was not pleased. 'I haven't got all the afternoon, Gavin,' she untruthfully announced. Mandy was listlessly removing rollers, and the client's hair was emerging as sausages the colour of custard.

'Back in two ticks, Mrs Whittington,' he said and hurried through to reception. On his way there, he nearly ran into Mrs Courcel, an immaculately turned out young woman for whom hairdressing was an obsession.

'Here I am for my usual,' she said as though presenting him with an especial treat.

'May have to wait a few moments,' he replied. Mrs Courcel came in nearly every day, and apart from tints, cutting, washing and setting and the purchase of innumerable pieces; a comb-out, her most frequent requirement, meant a long discussion on how her hair could be restyled. She was childless and bored, but his sympathy for her had long ago evaporated; she had nothing to do all day, and he could not help envying her those hours during which she did not have to earn her living and which he could so easily and interestingly have filled.

Mrs Buckmaster, a tweedy and commanding lady, rose from the white leather chesterfield.

'Ah – Gavin. I thought, before I made an appointment for her, that you might give us a teeny bit of advice. Cynthia!'

By the time he got back to Mrs Whittington, he found her testily examining *Vogue*.

'I ask you, Gavin! Can you seriously imagine anybody going out like that?' She held out the magazine, so that he could see the picture of a young girl wearing what seemed to be lilac sequinned culottes with wide sequinned braces that miraculously covered her nipples. The girl's strawberry blonde hair was blowing, and she stood poised by a Palladian bridge in some great park.

'Incredible, isn't it? What gal could ever go about seriously looking like that?'

He smiled pleasantly as he began brushing the custard sausages.

'I really don't know, Mrs Whittington.' He was wondering whether the bridge was from Stowe, or Stourhead, or Wilton or Blenheim.

'I mean, if one faces up to it, it's disgusting. It simply isn't on. If I had ever suggested to my daughter that she should go about in that state she'd have laughed her head off.'

Gavin had seen Mrs Whittington's daughter. Her appearance had struck him forcibly as that of a heavy-weight policeman in County drag. He had felt quite frightened at tackling her hair, which was dark, and painfully springy, like heather.

'It takes all sorts,' he suggested dutifully. Mrs Whittington did not care for unpredictable conversation.

'It must do.' He had brushed all her curls together, so that her hair looked like Instant Whip. 'Oh, well.' She gave a huge liberal sigh, discarded the magazine and told him a good deal about what she thought of the law on abortion.

After Mrs Whittington, there was just time to settle Mrs Courcel's discontent with her appearance for the day before he started a big restyling job upon a retired opera singer who wanted her long hair cut off and permed. Mrs Courcel had lost him his lunch.

Although it was in the middle of London, the establishment that Gavin worked for was not fashionable. It was no scene for the young: there was no music: glamorous personalities – such as models, pop stars or other people whose pictures regularly appeared in the press and on the screen – did not frequent it; its clientele were middle-aged to old. It combined experienced and highly professional service with more individual attention than was commonly to be found in the newer places, and therefore its patrons tended to stay; its staff to remain. The chief problem was getting juniors, as fewer and fewer girls (or men) were prepared to face the gruelling three years' apprenticeship – with one day off for the college every week – where they were expected to do only what they were told from nine to six; sweeping up, washing hair, handing rollers and pins for setting until their feet killed them for wages that were less than they could earn almost anywhere else. Already, Gavin and the other three hairdressers he worked with were having to do some of the shampooing and clearing up, and as the appointments they were responsible for did not diminish, they were all a good deal more tired at the end of the day.

Gavin, far the youngest, did not mind any of this; he had always been a hard worker and it suited him to work with and for people older than himself. The thought of a salon filled with the young and beautiful would have terrified him. He was thirty-one – had been in hairdressing for fourteen years now, and experience and expertise had slowly alleviated some of his agonizing shyness – in the salon, at least. Outside it, he reverted to square two – that is to say he had learned to conceal most of his terror – although he still knew nothing about how to get rid of it.

He had worked out a kind of Ladder of Fear that began with meeting people he already knew, and thence, step by step, having to talk to them, having to talk to *one* of them, meeting someone he *did not* know, and having to talk to *them* – until it ascended the astral plane of meeting a beautiful girl *alone* and having to talk to *her* . . . The Ladder of Fear only catalogued the problems and arranged them in order of strength from a mild breath of discomfort to the gale force of panic; it did not help in the least with their dissolution.

None the less, the years in the salon (where he had stayed on after his apprenticeship) had certainly improved his public persona: he did not any longer find it in the least difficult to talk to and advise women about their hair, or to listen to them about almost anything else. He found, indeed, that his middle-aged or aged clients made an interesting change from his parents, who, father and mother respectively, were dedicated to making money and keeping things nice.

In the train by six-twenty, he reviewed his evening. Home by five past seven, go and tell Mum he was back – of course she heard the gate and the front door but didn't count that as being told – up to wash and back down for the meal, a cup of coffee and a Wilhelm II and then . . . He might watch the programme on China, or play his new Strauss recording, or finish the latest Anthony Powell. And then – to bed.

When he got a seat on the train, he found he was opposite a young girl who was laughing and talking a lot to an older, plainer friend. She had short, curly, auburn hair, a creamy skin

– freckles, though – and pale, gentian-coloured eyes. She was
making her friend laugh a lot, and he wished he could hear
what she was saying, or enough of it to find out whether she
was really funny, or whether it was just girls being silly. Quite
soon he noticed that other people in the train were looking at
her too, in fact, all the men coming in and getting out of the
carriage looked at her, and some of them stared. She was really
– well, he would call her arresting to look at; not beautiful, but
then he had very high standards of beauty: he was not a person
who was easily pleased, in fact, where that was concerned, he
knew what was what. She had small, wide-apart breasts well
defined in her white orlon sweater. As she was sitting down, he
was unable to pass a serious judgement upon the rest of her
until he got to her ankles, and they were far from perfect. Her
friend was pathetic. He felt a twinge of pity for her, but there
it was. Beauty, the faintest shade of it, had utterly passed her
by.

His home was a good twenty minutes' walk from the
station: on wet days he waited for the bus, but he walked
whenever possible because one doctor had told him that fresh
air was just as important as diet if one was prone to skin
problems. He nearly always had a spot – no pun intended – of
trouble in the spring; lots of people had, though; it was
something to do with getting rid of the impurities of winter. It
was a lovely evening; for some reason this particular kind of
late spring light always made him think of the Suffolk coast:
mysterious and bland; a painter's light – Mary Potter came to
mind. He wondered whether the Dutch coast was the same:
whether it was simply the North Sea – a great deal of it – that
informed those skies but the only time he had been to Holland
he had been to the museums at Amsterdam and The Hague,
except when he had walked about parts of them later to look
at tarts sitting in the windows waiting for customers. A
thoroughly civilized arrangement he had thought at the time,
but, inevitably, the girls had turned out to be disappointing.

Still – a good idea, and he had enjoyed looking at them, even if they hadn't come up to scratch.

At home, the gate was sticking again, a lovely waft of the white lilac, and then, the moment he had the key in the door and before it was properly open he smelled (oh dear) curry. One of the things Mum hadn't got the hang of was curry. When he bent to kiss her he noticed that his dandruff was on the march again. He had never met – he had never even *heard* of anyone who was subject to such virulent and persistent attacks of this tiresome complaint, and if anyone ought to be able to deal with the problem it should be he. Nothing seemed to avail for long, and he had stopped wearing dark suits years ago. A good thing he was the sort of person who noticed this kind of thing about himself, because if *he* didn't, who would ever tell him? He patted Mum's shoulder, thereby dismissing as much of the dandruff as was tactful. His father was watching some violent, deafening film on telly.

The house was square, double-fronted and built by Gavin's uncle in 1937. Uncle Keith had been considerably older than Dad, had worked for a local builder all his life until he won three thousand pounds on the Grand National, whereupon he had started his own business – with Dad and a couple of men, bought himself a third-of-an-acre plot in a lane off the main road in New Barnet and constructed his own home upon it. He had had a profound and informed contempt for architects and, as he was not much of a draughtsman, the house was a simple rectangle – in shape much what might have been drawn by a child. But he had had, had *always* had, an eye for detail, and on this, his own home, he spared no detail that sprang to his mind. The surface textures of the house embodied every technique he could employ: three kinds of brick; tiles, pebble-dash, roughcast and timber beams; the front door had a porch with both rustic wood and stained glass of wine gum hues; there were casement and sash windows and even a pair with diamond leaded panes; the chimney stack had Tudor associations and, too tall for the size of the house, looked as though he had found it somewhere and not wanted to waste it.

Gavin's room was unlike any of the others in the house. This was partly because it was the two attics in the roof turned into one; partly because he had – naturally – been able to do what he liked with it. The roof sloped so that he could not stand upright at the sides of the room, but this no longer troubled him. He had painted the walls and woodwork white, and bought a second-hand carpet with flowers on it that entirely covered the floor. Books and gramophone records covered both end walls. He had built out wide window shelves for each of the four dormer windows on which he kept his cacti and ferns and one miniature Japanese elm. A screen concealed the wash basin: he had pasted it with postcard reproductions of pictures he had particularly liked, and sometimes buildings cut out of old *Country Life*s from the salon. His bed was covered with a rather tattered old Persian silk rug that he had come upon years ago in a junk shop. His – so far small – collection of Baxter prints, his shells (juvenilia, this, he sometimes thought, but, when it came to the point, he couldn't bear to part with them) were arranged on two shelves over the bed. There was a small kitchen table for answering his correspondence. He had put hardboard over the fudge-coloured tiles round the fireplace and his antique mirror – gold, with two doves and a wreath of roses roving round them – over it. He had bought an old chaise-longue at the same shop as the one where he had first seen the mirror – from the top of a bus. It had been very well upholstered in red velvet that had faded with age and the sun: only the bits behind the faded buttons showed you the original, royal colour. But he had not wanted to change it, which had driven his mother into a frenzy about germs and worse. She sprayed it angrily with fly-killer and had been known to dab at it with almost neat Jeyes fluid till he'd stopped her. She thought second-hand things equated with being poor and there was no shifting her, so he had simply said that he was funny that way, and that had turned out to be immediately acceptable. The room was certainly Gavin's rather than his parents'. Mum kept the rest of the house so nice that it was in a perpetual state of suspended animation – there was no sign that anyone ever read, sewed, talked, left things about, or even dropped or broke them – whatever they did, she cleared it up almost before they had finished doing it. Even meals were cleared off the table the moment their mouths – or possibly only plates – were empty. The garden was rather like that as well. It was so tidy and symmetrical that putting even one deck chair in it made it look lop-sided. Largely on the strength of these things, Mrs Lamb had the reputation for being a wonderful wife and mother.

When he had washed, he came downstairs to find that his mother had propped his post against his glass on the table. There was a card from the library saying that the book he had asked for was now in and also a travel brochure about Greece – the country he was planning to go to on his next holiday: a good post.

Supper was eaten in silence. Mrs Lamb did not realize the heat of the curry because she did not eat it. She hardly ever ate at meal times, and was not given to tasting the food she cooked. This meant that whenever she strayed from the family recipes learned from her own mother, her food became an anxious business for her consumers. She was particularly fond of trying out new recipes for 'foreign food' and various curries were a recurring hazard. But she also had the unshakeable notion that all printed recipes were mean: if it said 'one teaspoonful of chili powder and two of plum jam' she carefully measured these amounts and then chucked in a whole lot more for good measure. The results were extreme; scalding, dizzily sweet, briney beyond belief. Sometimes the skin was removed from the roofs of their mouths before they were blown off – sometimes not. Mr Lamb and his son dutifully ate as much as they could of whatever was put before them and kept their criticism to an heroic minimum ever since the dreadful evening some years back when Mrs Lamb, looking more like a nervy little witch than usual, had served them their first curry, asked what they thought of it, and on being mildly told that it had seemed a bit hot, had burst into wracking sobs and a tirade that beginning with their ingratitude had extended to the futility of her whole life. It had taken hours to calm her, and even then she had not been really appeased and they had been treated to tinned food served with sardonic sniffs and nasty remarks made to Providence for nearly a week. Afterwards, Gavin had realized that it had been the anniversary of Caesar being put down. As she refused to have another dog, Gavin and his father made a note of the anniversary, and were always especially bright and obliging on it, but they had also divined that criticism, however tentative, was not something that Mrs Lamb wished to experience. So, this evening they chewed their way through shredded strands of beef in coconut syrup and sultanas while Mrs Lamb sat, a little apart, crocheting a playsuit for a teddy bear; her small speedy hands in no way impairing her watchfulness: the teddy bear, clad in tangerine nylon fur, lolled beside her.

'Very nice,' Mr Lamb said at last. He drank the last of the water on the table and met Gavin's eye without expression.

'You haven't finished the coconut,' she said, without apparently taking her eyes from her crochet.

'You gave us so much, Mum.' Gavin got up to move the plates.

'You could finish it up on your pears,' she continued inexorably. 'They're waiting for you outside.'

They were indeed. Fruit out of a tin did not count as tinned food for some mysterious reason that had never been uncovered. There was a whole lot of nonsense in tins – and then fruit. The pears were in sundae glasses lying on what looked like raspberry jam and topped with custard. The kitchen was spotless. Salt evenings could be worse. He had a quick drink of water and switched on the kettle. In a minute or two, she would come out and make tea for herself and Dad and coffee for him.

'Don't you forget about the Castle puddings,' he told her as he returned with the pears.

'I won't.' She did not mind being admonished to make things they liked.

'Pears are good for your complexion,' she added, an unexpected number of minutes later. 'There's strychnine in pears.'

He knew that with peeled, let alone tinned pears this was most unlikely, but the occasional – and surprising – pieces of misinformation were yet another spice in his mother's life and he was very fond of her. It was Marge who argued with their mother; they could keep the same argument going for days – for weeks now that Marge was married and they met only at weekends, when she brought the kids over for Sunday dinner. They did not have rows, exactly, but neither of them gave an inch.

Mr Lamb was hurrying with his pears because he wanted his tea, and then his pipe so that he could get back to television before the programmes got too highbrow. A quiet man, he none the less enormously enjoyed violence in his viewing: sex, he often said, he had never cared for – his morality entailed knowing a great many things that were not right – but the sight of somebody being machine-gunned to pieces or battered to death afforded him genuine entertainment. He even enjoyed the news occasionally for this reason.

Mrs Lamb would sit with him whatever he watched, but she would not watch herself. This was not because she did not like television; she watched it in the afternoon when Fred was out building or repairing people's houses. It was simply that she disapproved of women doing anything *with* men: women – particularly wives – were meant simply to *be* there while their husbands spent their leisure hours as they pleased. Now, observing that they had finished their pears, she laid the playsuit carefully beside the bear, seized their sundae glasses and nipped into the kitchen. Gavin met his father's eye again: they had little in common, but in particular they shared a benign conspiracy geared solely to not upsetting Mrs Lamb.

'Yes, well – a nice cup of tea won't do any harm,' Mr Lamb said in a voice designed for his wife to hear.

Outside, an ice cream van jingled its Greensleeves way down the road and Gavin wondered fleetingly whether this was tremendously unfair to Vaughan Williams, or whether he would have regarded it – ruefully – as some kind of accolade – vox populi to the chime. This made him feel lonely: a spring evening with some hours in it that he could spend as he pleased. If he stayed downstairs, he would get 'The Streets of San Francisco': if he went up, he could be alone with Brahms and he did not quite want either of these alternatives. But, when he started to think of what he might want, he felt merely spasms of fear and a kind of despair – an almost irritable anxiety: there must be more to life, and could he stand it if there was?

The telephone rang and he leapt to answer it. 'I'll go, Dad.' It might be his friend.

It wasn't: it was a customer of Dad's, having trouble with a skylight. Mum had brought in their drinks and was now quivering with anxiety to see them drink them. To make up for the exasperating possibility that Dad's tea would be cold before he came off the telephone, Gavin scalded his already fiery tongue on his Nescaff. Appeased, Mrs Lamb handed him the *Daily Mirror*.

'No thanks, Mum.' He'd read the *Telegraph* on his way to work.

'You ought to *look* at the paper.'

'I've read one already. Anyway – *you* never do.'

She seized the playsuit. 'I've got better things to do with my time.' She never read any papers on the twofold grounds that she didn't believe a word they said and that they never had anything in them.

Mr Lamb returned from the telephone. 'There's no money in skylights,' he said.

'They make a nice light, though,' Gavin said.

'If they can't make do with windows, they can fall back on electricity,' said Mrs Lamb. She was watching to see whether her husband wasn't enjoying his tea because he had let it get cold. Mr Lamb was up to this, however; he signalled his enjoyment by wincing appreciatively at the first sip, drinking the rest in fairly noisy gulps and mopping his moustache with an old Army handkerchief – faded khaki – out of which fell a little clutch of washers.

'I wondered where they'd got to.'

'You'll wear your handkerchiefs out keeping things like that in them.'

'I said to Sid last night, "You got them washers?" "No," he said, "I 'aven't got 'em, *you* had 'em." "I 'aven't got 'em," I said and 'ere they were all the time!'

'Wearing everything to a thread like that, nasty sharp things' – she was cramming the bear's indifferently hinged limbs into the playsuit, twisting him this way and that: it looked quite painful, but Gavin noticed that his expression of wilful unreliability remained unchanged.

'Nothing sharp about a washer, dear, unless it's worn. Nothing sharp about a *new* washer.' He had finished filling his pipe and leaned back to pat for his matchbox in his jacket. 'These are new washers,' he explained reassuringly.

She darted to her feet to seize his tea cup. 'Tobacco all over the table!'

She was always one jump ahead, Gavin thought; no sooner had they laid one anxiety at rest than she pounced upon another and they lumbered after her shovelling sand into all the ground she cut beneath their feet: she called it 'Where would you be without me?' and he called it 'Understanding women'. It gave them both a sense of domestic strategy, Gavin thought, but it hadn't, exactly, anything to do with *him*. He decided to ring his friend, Harry King.

'Harry – '

'Oh, hullo!' There was a faint, but unmistakable crash of breaking china. 'Shut *up*, you silly quean, it's Gavin. We were just finishing dinner. Why don't you pop round for a cup of coffee?'

'Thanks: I'd like to.'

'I warn you, there's a certain amount of tension in the air.'

Another crash – it sounded like glass this time.

'Are you sure you'd like me to come?'

'*I'd* like you to come, dear boy.'

'Hadn't you better ask Winthrop?'

'No.'

'All right.'

'Come on your scooter, or you'll be all night.'

Harry lived in an extremely small block of flats in Whetstone. It was built of concrete which looked as though it had been severely pecked by giant birds; whether this was in preparation for some more indulgent facing or whether the concrete being some three years old had failed to stand up to the exigencies of the British climate, Gavin did not know: he *did* care, since he thought Harry – and even Winthrop – merited a lovelier home, but he had not liked to ask. There were only six flats in the block: each containing a living room, a bedroom, bathroom and kitchen. The living rooms sported balconies, large enough, as Harry had once said, to accommodate one deck chair or a medium-sized dog, or, alternatively, a dog in or on the deck chair – the space involved was described by him as fanciful. The building was rather surprisingly called Havergal Heights (years ago they had wondered whether it could possibly have been named after Havergal Brian: Gavin, who had just at that time finished reading *Ordeal by Music*, had said he hoped not, or if it was so, he hoped the poor old composer didn't know, and Harry said he thought it was perfectly in keeping with the rest of H. Brian's life). Winthrop had said who the fucking hell was Havergal Brown and then, when Harry started to tell him, said that Harry was patronizing. This evening sounded like another of those, Gavin thought as he immobilized his scooter on the concrete crazy paving and rang the bell marked F. King – highly unsuitable, as Harry always pointed out to newcomers.

'That you?'

'Yes.'

The buzzer went: Gavin leaned on the door but it remained shut.

'I don't think it's working.'

Nothing happened for a bit. Gavin thought what a good thing he knew Harry so well: it meant that, if nothing went on happening, he could ring the bell again without feeling bad about it, and also he could wait to see if something *would* happen without his mouth getting dry. But this thought, like so many of the few he indulged in that were of even a faintly consoling nature, only went to show him how many other people he would find it impossible to visit because of hazards of this kind. Listening, he could hear a quarrel, a spin dryer, Radio Four and a gun-fight on telly: the soundproofing in the flats was poor, to put it mildly.

The door opened suddenly and there was Harry. He was wearing his tartan sleeveless pullover and his shirt sleeves were rolled up.

'The bloody thing's always going wrong. When they mend it, it only lasts five minutes. How are you, dear boy?'

'Fine.'

As he followed Harry up the concrete stairs Harry said:

'Winthrop's having a bit of a moody. If I've told him once, I've told him a hundred times he must not use the Wok without oiling it. Pay no attention to him – he's just a child.'

The flat was one of the top ones. The sitting room – not

15

large – was furnished rather as Gavin imagined a small V.I.P. lounge at an airport would be. A large black leather chester-field, black glass-topped table, a huge – almost menacingly healthy – houseplant; two walls of black coffee; two of coffee with milk in it. The floor was covered by a surprisingly white, rather furry carpet (people were encouraged to take their shoes off before they came through the door). The only things that one couldn't expect to find in a bona fide V.I.P. lounge were the hi-fi equipment and the books. There was a hatch through to the kitchen.

'I was just finishing the washing-up to save any more disasters. Like some coffee?'

'I would.'

'French or Turkish?'

'Turkish – if it's not too much trouble.'

'No trouble at all. It's a bit late to be drinking it, but we all have our little vices.'

Gavin watched as Harry measured coffee beans and poured them smoothly into the electric grinder.

'Has Winthrop gone out?'

'No. He may have *passed* out. But he hasn't gone anywhere so far as I know. Unless he's jumped clean off the balcony, which, so far as I'm concerned, he's very welcome to do.'

Harry had a trick, with which Gavin was familiar, of lowering the volume of his voice with dramatic suddenness towards the end of a sentence, while using his mouth to enunciate the final syllables with the sort of care that he might have employed if he was teaching someone to lipread. This was something that Gavin had *noticed* many times, but now he realized that it was connected in some way to what Harry was feeling: his eyes were uneasily bright. He switched on the grinder and, in the few seconds that it took to chew and roar its way through the beans, little shreds of Harry played back relentlessly in Gavin's mind: like clips from a film: Harry describing the end of *The Ring*. Harry talking about his first evening in Venice: Harry telling him about picking up Winthrop . . .

'I wouldn't mind his tantrums, I wouldn't mind – well, to be scrupulously fair, I *do mind* – but I could put up with the fact that he is congenitally incapable of sticking to any arrangement. I've *always* known he's bone idle – he's always been quite honest about *that*. It has a certain charm and it makes you understand why he *can't* have any sense of time – '

'Look out!' The rich brown froth was starting to mushroom over the top of the pot. Harry whipped it off and lowered the gas.

'It's the *lies* he tells – '

'Lies?'

'You ask him if he's done something and of course he says, "Yes." It bears no relation to the truth whatsoever – ' without warning, he darted out of the kitchen.

'Shall I put the coffee back?'

'If you keep an eye on it. It should come just up to the boil twice more. Don't let it actually *boil*, though.'

'I put them out on the balcony: I was afraid they'd infect everything else. Look at them.' He dumped two flower pots on the draining board. One contained a stephanotis, Gavin observed, and one a fern. Both plants looked decidedly sick. The stephanotis was glistening with sticky drops – many leaves were discoloured, and one fell even as he watched. 'Looks like scale,' he said, and just caught the coffee in time.

'That's what it is: the fern's got it too. Caught it – it's wildly infectious.'

'Yes, I know.' Gavin put the coffee back on the gas determined to watch it whatever Harry said or did.

'He knows that perfectly well. If I've told him once, I've told him a hundred times. I've said, "*Don't* just buy any old plant off a stall, and if you do, *quarantine* it for a couple of weeks." Does his Lordship take a blind bit of notice?'

'You can try sponging the leaves with a weak solution of

paraffin and water. But I've never got rid of scale myself. I think the coffee's ready.'

'I'll make *him* do it. He loathes paraffin: serve him right.'

Harry had the wrong face for looking vindictive: with his small, nervous eyes, his long nose quivering, his narrow mouth braced with resentment, he only succeeded in looking like an anxious rat. Gavin who had owned a white one when he was considerably younger felt a surge of affectionate nostalgia.

'If you've got some rubber gloves handy, I'll have a go. Can't get paraffin on my hands, the clients wouldn't like it.'

'Me neither. No – let's play some Tchaik.' But, as if on cue, a blast of what sounded like four cowboys in a frenzy of self-pity burst upon them.

'My God! Watch the coffee.' Harry almost ran out of the kitchen, his spikey hair on end. Gavin stood in the kitchen: he did not like to go into the sitting room, since the bedroom led straight off it, but he could not help hearing . . .

'Winthrop! You miserable boy, you. How many times have I *told* you I won't have that row here!'

The music stopped as abruptly as it had started, there were sounds of a scuffle, a thud, and a shriek of pain. The bedroom door slammed. Gavin found a glass and had a drink of tap water: he was extremely thirsty, and the thought of a scene in which he might be expected to take sides, or at least some part, made his mouth even dryer than his mother's curry had already achieved on its own. He thought longingly of the more peaceful evenings when he and Harry, and even sometimes all three of them, discussed their holidays, and listened to records and worried about their mothers. Harry's lived with a senile brother in Potter's Bar and still worked as an office cleaner, and Winthrop's was an unwillingly retired prostitute with one leg – it hadn't been the absence of a leg that had impeded her career, but a nasty car accident that had otherwise affected her mobility. She lived in a Home with what she described as a not very nice class of person.

Harry and – more surprisingly – Winthrop were both devoted sons, visiting their mothers regularly, never forgetting their birthdays, taking them on outings and devising treats for them; more than that, they were unfailingly kind to each *other's* mother, discussing her respective welfare with a serious concern. He listened: they were talking, but things sounded calmer. He decided to take the coffee into the sitting room. As he did so, Harry emerged from the bedroom holding a handkerchief to one side of his chin.

'He hit me with that ashtray we brought back from Pisa. He knows I can't stand blood.' He sank on to the chesterfield and added unexpectedly:

'It's all right now, though: the air has cleared. No Stones and no Tchaik is the contract.' He poured the coffee that Gavin had put on the black glass table. 'He's coming to join us when he's done his hair. Just behave as though nothing has happened. How's the job going?'

'All right; just the same really. How's yours?'

'Well, it's nothing like the last one, but one does feel one is doing some good. The most embarrassing thing about my clients is that what with being out of condition and then having nothing but raw fruit or vegetables they're so full of *wind*. I don't mind, because I've come to expect it, but they get so embarrassed. And I suppose,' he finished honestly, 'that if they weren't – I mean if they employed a whole lot of sang froid about it – *I'd* feel embarrassed.'

Harry was a masseur: he had recently gone to work in a fashionable Health Farm because there had been so many rows with Winthrop when he worked at the Turkish Baths in Jermyn Street. For some reason Winthrop seemed to feel that the presence of at least an equal number of ladies in the clientele obviated temptation, although so far as Gavin could see, all it did was halve his chances. The coffee was good; he said so and Harry replied:

'The secret is to have it really fresh: freshly roasted, freshly ground: like everything else – it's no good if you don't take it seriously. Winthrop wants you to cut his hair, by the way – if you feel up to it.'

'I'm afraid I haven't brought my scissors with me.'

'*He's* got some. Humour him, there's a dear child, or we'll be having another moody.' He met Gavin's eye and winked – a desperate plea. Then more briskly, he said, 'I meant to ask you: I want to get a new recording of K.449. I'm through with Haebler. Gabble gabble. Who would you recommend?'

Gavin thought seriously. This was just the kind of question he liked to be asked.

'The performance I *like* best is Serkin. There was a nice one with Gieseking. Probably Haskill as well, but they aren't recent. I don't think Milkina's *done* it, or I'd have her, but Klein may have.'

'Klein? He's good, isn't he?'

'He's good. Worth asking. Of course there's Clifford Curzon – ' he broke off, and they both looked towards the bedroom door where Winthrop, clad in boxer's shorts, track shoes and a T shirt stood in a pose of theatrical patience.

'What the fuck are you two talking about?'

'A Mozart concerto, dear boy, in E flat.'

'Oh.' He prowled to the only armchair and cast himself upon it. His T shirt said SEARCH ME YOU MIGHT EVEN GET TO LIKE IT in three rows on his rippling chest. 'That sounds like a boring conversation to me.'

Harry pursed his lips. 'No doubt it might seem so to some of us.'

'Oh dear,' thought Gavin. He asked Winthrop how the job was going.

'Which job?'

'I thought you were demonstrating sports wear.'

'Oh *that*! I couldn't stand that. Get paid far more for a beer commercial – far less work – same money for a few hours' work as I'd get at any department store for a week.'

'But it's not *regular* work. There's no *security* in it.'

Winthrop looked at Harry with affectionate contempt.

'There he goes. If he had his way, I'd be at home all day churning out chutney for a health shop.'

'You make marvellous chutney, dear child. I don't know anyone who makes chutney like him – out of *anything* – he's got a real gift for it. You've got so many talents, Winthrop, you just won't use them.'

'Some of them I use.' The room became full of sly smiles, but the atmosphere had definitely gone down a peg, Gavin thought.

'Harry said something about you wanting a hair cut,' he said.

'I've changed my mind. I'm going out.' He got to his feet, ran a muscular hand through his auburn curls and yawned so that Gavin could see nearly all of his splendid teeth.

'Where are you off to, then?'

'I'm going to Town. You should care. Leave you to your fucking classical music.'

'I don't mind. Where are you going to?'

'Mind your own fucking business.'

'Please yourself.' Harry's eyes had filled with tears. 'I ask you a perfectly reasonable question and you get stroppy.'

'I'm going to a disco, if you must know. Satisfied?'

'It makes no difference to me *where* you're going. I only asked.'

'You only *asked*,' repeated Winthrop and disappeared into the bedroom.

'My God!' Harry's silky gold hair stood in spikes off his forehead and his nose was twitching again. Gavin's heart began thudding – he could not think of anything to say or do that would alleviate Harry's distress.

In an astonishingly short space of time Winthrop emerged in a bright blue windcheater over a white track suit.

'Ta ta,' he said, 'Don't do anything I wouldn't do. And

that means you can do fucking well *anything*.' He had two goes at slamming the front door, and they heard him running downstairs.

Harry burst into tears.

'Look here,' said Gavin; 'don't – I mean – he'll be back.' He groped for a Kleenex in his pocket. 'Won't he?'

'He'll be *back*. It's who he'll be back *with*.' Sobs convulsed him – the Kleenex was sodden before he had even blown his nose. 'He's got no sense of responsib*i*lity! Just a child! He really goes in for the rough trade – has all sorts back – I knew it was a mistake to get the chesterfield. I told him this is the lounge but he'll get up to anything anywhere you wouldn't treat a dog like you treat me sometimes and do you know what he said?'

'No,' Gavin said (what else could he say?).

'"Yap yap,"' Harry looked at his friend with streaming eyes. '"Yap yap." As though I *was* a dog: never mind my migraines. He's got a lovely nature underneath. I keep telling myself he's had a terrible childhood – well it's a fact – his mother's working hours being so awkward, and she filled him up with Milk Tray so all his teeth had to be crowned before he was eighteen and getting the money for that set him on the primrose path I can tell you, he couldn't be too fussy where he got it from.' He took a deep breath and blew his nose on the only other Kleenex Gavin had with him. 'When I got him back here the first time it seemed such a golden period of our lives. "Consider this as a haven," I said, and he cried. And I got the trouble with his back right. It took me three months – that's the time he got into Asian cookery and he even seemed to take an interest in Opera – his mind was like a clean slate. He didn't used to want to go out all the time then – he was quite happy with his photography and that rug he was making, and we used to make a lot of wine and have one or two people round – well, you remember how it was – an idyll. That's how I described it then, and it's how I'd describe it now. If asked.'

He looked hopefully at Gavin. Gavin, however, was far from sure that nostalgia would prove to be a comfort, and suggested a cup of tea instead. So that is what they had, and Gavin was pleased to find that he was right about the idea. They had three cups each and nearly a whole packet of chocolate digestive biscuits because Harry said that upsets made him hungry. Gavin, who loved chocolate, ate his share although he remarked that it played havoc with his spots.

'The trouble with you,' Harry said affectionately, 'is that you need a sexual partner. Clear your skin in no time.'

'I haven't found the right girl.'

'You know what I think?'

'Yes,' said Gavin because they'd had this out before.

'You're barking up the wrong tree. The reason you don't find the right girl is that you don't want a girl. If you did – you'd find one. You want a lovely young quean. Why don't you try it?'

'But if what you say about the girl is true – if what I wanted was a chap, wouldn't I have found one by now?'

'Not necessarily. You're inhibited you know. Shy: you underestimate yourself. And living at home doesn't make it easy: I can see that. But you'd probably find – after a bit of initial distress – that your mother would feel it was only natural for you to have your own pad – a nice little place of your own with a boy you can really rely on. I know you'd never neglect your mother, but you have got your own life to lead and it's time you made a start, you know. You should come out with me and Winthrop one night and see what we can find.'

'How's your mother?' It was a deflection, but Gavin felt all the horrible, and horribly familiar, sensations of a first-class blush – the kind that surged up from just below his collar bone, ignited round about his Adam's apple and exploded on his face, making the worst of his spots look as though their heads had been touched with luminous paint.

'She's having a lot of trouble with her food. What she

fancies, she can't keep down, and anything she *could* keep down, she really doesn't fancy. But she's all right in *herself*. Still working and putting up with Sydney which is more than most of us could do. He keeps on asking her the time and he won't throw anything away – hides things – she keeps on finding paper bags in his bed and God knows what was in them in the first place. She's been a good sister to him – leaving aside anything else. I got her some tropical fish for her birthday and they seem to have gone down very well, I must say.' He tried the now exhausted teapot and then said with a touch of sly severity: 'I have a feeling that a certain party didn't want to pursue a subject. It's understandable: I know you feel a bit shy about these matters.'

So, although in a sense Gavin had got away with it, in another sense, he hadn't.

'Tell you what, dear boy. There's going to be a little party shortly; perhaps you'd like to come to that?'

'I don't know. I'm not much of a one for parties.'

'Have a go. I mean you can't spend your whole life working and going on holidays alone and all that. Take the plunge: be open-minded.'

'I'll think about it. Have to be getting along.' Once a week he went to work at a quarter-past eight in order to wash and set a Cabinet Minister whose hair had to be done as she put it 'before breakfast'.

Harry accompanied him solicitously downstairs to his bike. 'Sorry about the slight difficulties earlier in the evening.'

'That's all right. I hope it'll all work out.'

'It'll work *out*. Deep down, we've got quite a lot going for each other. Mind you,' he added, as Gavin was unlocking his bike, 'if it is a girl you're after, and I'm wrong – if I am, mind you, you're not going to meet her in that salon of yours, are you? They all sound a bit long in the tooth there, apart from anything else. What are you doing on Sunday? Winthrop and I were thinking of that exhibition at the V. and A.'

'I've got to go to my sister's. Take my mother over.'

'Oh well – you mustn't miss that. Another time then. Look after yourself.'

'You too.'

The ride back was refreshing. But, if what had happened earlier was what Harry described as 'slight difficulties', Gavin trembled to think what full-scale ones would be, and the hazards of any close personal relationship – with either sex – appalled him. Even if he went to the terrifying lengths of finding somebody, how could he rely upon them not to behave with the dangerous unpredictability of a polar bear? It seemed to him that with all couples there was the placator and the placated, and he was pretty sure which he would turn out to be. He was far more like Harry or his Dad, than he was like either his Mum or Winthrop. He put his bike away with the uneasy feeling that he was not *up* to real life, although real life was supposed to be what he was in. It was quite chilly – felt like frost.

The house was dark, except for the lantern light in the hall, and it smelled faintly of curry; and Ronuk: 'keeping everything nice' did not extend to smells. His mother's activities could always be traced by smell: on Mondays, the washing; on Tuesdays, the furniture polishing; on Wednesdays, the disinfectant (on the rubbish bin after the dustman had been); on Thursdays, the cakes she made for the weekend; on Fridays, the fish. He went – quietly – into the kitchen and got himself a glass of Express Dairy orange juice out of the fridge; he felt it was good for his awful blood, and it was the size of whim that his mother fell in with. His thirst had not abated in spite of the tea. Breakfast was laid with military precision: his cereal by his place, his father's knife and fork at the ready for his fried bread and tomatoes. The sugar bowl had a muslin cloth weighted with beads on it; the electric toaster a linen cosy embroidered with a cottage and hollyhocks – his mother's precautions against flies and germs combined in the case of the cosy with a general feeling that things were more refined if they appeared to be other than they were. The lavatory was particularly like that. The seat was covered in candlewick, the paper in a felt box appliquéd with sequins. In the bathroom he cleaned his teeth, surveyed the battlefield of his face (his spots really were a case of swings and roundabouts – whenever half a dozen swings subsided, the roundabouts got cracking: nothing seemed to finish them off; if one generation succumbed to calamine, disinfectant creams or even surgical spirit, another thrived on just the same treatment). He had tried the school of 'don't touch them leave them alone', but this simply meant that they took their own interminable time to burgeon. He had tried the 'nip them in the bud' school which simply meant that they redoubled their efforts. Discrimination was the best method and careful timing. There came a moment with each one when it could be effectively squeezed, disinfected and left to heal. He dealt with two such, took out his contact lenses and bathed his eyes. After reading Huxley's book, he had taken to a modified version of the Bates method – the exercises, and hot and cold water bathing. His eyes were the colour of ginger nuts, and gave the impression of resting widely apart upon very shallow declivities – he had been called Froggy at school. Somehow, he thought wearily (because he had thought it so often before and knew that it didn't help), the things that were *better* about his face – a broad forehead with knowledgeable bumps, finely-arched brows of a pleasing bronze shade and high cheekbones – seemed merely to make the bad things worse. It was as though two conflicting forces had composed his features and a kind of angry democracy had ensued. He did not know that his smile made everything not only all right but unusually better than that. He never smiled at himself in a glass – could see nothing to smile at.

His room, the door of which he kept shut, did not smell of curry. He had tacked a piece of felt to the bottom of the door (to exclude draughts he had told his mother but really it was to shut out the various consequences of his mother keeping everything nice). He allowed her into his room once a week – on Saturdays, when he was there; she exclaimed over the dirt, barked his shins on the Hoover and wondered incessantly what things were *for*. He liked order, and did not mind dust.

Without his lenses, the Persian rug had a kind of suffused glow – its casual geometric patterns were all of the colours that reminded him of a really good azalea garden – startling but compatible pinks and oranges and reds and yellows – it made his bed look very inviting.

When he had undressed and laid his clothes for tomorrow carefully out on the red sofa he went to the dormer window the shelf of which was occupied by his little bonzai elm and opened the casement: fresh cold air streamed in. He hopped into bed and drew the rug up to his chin to enjoy its faint, musty smell. Then he turned out the light and shut his eyes.

Where was he? Oh yes – he always went back a little bit, so that he could recapture the last thrill from last time. He had been walking – well, here he was, walking along the cliff path. It was noon and high summer – the hot air spiced with thyme and the countless little flowering plants. The sky was serenely blue and the faint, chalky path – circuitous and full of small declivities and ascents – gave him a feeling of mystery and of purpose. The sea was not visible but he knew it was there, and part of the adventure was to find it. The path was ascending more and more steeply until he was using his hands to help him climb, and then, but suddenly, he was at the top – a spur of land curving away to his left and looking down upon a perfect little bay the shape of a scallop shell, invaded by a pale-green sunlit sea and edged with pure sand. In the centre of the bay and lying on the sand with her long red-gold hair fanned out round her head, lay a girl . . .

He enjoyed again that first powerful shock of discovery and delight, and then, because her hair was so beautiful, he put an iris-coloured towel under her to protect her from the sand. She wore – she was wearing a lilac cotton bikini with the straps off her shoulder, but even though she was lying on her back her breasts were well defined. Her skin was like pale brown eggshell and she did not know he was there. He lay down upon the turf to watch her. After a minute, she rose to her feet and walked – no, and then she *ran* down to the sea and cast herself upon the pale green water with a graceful abandon – but she was not a mermaid – she had beautiful legs. She dived, and when she emerged shaking drops from her streaming, coppery curtain of hair he saw that she had forgotten her shoulder straps and he glimpsed her breasts – like mother of pearl touched with coral. He waited; he wanted her to finish her bathe – to enjoy her pleasure in it. The cliff below him was steep – a good twenty feet – and he wondered whether it was possible to get down. His heart was pounding and he did not want to frighten her. But, when she came out of the water and was trying to cover her breasts again, she saw him. He waved so that she should know he wanted to be seen and she looked up at him and smiled – and when she did that she was suddenly much nearer – it seemed no distance at all – for he could see nothing but her face which was – her face was – well, as she was unlike anyone he had ever *seen* – how could he describe her? All the words seemed so *used*: she struck him, as though he was looking straight into the sun, and like the sun, even when he looked away, her face anonymously dazzling, was still before his eyes. (Tolstoy: never mind.) She was far away again, combing her hair with her fingers and, it seemed to him, waiting. Then she made a gesture which said 'Come down'. He looked at the precipice, spread out his hands with a gesture implying that it looked impossible. Then he called: 'Can you come up to me?' As he said that, he realized that the light was dying with tropical, theatrical speed; from gold to dark yellow to a rose-coloured dusk, to hyacinth to violet to silver-brushed indigo, and she was standing motionless, darker than the dying light. Then one of them called (he was not sure which, but he heard the voice), 'It's hard to go up – it's easy to come down,' and he was standing on the very edge of the cliff and she was holding out her arms and calling, but faintly, 'Just let yourself go,' and he felt fear like a cold heavy weight creeping up his body – turning first his feet, then his legs then his stomach to stone, creeping inexorably up him at an even pace and leaving paralysis and insensibility in its wake; he knew if it reached his heart he would be done for. And it was as though she understood the danger because she suddenly called out – and it was unmistakably her voice this time – clear and serene – 'Only trust me. Just let yourself go!' And he lifted his arms, spread them out and plunged down and down into the feathery warm dark.

CHAPTER TWO

'AND where is it to be this year, Gavin?'
The question, like the half-dozen she asked each week, conveyed such stunningly liberal unconcern for the answer, that as usual he hesitated before replying; puncturing the little bottle of Inerol and shaking its blue to purple, before he murmured that he was thinking of Greece.

'Ah, Greece,' she said, in exactly the same tone of voice that he felt she would have employed if he had said Madagascar or Wormwood Scrubs. 'Greece is still very good value, they tell me.'

Gavin massaged the setting lotion gently into her hair and then their eyes met in the mirror in front of her. 'Your usual?'

'Yes please, Gavin. You know me. I'm *not* very adventurous about my hair, I'm afraid.'

The ways in which The Rt. Hon. Mrs Veronica Shack might have been adventurous to make up for this lapse were unknown to Gavin, but he smiled gently and began combing out her hair. In his experience, most women were given to statements about themselves that required contradiction – flat, but with a roguish tinge – and since they usually contained some unpalatable element of truth which he was too honest – clumsy, he put it – to combat, he had learned to take refuge in kindly silence.

After he had secured the central front roller, he said: 'The most important thing for you is to have a hair style you feel comfortable with and that's easy to keep. I don't imagine you have much spare time.'

31

'That *is* my problem. I really wish there were thirty-six hours in every day.'

'I suppose that would help,' he agreed, while wondering what difference it would make.

'But I expect, if we had, we should simply fill up those extra hours with more meetings, whizzing about, decision-making and conferences. And you, I suppose,' she ended with the correct dose of personal touch, 'would simply be washing more people's hair.'

Gavin did not usually wash clients' hair; it was done by juniors; he made an exception in the case of Mrs Shack, because she wanted her appointment before the salon officially opened. He felt momentarily depressed that she did not seem to realize that he was doing her a favour: then he remembered reading somewhere that gratitude was only excited by new elements, and he'd been doing Mrs Shack's hair now for at least two years. If it was true that people could adapt to *anything* – the chances were that they would start with favours. This was interesting because, on the whole, favours seemed to be thinner on the ground than misfortunes: he would have thought that most people had less practice at adapting to them . . .

She was asking him what he thought about something – some social issue – (high rise flats? immigrants? the powers of the police?) – no, it was something about education – that was it; of course she was very keen on getting rid of Grammars . . . '. . . at the expense of the average children, don't you think?'

'I think most people are more broad-minded about things when they don't know about them.' He was engaged in fitting a pale blue nylon net over her rollers.

'That is a very good remark. I like that. I must remember it.'

Even her praise was tainted, but he knew by now that she neither meant nor could help it.

'Would you like some coffee?'

'That would be wonderful.'

He settled her under the dryer with her briefcase full of papers, and went to the small room at the back of the salon where the electric kettle sat on a draining board beside a sinkful of dirty cups: the juniors were supposed to take turns in clearing that sort of thing up, but they were extremely unreliable about it. He filled the kettle, and washed up a cup and saucer and was drying it on a paper towel when Daphne, the receptionist, came in.

'Morning, Gavin. Oh, aren't they the giddy limit! Don't you bother with it. Complain!'

'I don't know which one is responsible.'

'I don't mean to the juniors; I mean to Mr Adrian.'

'No – I'll find out which one it was and blow her up.' He knew from experience that if he told the owner of the salon *he* would be so tough with the culprit that ten to one she would leave – and any juniors were better than no juniors.

When he took the coffee through to Mrs Shack, the salon was coming to life. The telephone was ringing, two more clients had arrived and Iris, Hugo and Peter were getting out their trolleys of equipment for the day's work. Daphne put down the telephone receiver and called, 'Sharon won't be in today: her mother says she's eaten something.' Then she mouthed: 'Bet you it was her.' When his favourite junior, Jenny, arrived, he told her about the cups and asked her if she would mind washing them up before Mr Adrian arrived. Jenny, who with her short, dark golden hair en brosse and huge steel-rimmed spectacles, looked like a cross between a choirboy and a young owl, rolled her eyes and shrugged her bony shoulders, but clumped off in her absurd boots without a word to do what she was told. Daphne started arranging some tulips in the vase for the reception desk and Gavin had a quick look at the book to see what was in store for him. Fridays were always busy – mostly with regulars – but he saw that in his case there was one exception. Miss Muriel Sutton was booked for a cut and a permanent at two. His heart began to sink as he remembered who she was, and then plummeted. Muriel was his sister's best friend, older than Marge, worthy and unmarried. Marge, who was married and liked it, seemed to feel that Gavin should follow suit, and what had begun as her idle but none the less embarrassing family speculation about who he would marry, had, over the years, hardened into an obsession: heart to heart talks with him, frightful schemes to introduce him to a series of 'nice girls' with recriminatory follow-ups, or post mortems, depending upon how much she had been able to throw whoever it was and him together. In between what might be called the outsiders introduced to the field, Marge's undoubted favourite was Muriel. Muriel, she had told her brother, was really a good sort, was thoroughly domestic and maternal: she was worth her weight in gold, which Gavin had once considered must make her very valuable indeed. There was no nonsense about her: she was not flighty or preoccupied with her appearance; she thought of others; she was longing to get married. As time went by, Marge's claims about her friend's qualities verged upon the desperate: Muriel – deep down – was quite artistic – had won prizes for flower arrangement and even written some poetry – and, knowing how deeply Marge distrusted anything at all to do with art, Gavin recognised the lengths his sister was going to about the whole business. Sending Muriel all the way from Potter's Bar to have her hair done by him was a new manoeuvre: it was surprising in a way that she hadn't thought of it before, since it was clearly the only cast-iron method of forcing him to spend some time alone with Muriel. Still, it was in the salon: on the Ladder of Fear count he would not ever be *alone* with her.

'Miss Renishawe's in. Jenny's put her in Cubicle Three.'

'Right. Keep an eye on Mrs Shack for me.'

Miss Renishawe had been lowered into her chair by Jenny.

She still wore her navy blue knitted hat – now slightly askew, which went so well with her weatherbeaten face and keen blue eyes and made her look more like an old sea salt than ever.

'Just want it cut, Gavin – no nonsense.' Nonsense was rollers. He had just about accustomed her to having a blow dry although each time she asked him what was the matter with nice old-fashioned towels. Her hair was the colour of silver birch bark and she liked it cut extremely short, 'shingled' as she put it. She was a great gardener and Gavin found her conversation – when she indulged in any – a pleasant mixture of knowledge, opinion and personal rumination. Today she said nothing at all for about ten minutes and then suddenly as though she was in the middle of some argument asked:

'Do *you* go in for this new-fangled notion of having a *herb* garden?'

Gavin shook his head.

'My mother wouldn't see the point of that, I'm afraid.'

'Well, you can tell her from me that she's quite right. All very well when they were the family medicine chest: that's become nonsense when everyone's chock full of penicillin whatever's the matter with them. Herbs should be planted with other plants: gives them health and saves them from disease. Take roses, for instance. If you underplant them properly with herbs you'll save gallons of chemical muck. How would *you* like to be deluged in some revolting-smelling concoction the moment you felt poorly?'

'You mean like those disinfectant baths they give prisoners?'

She chuckled, and for a moment her face, equally composed of wickedness and innocence, had a fascinating beauty. 'People do stupid things, they must expect stupid things to happen to them. Plants are never stupid.' After a pause, she added: 'Extravagant sometimes, but never stupid. Get it nice and short, Gavin: I don't like it bothering me. I don't like to know that it is *there*.'

A bit later, she said: 'That little fair, bird girl. I like her to wash me. She doesn't scrubble me up like the others.'

'Right.' He called Jenny, and was just in time to comb out Mrs Shack, who, rollers removed, was showing that she was perfectly prepared to wait, like everyone else, even if she *did* have rather important things to do with her time.

By now, Mr Adrian had arrived. He was a very large man – even flabby: he wore heavy, horn-rimmed glasses and an extremely skilful toupee; his huge pale chins meandered down into his bow tie, and his suede shoes had thick rubber soles. He moved about the establishment with ponderous silence, but nothing escaped him; he had found out about the dirty tea cups by feeling the drying-up cloth which was far damper than it would have been if the cups had been washed up the night before. Mrs Silkin, who came to do the sandwich lunches and coffee for clients, had complained about the cloth; she always left everything nice, Daphne told Gavin that Mr Adrian had said Mrs Silkin had *several* times said. Instead of providing another cloth – which was urgently needed – Mr Adrian had gone straight for the juniors. Gavin could tell this by simply looking at them: Mandy was sulking which meant that she had to be asked to do every single thing, and then did it twice as slowly, and Jenny looked as though she was going to burst into tears at any moment. Mr Adrian beckoned Gavin over to the back of the salon where, in a small cubicle, he had a comfortable chair and read the racing papers.

'I understand that it was you who discovered the cups this morning.' He raised a huge white hand to prevent Gavin from speaking. 'I'm not blaming *you*. I've said the same to Hugo and Peter *and* Iris. But, if nobody tells me anything, how am I to know? I ask you, that's all.' He waited while Gavin didn't say that it didn't seem to make much difference whether people told him things or not since he had found out anyway.

'I don't think it was anything to do with Jenny. Or Mandy,' he added fairly.

'You needn't tell me that. I *know* the young lady respon-sible. And I tell you, quite frankly, that I have a suspicion that this incident will prove to be the Last Straw.'

Mr Adrian specialized in last straws, could even be said to be addicted to them, so Gavin remained silent.

'*If* that young lady condescends to put in an appearance tomorrow, I shall ask her for an explanation, but I'm afraid, even now, that I know what her answer will be. "I'm sorry, Mr Adrian, I forgot." His mimicry was offensively careless. He passed a hand over his toupee with practised caution and concluded, 'No. It will have to be O-U-T for Miss Sharon.'

'We're short of juniors now – ' Gavin began, when Daphne interrupted to say that she was sorry she was interrupting, but his client was in.

'Don't tell *me* that. I *know* we're short of juniors. Nobody knows we're short of juniors better than I do. I shall have to strain every nerve to find a replacement, and meanwhile we'll just have to take the rough with the smooth. But, Gavin,' he went on and on: 'keep them up to the mark. If you all keep them up to the mark, we might not have these little unpleasant-nesses.' He smiled with vulpine insincerity and said he must not keep Gavin.

As Gavin walked back to the reception he realized that his heart was pounding, and that this, for once, had nothing to do with fear. He actually hated Mr Adrian. All he ever seemed to do was to make nasty situations. He blew up petty little mishaps to the size where they upset even people who had nothing to do with them. 'Take the rough with the smooth' indeed! As he and the other hairdressers were the people who had to do this, they might at least have some choice about the rough. Almost *any* junior was better than no junior. If Sharon went they would be two short, and this simply meant that he and the others had to do a lot of extra unpaid work which entailed staying late and/or arriving early, which impaired their own work and which made Mandy and Jenny feel put upon.

And another thing that he hated about Mr Adrian was the way that, while he was quite prepared to be very tough and unpleasant to juniors, he had been trying to blame Gavin for the incident without actually having the courage to say that that was what he was doing. And he was mean. (Gavin had worked for him longest and he had always been forced into asking for any rise during that time, never once been offered one, and he found it agonizing having to ask. Often he only managed to do this after he had been goaded by the others who were thicker-skinned – 'braver'.) But, before he could start to consider the extent and degree of Mr Adrian's meanness, he was confronted by Mrs Wagstaffe and her irritable dachshund Sherry. Mrs Wagstaffe wanted a cut, but Sherry disliked anybody doing anything at all to her. He was a dog of few words, but he had a lightning snap, designed to harass and unnerve his target, rather than actually to draw blood. Gavin liked dogs – he had always wanted his mother to replace Caesar, but Sherry, after years and years spent with Mrs Wagstaffe who anthropomorphized him, had become much more like a nasty person than a dog. Now he sat, poised on Mrs Wagstaffe's tweed lap, rumbling softly – like the beginning of the storm in the last act of *Rigoletto*, Gavin thought.

'Now then, Sherry, good morning, Mrs Wagstaffe,' he said in that order.

'Isn't he amazing? He never forgets.'

Since Mrs Wagstaffe came in regularly every three weeks to have her iron grey bob and fringe trimmed, there seemed no earthly reason why Sherry *should* forget, but as a master of petty grievance he would probably remember if she didn't come in more than once a year.

'Let him smell you,' invited Mrs Wagstaffe, but Gavin had been had that way. The best method, he had found, was to vest Mrs Wagstaffe in one of the larger overalls so that the folds enveloped Sherry, on the general principle that what the eye could not see, the jaw would not snap at. The rumbling reluctantly subsided, and he snipped away while Mrs Wagstaffe earnestly discussed the differences between mange – something Sherry definitely did not have – and alopecia, a condition she suspected Sherry might be suffering from. Tinned food certainly aggravated his condition but, then again, hot weather, or other animals, or anxiety of any sort – he was very highly strung – or people he did not like (and, really, he only actually *liked* her) had much the same effect. Gavin switched his mind into what he called neutral as he worked. That is to say, he neither thought about the juniors, or Mr Adrian, or Muriel Sutton looming, or Harry's problems with Winthrop, or where, in fact, he would go for his holidays, or last night in bed, nor did he give his mind to the difficulties attached to Mrs Wagstaffe's relationship with her dog. He half-listened and agreed with her; years ago, he had learned that he could work better in this way: that the core of his attention was upon the way in which his client's hair grew: her double crown – like two opposing tides meeting – the patch, just north of her left temple where her hair was noticeably thin, the suggestion of side burns that, with a woman, were better concealed if not eliminated. In fact cutting was what he liked doing best; it combined skill bred of much varied practice with flair born, he supposed, of some alliance between his eye and his hands. In this respect, if no other, he could do what he could see to do – always with interesting provisions that no two heads were alike, and there was always the tantalizing possibility of doing better. It was perfectly possible to string along with Mrs Wagstaffe's monologue and do his best for her hair. When he had finished with her, Iris asked him to confer with her about a client who had rung to say that she wanted her hair cut off and the colour changed as soon as they could both fit it in.

'She wants a permanent as well, but I explained to her that she would do better to wait a fortnight after the tint for that.'

'How long *is* her hair?'

'Well, it doesn't reach her waist, but there's a fair amount of it. I know you like to do two cuts when it's from length.'

'It's usually more satisfactory – gives the hair time to settle.' Together, they pored over the engagement book. Iris, who was expert at her job – something of an artist, Gavin thought – was always heavily booked, and finding a time that fitted with his schedule was not easy and his next client had already arrived. Gavin, apart from respecting her skill, was fond of Iris: she was a gentle, middle-aged woman, devoted to her work, who unobtrusively lent a considerable air to the establishment. Her judgement and her taste were excellent; she never allowed her clients to indulge in the sillier caprices that would show their lack in these directions; they all emerged from her hands with hair that matched both their complexions and their ages. Although they had worked in the same salon for eight years, Gavin knew very little about her, and what little he did know made him almost afraid of knowing more. Her only child had died in a car accident; her husband, who was blind, had appalling arthritis and had undergone operations on both of his hips – one successful, the other not. They lived in a bungalow on the river, and Alfred, whose guide dog had recently died, was having a lot of trouble with the new one. The last time that Gavin had asked her anything about herself had been about her holiday on which he knew she had set great store. She had been saving for years to go to the Caribbean, but had had to cancel it because Alfred had got a bed for his second operation.

After some juggling, they agreed to slot Dr Blenkinsopp into the following Tuesday afternoon at one forty-five (bang would go another lunch hour, Gavin thought), and Daphne said she would offer the appointment and come back to them.

His next client, Mrs Blake, was a permanent. Her hair was in poor condition – very dry and with the ends splitting, and, strictly speaking, she shouldn't be having a perm at all, but his earlier attempts to dissuade her had met with an almost hysterical resistance, and sensing that she was very unhappy, he did not want to make things worse. He apologized for keeping her waiting, and as her eyes met his in the mirror he realized that things were much worse than usual. She wore far too much make-up – as though she was only meant to be seen at a distance, and her eyes, set in the peach and biscuit pottery of her face, had always seemed, like a clown, to provide an uneasy contrast, but today they gave him a shock – she looked as though she was in hell. He felt for his comb and cleared his throat.

'I've been thinking about your hair since we last talked, and I was wondering how you would feel about a short cut –' he ruffled her hair gently with the comb – 'fairly close all over the head, and then a light permanent? The style would suit you and be better for your type of hair.'

'Perhaps that would be the best thing.' He thought she smiled and he responded as though she had.

'Would you like a cup of coffee? Or would you rather wait until you have your sandwich?'

She shook her head and, as though the movement had upset them, tears filled her eyes. For a moment she sat, blind, holding her breath and resolutely smiling. Gavin wanted to put his arms round her. Instead, he drew a protective curtain round the cubicle, murmured something about fetching his scissors, and went to find Jenny.

'Get my client a cup of coffee, would you?'

'Mrs Silkin's in.'

'I know she is. Get *her* to get it. Quickly.'

'Okay.'

At that moment, Mrs Silkin minced past them carrying exactly what he wanted. 'Could I possibly lift that off you?' He lowered his voice to a conspiratorial hiss 'Client's up*set*'. Mrs Silkin's expression melted from '*Do* you mind?' to 'Poor thing!' and she made as if to follow him. He felt for the 20p tip Mrs

Shack had given him and popped the coins into Mrs Silkin's overall pocket. 'Here's her money.'

When he returned to the cubicle she was smoking.

'I don't know why I *offered* you coffee,' he said: 'clients who are having a perm get it for free. Seems a pity to waste it.' He put the cup in front of her, settled the towel round her neck, and with every appearance of extreme concentration began cutting her hair. After a bit, she asked him what he was going to do for his summer holiday and they talked a little about Greece: she had once been on a cultural cruise of the kind that provided lecturers to go with the sight-seeing. A bit too much like a school holiday, she said; she had never liked doing anything in groups. But, by the time he sent for Jenny for her first hair wash, she seemed much calmer.

'Use a nice lot of conditioner,' he said to Jenny, 'I'll take Mrs Wagstaffe out.' Mrs Wagstaffe insisted upon sitting under a hairdryer because she disliked being blown-dry, and with the shortage of juniors this was really a blessing. Sherry made a half-hearted attack on him, but Gavin recognized this as being more a matter of form than of purpose. Mrs Wagstaffe gave him 25p in a conspiratorial manner – almost as though she was slipping him some heroin – and, when he had helped her to struggle into her thickly-lined Burberry, he was free to have a quick coffee before dealing with the tricky permanent.

Peter had got in before him. This meant that he occupied the only stool in the tiny annexe off the coffee cupboard. Peter had recently got married after a three-year engagement to a girl who worked as a secretary to an accountant. For three years they had saved to buy a flat and, each time they thought they had enough to suit their mortgage company, inflation had put the whole thing a couple of thousand pounds out of reach. Gradually, they had given up everything: holidays, the squash club (they had met playing squash), visits to the cinema – except once a month – eating out, smoking, and going to the pub. He had gone to carpentry classes and she had learned upholstery. Even their eventual wedding had been conducted with the utmost economy and they had spent their honeymoon painting and papering, making bookshelves and laying lino.

They still seemed to spend the most strenuous evenings stripping paint off doors, sanding and polishing their sitting room floor and tiling bits of the bathroom. Peter had a beard, which added to his ravaged and rather missionary appearance, and this morning he looked more exhausted than usual. Gavin knew that the most casual question elicited floods of response (this was why he knew so much about the flat), and as he was feeling the need of a peaceful break, he smiled at Peter and leaned against the draughty window to watch two pigeons on the fire escape, remarking that they seemed to be getting on very well together. But for Peter, who was capable of relating almost anything to his personal life when he wanted to, this unfortunately provided the perfect opening.

'*You* can laugh,' he began bitterly: 'pigeons are one thing. You're not married.'

Gavin, who hadn't been laughing, felt less like that than ever. 'What do you mean?' he said – exactly (as he knew) he was meant to say.

'Spring, and nature and all that jazz. It's got into Hazel now. What do you think she said to me last night?'

Gavin shrugged, divided between wanting to look as though he didn't want to know, and feeling he ought to look as though he did.

'She told me – and we hadn't even finished getting the cork down in the toilet – she calmly told me that she wanted to leave the bank and start a baby! *Hazel* said that!' he added, as though it might have been better coming from anybody else.

Gavin, wishing that his coffee wasn't too hot to drink, murmured something about girls who got married often feeling like that, but this, so far from being oil on troubled waters, was more like setting a match to the oil.

'But it would throw everything out! You know we've got this five-year plan? We've done all the sums, everything worked out: we live on my salary, including rates, heat and light, etc., and hers pays off the mortgage and the H.P. payments on the fridge, *and* she saves a bit towards a larger flat. *When* we get the larger flat (by which time the H.P. payments will have been paid and hopefully a washing machine as well), *then* she can start to think about a family, but even then, as I pointed out to her again and again last night, there's bound to be some sort of mortgage on the larger flat, and if she's not earning anything we shall be pretty tight for money for a good five years after that. It's all in the book. We spent hours working it all out, and I got a friend of mine who's an accountant to check the figures so it isn't as though she can say the figures aren't *right*. But, if she starts acting up and just doing what she *feels* like, we're sunk. I knew women were difficult, but I thought she wasn't like them. She hasn't even worked out what it would *cost* to have a baby, quite apart from there being nothing to pay for it *with*.'

Gavin suggested that perhaps the actual baby wouldn't cost much, but Peter knew all about that. 'Oh, yes they *do*! They keep needing larger and larger clothes and all those gadgets to stop them doing anything. Pens and slings and high chairs!' he exclaimed. 'I don't want to spend all my night classes making those!'

Gavin gulped down his coffee and prepared to escape, but he'd left it too late.

'Tell you what. Come and see us. Have supper. We've worked out a rota for food to fit the budget, but I'll pick you a good night. If you admired the flat, *and* said how marvellous it would be when we've done X, Y and Z to it (I'll tell you what that amounts to), it might impress her. Coming from a complete outsider.'

The thought of his being able to persuade a newly married total stranger that she couldn't afford to have a child made

Gavin want to scream with terrified laughter: what he actually did was to mutter something about looking forward to seeing the flat one day and he must get back to his client. Later, as he wrapped the tapered wisps of hair in the paper soaked in the perming solution and fastened each into its small roller, he wondered fleetingly what it would be like if people actually behaved to one another exactly as they felt, instead of filtering their reactions until some suitable, thin response trickled through? Judging by his own double life in this respect, he thought it would frighten him, but as there seemed no chance of it happening, he allowed the little squib of curiosity and exhilaration its brief and secret explosion. He would have shouted at Mr Adrian. He would have smacked that dog. 'Don't you be so bloody patronizing!' he would have said to Mrs Shack. And he would not only have put his arms round this poor lady, he would have told her that she had all the time in the world to tell him what was making her feel so awful. If one thing led to another, these very different things would certainly have led to different things. He supposed that people couldn't stand one another much because they couldn't stand one another at all. And then, when people in plays behaved, as they sometimes did, without the filter, it was called artificial and not like life. One of the best things about art was it *not* being like life: surely most people knew that somehow or other? Take opera for example. But, before he could take opera, he realized that Jenny, who had been standing on one leg handing him papers, had run out of them and was simply staring into space, and since the timing of a perm was vitally important, he had to send her off at the double for some more, and however quick she was, this probably meant doing the head in two sections. He smiled reassuringly at the client and began squeezing more solution with a sponge on to the existing rollers. Yes, given the state of the hair, it would certainly mean that, he realized as he unrolled the test curl. Well, it was his fault: his business to keep the juniors up to the mark: blast it though, it was going to make the whole thing longer.

'It's a terrible smell, isn't it?'

'Not too good, I'm afraid.' It *was* awful: something like roasted rotten nuts: he never got used to it.

'I suppose you get used to it,' but she said it anxiously and he hastened to reassure her.

'It's all in the day's work. Jenny!'

Jenny scuttled back with the papers. 'Someone had put them back wrong. I couldn't find them.'

'You should have collected enough in the first place,' he said, but so mildly that she grinned as she apologized.

One way and another, Mrs Blake's perm took longer than it should, with the result that he began to get behind with his appointments. His twelve o'clock didn't turn up: she was a tiresome woman who was given to breaking appointments on the ground that she didn't feel up to it. She usually claimed that she was unable to let them know that she wasn't coming in because the telephone was always engaged, although, mysteriously, she was able to use it to make appointments. When Gavin had remarked on this to Iris, to whom Mrs Bletchley-Smythe also went, Iris had made a minute little drinking gesture with one hand and unexpectedly winked. 'How do you know?' Gavin had asked. Iris had looked at him in a kindly, almost pitying way. 'There are signs,' she said. Anyway, Mrs Bletchley-Smythe didn't turn up, but Mrs Courcel did, with three hair pieces: two of them to be cleaned and reset, and one which she wanted used to dress her hair after a wash and set, and he knew from experience that dressing Mrs Courcel's hair in a new way was a time-taking affair. He managed to get her hair into rollers before he set Mrs Blake, whose newly permed hair emerged from the wash basin in tiny corkscrews – he hoped not *too* tight, but it had taken very fast . . .

'I look like a rather expensive doll! My hair, I mean – not

the rest of me.' Well, at least she was noticing – it had taken her out of herself a bit.

'I'll set it on rather large rollers to give it a soft effect,' he said. 'Mind you, a perm's always a little bit tight to begin with. Or, if it isn't, it doesn't last five minutes. Would you like to order a sandwich now to have under the dryer? Egg and prawn's very nice, with brown bread. Mrs Silkin makes them with a little cress – ' but he realized that he was entering Mrs Blake's Danger Zone; she didn't seem able to stand anyone offering her things. This time she nodded, and started to frown, so he sent Jenny off to Mrs Silkin with the order, and bent over his trolley pretending to sort out the rollers to give her time to recover. But she didn't recover; tears were making two tracks down her face, she was holding her breath again, and, what both moved and frightened him, she began a small uneven rocking motion. This time, he took one of her hands in both of his, held it very firmly and remained quite still not looking at her face. It was meant to be a kind of repressive comfort; not the kind he wanted to give, but the only kind that circumstances would allow. Eventually, she let go of her breath in a long muttering sigh and then said, almost briskly: 'I shall have to blow my nose.'

He released her hand and stooped for her bag which was on the floor.

'Of course,' she said, 'if you stayed on one of the islands near Turkey – the Dodecanese I think they are called, you can get across to Turkey. You can get a boat from Cos, for instance, they tell me.'

'I don't think I'm going to be there long enough, you see. I mean, I've never been to Greece, and two weeks isn't very long to get the feeling of a new country.'

'Perhaps Turkey next year then.'

'Can you manage without me, Mr Gavin, because Mr Hugo wants me to wash his client?'

'All right, Jenny. But I shall want you at about two-fifteen, so mind you get your lunch in before that.'

Jenny rolled her eyes and, slightly overdoing it, said, 'Yes, Mr Gavin,' but he knew that, with her, it was the tail end of her apology for letting him down earlier. Mrs Blake, meeting his eye for the first time in the mirror, and clearly finding it difficult, said hastily: 'I like that girl; she looks about fourteen, though, doesn't she?'

'She does look young. She's twenty, actually.' He decided that Jenny was a good safe subject. 'But she came to hairdressing later than they usually do. Her father was a vet, and when she left school she worked with him for a couple of years, but then two of her brothers were passing the exams and said they were going to take over the business and they wanted her just to be a sort of receptionist and general assistant so she decided to have a different career.'

'Goodness! What a lot you know about her!'

'She's been here nearly three years.' While he finished the rollers and put on the net and ear pads he reflected that in a way it was funny that he didn't know more.

'Half an hour under the dryer should do you,' he said: 'one of the advantages of having shorter hair, you'll find.' He settled her in with a clean towel to protect her neck, told her that Mrs Silkin would bring her her lunch and hurried over to his next client, an anaemic young woman who stammered terribly (the stammer somehow neutralized the fear he might have felt about her youth). She looked up from her book (she was one of the very few clients who actually brought real books to read). They smiled at each other, and he picked up the book to read its title – he enjoyed and she liked his curiosity in this respect. '*Time Was*,' he read; 'Graham Robertson: don't think I've heard of him.'

'Erse erse uss uss *Sar*gent p – pppppp painted him when he was a young – ermmmmm man,' she said, and showed him the frontispiece.

'Oh yes. I know that one. Very fine portrait. Although, I think I'd rather have been painted by Whistler, wouldn't you?'

'Only when I was very old. The er er erra erra rest of the time, I'd rather ersa ersa *Sargent*.'

Her hair was very fine and she wore it in a longish bob with a fringe. She was one of the few people whom he preferred to cut dry, as, wet, it contracted to such tiny wisps that it was difficult to see its shape. It was a delicate business, getting her hair right, and usually protracted because, in her enthusiasm for what she was reading, and with a touching acceptance of her speech problems she would leaf through the book and show him some particular remark. Thus he got Mrs Patrick Campbell: 'My eyes are really nothing in particular, God gave me boot buttons, but I invented the dreamy eyelid, and that makes all the difference.' And: Once at a rehearsal Sir James Barrie, impatient at the impossible subtleties demanded of the players by a producer, called out to an actor, 'Mr—, I want you to cross from left to right silently conveying to the audience that you have an aunt in Surbiton.'

'Aren't they erwer erwer erwer erwer *un*derful?' It was indeed a bonus to be presented with entertainment of this kind: it also opened up the charming, if organized, vista of the late Victorian and Edwardian eras which he knew he had not explored enough. But, and perhaps this was because he felt a bit tired by now (although the day was barely half done), he also felt that somebody like Miss Wilming must be rather lonely if she felt the need to tell him, only her hairdresser, after all, what she was reading. He found himself worrying about her stammer, and how lonely this might make her; she might even be shy, poor thing . . . the terrifying thought occurred to him that *he* might have been landed with a stammer: God, if he had been, *he* wouldn't have been able to talk to anybody at *all*! He wouldn't have dared to do this job, for instance, he would have had to be a lighthouse keeper or something like that. Of course, people could get cured of stammering – look at George

VI and Demosthenes: on the other hand, Somerset Maugham, who loathed his stammer, had never got over it. Perhaps the need to orate was a spur, in which case he would probably have had his stammer all his life. At this point, just as he was realizing gratefully that not having a stammer was one thing he'd got going for him, he also realized that he'd taken off too much of Miss Wilming's hair behind her left ear and would have to do a general trim all round again to redress the balance. She was reading quietly, and he had to resist the host of other disabilities by which he might have been afflicted that crowded into his mind. Winthrop's mother, for instance; how on earth would he have managed with a cork leg? He certainly wouldn't have thought of being a prostitute: Winthrop's mother seemed now to him to have lived at the very top of the Ladder of Fear, and minus one leg to boot. Then there was a host of frightful diseases . . . shutting the door on leprosy and inherited syphilis, he wrenched his mind back on his work, conscious of a passing but real surge of gratitude for acne and dandruff – the first, after all, did recede from time to time, and the second was something that he had the professional knowledge to keep at bay.

'I'm afraid you'll have to stop reading for a minute or two while I cut your fringe,' he said. She put down the book and smiled trustfully at him: really, in a way, she was rather an attractive person – not his type, of course, but looking at her quite objectively he could see that quite a number of people might regard her as reasonably attractive.

When he had finished, she gave him a 50p piece in an anxious, almost supplicatory manner – as though she was afraid he might not accept it.

He thanked her warmly and then he had to rush over to Mrs Courcel, who had taken herself out of the dryer and was surveying herself with the unswerving interest that he had noticed she seemed always to have for her own face. Quicker to take her rollers out himself than wait to get Mandy or Jenny.

Mrs Courcel's hair was black and glossy and the gloss shone blue – like the flame from methylated spirit. It was really the kind of hair that looked best when it was dressed very simply, but when he had once suggested this, she had said to hell with simplicity, it bored her husband. Her hair piece lay on the shelf in front of the mirror like a dead raven. He brushed out her hair from the roller curls and then asked her what she wanted him to do.

'I want it all drawn back, but on top as well, and then the piece *right* at the back, with curls falling down each side. I've a dress with just one shoulder, so I want it sort of Grecian.' His heart sank. Getting the piece to stay on the back of her head (she hadn't really *got* a back to her head – it sloped alarmingly from the top) would be murder – however: never say no to a client. He parted her hair in the middle, fastened each side with clips and picked up the hair piece. Fifteen minutes later, he had achieved what she had asked. He was sweating but thank God it was over. He handed her the mirror and she began a minute survey of her head from every angle.

'It's no good,' she said at last. 'I thought it couldn't be: it didn't feel right and you can see – three quarters from the back – that I *look* as though I'm wearing a hair piece. It doesn't look like *me*.'

There was a brief silence: Mrs Courcel did not look in the mirror at him to see what he thought of what she thought: she continued calmly to gaze at herself, picking at pieces of her hair with her coral-painted nails, but Gavin looked fleetingly at his own face as a tidal wave of rage and hatred surged up his body and swirled about his throat, and was astonished to see that it was suffused with a weak (and silly) smile. He had been afraid that his fury would show – might even upset the client – but his idiotic expression filled him instead with self-loathing. 'Why don't you ever stand *up* for yourself?' Marge used always to say whenever awful things had happened to him as a child which they so often had. When they'd emptied his silkworms down the school toilets, when he'd won a pig at Barnet Fair and his mother had made him give it away, when his father had said there was no sense in paying for violin lessons, when he'd run a (sub-normal) temperature the night before he was going to the sea-side with Auntie Sylvia and his mother had cancelled the trip 'to be on the safe side', when Tony Williams had pinched his brand new bike and crashed it . . . he realized that he was taking down Mrs Courcel's hair, and glancing up from his hands to the mirror again he saw with relief that the smile had vanished – indeed, he had no expression at all.

'I think if you tried the piece on top of my head with the curls below it it may work better,' Mrs Courcel said. He set about trying that: it was what he had been going to do in the first place. As Mrs Courcel relentlessly followed every move he made – and he was now working against time because Mrs Blake was due out of the dryer any minute with no Jenny to hand him pins or hold pieces of hair – he felt his stomach contracting with nerves, and knew that even if he managed to get time for lunch, he wouldn't feel like eating. 'God!' he told himself; 'you've been doing this job for nearly sixteen years and you *still* let a little thing like this get you down!' She was just a difficult client; selfish, self-absorbed and narcissistic. He thought of a few more things that she was, and then his dogged sense of fairness – misplaced, in this case, for all he knew or did not know – rushed to the attack. For all he knew, everything she cared about might have been taken from her: her obsession with her appearance might be nothing more than a gallant attempt to keep going; she might have *had* a child who had died; her husband might be off with another woman and she was trying desperately to hold his attention; she might be so frightened and lonely that she was in danger of going mad. The thought of a life that could entail a pointless visit to the hairdresser every day opened up vistas of boredom and isolation that any ordinary person like himself would find appalling.

Look how fortunate *he* was, with a good job, Mum and Dad to go home to, a nice foreign holiday every year and tons of interests, and it wasn't as though he felt marvellous all the time in spite of all that. He stopped there, because he found himself not wanting to contemplate his opposite of feeling marvellous – not in the salon and especially not when he was dressing Mrs Courcel's hair. He hoped that Mrs Blake would not start crying again (a distinct possibility if he was too nice to her when he combed her out) and, beyond Mrs Blake, Muriel Sutton loomed. As he handed Mrs Courcel the hand mirror for the second time, he said: 'I think that's about the best I can do for you today.' (Bloody well like it, or leave it.)

After prolonged scrutiny, she agreed that it was better, and before she could qualify her cautious approval he begged to be excused and wheeled his trolley smartly over to the patient Mrs Blake who was still baking under the dryer. As he did this, he noticed that Mr Adrian had emerged from his lair, had seen Mrs Courcel being abandoned and was now padding over to her. This was going to mean trouble of some kind or another, but he decided to concentrate upon Mrs Blake.

'Sorry to keep you waiting,' he said: 'but at least it will be thoroughly dry.'

'I don't suppose I shall know myself,' she said as though this would be an inviting prospect. He smiled but did not reply: he felt that the best technique with Mrs Blake was to look as though dressing her hair occupied the whole of his attention. The large rollers out, he brushed the curls thoroughly while – from the corner of his eye – he saw Mrs Courcel escorted to the reception desk by an obsequious Mr Adrian (she was an account customer and of course she spent a lot): she did not come over to tip him, and he knew that that was a bad sign. No parting, he thought, and he would back comb the sides a little to give extra width. The perm had taken very well: wasn't too tight considering.

'When you've finished, I'd like a word with you, if I may.'

'Right,' he said. Mr Adrian hovered a moment more and asked if Madam was pleased with her perm.

'I'm sure I shall be. Gavin's been wonderful: I've got such difficult hair and he's made it look positively luxuriant.'

Mr Adrian smiled, showing a large number of small, unnervingly white, false teeth and glided away. Gavin felt a surge of gratitude to Mrs Blake.

When he had finished with her, she really looked much better: the slightly windswept look made her look more hopeful and alive.

'There we are,' he said briskly as he handed her the mirror. 'Of course, it'll take a week or two to settle down.'

'Thank you so much.'

Fearing that she might be reaching danger point, he took her quickly to the desk, handed her over to Daphne. When she thanked him again he gave her a cheery wink – as a kind of telegram to keep her pecker up. Pity there was nobody to wink at him, he thought as he walked to Mr Adrian's lair, or, pity he couldn't wink at himself.

He knew exactly what Mr Adrian's 'word' would be. Mrs Courcel was a very good customer: he – Mr Adrian – did not keep the kind of establishment where clients were abandoned the moment their hair was dressed: no – in his establishment (and perhaps he ought to remind Gavin whose establishment it was) clients were conducted back to the reception desk, where, if there was not a junior available, they were helped into their coats. It might sound funny to Gavin, but good, old-fashioned courtesy made a world of difference. Some clients were more fussy than others, but that, as Gavin must know, was the way the cookie crumbled – his teeth put in an appearance here . . .

'Perhaps you could suggest to Mrs Courcel that she make appointments instead of dropping in – '

Now now, Gavin knew that she usually did make appointments –

'She doesn't! She makes about one a week, and comes in at least three other days. She upsets my bookings, and then, when she wants her hair dressed *twice*, I get short of time.'

Mr Adrian had looked at the book, and as far as he could see but correct him if he was wrong, Gavin had not got another client until two.

'Mrs Blake had to be finished off.' But Gavin knew that Mr Adrian, by putting him on the defensive and ignoring his lunch break, had won some sort of murky point. Gavin was at least too experienced in Mr Adrian's little ways to *mention* his lunch. He knew if he did that exactly what he would get. Oh – of course, Gavin's *lunch*! We mustn't forget the all-important point of your *lunch*! Then there'd be a lot more stuff about how, in this modern age, the client was of no importance compared to employees *having* to have a disproportionate amount of time off to eat a sandwich, when he thought of *his* youth . . . no, Gavin's only victory was not to give him that opening.

'Right,' he said with great firmness but apropos of nothing at all. 'Point taken: I must be off now.' And, before Mr Adrian could take his feet off the chair on which he usually kept them, he'd gone.

Now he'd have to go out to lunch – well, go out, anyway. His watch said twenty-five to two. There'd be queues at all the local sandwich shops – his only hope was the pub.

It was, as usual, crammed – with the sort of people who seemed only to manifest themselves in pubs: large sweating men in tweed suits; middle-aged women wearing diamanté clips and fur jackets, with most of them shouting and laughing. Jokes about Irishmen, Welshmen and Scotsmen and just any old person who was tight were being bandied about; there was a smell of drink and hot clothes and the air was filled with smoke. There was nowhere to sit (which he minded because he was on his feet all the time he was working) and the only sandwiches left were cheese. He bought one and a tomato juice to wash it down. Then, by great luck, he saw a seat in the corner being vacated and managed to seize possession of it. Once in it, he thought things would feel better, but in fact they got worse, or, rather, getting somewhere to sit and having something to eat freed his attention for how horrible the rest (and most) of life was being. If Mr Adrian had ever spent his youth working like a galley slave – one of his many ways of putting it – he had certainly made up for that ever since. But it was more, or worse than that. He could stand Mr Adrian lolling about all day with his racing papers, it was the way he turned everything sour that was unforgivable. The only person in the whole salon whom he never dared to snipe at was Hugo, who was the oldest of them. It was difficult to put an age to him since he had had silver white hair, a white moustache and brindled eyebrows ever since Gavin had first seen him. For a brief moment, Gavin considered leaving, getting out, starting somewhere else, but the mere thought of such a cataclysmic change frightened him nearly as much as the thought of being left entirely alone with some unknown female. He wouldn't know what was going to happen every day – he might never know what was going to happen again! The unknown couldn't be good: it would be like freewheeling on his bike down a steep hill in the dark . . . faint echoes of last night recurred then, but he shut down his memory of it . . . he had only himself to trust and he was always letting himself down. It was easy to go down. No, he'd have to stick Mr Adrian. He could blow off steam to Harry who was wonderful about it, listened with the utmost attention, clicking his teeth and twitching his nose. 'The old *bitch*,' he'd say; and almost admiringly, 'I don't know how you stand it.' His work wasn't his whole life, after all; there were tons of things he was interested in. Five to two – he must get back to Muriel Sutton.

She was waiting for him, of course; she was early, sitting on the reception chaise-longue.

She wore a polyester dress of a green so shrill that, after the first assault, he tried to concentrate upon anything else about her: white shoes, white handbag, white gloves. Her face always reminded him of a kitten's peeping out of an uncooked bun, small, playful eyes, a tiny, podgy nose, with the shortest possible upper lip all set in a vast expanse of seemingly boneless white flesh – whiskers and some fur, even pointed ears would have lent piquancy that was sadly lacking.

'It's all right, Gavin, I was early,' she said with a knowing indulgent smile that was meant to put him at his ease. As he put the cape round her and conducted her to a chair he reflected that the salon was full of *other* people, including his colleagues, it would be impossible for her to confront him with any really terrifying intimacy: he resolved to be extremely professional.

'Now,' he said; aware of her gazing at him in the mirror. 'What have you got in mind?'

She pursed her little, bright pink lips.

'Well, you know how it is: I just felt like a change.'

He combed through her hair experimentally – to get the feel of it. It was dark, fine and rather greasy; had been cut square to shoulder length and permed rather badly about six months ago, he guessed. She wore it scraped back from her face by a tortoiseshell band. He tried a side parting, rather high up – no, that would create problems about what to do on the parting side. The thing was to get her hair to conceal the featureless areas of her face – to give the built-up bits more of a look in.

'Supposing I cut you a fringe – from fairly far back, and then I layer the back and perm it to curl upwards?'

'Whatever you say, Gavin. Marge told me to put myself completely in your hands.'

'Right. Well, we start with a shampoo, and then I'll cut you wet. Jenny!'

But there was no sign of Jenny. He made signs to Daphne to get Jenny, and Muriel, with the same smile, said, 'I've got all the time in the world. Don't *worry*!'

Daphne said: 'She's not upstairs: I don't know where she is.'

He went to the back of the salon – partly to get away from Muriel – before he retorted that he wasn't worrying, but *he* hadn't got all the time in the world thank you – and found Jenny cleaning one of Mrs Courcel's hair pieces. 'Mr Adrian told me to,' she said.

'Well, you'll have to shampoo my client first,' he said. Jenny grinned.

'Glad to.' He knew she hated Mr Adrian although nothing, of course, would ever be said.

While Jenny was shampooing, he slipped out to the back to get a cup of coffee from Mrs Silkin. The mere thought of being properly alone with Muriel was intimately nerve-wracking, but he now realized that when he was with her when there were other people present she simply maddened him with her 'you and I know that I know all about you' demeanour. When, however, he *thought* about her, unthreatened by the prospect of actually seeing her, he just felt extremely sorry for her. Just! Feeling sorry for other people was one of the most overwhelming sensations he had about them that he knew – a time when he felt powerlessly sad, when injustice seemed to have a casual, but all-embracing whip hand: why should Muriel weigh fourteen stone *and* be seemingly unaware of her actual effect upon people whom she most wanted to move or impress? It was different for him; what he wanted was probably unattainable – out of the question – but she just wanted to capture the devotion of a perfectly ordinary chap like him (well, due to Marge's formidable influence, he suspected that she'd narrowed her sights to it being actually *him*) and settle down – subside into some sort of innocuous routine of providing for the creature needs of a family. She didn't even want a Prince

Charming; Fred Charming would do her perfectly well. Well, he must be kind to her, but the drag of that dictum included the feeling that, apart from being hard work, being kind to her wasn't even good enough: being direct to her was a sort of long-term kindness that he had not got the energy to employ . . .

'She's washed and combed out.' He felt for his comb and followed Jenny back into the salon.

'Now,' he said, with as much breezy good-will as he could muster: 'let's see what we can do.'

She asked him whether he had seen Marge lately. He nearly fell into the trap of saying that he went on Sundays – was, in fact, going to lunch this Sunday. He knew that would mean that she would get herself asked along if he did. So he said, not since last week. She said she often wondered what he did with himself at weekends. Not much: caught up on his reading, got some exercise, saw a few friends. She always thought that weekends was the best time to see friends. She didn't know about Gavin, but most weekday evenings by the time she'd coped with the rush hour back from the office, all she felt up to was cooking supper and watching a little television possibly – of course she didn't watch just *anything* – she was pretty choosy when it came to television, but documentaries often opened up new vistas and she had to confess that she was a bit of a romantic and loved a good old Hollywood film with a proper, old-fashioned story – nothing violent. Of course it wasn't the same as going to the cinema, didn't he feel there was nothing like having an evening out and going to a film? Barnet Odeon had three screens and there was quite often a worthwhile film showing on one of them. Marge had told her how interested he was in films. He belonged to some society, didn't he, that showed the real oldies on the South Bank somewhere? Yes, but he hardly ever went these days. It *was* difficult to keep up with all one's interests wasn't it? She had her flower arrangement class and she visited one Old Person in

Barnet General every week, and last year she had made every single one of her Christmas cards, verses, decoration, the lot, and then she was very keen on making her own pickles and jams – time flew without one realizing it. It must be three months since she'd seen Gavin – no *more*! – it had been on Boxing Day, hadn't it; they'd had such fun – all those games with Stephen and Judy, such lovely kids – not that Marge didn't deserve it, she and Ken made a lovely couple, did Gavin remember the wedding? When all the sausage rolls had been off because of the weather and they'd had to rush off and get some ham? But Marge had made a beautiful bride and she had felt quite embarrassed being the only bridesmaid and did Gavin remember Lionel – the best man? Well, it was all water under the bridge now but she didn't mind telling him that after the reception Lionel had been – well, you know – he'd made ever such a pass at her (here she mercifully lowered her voice), he'd got her at the end of the passage coming out of the bathroom and she simply *had not* been able to get by . . . She hadn't set eyes on him from that day to this. Just as well, really, because she did like things nice between people – quite frankly, she found all that grabbing and pawing distasteful – there were things of the mind, after all, and personally she didn't hold with love at first sight, she felt it was something that ought to come slowly – often two people might not be aware of how they felt for years, or one of them might feel too shy to say anything. Here, her dark little eyes flickered at his for an instant in the mirror and her mouth, as moist and pink as an uncooked chipolata, curled into its miniature smile. But her hair was cut, ready to be dried before he permed it. He had got by with a kind of absent-minded acquiescence and by an over-attention to the job. The back of his neck felt burning, and his face ached with the passive half-smile he had adopted, but that was a small price to pay. The worst was over, in a way; he could insist upon the presence of Jenny for the perming process – and make her hand him the rollers for the set after it. He hadn't got trapped into *seeing* her; her monologue had been too much of a landslide for any particular notion to get lodged long enough to confront him with the need to reply. He knew that Hugo, working on his right, must have heard a good deal of Muriel, but tact about such matters was unwritten law. Without being told, Hugo would have known that Muriel was some kind of private connection and this always meant that you pretended not to have heard anything and never passed any remarks afterwards. Hugo had a terrifyingly old relative – aunt, Gavin supposed she must be – who treated him as though he was a small unreliable boy all the time he cut and set her iron-grey waves. And Peter had a sister who acted as though she owned the place because her brother worked there. He wouldn't get ribbed about Muriel.

While Muriel was being dried, he cut the hair of a four-year-old child – the daughter of an old client who alternated between an almost regal immobility and sudden convulsive movements when it seemed as though it was going to throw itself out of the chair. Every time it did this and was reproved by its mother, its fine, ash-blonde hair had to be combed out again to provide a line to cut from. He became afraid of nicking one of its ears; felt oppressed by its silence and depressed by his inability to capture its attention. When it came to trimming its fringe he was sweating with nerves. 'You really *have* got to sit still for this bit,' he enjoined. At this, the child lowered its eyelashes over its amazing brown velvet eyes and put its head in its lap. 'Susannah! Gavin can't cut your hair like that.' And so it went. As he pocketed his 20p tip, Gavin resolved for the hundredth time never to cut a child's hair again.

By then, Muriel was ready and waiting for him with her conspiratorially indulgent smile. So, when Daphne came and said that there was a telephone call for him, he didn't even ask who it was, but went to answer it as a kind of respite.

It was Harry. 'Know you don't like being rung up at work,

but there's a little party on Saturday night that Winthrop and I think you might really enjoy. Okay?' And, without waiting for an answer, he went on: 'Come to our place at seven, and we'll all go on from there. We're getting a lift: it's all arranged. Bye,' and he rang off.

So when, what seemed like hours later, Muriel really came out into the open with an invitation to supper with her on Saturday, Gavin, who had not had the slightest intention of accepting Harry's invitation (who had, in fact, felt cross at not being given time on the telephone to refuse it), found himself saying that he was already going somewhere that evening – he was afraid.

CHAPTER THREE

GAVIN spent a good deal of Saturday trying to think of legitimate ways of getting out of Harry's party. In his private Court of Law (where petty cases against Gavin Lamb were tried from morning till night practically every day of the week) there was really no case at all. He had committed himself to going to the party because he had told Muriel that he was going out, and his brand of honesty precluded his staying at home after that. Unless he was ill; but he wasn't ill. On the other hand, he hadn't actually *said* where he was going, so wouldn't simply going out somewhere – anywhere – do? But that didn't feel right: if he didn't go to Harry's party, he *could* have had supper with Muriel. Never mind whether he *wanted* to or not – the court didn't care in the least about want, it was only concerned with the rights and wrongs of the matter. And, as usual, there was evidence of the accused evading an issue to the point of dishonesty. Sentence passed was that he go to Harry's party *unless* he cared to ring Muriel and tell her that he could make it after all. Options presented by the court were usually of the kind that made him feel mild guilt for choosing the lesser evil.

Otherwise, Saturday was much as usual. He got up later, had a boiled egg for breakfast, got through his mother doing his room – 'Books are very *dirty* things, you know – they collect the dirt I don't know why you want so many of them'; went to the cleaners to collect his best brown trousers and spring jacket; collected the new records he'd ordered; and bought a bunch of tulips for his mother. For lunch, there was boiled beef and

63

carrots and dumplings – followed by Castle puddings which, since he'd mentioned them only the night before, he had to eat in quantity. The meal had to be demolished fast because Mr Lamb wanted to watch an old war film and Mrs Lamb wanted to get the washing-up done. There was nearly a disaster about one Castle pudding being left; before either Mr Lamb or Gavin could conceal or dispose of it, Mrs Lamb flitted in from the kitchen where she had been washing their beef plates.

'Which of you is going to eat that,' she commanded. Mr Lamb shrugged, but he met Gavin's eye uneasily. 'Three's my lot,' he said; 'and very nice they were too.'

'Well, I've had four. Wouldn't it warm up, Mum?'

'Warm up? Warm *up*? Since when have you known me serve warmed up food? In this house,' she added, as though she might do it anywhere else. 'Cold food's one thing – warmed up is quite another. A lot of elderly people drop dead from warmed up food: they may think it's easier but they soon find out their mistake.'

The wildness of this lie warned Gavin and his father that, if they didn't want things to go too far, they'd better recognize that they'd gone quite far enough.

'We'll share it,' Mr Lamb said. Taking the initiative meant that he could divide it and take the smaller piece.

'All that fuss about one Castle pudding,' Mrs Lamb scolded as she poured all the rest of the golden syrup on to their plates. 'I'll bring your tea into the front room if you want to watch the match.' She popped back into the kitchen.

' "People have been known to drop dead!" Where does she get it all from?'

'I don't know, Dad.'

'If you ask me, it's the women's magazines – all those books she reads every week. They're always putting people into *classes* – and full of all that do-it-yourself nonsense. The trouble *we* get with that! And fancy meals. And there's another thing about them. Don't tell your mother, 'cos I don't think she's noticed, but they're full of *sex*. What good is that? They may call it romance but it's nothing of the kind. It's dressed up sex . . .'

'Dad, if you want to watch the match – '

'It says, "You may be presented with a difficult choice and if you continue to be in doubt you should do nothing – let events speak for themselves." Here's your tea.'

'All right, Mother.' He took the tea, winked at Gavin and went into the front room. 'It' was their horoscopes in the *Mirror*; Mrs Lamb read them every day and seemed always to know them by heart. They were allowed to wink or smile about them – to tease her very gently in return for seeming to believe them.

'What about mine then, Mum?'

'"You will have a quiet, socially rewarding day, but beware of rash impulses that could result in embarrassment." Going to take your tea up for a nice read, are you?'

'I thought I'd mow the lawn first.'

She liked the lawn mown within an inch of its life, so this suggestion found favour. While he marched up and down, he wondered anxiously about the rash impulses. Whatever they were, he determined to beware of them since he could certainly count on the embarrassment. Ordinarily he would, metaphorically speaking, have winked (one did not wink *at* Mrs Lamb), would have risked a little nudging pat on her shoulder, but the threat of rash impulses froze him. Perhaps it was rash to go to Harry's party, but if it was, the impulse had been yesterday's.

The rectangular garden had wallflowers, pink tulips, and forget-me-nots planted in the two beds which contained standard roses of peculiarly fluorescent colours – not in flower yet, but once they started they went on and on. They were the pride of both his parents: Mr Lamb pruned and fed them with ferocious care; Mrs Lamb sprayed them repeatedly against every known pest. The wallflowers and forget-me-nots were a concession to him: they really preferred bare, weedless beds symmetrically planted with staked and regimented dahlias and chrysanths. At the far end there was a small greenhouse where Mr Lamb grew tomatoes and cucumbers, and, outside it, two rows of runner beans behind which was the compost heap. Gavin only had to go there twice with the mowings. When he had finished, he wondered whether to get a chair and his book to read out of doors, but the rather fitful morning sun had given up, the sky was a pale, dense uniform grey and the neighbour who had recently embarked upon learning the electric guitar was well away with his explosive and irregular tonic dominant chords. Mowing the lawn had helped to get his lunch down anyway.

He watered his plants, and after wandering round his room picking at books to see what he felt like, took one of his favourite catalogues – of an exhibition he had seen years before in Paris – on to his bed. It was beautifully produced and he was easily plunged into the lyric composition of early summers, of sunlit waters and orchard greens, and pieces of domestic behaviour caught with brilliant intimacy. It was the girls he loved: girls brushing out their hair, cutting their toe nails, putting on their stockings; cast in languor upon grass, upon chaises-longues, upon orientally coverletted beds; sitting self-consciously erect upon small severe chairs in a café, one girl sewing the collar on to a flowered dress, one washing cherries at a wooden table, one reclining in a white basket chair nursing a baby whose head, round and brown like a hazel nut, pushed against her breast. If those girls existed now he would be in love: there was something both festive and gentle about them whereas he felt that most girls today were as joyless and difficult as Everest – to be conquered by anyone who did not mind discomfort and recognized that they were there. He let the catalogue lie and closed his eyes . . .

He was walking up a very short, straight drive edged with young poplars towards a white house with green shutters whose door was open. The sun was hot and the house marvellously cool and still, except for the sound of a large walnut clock ticking. A straw hat trimmed with daisies and narrow green velvet ribbon lay on the chest below it and he knew this meant that he could go up. Her door was also open, but the shutters were closed, making bars of aqueous light across the white bed. She wore a muslin wrapper of pale green and white so that the bed was a marvellous confusion of stripes and her white skin was blossomed with green and gold reflections. She lay half on her side with her face resting in the palm of one hand: at affectionate ease with herself, she was asleep. On the bed beside her lay a painted paper fan open as it had fallen from her hand. (He remained quite still to watch and enjoy her – to store and print the detail of her in his mind so that it would be easier to return to her in the future.) Her heavy dark hair, cut short on her forehead, was long and undressed – tied back with a piece of white braid; a thin gold chain with a cross on it lay slanted on her neck. Her ankles were negligently crossed, her feet were bare. How should he wake her, and what might happen when he did? She would speak French, he realized with sudden panic: he would not understand her. No – she would speak just enough English; or perhaps they need not speak. He put out his hand to touch her forehead . . .

There was a banging on his door.

'You never drank your tea after dinner.' Before he could sit up, she was in the room with a tray, and stood over the bed waiting for him to clear the bedside table of books so that she could deposit it. She wore her spectacles and three rollers at strategic points in her hair and he could see her darting professional glances round the room to see whether he had managed to untidy anything since this morning.

'You shouldn't have bothered.'

She took this as a compliment. 'It will be a fine time when

I can't bring my own son some tea. There's those shop cakes you like. You can bring the tray down when you're done with it. Don't let it get cold.' And she went.

The tray was a round tin one with a cat crouching in some buttercups printed on it. The teapot was encased in a knitted cosy the alternating colours of a ripe banana. There were three cup cakes arranged on a paper doily on a plate. The milk jug was shaped like a yellow chick from whose beak the milk was supposed to pour (Marge had given it to his mother at Easter), the cup was one of her best square ones whose handle was too modern to have a hole in it. Even before he lifted the shrouded teapot he knew it would be the one with feet – amusing china boots upon it. The whole tray was crowded with her affection – never expressed in words but in countless domestic deeds of this nature. He got up from the bed and fetched his secret cup and saucer from a cupboard. It was a piece of early Copeland with painted violas and butterflies, the rims richly gilded. He drank his tea out of it and wondered whether he could ever get his mother to believe that he liked China tea. She would give it to him if he asked for it, but she refused utterly to *count* it as tea, so if he had it, it simply meant that he had to drink twice as much. He still felt so stuffed with food that the cup cakes were a problem. In the end he wrapped them in a handkerchief to take to work. He started to feel nervous about the party as he was washing his cup in the bathroom, and decided to have a bath and listen to some music while he catalogued his newest batch of records to take his mind off the evening.

He had a long bath, washed his hair – did some Bates work on his eyes and had a thorough inspection of his face and neck. His face wasn't too bad, but there was a corker coming up on his neck – too high to be concealed even with a scarf round it. He scowled at himself in the glass so that he could see how much better he looked when he stopped. Not much better, really. The bathroom now smelled of bad eggs from his dandruff treatment and he was glad to leave it. He opened the window, tucked the curtain out of the way to air the room, and padded upstairs back to his room.

The catalogue lay on the bed where he had left it – open at a luminous Vuillard interior of a girl in a rocking chair looking out of a window. He shut the catalogue and put it away. She was always interrupting him: the only long privacy he could count on was at night.

He decided that Chopin would be good music to play while he did his catalogue, and opted for the mazurkas. It had to be music that he knew extremely well, but not of a kind that required intellectual attention: Chopin he could now – from love and familiarity – absorb through his skin. His cataloguing was a simple but ingenious affair. A loose-leaf book indexed under composers with each record numbered as he collected them and then entered in the book with its number and details about performance. Thus he could turn to S. find Schubert, or Strauss or Scarlatti – look for songs or operas or sonatas – find the number of, say, *Ariadne auf Naxos* and then seek it from the records on the shelves as they would be arranged purely in numerical order. He had taught Harry this system and Harry took every opportunity of praising it to friends in front of Gavin until he felt quite embarrassed. He had got to record three hundred and thirty-two, and with the new song cycle he had bought of Somervell's 'Maud', and the reissue of Rachmaninov playing an assortment of piano pieces, and Tuckwell doing the Mozart horn concertos, he was going to get nearly to the forties. The problem was soon going to be one of space: he would have to shift things round a good deal in order to build a new record shelf. If only he wasn't going out! He was longing to play the new records. Well, this time tomorrow he'd be safely back from lunch with Marge and have time to himself.

At half-past six he was dressed: cream shirt, brown trousers, brown and coffee-coloured Indian scarf failing to conceal newest eruption, brown windcheater unzipped (it was quite warm) and the faint feeling of malaise he associated strictly with going to parties. His parents were both in the front room. Dad was asleep in front of an earnest programme about New Towns; Mum was making a jockey cap for the bear out of scarlet felt.

'I'm off now.'

'Got your key?'

'Yes.'

'I hope you have a good time.' But she said it as though this would be very unlikely.

'I'll do my best.'

'Don't do anything I wouldn't do.' Dad had opened his eyes.

'Of *course* he won't. Anyway, why shouldn't he? You enjoy yourself,' she advised.

'Going to Town, are you?'

'I don't know. I'm going to a party with Harry.'

'Leave him alone! He's got a right to his own life, hasn't he?'

'I never said he hadn't. I only asked.'

'If you was all dressed up for a party, you wouldn't thank people for prying into your affairs. Now would you?'

'I ought to go really. Mustn't be late.'

'See what you've done? Driven the boy out with your nasty inquisitive questions.'

'It's all right, Mum. I don't mind him asking. It's just I don't know where the party is.'

'You see?' A thought struck her. 'You're going to a party and you don't know where it *is*? How can you do that? What sort of party can *that* be?'

'I don't *know*, Mum. Harry asked me to go with them.'

'Them? Who's them?'

'Winthrop, Mum.'

'And who's them beside Winthrop?'

'*Harry*. Winthrop and Harry.'

'No need to raise your voice with me.'

'Who's asking questions now?' Mr Lamb was enjoying the turned tables. He should have known better. She rounded on him. 'I only wanted to know. And who started it? Gavin didn't mind me asking, did you, Gavin? I only asked. Don't you take that tone with me. You surprise me sometimes, you really do, with your nasty nature, I wonder where it all comes from.'

Gavin met his father's eye warningly. Then he leant down and gave his mother a quick kiss. She jumped.

'Now look what you've made me do!' She held out a little horny thumb on which a bead of scarlet blood was forming. 'Two inches further down and a bit to the left and I might have had lockjaw! Where are you off to?' Mr Lamb had levered himself to his feet.

'Get the iodine.'

'Sorry, Mum.'

'All this fuss about a little prick.' But she was appeased, and Gavin was able to make his escape.

On his scooter, he reflected that really his mother was an excitable person who was short of excitement. She could do all that she had to do with one hand tied behind her back, in half of her day, and then she was left with solitary hours that neither her upbringing nor her intellect had equipped her to fill. He wondered how many people were bored without realizing it. Because surely anybody who recognized their boredom could do something about it? Perhaps that was much more difficult than it seemed. Boredom might be a kind of evil, ubiquitous secret that people called by any other name that suited their nature and view of themselves. Discontent, dissatisfaction, being a square peg in a round hole, envy – wanting, while still themselves – to lead someone else's life, unhappiness . . . he felt less sure of unhappiness as he did not know enough about it. His knowledge was gleaned chiefly from reading – from opera and the theatre, and again none of that was exactly like life: although, if good, it gave the appearance of it, at the same

71

time confirming that it did not matter so much what you did, or even what happened to you, so much as it mattered how you felt about it. Unhappiness in real life must be largely a matter of feeling that you were struck and caught by some circumstance that you were unable to escape from or resist. And he supposed that if you went on being unhappy about the same thing in the same way some kind of boredom would ensue. Boredom in fact, seemed to have something to do with lack of movement. But then, people could have what seemed to be very boring lives and not be bored by them. Look at him, for instance. He was just a hairdresser still living at home with his parents with two weeks' holiday – well, three now – a year – nobody could say that his was a very exciting life. *He* wasn't bored. On the other hand not enough happened for him to be unhappy in any sense that he understood what was meant by that. He wondered whether he could bear it if he was, but he was approaching Havergal Heights, and all the known – and, worse, unknown – possibilities that attached to a party were really upon him now. He dismounted his bike with a dry mouth and the feeling that he had lost the knack of breathing properly.

He felt momentarily comforted by the sight of Harry who was looking friendly and smart in his purple shirt with a pale pink scarf round his neck and his hair sleeked back.

'Welcome, dear boy. The others haven't arrived yet and Winthrop's had trouble with his jeans. I *told* him they were too tight when he bought them. "You'll do yourself an injury," I said when he tried them on, but his Lordship's vanity prevailed so we shall all have to hope for the best.'

The room looked very tidy with bowls of peanuts and Twiglets on the blackglass table and all the cushions carefully askew on the chesterfield.

'You're looking very good, if I may say so. Sit down, dear boy, I'm going to get us a little drink.'

Gavin sat down and ate a peanut to take his mind off

things. The windows on to the balcony were open, but the curtains, that looked as though they were made of yellow fishing nets, hung motionless. Another thing about parties, he recalled, was that he nearly always felt too hot at them.

'Close, isn't it? Thunder about, I think. Now, you can have whisky, or my little concoction. Winthrop and I got rather attached to it when we were in the South of France.'

'What is it?'

'It's called Kir. Have a go and see how you like it.' He poured a faintly pink liquid from a jug. Gavin tasted it. It was cool, a bit fruity and rather nice.

'It's just white wine with a spot of blackcurrant cordial. Like it?'

Gavin nodded, decided to have a Wilhelm II to calm himself and asked who were the others.

'Just Stephen and Noel.'

'Is the party here then?' He began to feel better at the prospect.

'No, no. They're coming to pick us up – give us a lift. The party's in some flat that belongs to someone who's a friend of one of Winthrop's friends but he's away. Somewhere off the Cromwell Road,' he added as though this pinpointed it. 'It's a mixed party – it's not just us. The field will be wide open, dear boy.'

Gavin tried to smile, but he began quite wildly to wish that he was getting 'flu, or, better still, was an asthmatic with an incontrovertible attack coming on.

'Perhaps I'd better take my bike?' This would mean that he had at least the means of escape. But before Harry could reply the buzzer went and Harry rushed to answer it.

Winthrop emerged from the bedroom while Harry was dealing with the door. He wore a black T-shirt with GET LOST in green on it, and the tightest pair of white jeans that Gavin had ever seen. This made him move rather stiffly – like Frankenstein's monster – and when he sat down, which he did at once, it did not seem possible for him to bend his knees. His auburn hair was wet and hung in tight shiny ringlets.

'Hi,' he said amiably. 'How's tricks?'

Wondering what Winthrop might think his would be, Gavin said they were fine. Winthrop heaved himself into a position that enabled him to pour himself a drink. To Gavin's surprise he chose whisky – about two inches of it. He caught Gavin's eye, and winked.

'Barnet's wet,' he said: 'don't want to catch cold.' He downed the drink just as Harry returned with the newcomers. There were three of them.

'Bloody door's gone wrong again.' He looked flustered. 'This is Stephen and Noel – and Spiro – from Greece. Gavin.'

'And fucking little me,' said Winthrop. He looked ominously at Harry. Harry blushed. '*You* know Stephen and Noel. I don't have to introduce you.'

'I don't know Spiro. Do I, Spiro?'

Spiro, who was extraordinarily young and extraordinarily good looking, smiled so that Gavin could see that his teeth matched the whites of his eyes, tripped over to the chesterfield and shook Winthrop's hand.

'Is British to shake,' he said.

Stephen, who was short and rather bald, but wore sideburns and a moustache said: 'He's only been here a week, hasn't he, Noel?'

'Six days, Stephen, actually.' Noel was Australian. He was wiry and with a crew cut and huge, pale blue eyes whose expression was alternately vacant and sardonic. There was a rather wary silence while Harry got everybody drinks, and Gavin wondered how on earth he would be able to think of things to say when conversation did break out. Spiro had perched himself on the arm of the chesterfield looking around him with frank curiosity and smiling if anyone looked his way. His mouth, when he wasn't smiling, was curved and chiselled like the best Greek sculpture. Indeed, Gavin thought, he was more than good looking, he was handsome to the point of beauty – probably the most beautiful creature that he had ever met in the flesh. He became aware of Noel observing him.

'Staggering, isn't he?' This remark seemed most unfortunately to focus everyone's attention upon Gavin, and he felt his face getting hot. He mumbled something about Spiro being very good looking, and Spiro, hearing his name, stood up, moved gracefully over to Gavin, and shook his hand. 'Ello – Hav*in*,' he said, and there was a friendly murmur of approval from the others. Gavin felt that he was being propelled along what could only turn out to be a sexual cul-de-sac and that they would all turn on him when they realized his dishonesty, but he also felt that there was nothing he could say to explain himself that would not sound wrong. Kind Harry rescued him.

'Gavin's not quite sure where he is, so don't upset him: he's one of my oldest friends. How about this party, then? Stephen, over to you.'

Stephen, who had also looked kindly at Gavin, said that he'd got his car and he thought they could all fit in, but Winthrop said that he was taking his bike. 'And I know who's going with me,' whereupon Spiro positioned himself behind Winthrop, bent his knees and went 'vroom vroom!' This delighted him, and he repeated it several times until Winthrop turned round suddenly and put his hand under Spiro's chin tilting his face upwards. There was a very short, loaded silence, and then Winthrop said, more gently than Gavin had ever heard him speak: 'Come on then,' and they left the flat. Gavin looked at Harry, who wore an expression of stalwart gaiety, but all he said was: 'I suppose he knows where the party is?' and Stephen said yes, he did, he knew the owner of the flat.

'He knows Joan. He doesn't know Dmitri, Stephen, actually.'

Gavin sat in front of the car with Stephen, who was driving, and Harry in the back with Noel. Gavin nerved himself eventually to ask Stephen what kind of party it was going to be.

'Well, it's a beautiful flat – a penthouse – and when Dmitri's in town he throws pretty good parties, but he's away, and Joan, that's his wife, told John to invite whoever he liked. They're very generous – '

'They're loaded.'

'Yes, but they're also generous, Noel. You have to admit that. People can be loaded and mean as hell, but Dmitri's not like that – '

'It isn't his money. It's Joan's money, Stephen, actually.'

'Well anyway, they spend it. They've got a fabulous place in the country. Noel and I went for a weekend once. It was amazing. They've got an indoor pool and sauna, squash court, colour TV in all bedrooms – the lot.'

Harry asked: 'What does Dmitri do then, when he's not at home?'

'Something to do with interior design, isn't it, Noel?'

'That was Joan's idea. She thought it would keep him at home more, but he got the idea of doing yachts so it hasn't really worked. He's always popping off to Monte or St Trop and he's away for weeks.'

Noel's voice sounded as though the situation amused him, and Gavin felt uncomfortable. Stephen, who seemed to sense this, said: 'Joan's all right. She knew what she was in for. She married him with her eyes open.'

'She's had to keep them shut ever since, Stephen.'

'That'll do, Noel. If you dislike her so much, you shouldn't go to her parties.'

'I like her all right. She's a bit of a cow, but I don't mind her.'

'She's a good cook.'

Harry said: 'You should know. Stephen's a chef,' he added for Gavin's benefit.

In the silence that ensued, Gavin wished desperately that he hadn't just weakly *suggested* that he should take his bike; he should have *told* them he was going to; then he would have been able to escape whenever he wanted, which, given his present feelings, would be about thirty seconds after he arrived.

'Here we are,' Stephen announced – quite suddenly.

It was a large, modern block of flats. Stephen pressed the buzzer and a voice instantly answered. They were through the plate glass doors into a carpeted hall and facing two lifts with heavy bronze doors. Stephen pressed the top button and, without any sense of movement, presumably up they went. Harry gave him an encouraging grin, and Gavin tried to grin back.

The noise of the party – like human surf – burst upon them as the lift doors opened. The doors to the flat were open. Someone, the stature of a child, but with a doll's face and dressed in maid's uniform flitted towards them to take their coats. Gavin parted with his windcheater; his anxiety had reached the point of recklessness; he felt he might never see it again, but that that would be a small price to pay for not being too hot until the imminent instant flight that he knew might become necessary. Harry took his arm, and following Stephen and Noel propelled him into the main room which seemed to be absolutely full already of people – of both sexes – although with a preponderance of men. A tray of drinks was offered them by a tiny little man in a white jacket who looked as though he might be some relative of the person who had taken their coats. Both looked vaguely foreign, but Gavin could not place them at all. He saw that the room, which seemed to be very large indeed, had glass doors that were open on to a terrace: there were people on that, but at least it would be cooler.

'. . . Harry King, and this is Gavin – 'fraid I don't know your other name. Gavin, this is our hostess, Joan.'

Immediately in front of and well above him was a vertical

tube of silver lamé on top of which was a flaming head – like a shaggy chrysanthemum – of the most blatantly orange hair even he had ever seen in his life. Orange lips were smiling from above (she must be well over six feet, he thought), and a pair of diamanté spectacles that seemed to be glazed with plate glass were beaming down at him.

'Why, Gavin, it's wonderful to have you here,' she said, in a throaty voice whose accent reminded him of someone out of a play by Tennessee Williams. At least she wasn't young: at least he wasn't alone with her. He had spoken too soon. She linked an amazingly muscular arm in his and saying simply, 'Come with me,' bore him off – away from Harry and Stephen, and even Noel – anyone he knew at all.

'Have you a drink? Oh dear! Where are those Filipinos? I have them for big parties, because they can burrow through the crowd more easily. Either you have to be small, or else like me, and I've never found any decent waiters my size. Anyway, we're heading in the right direction for a proper drink.'

They had reached the hall again, which Gavin now saw was extensive with a great many doors leading off it. Joan steered him through one of them into what looked like some kind of study. A regiment of bottles stood on a table at one end of a sofa. She shut the door.

'Now: you can have anything you like, but I'm going to have a brandy and ginger ale on the rocks.' As she moved away from him, Gavin saw that she really *was* tubular: she seemed to be corseted from just below the neck to just above her knees. She had long rather elegant masculine legs (Barry Humphries as Dame Edna came to mind) and long, pointed court shoes with very high heels that seemed to be made of multi-coloured sequins. When she had poured her drink, she opened what looked like a pineapple made of solid silver and put three blocks of ice into her glass. Then she turned to him. 'Now – and this is going to force you to speak – what will you have?'

'Perhaps I could try what you're having. I've never had it.'

'A pioneer drinker: I like that. You have this; I'll make another. Then we can sit soft for a while and you can tell me things. Or,' she added, as she turned back to the bottles, 'if you think that idea devastating, I'll tell *you* things. I always find that general conversation is a bit of a strain with a stranger.'

There was another sofa near a second open door in the room and she went and sat upon it. It was clear that she intended Gavin to join her, and after a moment's hesitation (but what else could he do?) he joined her. She took a swig of her drink and motioned him to do the same. Then she said: 'You don't like parties, do you?'

Mesmerized by her directness, he said no, they made him nervous . . . The moment he had said that, he felt slightly – but not much – more at ease.

'How's the drink?'

'Very good. Pretty strong, though, isn't it?'

'I hope so. Let it steal through your veins, as they say in adventure stories.'

Gavin drank some more: it managed to taste exactly half of brandy and half of the ginger ale and it was certainly true that he could feel it warming him inside.

'Have you ever played a game called Secrets?'

He shook his head, and something of his alarm must have shown, because she smiled and said: 'Oh, it's risky all right, but there's a kind of balance of power about the risk and that lowers the price.'

This didn't strike him as reassuring. 'Look – it's very kind of you to take so much trouble about me, but won't the others miss you? I mean, it is your party – '

'Oh – they're all as happy as clams! They don't come to see me: nobody in their senses would do that more than once. I picked you because I was watching you because you were the only person I could see who clearly wasn't enjoying himself. I'm a hostess and you struck me as something of a challenge. Have another swig, because we're going to play, and I'll begin.

The rules are that I have to share one secret about myself, and one secret about you.' There was a brief silence during which, as she did not look at him, he felt able to look at her. Her hands, folded round her glass, were trembling.

'I weigh nearly fifteen stone. When I first saw you, I thought you were homosexual.'

There was another pause, and she said gently: 'It's better to play fast.'

'I'm thirty-one and I've never been to bed with anybody.' To his own amazement, as he said this, it was as though he had released some vociferous prisoner trapped and gabbling from within; somebody who was much better out. They had turned towards each other and she was gazing at him with impassive attention. He said: 'I thought you were terrifying.' With an effort, he added: 'I mean I thought you might be a man in drag.'

She lifted her glass to him and they both drank. Then she said: 'The only sex I've had in my life I've paid for. I thought: I suppose you're another hanger-on. I wonder what lies you'll tell.'

'I pretend that no one's good enough for me because I'm such a coward. I get spots all the time and I'm afraid that she would laugh at me. Is that too much?'

She shrugged, but her attention did not waver. 'Feel free.'

'I do.' It was a discovery. 'I pass about you,' he said.

'You can't do that, rules.'

'*Orange* hair. Why on earth do you have orange hair?'

'It's a wig. When I'm very unhappy I drink so much I'm sick. Or I buy things. You may be a prig.'

'I don't think you should say I might be; I think you should say I am.'

'Right. I think you are.'

He finished his drink. Then, with a final effort, he said: 'I invent girls who are in love with me. Girls who'll do anything

I want. You're the kind of person that, in a different way, I'm afraid I am.'

'I'm grotesque. I underline it, so that everybody else will know that I know I'm grotesque. I make the most of a bad job. I love men – particularly beautiful men – and I'm sorry for myself. When I saw you, I wondered what you'd cost.'

There was a silence between them during which Gavin became conscious of his total absence of fear. He could look at the figure before him – at the orange hair and orange mouth painted on to a dead white face, the plate-glass diamanté spectacles, the corseted bulk of the silver lamé – simply as part of the pieces of declared truth about her which neither of them felt the need to judge or disclaim. It was as though she had made herself transparent; as though what ordinarily constituted the brick walls of personality had become like glass – or even clear water. Had he become like that for her? Had she accepted those fragments of truth about him, and if she had, what might happen next? Some of his exhilaration ebbed and he felt a familiar spasm of fear.

She seemed to sense where he had got to, as she said: 'It's your turn, but we can stop if you like. Would you get me another drink?'

He took her glass. While he looked for and found the right bottles, he asked: 'Do you mind if I ask you a question?'

'I forgot to tell you the other rule: no post mortem.'

'I don't think that what I want to ask would be that. If it turns out to be, you needn't answer.'

'I don't *mind*,' she said, 'and I shan't, if it is.'

'You've played before?'

'Once or twice.'

'Well – ' but, before he could find the right way to ask, she said: 'But it's odd – it's never in the least the same. It's more as though certain kinds of truth attract one another. Was that what you meant?'

'Yes.'

'Otherwise it wouldn't be fair on the new player.' She accepted her drink and added: 'It isn't a game you can play with anybody.' It was difficult to see her expression behind the glasses, but her voice sounded weary, as she went on: 'Most of the people here, for instance.'

He thought of Noel in the car, what seemed like hours ago.

'Don't you want another drink? There's a lot of food laid out in some of the rooms. I'm not trying to get you to go away and eat it: I just thought you might like to know.'

Before he could reply, there was a frenzy of tapping on the door and one of the Filipinos appeared. He looked very agitated. 'Please, Madame, come,' he said.

She got to her feet. 'I shall have to, because he hasn't enough English to tell me why.'

'Is there a bathroom somewhere?'

'Dozens. The nearest is through there.' She indicated the door behind them: the sounds of the party – like distant good-natured roaring – were again to be heard, making him realize that he had forgotten that there was one. Joan had gone, but she had left the door open. After a moment's thought, he went and closed it. He did not feel like rejoining the party yet, and leaving the door open might mean that some of it would join him. He looked at the room. It was furnished as a kind of study/library in a rather theatrical manner more as though it had been designed to suit its name than its calling. There *were* books – on the whole of one wall – but they seemed all to be sets bound in leather with gilded lettering. His own books that he used and read did not look at all like that. Apart from the two sofas, one each side of a fireplace where no fire would be likely to burn, there was a large leather-topped kneehole desk, empty, except for silver and leather desk furniture upon it – a blotter, writing paper holder, ink stand, a pair of lamps with green glass shades and a large photograph in a silver frame. He looked at the photograph. It was a head and shoulders studio portrait of a man whose swashbuckling good looks made him think of Errol Flynn playing one of the Three Musketeers. It was inscribed in writing like an exuberant spider with spurting black ink: 'Joan – all my affection – D M I T R I' . The Dmitri was twice as large as the rest of the writing. He went through the door that she had indicated led to a bathroom.

It didn't seem to, at first. It was obviously her bedroom and smelled of chocolates and flowers. It was decorated all in rose and white; again the theatrical décor for a romantic young girl's bedroom – he thought of *Spectre de la Rose*. The lights were shrouded and very low, but he had a general impression of drifts of white muslin – round the dressing table and the window; a rose-coloured carpet stretching in all directions; bowls of white pinks, a very long striped day bed, what looked (could it be?) like a Marie Laurencin in an alcove between two doors or cupboards and, in the far corner, an enormous bed – a four poster with elaborate hangings – swags of pink silk curtains edged with white fringe and an immense rose-coloured coverlet in considerable disarray. Indeed, the bed looked as though it had been romped in and abandoned – bedclothes humped, pillows scattered. Perhaps the doors *weren't* cupboards: he went to see. The left-hand door opened and he walked into a palatial bathroom – with black marble and silver walls, taps shaped like dolphins and a carpet that seemed to be embroidered with them. This, too, had two doors (he began to realize that the flat must occupy the whole of the top of the block – was probably two, or even three, apartments thrown into one). Again he chose the left-hand door, and there was a lavatory – entirely black: luckily, he never had to search for any lights as they were always on. When he had relieved himself, he decided to wash his hands and put a comb through his hair. This was partly because he had never been in such a bathroom before in his life and felt it would be a pity not to make some use of it. He wasn't sure if his face looked the same, but he felt different about it. His eyes looked very bright, and his newly washed hair actually shone. From somewhere inside him, a voice muttered: 'You're all right.' It was unusual – and encouraging. Exhilaration – a touch of excitement and finding himself where he was and feeling all right about it – gave him the courage to explore. He tried the second, right-hand door. It opened on to a yet more amazing bathroom, whose floor, walls and ceiling were all of glass. In the middle of it was an oval sunken bath, and in the bath were Winthrop and Spiro. Winthrop lay on his front and Spiro was astride him soaping his back. With the glass this scene was repeated all over the room with variations of angle that gave the impression of a piece of film. Their heads were both turned in his direction, and, seeing him, Spiro smiled his smile betokening angelic jolly mischief and said: 'Ello, Havin! Vroom, vroom!' and then collapsed laughing.

Gavin said: 'Sorry! Sorry to have barged in – ' he couldn't think of anything more to say.

Winthrop smiled amiably: 'Think nothing of it. We got a bit sweaty, one way and another, and Dmitri's bathroom is always good for a wash and brush up.'

Gavin reiterated some muttered apology and retreated, shutting the door behind him. Back in Joan's bathroom, he sat on the edge of the bath a moment to recover. They had given him a fright as well as a shock. Then he thought of Harry and his fright turned to anger with Winthrop – going to a party with Harry and behaving like that. *Anybody* might have gone through the door: Harry might have! He had an obscure feeling that, since they could so easily have locked it, they must have left it unlocked on purpose. *They* hadn't looked shocked when he walked in. They'd looked almost as though they'd liked it! He found himself wondering what Joan would think; then he wondered whether, by any chance, she had returned to the study/library to find him. If she hadn't he supposed he ought to join the fray. He went back to the rosy, scented bedroom, thinking – rather defiantly – that he might as well see if it was a Laurencin – well, of course it would be that, but whether it was a reproduction or the real thing – but as soon as he got into the bedroom, he realized that something else, disturbing, but quite different, was going on. Somebody, unmistakably feminine, was sobbing. The sobbing came from the bed. As he turned round from the Laurencin to face it, the hump of disarranged bedclothes moved and a girl sat up holding a good deal of rose silk coverlet round her. When she saw him, she gave a little wail of disappointment – it almost sounded like rage – and cast herself back on to the bed. Gavin suddenly felt that this was too much. Men cavorting in Dmitri's bathroom was one thing, but *girls* in poor old Joan's actual bed was surely another.

'Look here,' he said – unable to recognize his own voice and proud of it, 'what on earth do you think you're doing?'

'Shut up! Mind your own business – go away!' There was a second's pause, while Gavin battled with his reflexes, and then she said: 'Actually – don't.' She sat up again.

'I might need you.'

In spite of himself, he took a step nearer the bed. 'What for?' He felt wary and sounded sullen.

'I'm not supposed to be here.'

'I should think not.'

'I don't mean *here*,' she patted the bed, and the coverlet slipped, revealing bare, very bony shoulders the background to which was a lot of dark tangled hair. 'I mean at this party.'

'Why did you come then?'

'Love,' she said resentfully. 'It's so awful – that the quite awful things one does because of it don't seem so bad, don't you find?'

'Don't they?' He had the sensation of being treated as though he was somebody whom he hadn't even begun to be. 'I don't know,' he finished more honestly.

'Don't *know*?' Her high, rather childish voice rose to a

squeak, and he moved towards her again making a movement of his hand to quieten her.

'There are some people in there.'

'I *know*! That's why I'm here. I sent a message to him. I wrote it because those Filipinos can't take messages. I told him to meet me in here and then I hid, to be a lovely surprise for him. But then he came with – with someone else – ' her voice tailed off: 'and they had an awful time on this bed for ages, and then they went in there.' To Gavin's dismay, large pear-shaped tears began slipping down her face. After a moment, he said:

'But why are *you* in bed? I mean you can't have hidden in it, surely?' The thought appalled him. But she retorted: 'Of course not! What an idiotic idea! I got into bed to cry. I can't cry properly unless I'm lying down. My heart was broken,' she added as an afterthought. He noticed that she looked at him intently as she said this. Her eyes were pale blue, wide apart and nearly round. He also noticed that the coverlet had slipped so that one very small naked breast with an apricot nipple showed; he noticed the apricot because of the pink coverlet. Wondering how on earth young she was, he said accusingly: 'Aren't you wearing anything?'

She looked defiant. 'Of course not. It's dirty to get into people's beds in your clothes. How would *you* like it?'

'I wasn't wearing much, anyway,' she added. 'And when I heard you come in – of course I didn't know it was you. I hid under the bedclothes. I stifled my sobs.'

She was looking at him again – again intent. When, because he couldn't think of anything to say, he said nothing, she said: 'Well, you couldn't hear them, could you? So they must have been stifled . . .'

'I think you'd better get dressed.'

'All right.' She replied – almost gaily. Then, without any warning, she threw herself face downwards on the bed and wailed: 'You're taking my *mind* off it!'

'Off what?' One incredibly thin arm – well, skinny, really –

was clutching the top of her head, and she moaned: 'It's hopeless! He's the most beautiful man I've ever met in my life. When he smiles! I thought, if you really loved somebody, the fact that you don't speak the same language doesn't matter. They automatically loved you back! You bet they don't. All the things you read about let you down when you come to the point. But he didn't even give me a chance! It's juvenile to go thrashing about with a stupid common jerk when there's a perfectly good girl. That's what it is – *juvenile*!' She said this last as though it was an unanswerable insult that gave her some satisfaction. 'He ought to grow *up*. High time,' she finished, but as she seemed to have done, Gavin decided to be brisk.

'If you'll tell me where your clothes are, I'll give them to you, and wait next door while you put them on,' he said. He had decided that if it was Spiro she thought she loved, and the smile and lack of language seemed to indicate that, the sooner she got over him the better.

'I want to wait till he comes out.'

'That's up to you, but I'm not going to wait with you.'

'Please do. I beg you to.' She put a bony little hand on his arm, and he noticed that she bit her nails. 'He's got some awful olive-skinned boy with him; it's two to one; I won't stand a chance on my own.'

'Look here, if it's Winthrop you're so keen on, you won't get anywhere.'

'How do you know?'

'Because the person he lives with is a friend of mine. Honestly. He's not interested in girls at all.'

'You might be telling frightful lies: people do, if it's worth their onions.'

'Well, I'm not,' he said, too anxious now to take her up on the onions. 'Where's your dress?'

'Under the bed,' she said sulkily.

He bent down and it was. A rather skimpy dress of red cheesecloth.

'Stay while I put it on.'

'All right.' If he didn't stay, she might *not* dress, and he still felt that he owed it to Joan to get her out of the bed.

He walked over to the Laurencin – the heads of three doe-eyed girls.

'What's your name?'

'Gavin,' he said, without turning round.

'Gavin what?'

'Lamb.'

'How old are you?'

He told her.

'What do you do?'

'I'm a hairdresser.'

'Oh good.' She seemed mysteriously pleased. 'Okay, I'm dressed.' She giggled, an unexpectedly pleasing sound, and said: 'It's quite easy, because I don't wear knickers.'

When he turned round, she was sitting on the side of the bed fastening her very high-heeled red sandals. Then she stood up and held out her hand. 'I'm Minerva Munday; how do you do? Lady,' she added. She was looking straight at him again – to see if he was impressed, he thought. What *did* impress him about her was her thinness; she was about the thinnest person he'd ever seen in his life – far thinner than Jenny at work whom he had always thought too thin for her own good. He remembered that Joan had said there was a lot of food laid out somewhere, and then he remembered that Minerva (Goddess of Wisdom, his foot; she seemed to him no Goddess, and ridden with folly) had not been asked to the party at all – was a gate-crasher – still, perhaps with all those people, she would not be noticed . . .

'. . . seem to be rather impressed. Haven't you ever met a Lady before?'

'I cut their hair from time to time; I don't suppose you'd call that meeting them. Anyway,' he ended kindly, 'of course I'm impressed.' He was moving towards the study/library door having considered making the bed – nicer for Joan – and discarding the idea on the grounds that Winthrop and Spiro might make an appearance, and a scene ensue – nastier for Joan.

'Where are we going?'

'To find some food.'

'How do you know I want any?' But they were safely out of the bedroom and he had shut the door.

'*I* do,' he said in his new, firm voice.

'Oh – all right.'

'Don't you think you'd better comb your hair?'

'Haven't got a comb.' She turned back to the bedroom.

'You can borrow mine.'

She seized it, and dragged it through her hair so violently that it broke. She held a piece in each hand and made a hideous – and very funny – face at him. 'Some comb,' she said.

He took the larger broken piece and started to deal with the tangled mass. Even with her heels, she was not taller than he, but they were so high that, however gently he combed, she seemed to be in danger of losing her balance. 'You'll have to sit.'

She perched on the arm of the sofa he had sat on with Joan a hundred years ago. 'Pity you didn't let me do this in the first place,' he said after a bit. 'You've got very thick hair and you've got it in a right old mess.'

'I forgot you were a hairdresser. Are you really one?'

'I told you I was.'

'You might have been making it up.'

'I'm not given to that kind of thing.'

'Oh, nor am I. But what actually happens is much duller than it need be a lot of the time, don't you think?'

While he was still thinking that, this evening, no, it certainly wasn't, she said: 'Or are you frightfully grown-up about it – contented with your lot and all that?'

'I'm not bored, if that's what you mean.'

'I am. And I'm never sure what my lot is, but I must say I dread finding out.'

'Why?'

'Because then I'd be stuck with it, wouldn't I? Ow!'

'Sorry.' He'd been combing the full weight of her now untangled hair back from her forehead where it grew in a sharply defined widow's peak a little off centre.

'It's all right; you're pretty good, really. I once bit somebody who combed my hair. I was much younger, of course. My nursemaid – '

The door opened and three people, two men and a woman, came into the room carrying plates of food and glasses of wine. 'Plenty of room here,' one of them – the one who opened the door – said. They smiled guardedly at Gavin and Minerva as a way, Gavin felt, of not having to do anything else about them, and the woman said earnestly: 'But can't somebody *tell* Christopher that that sort of behaviour simply isn't *on*?' 'My dear Mollie, he's got Production behind him!' The second man said: 'Well I just hope I'll be on location before Jake finds out – that's all.'

As Gavin reached the door, Minerva put her hand in his and said:

'Do you know a lot of people at this party?'

'No.'

'Let's just go; let's not eat.'

But Gavin had started worrying about Harry, and whether he knew about Winthrop and Spiro, and whether he was feeling awful about it and needed support. 'I can't go until I've seen one person I do know,' he said, 'and they'll probably be eating.' Harry was anyway fond of food, and he invariably ate when he was anxious which was the least Gavin expected him to be.

It was quite clear where all the food was, since a trickle of people was emerging from a room down the passage, and each of them held a plate or was eating something, so he – very mildly – dragged her in the right direction (he was surprised to find himself doing this, and surprised also that he *could* do it).

The dining room – if that was what it was – had a long table down one side of it covered with bowls and dishes and plates of food. A good many people seemed to have eaten (there were about a dozen still in the room) and the food had that wrecked and plundered air: cold birds like shipwrecks; semi-spectral fish, ravaged mousses, a chocolate cake like some bombed building – crumbling brown rubble pocked with cream; and various salads fainting gaily in their bowls. Gavin saw Harry at once – sitting in the corner with a plate piled high and talking earnestly to an elderly man with a pointed beard. Harry registered Gavin's arrival instantly and Gavin realized that this was because he was very much on the watch – had positioned himself so that he could see whoever came into the room.

Minerva said:

'He's not here.'

'Who isn't?'

'Winthrop.'

'Never mind. You get yourself a plate of food. You could get me some too, if you like,' he added, hoping to keep her busy. He had decided that it would be better if she and Harry did not meet.

'All right.' She turned obediently to the table and he went over towards Harry. He was still talking.

'. . . and *when* the 1945 Government nationalized the railways what they didn't seem to recognize for quite some time was that they automatically took over thirty-five per cent of the canal system, much of it of course unnavigable, and a lot *they* cared, since fifty per cent of navigable waterway in the British Isles had fallen into complete desuetude and it had become fashionable to regard them as an outmoded form of transport. Oh, hullo, Gavin – you haven't seen Winthrop, have you, by any chance?' – his nose was twitching and he was elaborately casual.

'Not for some time. I know he's here, though.'

'Oh. Oh well, that's all right, then. This is Eustace Parker, my friend Gavin Lamb. Eustace makes documentaries on popular holidays. At least, I don't suppose he does that all his life, but that's what he's doing at the moment. I was boring him a bit about canals – '

'Eustace! Good Lord!' A squat and gnomic lady, in one springy pounce, had settled herself plum in front of Eustace, and by sitting cross-legged, and placing both her hands upon his shrinking knees, made it impossible for him not to notice that she was there. He looked at her with alarm and distaste.

'Biddy! Long time no see.'

'Oh my dove, I *know*! Auntie keeps sending me all over the place doing these filthy programmes that I told you in Manchester I was afraid Cyril was going to wish on to me; I've got contemporary poetry coming out of my *ears*! I feel if I have to record another poet, I'll go out of my mind. I do hope neither of you are poets,' she added, including Harry and Gavin a bit. They said they weren't and she turned her full attention back on to Eustace whose continuous smile, Gavin thought, was not unlike a cat's purr – it seemed effortless and he couldn't think how on earth he could breathe at the same time. Harry telegraphed his desire to get away, but Gavin pretended not to understand him: he still shrank from the idea of Harry and Minerva meeting. On the other hand, unless he escaped altogether, he began not to see how this could be avoided . . . unless he could manoeuvre the girl and the food to somewhere else pretty quickly. He walked briskly over to Minerva who had assembled two plates on one of which was a drumstick and a piece of the chocolate cake and on the other some of what looked like very nearly everything on the table.

'I thought you were never coming; I thought you were

trying to ditch me.' She did not sound accusing when she said this, but rather surprisingly humble.

'Let's go and eat it on the terrace,' he said.

In the passage they met Noel and Stephen having a muted row. Noel seemed drunk as he looked at Gavin with no sign of recognition, but Stephen gave him an apologetic smile. But this meeting renewed Gavin's fears about uncomfortable encounters. They might meet Winthrop and Spiro anywhere, at any moment, and while Minerva seemed to have calmed down remarkably quickly about them, there was no knowing how she might respond if they did. He led the way through the first large room he had been in, the one which had the open doors on to the terrace, and found a relatively dark corner where they could sit.

'Which was your friend; the one with the beard or the one with the spikey hair?'

'Spikey hair?'

'Is he working class, like you?'

'He's like me, but I don't think we're working class – we're more bourgeois than that.'

'Sort of lower middle?'

'More or less. I don't know about Harry's Dad, but I suppose mine *was* working class – at any rate until he got his own business.'

'So you've moved up a class then. Are you going to keep your accent?'

'Why not?' It was odd; he'd never thought of it like that.

'I want to move *down*,' she said.

He felt she was looking at him again and said: 'I think you say a lot of things just for effect, don't you?'

'Not only for that. But it would be pretty stupid if everything I said wasn't meant to have any effect at all. There are people like that but they're ghastly dull.'

He decided to drop that for the time being.

'Why aren't you eating?'

'I don't like eating much. I mean, I don't much like eating anything. But I rather go for bones. I like gnawing.'

'Gnaw it up then,' he said.

It was cool on the terrace: there was a pleasant background of music – Billie Holliday – unmistakable even at such low volume, and the dwindling numbers on the terrace were leaving them in peace. He discovered after a few mouthfuls that he was very hungry and was tackling some very good fish with cucumber round it and also watching Minerva stripping the skin off her drumstick with her small, white teeth, when he felt a hand on his shoulder, looked up with a start to see Stephen's face looming down at him.

'Sorry to interrupt, but there's a minor crisis and I told Joan I'd find you. It's just a touch urgent.'

He put his plate on the tiled ground, got to his feet and said to the girl – who looked as though she was poised to come with him: 'You stay, I'll be back.'

Stephen held his elbow, almost as though he expected Gavin to escape or lose his way – while they went through the big room, and into the passage.

'What's up?'

'It's Winthrop.'

'Why didn't you get Harry?'

'He wouldn't be enough. Anyway, I don't want him to get hurt.'

They had, predictably, Gavin felt, reached the study/library door which was shut.

Stephen said: 'The thing is to be perfectly calm, but firm. And tough,' he added: he was trembling. He opened the door, shoving Gavin ahead of him into the room.

The room – although it had other people in it – seemed to be full of Winthrop. He stood, at one end of the big chesterfield, leaning slightly forward, with a hand on the end of its arm and its back; he stood easily poised on the balls of his feet, and his gaze menacingly intent, was fixed upon Spiro, who seemed to have shrunk, to be much smaller than Gavin remembered him and who was half crouching at the other end of the sofa with his hands also upon its arm. His eyes, which looked enormous in his ashy face were fixed upon Winthrop and at irregular but fairly frequent intervals he uttered a strange little grunt – half conciliatory, half denying – which sometimes exploded into a high-pitched nervous giggle. Seated at the huge desk, wielding the gold telephone, was Joan whose voice sounded almost brazenly calm.

'No, darling, just one of the usual parties. No, I told you, it was a lamp falling over. They were playing some weird acting game, I think: listen, supposing I call you back, I'm so longing to hear how the plans are going for Bobby's yacht – ' here Spiro's giggle ended in a shriek of terror as Winthrop made a move towards him. 'Sorry, I didn't absolutely hear what you said. No, darling, I told you – they're playing that silly acting game – hold on a minute I'm going to talk to you from my bedroom – much quieter – ' She motioned to Gavin to come and hold the receiver for her, saying, as he took it: 'It's Dmitri: he hardly *ever* calls me, and I must at least find out where he is. Put it back when you hear me,' and went into her bedroom, shutting the door behind her.

Gavin did as he was asked. This meant going either round Winthrop or round Spiro. He chose Winthrop, whose attention flickered from Spiro for the split second while he registered that Gavin was, in fact, simply going to the telephone. It was, however, long enough for Spiro to make a lunge round the sofa towards the door – a fatal error since the moment that there was less than the length of the sofa between them Winthrop sprang upon him and with the powerful certainty of a leopard seized him by the throat. Spiro's voice was cut off in mid-shriek, and Gavin, aware of Stephen's plaintively ineffectual protests, moved instinctively to try to stop Winthrop. This was no use at all; Winthrop simply removed one of his hands from Spiro's throat to send Gavin spinning across the room until he fell against the cornice of the mantelpiece and collapsed among the artificial logs in the fireplace. Although he was not knocked out, pain and shock overwhelmed him; his eye felt as though he had been hit by a cricket ball; his darkened vision doubled and a display of fireworks seemed to be set off from inside his head; his mouth tasted of thick salt and surges of pain, as dazzling as the beam of a lighthouse, regularly swept his right shoulder. He made an attempt to heave himself into a sitting position and as he did so, his shoulder thrilled with a pain so sudden and sickening that he was on the edge of fainting, but at the end of it, through the cold sweat and distance, he was aware that something that had been put out by his fall was now back. Gingerly, he made a second effort to sit up.

Things had changed; they had probably changed very quickly, but he had not seen them happening. Winthrop now had Spiro by the scruff of his jacket collar and had literally turned him upside down. Spangled on the maroon carpet were what looked like pieces of jewellery and, as Gavin watched, Winthrop gave Spiro yet another experienced little shake and a couple of coffee spoons, gold, with enamelled backs, fell from his pockets. Gavin became aware that Winthrop through clenched teeth was emitting a stream of imprecatory abuse.

'. . . you fucking little fly-blown piece of shit where are your morals? Answer me that! Dirty little crap-ridden wog didn't your arse-holing bitch of a mother teach you anything? I'm surprised at you – ' he went on but not more mildly, his surprise simply galvanized him into starting to beat Spiro up – 'think you can *come* to this country and *waltz* about sticking your filthy fingers into the *private* belongings of a lady who's kind enough to have you to a *party* – you got no morals you fucking little reptile – *and* what's more – you mother-fucking little creep – you got no more integrity than a louse.' He shook him again, but this time nothing fell out, and Winthrop let go of his ankle, at the same time kicking him sharply in the midriff so that Spiro lay winded, his intermittent wailing gasps stopped. In the silence that very briefly followed, Gavin became aware the audience no longer consisted of Stephen and himself. Harry, his arms tightly folded, stood by the door, and Minerva, still holding the turkey drumstick, beside him. Stephen, clucking, had edged forward and, on his knees, was picking up the various pieces – a charm bracelet, a gold watch, earrings and the spoons.

Before anyone seemed to have a chance to move or speak Minerva rushed over to Winthrop and threw her arms round him.

'Oh, darling, I could have told you he was a creep!' she cried. 'I never take things out of people's *houses*! I *knew* you'd see through him!'

Winthrop made some brushing movements to get her off him as though she was a fly, but she wasn't a fly and – in spite of the drumstick in one hand – she clung.

Then he said: 'Piss off – whoever you are.' He picked her arm off him like a bramble; then leaned over Spiro who had been lying in a foetal position moaning softly, but who was beginning to show signs of movement. Before he could do or not do anything, Minerva bent down and rapped him smartly on the head with the drumstick and, like a clown in a silent film, Spiro instantly fell back motionless, as though knocked out. 'I hate you – you cringing little queer!'

'Who do you think you're speaking to?'

'Oh, not *you*, darling Winthrop. I expect he blackmailed you, isn't that what awful people like that are always doing? Look at me! Don't you remember?'

Gavin, who felt that things were managing to take a turn for the worse, noticed that Joan had come back into the room and was towering quietly by the bedroom door and that Stephen was rearranging all the objects he had picked up on to an enormous black glass ashtray.

'That ad we did where you weren't ever alone because of

your pipe. I was one of the girls who got locked out, don't you remember? And afterwards we met at the coffee machine and you were talking to somebody else about this party, so I thought I'd come to it, and when I said I'd see you there you said okay. So here I fucking *am*.'

'Don't you use that language to me. It's disgusting: it's not right.'

'You use it. It's what *you* say.'

'That's different.'

'I don't think you are in at all a good position to criticize other people's behaviour. Gavin and I were jolly shocked at what you did with Spiro in there.' She indicated the bedroom, and was momentarily disconcerted to see Joan.

'Do you *mind*?'

'No, I don't – well, of course I mind that. I thought that was disgusting. Unnecessary,' she added with an attempt at loftiness, which collapsed the moment Winthrop turned on her, which he did at once.

'You mean you were actually in there? Fucking *hiding* in there?'

She nodded, but she backed away from him.

'You ought to be locked *up*! I think you are, without exception, the most disgusting person I've ever met in my life! You're a vulgar, nasty little bitch!'

She stood rigidly beside him, rubbing her eyes with her knuckles, in spite of the fact that she'd still got hold of the drumstick, and Gavin began to feel that everything was going to go on for ever, when Joan, who had been silent up to now, said:

'I have a sort of feeling that we've rather lost the party atmosphere, and so perhaps we should call it a day. Thanks for collecting the loot, Stephen; no, leave it there. The only thing I ask, really, is that you shouldn't leave anybody behind.'

Stephen nodded and went to Spiro, bending down to pick up one end of him, but Winthrop interrupted: 'Don't bother with that; he can stand, all right.' He gave Spiro a casual kick on the bottom and Spiro shot to his feet, and fell against Stephen, who fielded him with a nice blend of arrest and protection.

Winthrop said: 'Where's Noel?'

'He went down to the car. He's not quite himself, I'm afraid.'

'Can you manage him on your own, or shall I come down with you?'

'I can manage.'

'If you give Stephen any trouble, I'll have your balls for research.'

Spiro rolled his eyes and muttered: 'Ello – *no*,' and Stephen took him away.

Winthrop walked over to Joan, put his arms on her shoulders and gave her a kiss. 'Sorry about all that, my love,' he said, and Gavin noticed that he really did seem to be and that Joan knew that and liked it. 'That's okay,' she said. Winthrop turned to Harry who, with his arms still folded, had been staring at the carpet for a long time.

'My bike's outside. You coming?' He took no notice of Gavin as well as pointedly ignoring Minerva. Harry's face quivered; he nodded and, without looking at Joan, said with a kind of clumsy brusqueness: 'Thanks for having me.' Then he looked at Gavin, but before he could say anything Winthrop intervened: 'Don't worry about *him*: he's ganged up with that tonto little tart – he can take her with him. Come to think of it, Joan said everyone out, and it's her place – so, everyone out.' He moved over to Minerva, placed a hand in the small of her back and steered her straight at Gavin: 'Go on, then, out!' As the girl almost fell against him, he felt Winthrop's grip on his forearm, and, awful seconds later, they were all four in the lift, out of it, through the plate glass doors and into the street. Harry broke the silence. 'How's Gavin going to get home?'

'That's up to him, isn't it?'

'He came in Stephen's car. Perhaps it hasn't gone.'

But it had. Gavin, who felt as though his personality had been seized and held under some black water by Winthrop's unpredictable hatred, found his voice and said he'd be all right, don't worry about him.

'Night then.' Harry said it as clumsily as he'd thanked Joan and followed Winthrop to the bike. They had roared off into the night before he realized that he still had hold of Minerva's arm.

CHAPTER FOUR

THEY were standing – opposite the building they had come out of – beside the railings of a square garden. A white cherry tree shifted above them in a small breeze that seemed to have begun with the silence after Harry and Winthrop's departure, and a flurry of petals fell fast, and then more slowly, round them.

'What shall we do?'

'Do?'

'Don't be silly. Next.' She wriggled free of his hand and pressed herself against the iron railings. 'We could go in there. Look – there's a little hut we could use.'

'What for?'

She turned to face him. 'A friendly little screw? To soothe us. It wasn't a very nice party, was it?'

The suggestion seemed to Gavin so preposterous that, at first, it hardly frightened him. He murmured something like 'No thanks', and then fear – like an attack of dizziness or the beginning of being drunk – struck.

'Are you stoned? You look very odd . . . Odder than usual,' she added, as though she'd known him for years . . .

'You can't get into London squares; they're always locked.'

'That simply means we wouldn't be disturbed. I could almost get *through* these railings, and you could climb over. If you wanted to.' She clutched the sleeve of his jacket and, painfully, a bit of his arm. 'Don't you like me?'

'Of course I like you,' he said at once, at once wondering whether that was true.

'You don't sound at all sure. Is it sex you don't like then?'

'I don't feel like answering that question.'

'Oh – all right: I can see you're not in the mood.' She started to walk him along the side of the square. 'It was just an idea. Forget it.'

Forget it! How on earth was he to do that! He realized they were walking. 'Where are we going?'

'Where do you live?'

'Barnet. I ought to be getting back: catch the last train.' He couldn't just walk off and leave her on her own somewhere in South Kensington at night. 'Where do you live?'

'Actually, I'm not sure how much *I* like sex: I adore what it stands for, though. Being stroked and people making the best of me. But the actual *thing* seems to need a lot of practice – it's much trickier than people tell you . . .' She shivered and, to change the subject, he asked her whether she was cold.

'I'm always cold. I'm cold so much of my life that usually I hardly notice it.'

He thought of saying, well why didn't she eat more and wear more clothes, but he also thought that this would provoke some dull answers that he felt too tired to argue about. Really, he wanted to go home – get shot of her and get back to his bed.

She had stopped in front of a battered and travel-stained Mini and immediately opened its boot.

'The key's in a packet of Smarties,' she said. The boot seemed to be loosely packed with old bulging carrier bags.

'I didn't know you had a car.' This was a relief; it meant she was independent – he could go.

'It isn't *my* car,' she said. '*I* wouldn't have a crummy motor like this. It was lent to me. I borrowed it as they were away. Here it is!' She opened the cylinder of Smarties and shook out the key. 'You can't get in through the passenger door, the handle's gone. You'll have to come through my door.'

'I've got a train to catch,' he said, 'I can walk to South Kensington.'

'Oh, do let me give you a lift! It's the least I can do. You want the Northern Line anyway, don't you? I'll take you to one of its stations.'

She had tugged the driver's door open and now held it for him.

'Which way are you going?' He hadn't wanted to get in, but he did.

'Oh – northish.' She wriggled in after him and took off her shoes. Inside, the car was, if possible, even dirtier – and, while he was thinking this, she said: 'A friend of mine said it's rather like being inside an ashtray.'

As they set off, he realized that she hadn't answered his question.

'Where *do* you live?'

There was a pause, and then she said: 'A secret. So I can't tell you.'

'It seems a funny thing to have a secret about.'

'Does it?'

They were approaching the Victoria and Albert Museum and Gavin thought how marvellous it would be to have the whole museum to himself: he supposed that would mean going at night – like now; they would turn on all the lights for him and he would have the freedom of the whole place.

'Do you like being a hairdresser?'

'I like it all right.'

'You don't sound very sure.'

'I've done it for so many years; I'm used to it, you see . . .'

'Are you ambitious?'

'What about?'

'*You* know. Do you want to be the world's best hairdresser – opening salons in New York and Paris and Palm Beach – being photographed with film stars and models – all that sort of thing?'

'Good lord no!'

'Do you have your own salon now?'

'No. I work for someone, I wouldn't be any good at the business side of it.'

'So you're not ambitious about that. What *do* you want?'

As he answered mildly that he enjoyed a lot of things he became aware of how irritated she was making him feel. She kept trying to have conversations with him on too intimate a level: a chance encounter a few hours ago didn't rate her hectoring, childish curiosity. He remembered Joan and the astounding sense of ease and intimacy he had felt with her, and then wondered fleetingly whether he had dreamed all that. The thought was painful and he withdrew from it. That left him with the irritation. She was jabbering on about enjoyment having nothing to do with ambition.

'Look,' he said, 'just drop me off at any old tube. I can find my way home. Marble Arch will do nicely.'

'That's not on the Northern Line. I'm going to take you home.'

'I'm not going home. I've got to collect my bike.'

'Where's your bike?'

'It's at Whetstone.' He wasn't going to mention Harry because of Winthrop.

'Where's that? Is that on the Northern Line too?'

'The station's Totteridge. It's miles. It's probably miles out of your way.'

'No! Not a single mile!'

Due to the wretched door, he couldn't get out of the car anyway . . . Resolving to stand no more personal nonsense from her, he tried to find a more comfortable position for his legs.

'Do you like animals?'

'Yes. Why do you ask?'

'Just trying to find something you don't mind talking about. I thought of animals because I know your seat's too far forward. It's my parrot in the back.'

'A parrot?' He didn't believe her.

'Yep. If you don't believe me, feel behind your seat for his cage.'

'Mind his blanket,' she added as his hand reached the wide bars of the cage.

'He's very quiet.'

'It's his sleep time. He can be very noisy especially if he gets hold of any drink . . . He loves whisky. He gets very noisy when he's drunk.'

'Should he drink whisky?'

'He doesn't exactly pour it out for himself, you know. And I don't either, if that's what you're thinking. It's just if – well, if we're at a party and other people are drinking it. Then he just whizzes over and sinks his beak into their glass . . .'

'Why is he in the car?'

'He goes everywhere with me. That's why. He's my worldly good. An Admiral gave him to me,' she added as an afterthought. They were stopped at signal lights and she turned towards him as she said this. The street lighting made her eyes look much darker and the rest of her face waxen. He wondered fleetingly whether she was a little mad, and realized that he had several times wondered this already. Her eyes, intent, and rather knowing, seemed like lenses photographing his response. People one met at parties need not become friends, if one didn't want them to. He needn't ever see her again. This made him feel sorry for her.

'Do people actually call you Minerva?'

'Not much. Only if they're cross with me, so some people,' she giggled – 'yes, *do* call me it quite a lot. At the agency they call me Munday, but they spell it like a day of the week. They think it sounds chic.'

'What's the agency?'

'For modelling. Cheer up! You are being driven home by a model. Although, really, of course, I'm an actress. But I've been ill, so it's been silly to look for work.'

'Are you queer?' she asked some minutes later.

'Why do you want to know?'

'I don't particularly want to *know*. I don't *care* what you are. But you look as though you might be – a hairdresser and all that – you needn't think I'm not broad-minded. I know it takes all sorts to make a world, I just like to know which sort I'm dealing with.'

'I'm not queer.' The moment he had said that, he wondered whether it was true – whether Harry, who, after all, knew him better than anyone, mightn't be righter about him than he knew how to be about himself. After all, here he was with a girl who had offered to go to bed with him, not feeling anything like as frightened of her as he had always told himself he would be, but certainly not feeling – well – anything about her that would lead to anything. Irritated, more like. But the thought of Harry being right induced new waves of terror: how *could* he cope with people like Winthrop; the scenes, the tantrums – the seemingly continuous search for someone more attractive. And even if things were going well . . . the sight of Spiro astride Winthrop in the bath recurred – something he had really tried not to think about since he had seen it. Never, in a thousand years, would he find himself in that sort of situation unaccompanied by anything but terror and disgust. Was this true though? Was he suppressing all his *real* feelings (the kind most vulnerable to suppression, they all said); was the disgust a mere rationalization of terror? It occurred to him that perhaps sex was some kind of addiction – like alcohol or drugs – you did it – not initially for enjoyment, but because of the effects, which once experienced became more and more desirable, and, eventually, indispensable: in the end, you would put up with anything in order to have it. Or, perhaps sex was simply an experience whose fearful intimacy could only be endured because other feelings for the person transcended . . . There was nobody about whom he had had any of those feelings – indeed, he was not sure what they might be. Perhaps it was simply for breeding purposes. Many species of animal didn't seem to enjoy it much – if at all . . . Take the mink, for instance. They were simply driven by powerful instinct. When it came to powerful instinct then, he seemed to be stationary – completely unmoved . . . These ruminations ended, as he found they usually did, with some anonymous, irascible comment of the 'what on earth was *wrong* with him?' variety.

'Perhaps you're not anything.'

As he rather surprisingly retorted, 'Don't be silly,' he thought, goodness she couldn't have *heard* what he'd been thinking surely? Of course not. He just wished that he was safe and comfortable and alone at home.

'This is Golders Green,' she said in her humbler voice. 'Up there's where they burn people. I went to a cremation there once. My goodness, that's an awful way to end up. Canned music and teeny little services, and afterwards relatives walk about reading wreaths. Are your parents alive?'

'Yes. What about yours?'

'Well – they're not actually *dead*. If you saw my mother, that might surprise you. She looks as though she *ought* to be dead. Neither of them cares for me at all. I should think they're very sorry they adopted me by now.'

'Are you adopted?'

'I've just said I was. I wasn't a baby,' she added: 'I can remember things.'

'What sort of things?'

She paused: 'Someone in velvet and diamonds crying a lot; and stone passages. And servants saying to each other how sad I wasn't a boy. That's why I had to be adopted, you see – my mother had to have a son or nothing. Do you know what I think happened? I think some coarse common child was adopted and I was sent off in his place. To coarse common parents . . . I don't *feel* like them at all. I've never felt like them.'

There was a silence. Gavin really didn't know what to make

107

of it all; wasn't, indeed, sure that he wanted to make anything of it. Then he remembered that earlier she had said she was a Lady; thought of taking this up with her and decided against it. He felt rather than saw her looking at him as she said: 'Don't think I'm a snob: nobody can help their birth.'

As he still said nothing, she drove rather faster for a bit, until, waiting for the lights to change, she said:

'You're not very easy to talk to, are you? What do you like most in the world?'

Because he always thought people meant him to say what he meant, Gavin found these blanket questions outfacing – the sort of thing an old and intimate friend might work up to, and this girl was hardly a friend at all. 'I don't know.'

'Don't *know*?' she predictably shrieked. 'Don't know? You must have some idea!'

'I mightn't feel like telling you.'

'Oh! Something to do with sex. I thought so.' He didn't answer so she went on: 'Because men think about sex all the time.'

'And what do women think about?'

'Men – thinking about sex. I expect. It really doesn't interest me. There must be something to it or else it's some sort of fabulous conspiracy: everybody *knows* it's no good really, but they get on with people more easily if they pretend it is.' There was a pause, and then, in a manner that was engaging in its genuine disappointment, she said: 'I was hoping you'd tell me something true about it.'

Every time he'd begun to feel that she was absolutely impossible, she said something unusually possible. 'I'm sorry I can't,' he said.

'Okay.' The following silence was more comfortable: imbued with that nervous good-will that comes out of just managing to understand each other in time. She was simply confused, he thought; he knew what that felt like, and naturally it took her another way from the way it took him . . . 'I like music,' he said suddenly, offering her what intimacy he felt he could afford.

'What kind?'

'Several kinds. Classical mostly. Some jazz. I've no time for pop.'

'You mean you're a snob.'

'I don't think so,' he said mildly. 'I just don't enjoy it.'

'I mean you're a snob about music. I didn't mean a general snob.'

'I know you meant that. And I still don't think so.'

'Pop is the people's music.'

'Nonsense. Everything's the people's everything.'

'Someone said that to me: I didn't make it up.'

'Does your parrot talk?'

'*He* didn't say it to me, if that's what you mean.'

'You have to turn off in a minute.' He had realized suddenly that they were in Whetstone, and nearing Harry's flat. 'Here.'

'He says a few boring things – like "hello", and "how *are* you".'

'You go right here.'

Havergal Heights was now in view, and Gavin noticed that the lights were on in Harry and Winthrop's flat. A quick, quiet get-away was the thing to aim at. 'Here we are,' he said, 'that's my bike over there. It was very nice of you to bring me so far.'

She got out of the car to let him out from her door, but, as his feet touched the pavement, she clutched his arm, and said:

'When shall I see you again?'

'I don't know.'

'We must make a plan.'

'Well, if you give me your telephone number, I'll ring you.'

'Haven't got one.'

'Your address, then.'

'Oh no! I can't do that.'

'Well, I expect we'll meet.'

'Tell me your telephone number.'

Ashamed of having just lied to her, he gave his home number. She licked her finger and wrote it on the extremely dusty bonnet. 'I must say, you don't sound very keen about seeing me,' she said and, not for the first time in the evening, she sounded humble rather than sulky.

'I think I'm just a bit tired,' he said: 'as you said earlier, it wasn't exactly a relaxing party. Well – cheerio, and thanks again for the lift.'

'That's okay.'

'You get back in the car: you really do look cold.'

'Yes.'

He walked across the road and up to the fence by the flats where his bike was chained. He felt her watching him while he undid the padlock and got on to the bike. When he wheeled it round back into the road, he saw that she had got into the car but hadn't moved off. He started the bike, waved to her and set off . . . It was a one-way street, so he had to go round the block, and he realized that she was behind him. There were lights at the main road, and he tried to remember whether she would be able to turn right there – back to London. He would give her a final wave as he turned left . . .

The lights were green, and there was no barring of a right turn but she didn't turn right – she followed him. Perhaps she didn't live in London after all: perhaps it had actually been on her way to take him to Whetstone? Well, he'd turn right at the next lights and go the back way home – that way she *couldn't* be going.

She followed him. With a gasp of nervous rage, he accelerated; if she thought she could play some silly game tracking him, he'd simply leave her behind and then she'd be lost – and serve her right. He roared down the wide suburban road: it was set on either side by large, detached houses now for the most part dark – its only disadvantage being that for some way, at least, there were no turnings off it. The road curved gently downhill and a quick look behind him confirmed that she was out of sight. It occurred to him that if he simply stopped the engine and wheeled his bike inside one of the Edwardian drives she would rush past him and he would lose her ... But his bike was much faster and he was losing her anyway and owners of whichever drive he might choose might come out and ask what he was up to ...

As the corner became sharper, the road narrowed: the houses ceased and on one side there was a high brick wall, on the other a wooden fence bounding some waste land advertised on a hoarding as an industrial site. The T junction was less than half a mile away and, once he reached it, she would have no way of knowing whether he had gone right or left ... He began to enjoy the fresh night air and the feeling of freedom. He could put down tonight's adventures to experience. This made him wonder briefly whether possibly most of the things that happened to people that were remotely outside their everyday experience were really only satisfactory in retrospect, but before he had time to consider this rather depressing possibility, a sign heralding road works signalled his luck running out. Sure enough, the road became a single lane and the temporary traffic light on its tripod was red ... He stopped. It was impossible to see whether anything was coming from the other direction and the thought of flouting the red light occurred to him only as something he could not conceivably do. He waited while nothing came through and the light continued to be red. Just as he was wondering whether the signal had broken down, or did not operate at night, he heard a car behind him and knew it was the Mini ...

She drew up on his left and pulled down her window. 'I nearly lost you,' she said. There was a kind of gaiety in her reproach that he found infuriating.

'I can't see why you're following me. Because that's what you're doing, isn't it?'

'Well, in a *way* I am.' She said it as though with the utmost liberality she was conceding a doubtful point.

'Why are you?'

'I thought perhaps you might put up with me – put me up for the night. I've got nowhere to stay, you see.'

'What do you mean "nowhere"? You must have somewhere!'

'I haven't! I haven't anywhere at all! Unless you count the Mini.'

'What would you have done if you hadn't met me?'

'*I* don't know. What's the point of asking that? Look – the light's gone green. Let's talk when we get to your flat. Let's go.'

He was so stunned by her improvidence that he did as she suggested. He needed anyway to get away from her – even for a few minutes – to think about what on earth he could do. Mrs Lamb's reactions to a strange girl turning out to have spent the night at Plantagenet Road were unknown, the only thing he could be sure of was that they would be unfavourable and prolonged. She would dislike the whole idea, largely on the grounds that it had never happened before – a key reason with her for hostility. Her (possible) random objections began to bombard him; accusations of seduction, *rape*, even of being in love, of wanting to get married of leaving his nice home . . . And everything he might say back could only make matters worse. Nowhere else to go? Why not? What sort of girl could she be if she had nowhere to go? What sort of house did he think 206 Plantagenet Road *was*? Did he think that, every time he went to a party, he could bring back anyone he fancied bringing back? (Another of Mrs Lamb's less comfortable delusions was that, if something that she did not like happened, it was going to go on happening: she was a great thin end of the wedger.) His father would be of no help. He would fill his pipe with obsessive care, wink in a weakly conspiratorial way to Gavin out of Mrs Lamb's presence, and, if they were alone together for longer than a wink, say there was no accounting for taste and wonder what the world was coming to. And anyway, if she stayed tonight, how was he to get rid of her tomorrow? Sunday! He couldn't escape by going to work. And there was family lunch with Marge – she'd *have* to go: he couldn't possibly take her to that.

As he halted by the war memorial while a night lorry thundered up the main road, he suddenly realized a possible escape route. *She* didn't know that he lived with his parents: she clearly thought he had a flat on his own. Once she realized that he had neither the freedom nor the privacy for this sort of venture, she'd go away to wherever it was that she must surely have secretly in reserve. Thank God he *did* live with his parents – if he had got a place of his own, he'd have no excuse, and things would be much worse. Once she realized about Mrs Lamb . . .

Gavin was rattled; he was tired as well; a good many experiences of the evening had been entirely new to him, and some of them had been unpleasant: but for much or most of this, his intelligence would have told him that Mrs Lamb was not somebody it was easy for a stranger to appraise. He had had a lifetime's practice of his mother's responses to practically everything, but this really only meant that he didn't think her particularly eccentric – assumed more or less that she was much like everybody else's mother, and, that being so, of course Minerva would understand that a sudden visit was out of the question. Some sharper instinct, however, prompted him to stop a few doors away from No. 206 (where he could see that all lights were out), and this turned out to be well advised.

He parked his bike at the kerb as the Mini drew up behind him, and went over to her.

'Look,' he said, 'I'm afraid I didn't make this clear to you, but I don't have a flat or anything of my own: I live with my parents . . .'

'How extraordinary! Do you like it?'

'It's all right: fine. But I'm sure you see it makes a difference.'

'I bet it does. My things are in the the boot, and it's a bit tricky getting it open.' Before he could stop her, she sprang out of the car, and began tugging at the boot handle. He followed her.

'What I'm trying to say is that I really can't have you to stay. It's not my house, you see.'

She stopped trying to turn the boot handle and put the ignition key into its lock. 'Must be locked. I'm sure they won't mind. Not just for one night.'

'They would. I'm telling you they would.'

'You promised!'

'I didn't! You said, "Let's talk about it."'

'If they *knew* I was absolutely destitute! If they knew I had nowhere else to go!'

'They wouldn't understand that. And honestly, you *must* have somewhere.'

To his intense alarm, she sank to her knees in the road, and still hanging on to the boot handle burst into loud childish, wailing sobs.

'How can you be so – you don't know what it's like!' she wailed at what seemed to him the top of her voice.

'Oh – don't make so much *noise*!'

At once she subsided into a choked sob, but went on crying quietly which made him feel much more worried about her and much worse.

'I'm *cold*! Nothing's turning out right! I don't know what to do!'

The boot suddenly opened and she fell back against his knees. He stooped to help her and she threw her arms round his legs. 'Oh, do help me. Honestly!'

'Look,' he said gently, 'you must have somewhere. You must have *come* from somewhere. Where were you last night?'

'In hospital. It was so horrible I left. I truly couldn't bear another minute.'

'Are you ill, then?' His alarm was fanning out; there was

beginning to be nothing about her that he could regard with equanimity. Ill! She might be dying for all he knew. If she stayed the night and *died*! How could he be so callous! He tried to imagine what she must be feeling, and felt so frightened that he couldn't feel anything else at all. '*Are* you ill?' he repeated. She looked up at him and he saw that her neck was streaked with tears running down into the red cheesecloth.

'*No*-o!' She said it as though he had asked the question hundreds of times and she was fed up with answering it . . . In the boot were two tattered plastic carriers stuffed with what looked like washing. 'There's absolutely nothing wrong with me.' She ran her wrist and the back of her hand across her nose and said: 'I just want to get out my sweater. I'm just freezing to death.' She burrowed in one of the carriers and pulled out an Aran sweater – greyish, even in the street light.

'I could make you some scrambled eggs if you like; I put onion in them; people tell me they're delicious.'

'No thanks.' The thought of his mother smelling onions cooking in her own kitchen in the middle of the night made the back of his neck feel cold.

'Well, what do you want me to do?' She'd extracted one of the carrier bags and shut the boot again and now faced him. The sweater, which was not only dirty, but far too large for her, made her look like a fisherman waif.

'If you've really *got* to spend the night here, you'll have to be really quiet and do everything I say. And no giggling or crying either.'

'I'll be as quiet as a mouse. Although on linoleum they sound as though all their bootlaces are undone – not quiet at all. But I see what you mean,' she added hastily, seeing his face.

'What about that parrot?'

'He won't make a sound either. You open the door while I get him out.'

'No, I'll take him. This isn't my house. I live a few doors down.'

'That was rather scheming of you.'

She was a fine one to talk. He made no reply.

The parrot cage was heavy and tended to rotate when he picked it up by the ring on top and he felt rather than heard the creature shifting inside. He had to put it down twice: once to open the gate, and then to get the latchkey in the lock . . . He switched on the hall light and turned back to Minerva who was standing so immediately behind him that he almost fell over her. 'Shut up!' he hissed. Her answer to this was to take off her shoes, kicking them somewhere into the dark front garden. Even when she was trying, she seemed to get everything just wrong.

Ever since he'd given in about her staying, he'd been desperately reviewing possibilities and discarding them. He *wouldn't* put her in his own room, because it was his – and private. He couldn't put her in the lounge, because either of his parents might – just *might* – wake up in the night, fancy a cup of tea and go down and find her. There was a spare bedroom – that had been Marge's – but his mother kept that in such a state of shut-up suspension that he didn't feel equal to finding bed linen and removing furniture from off the bed where it was kept so that the floor was easier to polish. It would have to be the ground floor room – the spare lounge or best sitting room – also kept in wraps against the few days in the year when it was used, but further away from his parents' room, and since there wasn't a bed in it, he couldn't be expected to find bedclothes. He opened the door to this and switched on the light. The suite was covered with polythene sheeting, the blinds and curtains were drawn and the room smelled of rubber (the underlay of its new and frenziedly geometric carpet). Gavin motioned Minerva inside and shut the door. He dumped the parrot cage as gently as he could and moved briskly to the three-seat sofa and peeled off the polythene.

'This is where you'll have to sleep, I'm afraid.' He almost whispered, to keep her quiet.

'Okay.'

'I'll get you a blanket.'

'I could manage without one. It smells quite warm in here, but funny. Rather like a new car,' she added appeasingly.

'I'd better get you one. You stay quiet till I get back.'

'Could I use a loo, do you think? If I don't pull the plug?'

He looked sharply at her, to see if she was taking the piss out of him, but she wasn't. It had been an honest suggestion.

'Yes. Follow me.'

He showed her where the downstairs cloaks was, indicated that she should return to her room after she had used it, and tore silently up to his room for a blanket. When he returned with it he found that she had made a pillow of her carrier bag and curled up on the sofa. She was still wearing her Aran jersey and he felt touched at her offer to manage without a blanket. Her feet were bare and rather dirty, the nails painted the same red as her dress. She had long, articulate toes. He wondered whether he could get her to wash her feet before his mother saw them.

'Will you be all right?'

'I expect I'll just go to sleep.'

'Would you mind just staying in here until I come and fetch you in the morning?'

'Okay. When will that be?'

'Quite early.' He knew his mother did not get up before eight-thirty on Sundays and he planned to be down first in order to tell her. 'Promise to stay here then?'

She drew her finger across her throat, and then, not looking at him, she said: 'Thanks for having me.'

'That's all right. Hope you sleep.'

'And you,' she responded.

He turned off the light and shut the door, turned off the hall light and crept upstairs to the bathroom where he cleaned his teeth. The last time he'd looked in a mirror had been in Joan's bathroom before he'd come upon Winthrop and Spiro, *before* he'd encountered her. It seemed weeks ago: anyway, he neither felt nor looked as he had felt and looked then. Present feelings were far more familiar – how to stop an alarming situation from becoming downright terrifying. *He* hoped he'd sleep, but the prospect of dealing with his mother before breakfast, followed by breakfast having dealt with her, didn't make him feel at all relaxed.

In his room, he set his alarm for eight to be on the safe side, and then lay in the dark reflecting that he seemed to spend his life trying to stay on that side, or to get on to it. Safe meant knowing what was going to happen next: he could only stand adventure when he was entirely alone – when he was what he called to himself 'wake dreaming', in charge of the dream. But those dreams seemed always to gravitate towards his looking for somebody else to share the adventure with him, which argued that he didn't really like being alone. What on earth was he to *say* to his mother in the morning? One of the worst things about people was how easily they didn't go together. He became conscious of his head aching, as he thought crossly that he was the only person he knew who was prepared to get on with anybody as long as he didn't have to get on with them too much. He got up, put on his lamp and took an aspirin – something he very rarely did, but he had the feeling that his headache might climb to the proportions of a migraine. He couldn't cope with his mother or the girl – and Dad at breakfast – if he had a migraine. He turned off the light again, got into his sleeping position on his side and tried to go back to the previous night – on the sea shore having plunged down to the beautiful, reassuring girl with red hair . . . It was no good because, the moment he began to see her, he was sitting at the breakfast table with Minerva and his parents, and she was saying: 'I asked him if he'd like a friendly little screw as it hadn't been a very nice party but he didn't seem to want to,' and his mother's face going into a kind of puffed and silent scream – like a Francis Bacon. Please God let her not say anything like that. Just as he got to the point of wondering why he only asked God for things when he felt extremely uncertain of getting them by ordinary means, he lapsed into unconsciousness . . .

'Why are you up so early?'

He muttered something about not sleeping well, and wanting a cup of tea.

'If you'd lain in bed, you'd have got your Sunday tea – same as usual.' She wore a crimplene housecoat in traffic warden yellow and a turban over her curlers which were always kept in until the last possible moment before she went to lunch with Marge. He took his tea to the breakfast table and sat down with it.

'You don't look well. Are you sickening for something? You look a funny colour to me.'

'I was late last night. I told you. I didn't sleep well.' This was true: he had slept heavily, but he'd woken feeling even tireder – a bad sleep.

'How was your party then? I expect the food didn't agree with you. It's a wonder what people will give people to eat at parties nowadays,' she added, as though she had given them up for this reason.

'The food was okay. It just went on too long. I had to get a lift back to Harry's for my bike . . .'

She was separating sausages with the kitchen scissors. He'd got to tell her before she got worked up with cooking.

'Listen, Mum. I had to bring someone back here last night. It was too late for them to go home, you see. I put them in the front room. Not to wake you up, you see.'

'In the front room? Who've you put in there? What a funny place to put them.' A thought struck her. 'You've never done that before. Why ever did you do that?'

'I told you. Because it was too late for her to get home.'

'Her! You never told me it was a girl! A *girl*? Whatever are you doing bringing a girl home?' She began stabbing the sausages with a fork with quick, deadly little movements. 'This is your *home*, you know. I should have thought you'd have remembered that.'

'I'm trying to explain, Mum. She couldn't go home because it was so late.'

'She should have thought of that before, shouldn't she? She doesn't sound a very nice type of girl to me, how long have you known her, what is there to be so secretive about?'

'I only met her last night. I'm not being secretive, I'm telling you. She's just stayed the night – that's all.'

'You mean you don't know anything about her!' She seized a frying pan and cut a knob of Trex to put in it. 'Well – I never! She might be – ' but, here, either the enormity of her imagination or its sudden absence seized her up, and she pounced upon the sliced loaf and began cutting off the spongy crusts with a knife nearly as long as her forearm. After a moment she said: 'Only someone rather common would do a thing like that.'

This gave him the cue to play what he had only a moment before recognized would be his trump card. 'As a matter of fact she's not particularly common. Her name's Lady Minerva Munday.'

The knife became motionless, poised a moment in the air before she laid it down. 'You mean she's got a title? Lady

Munday? She's not a girl at all? Why ever didn't you say so before?' And, before he could speak, she was sweeping the breakfast things off the table on to a tray at such speed that Gavin became quite frightened.

'She *is* a girl, Mum; she's only about twenty. She's a bit eccentric – unusual, if you know what I mean.'

She was tugging open the bottom drawer of the kitchen unit out of which she drew and unfurled a tablecloth painstakingly embroidered with rabbits. Shaking it furiously before throwing it over the formica table, she said:

'I expect she's just like any other nice girl if you only noticed. There's no difference between Them and Us, it's nothing but class distinction. I should have expected a more modern outlook from you with all your reading really I should . . .' Ideas were attacking her from all directions. She was now routing out the best china, white, with silver ferns, last used, as far as Gavin could remember, when Marge's in-laws came to tea. 'And you mean to say you put her in the front lounge? When there's a perfectly good spare room upstairs? With a *bed* in it, in case you've forgotten. You're not going to tell me she passed the night on the settee?'

'I told you, I didn't want to wake you and Dad. And she's got her parrot with her.'

She darted him a look of total incredulity, changed her mind and retorted: 'You needn't think that surprises me. She's bound to have *something* with her. She's bound to have some different ways. The world,' she added shakily, 'would be a funny place if everyone was exactly the same!'

'Yes, Mum, I know it would. Look, Mum, don't worry too much. She's not the Queen, you know.'

'Gavin, there's no need to remind me that she is not the Queen. And if Her Majesty *was* coming to breakfast, I should make no difference; I should continue my normal life just as I am doing now.' She finished polishing the electroplated cruet and set it on the fern-ridden table. 'Although I grant you, naturally, I'm familiar with Her Majesty from the television. That's one thing I *do* see. What are you *doing* fidgeting about?'

'I'm making her a cup of tea.'

'I'm not taking it in to her like this.' She felt her turban. 'I shall have to go up anyway and warn your father. What time is she expecting her breakfast then, because I can't be in two places at once?' She seized the kettle and poured water on to a tea bag that was waiting in a cup. 'That's for him. You can. use one of the cups off of the table for – what did you say her name was?'

'Minerva Munday.'

'Lady Minerva Munday. Sometimes, Gavin, I do wish you'd have a little consideration and not spring things on people.' She poured milk and put three lumps of sugar into the cup. 'It's no good expecting breakfast yet: I'll let you know when she can come out.' She ran out of the room and he heard her nipping upstairs.

So far so good. He had known for years that she was fascinated by anything to do with royalty or titles – reading all the bits about them that she could find in newspapers and magazines, but he hadn't bargained for quite such a violent reaction. He only hoped that Minerva could live up to it. She had *said* she was a Lady Minerva, and he hadn't thought about it since then, but *come* to think about it, he had doubts. He had a feeling she said a variety of things simply to impress him, and that might have been one of them. But what he *couldn't* have now . . . what she mustn't do would be to spill the beans – if there were any – at breakfast. He made the tea for her and went to her room.

She was fast asleep, and took a good deal of waking. He had plenty of time to observe her feet again; they looked even dirtier in daylight after he had drawn the curtains. What he could see of her looked altogether grubby, and her hair wanted a good wash. Just when he thought she was awake, she groaned and turned away from him on the settee, burrowing into the blanket. He put the tea down and went to the parrot's cage. Poor thing – he'd probably like to be called. He took off the cloth and there was the parrot, green with a yellowish head, standing on his perch apparently waiting for him. He turned his head in order that he might observe Gavin with one eye. While he did this, the feathers on his head slowly rose and fell again but he was otherwise motionless. Gavin said 'Hullo!' but there was no answer. He turned back to the girl.

This time he shook her gently until she sat up.

'I've brought you some tea. You've got to wake up now.'

'All right. What kind of milk's in this tea?'

'I don't know. Perfectly ordinary milk.'

'Oh. That's what I thought. I'm afraid I only drink skim. Or cream, if I have to.' She put the cup down.

Suppressing his irritation – he needed her cooperation badly for the next hour or two – he said: 'Listen. I've told my mother you're here.'

'How did she take it? Am I supposed to be engaged to you or something?'

'Nothing like that.'

'Sorry, you gave me the impression that she was a bit old-fashioned.'

'She's – well, anyway. What I told her was that you were a Lady.'

She burst out laughing, and then, seeing his face, put her hand over her mouth.

'Well – you told me you were one. *I* don't mind, but it's the sort of thing that she . . . that she rather – '

'You mean she's hooked on titles and all that jazz?'

'That's more or less what I mean.' He felt slightly ashamed of saying it; a bit disloyal. He loved her and he didn't want anybody who didn't to laugh at her.

But she said: 'That's all right. You'd be surprised how few people who haven't got titles haven't got an attitude about them. Of course, most of them pretend like mad that they haven't.' She swung her legs over the side of the sofa and began rummaging in the carrier bag.

'So it's all right, then? You'll keep it up? Just for breakfast?' She stopped rummaging and opened her eyes very wide. 'What do you mean, keep it up? It's up.' She put her hand under her jersey at the neck and began scratching herself vigorously. 'I must say, this sweater's no good for sleeping in: I itched all night.'

'Would you like a bath?'

'Not much. Baths are what I have the evenings I'm not going out. I hate rushing them. Where was I? Oh yes.' She dived into the carrier again and pulled out a battered sponge-bag. 'I'd better clean my teeth though.'

'Have you any other clothes?'

'They're in the other bag in the car.'

'I'll get them. You go and wash. Your shoes are out there somewhere too, aren't they?'

'Yes. But I shan't need them while I'm in the house.'

'Oh, won't you?' Gavin thought as he hurried out to the car. He felt his mother's illusions were at stake, and, while eccentricity – like the parrot – was digestible, grubbiness was not. And, even if she took off the Aran sweater, the red cheesecloth was revealing in all sorts of ways that would certainly not prove acceptable. He collected the second carrier bag and her shoes from the front garden. She had taken off the sweater in order to be able to scratch herself more easily.

'What other clothes have you got?'

'A bikini.'

'Don't be silly. You can't have breakfast in a bikini.'

'And a pair of jeans. Honestly, you'd think I was having breakfast with the Queen.'

'You're having breakfast with a nice, lower middle class family: you let yourself in for this, not me, and it was you who started the title lark.'

'Goodness! I didn't mean to make you cross. I'll wear the jeans. I think I've got a shirt somewhere. I won't let you down. Can I go and wash now?'

'All right. And then come back in here.'

As he left her to see what his mother was up to, Gavin reflected that what he had thought of as being nasty to people was often just saying what you meant – even if they didn't always like it, it didn't actually hurt them. Then he just had time to think that it was funny how he always seemed to make these discoveries when he hadn't really got time for them, before he was back in the other room.

Mrs Lamb had certainly not wasted *her* time. The table was now fully laid, including a cut glass vase with three tulips in it. The sundae dishes were also out, filled to the brim with tinned grapefruit. Mrs Lamb was cooking furiously. She had taken out the rollers and her black hair was a riot of curls. She wore her floral dress in various shades of cyclamen and her uncomfortable shoes and her face had an unnatural pallor, due, he saw, to a thick coating of whitish pancake which contrasted strongly with her cyclamen lips and little brown neck below it.

'I've had a job to get your father into his suit, and I haven't had time to mitre the serviettes. Have you brought the papers in? Although I expect Lady Munday knows all the news.'

'Why should she do that, Mum?'

'Privilege,' she said sharply. 'It's Them who tell us what's going on.'

Gavin fetched the papers from outside, and also the milk. Mrs Lamb pounced upon the latter and whisked it out of sight.

'There's just the marmalade to put in that nice pot Marge gave me for Christmas.'

'I'll do that.'

She let him, which was an indication of her state of mind. 'Not the beehive pot; that's for honey. The one shaped like a cottage.' She wore her charm bracelet which kept slipping down her knobbly wrist threatening to plop into the frying pan. Her desperate excitement about this occasion touched him then about the rest of her life. 'It'll be a lovely breakfast, Mum, I know it will. There's no need to worry.'

'It'll be a perfectly normal breakfast – same as we always have. Worry? I'm not in the least worried. Not worried,' she repeated, shaking the sausages – like a terrier – to death in the pan. 'Don't hang *over* me – you know I don't like being hung over.'

So he went to see how Minerva was getting on. She had put on the jeans and a relatively clean but extremely crumpled white shirt, and was tearing at her heavy hair.

'Sit down and I'll do it.'

'Will I do?'

'You look fine.' What else could he say, and she did look better.

'You've made me feel quite nervous.'

'Everything'll be all right. Just don't – I mean don't discuss anything to do with sex.'

'Don't be stupid. I never talk about it at meals – specially not at breakfast.' Although she was clearly sulking, he felt he had to add: 'And I never tell them much about what happens at parties. I mean, they wouldn't understand.'

'All *right*!'

Shortly after that, his mother – in tones that he hardly recognized – called: 'Gavin! Breakfast is served!'

Half an hour later, Gavin felt that they had been having – or, in the girl's case, *not* having – breakfast for at least a week, and yet they seemed to have got no further than the grapefruit. Gavin knew that his mother had no intention of eating; the girl was picking at hers, and every time Mrs Lamb asked her a question, she put down her loaded spoon untouched in order to answer it. Mr Lamb, usually a most reliable and steady eater, seemed to think it would be rude to chew while the guest was speaking, so whenever Minerva opened her mouth his jaws became motionless while he stared at her with unwinking attention except when she looked his way, whereupon he coughed and his eyes did a world tour of the room. Mrs Lamb led the conversation, alternating between boasting about Gavin – 'Of course, Gavin really sees the world at his work, his salon's in the West End, you know' – with questions that, while they were cunningly phrased to sound as though she knew the answers already, merely wanted confirmation as it were, were actually, Gavin realized, designed to inform her curiosity about glamorous upper class life: 'I suppose your family only use their Town House during the Season?' Minerva rose gallantly to all these sallies: 'As a matter of fact we've rented it to some people from the American Embassy. Daddy hates London, anyway, he says there's so much more to *do* in the country.'

'I expect he has a lot of Estates to see to.'

'Oh yes: he's got them all right.'

'Not to mention the Stately Home?'

'It's nothing like as Stately as it was. Falling to pieces – most of it. We had a lot of death in the family, you see. So there were Death Duties.'

'What a shame!'

'My great-uncle and then my grandfather one after the other – like ninepins. My great-uncle got kicked to death by a frightful horse that the groom warned him not to ride.'

'Well I never! It just shows you, doesn't it?'

'It was rather awful, because afterwards the groom was told to shoot the horse, so of course he had to, and then he shot himself. A bit like captains going down with the ship.'

There was an awe-struck pause, during which Gavin wondered whether it was better when the ball stopped rolling, or better when it seemed in danger of rolling off the table.

'What happened to your grandfather then?' asked Mrs Lamb when she felt respect for the dead had had its due.

'Oh – he died of port. The doctor warned him, and he tried mixing claret and brandy, like Queen Victoria, but he never got to care for it. So he fell back on port. Then he just fell back.' She laughed in a social manner, and then met Gavin's eye by mistake.

'Shall I get the sausages now, Mum?' He had tried shooting Minerva warning glances, but she simply looked at him with wide, blank eyes.

'If everybody's had sufficient, you may.'

'Shall I help?'

'Gavin can manage.' She could not bear to miss a moment. 'It's all in the plate-warmer, Gavin.'

Sausages were brought. They lay on a huge Pyrex dish surrounded by fried tomatoes and fried bread, fried eggs and fried bacon. He placed this doubtfully on the table and fetched the plates. The whole thing reminded him of the carpet he had managed to stop his mother buying for the best lounge.

'Lady Munday would prefer coffee to tea, Gavin. Gavin fancies coffee for his breakfast, don't you, Gavin.'

Gavin said that he would make some and retired to the kitchen, where he discovered that he was sweating. While he boiled water and spooned Nescaff into cups, he heard her going on and on and on: the East Wing, the West Wing, the haunted tower and the lady who walked in the deer park . . . Surely, any moment, she would go too far, or rather, since she had done that almost from the moment she opened her mouth, she would be *seen* to have gone too far, and then what would happen? His mother would be humiliated, and almost certainly very angry as a result. He was honest enough to admit that he was frightened of her anger, but he also did not want her to be humiliated. The terrible dullness of her life assailed him and, as usual, he suffered from it because he made himself mysteriously responsible. His father was a kind of eating working machine whose social life – such as it was – was conducted outside the house. His mother – a pool typist, up from Swansea – had once worked for three months in an office in Barnet, had met Dad and had married him when she was twenty-one, and from that moment all she had ever been allowed to do was to keep house and have himself and Marge. She had fought for her children to have advantages often with no very clear idea of what they might entail, or even what they were. At one point she had taken a job in Boots to help pay for Marge's private schooling, but the rest of her married life had consisted of cleaning this house and feeding them all. Since Caesar had been put down, she only went out to shop. He took the coffee back to the table full of resolutions about giving his mother a new dog. The sausages and eggs, tomatoes, bread and bacon had now been arranged upon four of the ferny plates. Minerva had levered her egg on to her piece of fried bread and was now absently stabbing at its yolk with her fork as she answered Mrs Lamb's questions.

'Daddy simply hates the House of Lords,' she was saying. 'No wonder they have to pay them to go there. Sitting about in mothy old ermine and coronets all day: Daddy says it's no life for a man.'

'Do you want milk in your coffee?'

'No thank you, Gavin. I prefer it black. I'd love some sugar though.'

'Pass Lady Munday the sugar, Fred,' Mrs Lamb ordered sharply. 'Well, we have to have a government, don't we, or else where would we be?'

Minerva said, 'Goodness knows,' and put four lumps of sugar into her cup.

'Over-run by foreigners, that's what,' said Mr Lamb unexpectedly. Everybody looked at him and his neck went red.

'All capital cities have a lot of foreigners, Dad.'

'Not like us, they don't.'

Minerva who had drunk her coffee and was now spooning out the sugar said:

'I must say, some of them have awfully pretty clothes. And it must be such a relief, if you are really plain and spotty, to wear one of those black face masks every time you go out. Everybody would think you must be ravishing underneath, or your husband wouldn't bother with it. But they do have awful operations. If you're at all well born you have your clit sewn up so that you can't feel anything.'

Gavin felt himself going scarlet. In spite of not immediately and precisely knowing what she meant, he knew enough of what she meant to feel acute anxiety about what on earth would happen next, but both of his parents' faces were bland: his father had stopped chewing, but that was all, and his mother was listening and nodding in the way that she always did when she didn't understand what was going on and didn't want people to know. (She did this quite a lot with Ken Goshawk, Marge's husband, about politics, so it was easy for Gavin to recognize.) 'People have their little ways,' she now said. 'It wouldn't do if we were all the same. We have to remember that they don't have a National Health service,' she finished, polishing off a subject clearly unwelcome to her only because it was unknown.

Gavin shot Minerva a repressive look and she put her hand over her face and then actually scooped up a bit of tomato with her knife and put it in her mouth. This, Gavin saw, *did* shock his mother whose expression became almost wilfully broadminded.

'Eat up,' said Gavin. 'Remember you've got to be on your way in about half an hour, or you'll be late. And you promised me not to let you be that.'

'Okay.' She knew that she had gone too far and now cut the white off her oozing egg and ate it with the rest of the tomatoes quite quickly.

The rest of breakfast consisted of Mrs Lamb extolling the comforts of her spare room, and lamenting Gavin's masculine incompetence in putting her in the lounge.

'Oh, I was perfectly comfortable,' Minerva said – several times. 'It was such a lovely change from home,' she added, nearly spoiling it. 'Damp sheets and all those indoor draughts,' she hurriedly explained. 'One only has to put a hot water bottle in one's bed to see the steam simply rising.'

Gavin got to his feet. 'Come on: I'll help you pack the car.'

'Why have I got to go *now?*' she wailed when they were back in the best lounge.

'You promised you would last night. It's not safe to have you about. Look at what you said at breakfast.'

'It just slipped out,' she said sulkily. 'Anyway, they didn't seem to mind. And wasn't I marvellous about everything else? I do think you might thank me.' She was rolling the red cheesecloth dress into a ball before stuffing it into one of the carrier bags that, Gavin noticed, seemed to be overflowing however much she took out of them.

'I tell you what! Why don't we go for a picnic? That's quite a good Sunday thing to do, isn't it?'

'I can't. I'm driving my parents to lunch with my sister.'

'Oh.'

'Can't you find some nice friends to spend the day with?'

'Haven't got any *nice* friends.'

'Well then, you'll have to go home to Daddy and the deer park.' He picked up the parrot's cage, took her by the arm and started to propel her out of the room.

'You needn't pull me about like that: I'll go, only I do think I should say good-bye to your parents and thank them and all that.'

'All right. After we've packed the car . . .'

When the parrot and the carrier bags had been crammed into their respective positions she turned to him and said: 'I must say, you are somebody who makes the least of everything that happens to you. Look at me! You've simply wasted me, really, haven't you. But I suppose if you're contented with your boring old lot, there's no more to be said.'

This turned Gavin's self-reproach from nasty remarks passed inside himself about his brutal and callous attitude to a young girl, into loud jeers about how chicken he was about Life in general . . . He followed her silently up the crazy paving to the front door. She *had* done her best at breakfast – according to her lights (which meaningless phrase simply exempted her from behaving as *he* would have done in the circumstances).

Mrs Lamb met them in the hall. 'Very pleased to have *met* you,' she said warmly and several times. '*Any* friend of Gavin's,' she had added rather wildly. 'Fred!' But after an uneasy pause, with more calling followed by a small search, she was forced to say: 'I'm afraid he's – engaged – at the moment. I shouldn't bother to wait if I was you.' Gavin knew that she was terrified of his father flushing the toilet and emerging, which would make indelicately clear the nature of his engagement.

'It was awfully kind of you to have me for the night, and breakfast – and everything. Thank you so much.' After a moment's hesitation, she leaned down and kissed Mrs Lamb's white pancake make-up with the result that it became suffused with a tide of lavender as she blushed with pleasure.

'It was very nice of you to come. And I hope you find them all well at home, dear. And, next time you come, I'll have the spare room all ready for you. Just give Gavin a call – either here or at Mr Adrian's. All the best.'

She followed them to the door, watched them down the path and waved frenziedly – Gavin knew she wanted to see them off before Mr Lamb emerged.

'How do I get back on to the main road?'

He told her, and without a word she got into the car.

'Have a good journey,' he said awkwardly.

She smiled. 'You mean "have a journey at all",' she said. 'Get the hell out. Well, I am. Thanks for everything.' She did not look at him while she said this, but quite suddenly started the car and drove rather jerkily off down the road.

He stood for a few moments watching her – round a bend and out of sight. He felt awful. He'd managed to be both hard and feeble – it showed what a rotten character he had. Anybody else would have risen *above* minding whether she upset his parents – well, him really, he was even hiding behind his parents. She'd done her best: she was a poor little thing, probably quite ill, since she had just come out of hospital, and she hadn't really eaten her breakfast at all. And he'd simply been grudging, ungenerous about the whole thing; worrying about appearances, as usual, and not her feelings. He went on and on to himself about adventure – a fantasy life where wonderful things happened, and then when anything actually *happened* he behaved as though it was a disaster that had to be suppressed.

The trouble about real life, he reflected gloomily as he shaved, was that you didn't seem to be able to choose what happened, but only how you responded to whatever it was. It turned you into a kind of second-class power. You were allowed to make anything you liked of a job, but ten to one it would be a bad one in the first place. But how was he to know that poor little Minnie was a bad job? The moment he called her Minnie, he felt pity and affection for her. Minnie! He wondered whether other people called her that. Then he realized that he had no way *at all* of getting hold of her. So he couldn't even say he was sorry if he'd been rough on her. This made him feel more to blame than ever, and he got ready to drive his parents to lunch with Marge in a state of masochistic despair. He didn't expect to *enjoy* it at all: it was, as usual, the least and easiest thing to do.

CHAPTER FIVE

THE drive to Marge's did not improve Gavin's state of mind. Mrs Lamb was too excited, and as the treat, so to speak, was now over, her regrets took the form of strong criticism of Gavin for not warning her that her Ladyship was arriving, until after she had arrived, and of her husband for sticking to his ritual of the lavatory after breakfast no matter what.

'Anybody would think you was nothing but some sort of machine,' she scolded, 'and what was I to do once I realized you were in there, liable to come out at any moment with the toilet flushing? I ask you!' Mr Lamb, in the back of the car, murmured something harmlessly defensive, but this only made things what they usually became – worse – when he did that.

'And we all know you go in there just to read the Sports pages. It's not as though you have a Call – it's just habit.'

'Oh, Mum! It all went off very well. She enjoyed herself.'

But this was no good either, for the simple reason that when she was upset she was always a move ahead of them on the wrong track.

'There you go! Taking your father's side!'

'He wasn't!'

'Wasn't what? Who wasn't?'

'Him,' enunciated Mr Lamb with ominous clarity, a sure sign that he was heating up. 'Gavin. He wasn't taking my side. He was merely remarking.'

'I don't see what he has to do with it at all. *I* was just remarking that when you have people to stay – *whoever* they

135

may be – you don't go locking yourself in the toilet the moment they want to say good-bye. It's not done. People do not-usually-do-it,' she finished.

There was a dank silence. Then she said: 'But, if people want to be common, I suppose there's no stopping them. Poor Lady Munday.'

Gavin said: 'Actually, Mum, she's not Lady Munday. She's not married, so she must be Lady Minerva.' This proved a happy deflection, and Gavin elaborated. Mrs Lamb, after some gallantly casual rumination, decided that Lady Minerva must be the daughter of an Earl rather than a Duke! 'Not that there's any difference. Earls and Dukes, they're all of a piece, aren't they? I must say, I was a bit surprised at her costume. I expect it's a very different story when she's at home. She never wore those clothes to the party, did she?'

'No, she didn't.' She turned to Mr Lamb in the back as a conciliatory gesture, but she turned the wrong way and simply came face to face with the bear in his lurex sunsuit who was lolling beside her husband . . . 'I told you, he's too big to wrap up,' she cried. 'You promised you'd bring back some of that polystyrene from the works.'

'I'm sorry about that. I didn't understand there was a rush. Thought you were keeping him till Christmas.'

'Christmas!' she shrieked. 'Now, do you think I'd be wearing my fingers to the bone trying to dress a bear with all that time ahead of me? It's for Judy's birthday in case you'd forgotten.'

'She's a big girl for a bear,' Mr Lamb remarked.

'No, she's not. It's not a bear you take to bed with you. It's a bear you keep sitting about. She can take it to her new home when she's married.'

'How old is she? Nine, isn't it?'

'She will be nine next Tuesday. And you ought to give her something, Gavin: you are her Godfather, after all, not to speak of being her Uncle.'

'I'll give her some cash.' He remembered how very much better cash had been than most of the things they thought of to give him.

'Please yourself.' But she was deflected, not to say mollified.

Marge and Ken lived at Potter's Bar in a very new house. They had started married life in a flat, but with the advent of Stephen and Judy they needed more room. Ken worked for a small electronics firm: he was an engineer with political views of which Mr Lamb strongly disapproved. Marge had been a schoolteacher before she married; had given it up for five years after Stephen and then Judy were born (during which time she had fostered several children), and now worked in a small unit that taught educationally sub-normal pupils. Gavin admired his sister; she also made him feel inferior. She had such energy, and was so dedicated to helping other people; she felt, he thought, that everything was simple if only you went at it hard enough, whereas he felt that everything was so difficult that he hardly dared to move in any direction.

Ken was polishing his car when they arrived and Stephen was helping him. They both stopped momentarily at the sight of the Lambs: then Ken said something to his son, and Stephen polished harder than ever. Gavin had the impression that they had arrived too early – as they usually did. Mrs Lamb was so anxious that they should leave on time that they ended up by leaving long before it.

'Polishing your car, I see.' Mr Lamb was not noted for the originality of his conversation.

'That's right . . . Stephen, say hullo to Fa-fa and Gran.'

'Hullo, Fa-fa. Hullo, Gran.' But he went on polishing.

'Stephen!'

He stopped polishing and presented his sweaty little face with its beaky nose and bulging forehead to Mrs Lamb. He was a complete (though smaller) replica of his father, Gavin thought.

'Hullo, Uncle Gavin.'

'How are *you.*'

Stephen looked at him for a moment as though he was mad, and then answered: 'I don't know.'

'Don't be cheeky, Stephen,' said Mrs Lamb, but she hardly meant it.

'You'll find Marge in the house,' said Ken encouragingly. He wanted to finish off the car.

The house smelled of roast pork and Marge, in a butcher's apron, was in the kitchen emptying the washing-up machine. Judy, also in a butcher's apron that reached her ankles, was rolling a small piece of grey and disheartened-looking pastry.

'I'm making pastry,' she said immediately. 'I'm making pastry for afters for lunch today . . . I'm making it as hard as I can.'

'Hullo, Mum. Dad. Gavin. You're looking smart.' Marge straightened up from the machine, with a wire tray full of cutlery, to kiss her parents. She wore her hair in a pony tail like her daughter. Then she gave Gavin a little hug.

'I'll put those away for you,' said Mrs Lamb who had taken off her outdoor coat in a twinkling.

'No, Mum, you go into the lounge; there's a nice fire and Ken's put the sherry ready. And there's a bottle of Bass for you, Dad.'

'Mustn't keep *that* waiting.'

'Can I put lemon curd on it?'

'I told you – it's all gone. You'll have to use the strawberry jam.'

'No, I can't! I can't ever use that! You know what Stephen said!'

'I'm sure he didn't mean it.' Marge was hunting in the cupboard and now produced a pot of jam. 'There you are.'

'Accident jam! It's made of people. I can't possibly use it!'

'No, Judy, that's not a nice thing to say!' Mrs Lamb's reproofs were diluted by her doting, and her grandchildren never took them seriously.

'There's jam all over the road after a bad accident. That's what he said. He said he'd seen it! He said – '

'Will you have marmalade then?' Another pot was proffered.

'Don't like hot marmalade. How do they scrape it up, Mum? Off of the road, how do they?'

'Off the, Judy – not off *of*.'

'Fa-fa says off of. Sometimes he says eff off to be quicker.'

'That's enough, now.'

Mrs Lamb, who had met Marge's eye, added: 'Little girls don't use the same language as men.'

'Course they *do* or they couldn't *talk*. Mum, could I have ketchup in it?'

'Don't be silly, Judy. You'll use this nice jam, and if you don't get it in the oven quickly, it won't be done for lunch.'

Judy's brilliant pink and beaky little face (*she* was like her father too) went scarlet. 'You said if Stephen was allowed to wash the car, *I* could cook with you. You *said* it!'

Marge who had spread the jam in the middle of the grey pastry and was now rolling it up, said: 'And, next week, Stephen will be doing the cooking, and you shall clean the car with Dad. Now wash your hands and take Uncle Gavin into the lounge for a drink.'

Gavin, who had been leaning mindlessly against the fridge during the pastry dialogue, came to with a start. He had been, as people who dislike abstraction would have said, 'miles away'. Actually it was not very many miles or even hours. He realized that he had been wondering about Joan. Presumably alone in that huge flat littered with all the ash trays and chicken bones and wilting flowers – or perhaps the Filipinos cleared everything up overnight? Then he had discovered that he was wondering whether it would be more lonely to wake up amid the refuse of a party, or somewhere scoured clean of any signs of one. But probably if you were lonely you regarded your scene – whatever it was – as merely ironical emphasis, tidiness would mock you, wreckage would underline it. She must be very lonely, or she wouldn't have talked to him – of all people – like that. If the thought didn't make him feel so frightened, he would like to have seen her again.

'Gav*in*!'

'All right, Mum.' He followed her obediently into the lounge, where his father was standing in front of one of the picture windows with a glass of beer, staring wistfully at the blank television screen. These Sunday lunches often meant that he missed the football. 'Here we are then,' he said with an heroic attempt at sociability.

'Like a drink, Mum?'

Mrs Lamb parked her glossy best handbag on the glass-topped coffee table and looked proudly at the cocktail cabinet.

'A very small ver*mooth*,' she said, as usual. Gavin smiled to himself as he poured his mother's drink, not forgetting the maraschino cherry from the Heinz jar and the wooden stick with which to spear it. One of Mrs Lamb's greatest pleasures in life was these regular encounters with her daughter's luxurious and elegant way of going on. A drinks cabinet, drinks before meals in small glasses, was to her living proof of her Marge having bettered herself; having, as her mother would most innocently have put it, taken advantage of her advantages; that who had given her, but Mrs Lamb?

'Here you are, Mum.'

'I'll have a cigarette with it.' She settled on to the hairy, tweed-covered settee, crossed her sharp little ankles and opened her handbag.

There were sounds of altercation in the kitchen followed by the fleeting sight of Judy running stampingly upstairs. Mr Lamb took his pipe out of his mouth and said, 'Temper.'

'None of your business,' retorted Mrs Lamb sharply, so he put his pipe back in his mouth.

Marge came in: she still wore her butcher's apron over what Gavin recognized as her Sunday winter dress – cream-coloured jersey with a cowl neck . . . 'Everybody got drinks?' she asked. 'Gav – what about you?'

'Let me do you first.'

'I'll have a sherry. She's lost her plate: she will take it out for meals, and then she never knows where she's put it . . . Whatever's happened to Stephen and Ken? They've been out with that car for hours.'

She was restless, like her mother, but in a more sophisticated manner. Gavin saw her eyes run over the room to make sure nothing was out of place, but on the other hand there were things in it that *could* be; the Sunday papers neatly ranged on the table by the other picture window – as they might be in a dentist's waiting room; her sewing, which hung in a Greek bag from the arm of her rocking chair; the plant-watering can by the Magicoal in the fireplace. She took the drink Gavin proffered and sat on the arm of the settee the other end from her mother. She had good legs and always wore rather daring stockings – webbed, or striped, or dotted – today they were sheer and dark brown. 'We can't have lunch yet,' she said, 'we're waiting for Muriel.' She avoided Gavin's eye as she said this.

Mrs Lamb cast a lightning glance at Gavin, and blowing out her smoke – she never inhaled – said: 'Is that Muriel Sutton? Your friend? Still working in that office, is she? The one who was bridesmaid at your wedding? The one who lives in New Barnet? The one whose mother had that nasty accident?' No check could have been more thorough, Gavin thought gloomily, and of course she knew all the time.

'That's right, Mum. Stephen! Have you washed your hands?'

'I couldn't. Judy's in the bathroom. She's crying. She won't come out . . .'

'Use the downstairs one.'

'Can't. Dad's in it.'

'Gavin! That reminds me. I've left that B-E-A-R in the car.'

'I'll get it.'

As he left the room, Stephen said: 'You got a bear in your car?'

'You're so sharp you'll prick yourself,' said Mrs Lamb adoringly.

'I don't mind Judy having a bear. She's only a girl.'

Needless to say, Gavin had just levered the purple-clad bear from the car and was trudging up the crazy paving with it in his arms when he heard Muriel behind him.

'Yoo hoo!' she said. It was a greeting on a par with musical chimes at the front door, Gavin thought: utterly maddening and in this case unanswerable.

'Hullo,' he said. He had to turn round to say it. Muriel was dressed in electric blue with fuchsia trim and high heels.

'Aren't you the wonderful Uncle? What a lovely teddy!'

'It's my mother's present for Judy.'

'Well – I didn't think it was for *you*. You're just a little bit old for teddies, aren't you? I hope I'm not late. I couldn't catch the first bus that came along for reasons which I'll unfold later. Oh dear!' She gave an operatic shiver, but Gavin was close enough to her now to see that she was actually much too hot. 'I got some chockies for her,' she said. Gavin was close enough to her now to realize that she smelled partly of Evening in Paris.

'After you.'

'Thanks.' She tripped ahead of him, reiterating her version of a Red Indian, or was it a cowboy? Fortunately, Ken emerged from the gents off the hall and, while she was greeting him, Gavin was able to escape ahead of her to the lounge to deposit the bear. This meant, however, that, as self-imposed barman, he was bound to offer Muriel a drink (Ken had mysteriously not come into the lounge – what on earth could he be *doing*?). Anyway . . .

'What would you like to drink?' he said to Muriel, not looking at her which didn't help, because she teetered across the Afghan rug until she was not shoulder to shoulder exactly, more bosom to shoulder blade.

'Let me see,' she said. The others, Gavin heard, had begun to talk about gardening, and although he knew it was *paranoid* of him there seemed to be something conspiratorial about that: as though they were throwing him and Muriel together.

'You can have sherry, or gin, or red Cinzano,' he began tonelessly; 'or any combination of those that you feel like.'

'I'd like a tiny little gin and tonic, Gavin, please!'

And, while he was pouring it out wondering irritably what she meant by tiny, she said – and now *she* was being conspiratorial: 'I can't wait for you to tell me about the party.'

'What party?'

'*The* party. The one you went to last night. The one that was the reason why you couldn't come to dinner.'

'Oh, *that*. It was okay. Nothing much.' Two pictures – one of Spiro astride Winthrop in Joan's bathroom, and one of Minnie sitting up naked in Joan's bed – shot on to his mind's screen, and he blinked them out as he added: 'It went on rather late.'

She gave a knowing laugh. 'Got a bit of a hangover, have you? I thought you looked a mite peaky.'

Then he was saved by Ken who helped himself to a glass of cider: he played games and never drank spirits. Muriel went over to Mrs Lamb who was levering the bear's joints in an attempt to get him to sit upright instead of lolling which had always been his wont. She kissed Marge, who was so anxious about her size and single state that she responded – for her – with undue warmth, and said 'Good morning' to Mr Lamb who took his pipe out of his mouth to say 'Pleased to meet you' although he did not look it. Stephen came in and said:

'Mum, it's in the goldfish tank and she can't get it out.'

'Why can't she?'

'She's afraid of the catfish. She's only a girl,' he explained to his mother.

'Well – *you* get it out for her and tell her to come on down for lunch, if she wants any. And, Stephen! I've had enough of this "only a girl" business. And wash your *hands!* Little male chauvinist!' she exclaimed after he had left the room.

'It's only a phase,' said Mrs Lamb. She did not know in the least what Marge meant, but felt bound to defend her beloved grandson. 'He *is* a boy, after all,' she reminded her daughter.

'Men are all the same,' declared Muriel. She looked challengingly round the room for opposition to this remark and Marge instantly said: 'Ken isn't like that, are you, Ken? You believe in equality between the sexes, don't you? You don't think women are inferior to men, do you? I mean, you think that we should do jobs just like men, and men should do their share of domestic chores?'

'That's right,' said Ken stoutly, but he looked bored, or rather, Gavin thought, he looked as though he was afraid he might be going to be bored . . .

'That's all right then. I'll go and dish up.'

There was a silence after she left the room, but Mr Lamb's mind was almost audibly ticking over, and eventually he said:

'You don't get many women bricklayers.'

'Of course you don't,' exclaimed Muriel soothingly. 'The idea!'

'And you don't get many masons, either.'

'We know that!' said Mrs Lamb sharply, she wasn't quite sure which way the conversation was going now, but she'd had great practice at putting Mr Lamb in his place.

'And, between you and me, I'd be surprised if I met a woman plasterer.'

'I should – jolly – well – think you – would,' said Muriel almost as though she was humouring a mad child.

'That's not the point, though, is it really? I mean women haven't had a chance to do those jobs – up to now. In the Soviet Union they do. In the Soviet Union they do all the same jobs as men.'

'They don't get to be President, do they?' said Mrs Lamb with unexpected acumen. 'They don't get a chance at the top jobs – oh dear me, no. I don't suppose there are many Russian women Admirals or Bishops or . . . or Heads of Firms. Name me a Russian woman Admiral!' she demanded. Mr Lamb was not deflected.

'And joiners now. You don't get many women joiners, I wouldn't say.'

'Lunch is ready!' called Marge.

They went into the dining room for lunch.

They had finished the pork, and were demolishing damson pie with double cream (Marge was a great bottler of fruit). Conversation had been – not exactly sticky – but exhaustive. Mr Lamb, once wound up, was hard to stop: he had run through every conceivable job in the building trade where it would be funny if you found a woman. Mrs Lamb who sensed that she was on to a good thing with the Russians had retaliated: in her case, she was not bound by a trade, but able to range over every profession she could muster, and they had been many. Gavin had mentally gone through all the arts and surprised himself by finding how few women painters, sculptors or composers – even poets – resulted. He had just got to Berthe Morisot, and on to the notion that the Impressionists painted a good deal from a woman's point of view – take Vuillard's interiors for instance – but before he could give them as examples he was jolted out of his private mind by an entirely new hazard: Ken had made some scathing reference to the English class system. Usually, this salvo – shot across Mrs Lamb's bows as it were – would have resulted in her fiery defence of the Royal Family, with Gavin broadening the argument into popular myth, and the concept of most people requiring a figurehead, anyone from a god to a pop star, etc. (there were several well-worn jungle paths trodden each

Sunday by different combinations of protagonists), but this time Ken had gone too far, or rather had gone exactly the right distance, to provide Mrs Lamb with the opening that Gavin immediately realized she had been waiting for ever since they'd got out of the car.

'It might interest you to know,' she said, 'that there's no difference between Them and Us at all. As I happen to know. At first hand,' she paused grandly.

Everybody looked at her. 'That nice girl you brought home last night, Gavin. Lady – what was her name – ever so nice she was – Lady Minerva Munday!'

There was a satisfactory silence spoiled by Mr Lamb saying: 'You wouldn't catch *her* doing any making good.'

'We're not talking about the building trade, now, Fred. That subject is closed. We're on to something else.'

Marge said: 'Goodness me, Gavin, what have you been up to?'

It was her nature and practice to defuse any situation that she felt was becoming what she called 'personal', but this time there was a touch of genuine curiosity in her voice.

'Nothing much.' Gavin felt peevish – he would have said bored, but his face was heating up – particularly as he felt Muriel's currant eyes on his face . . .

'Gavin wasn't up to anything,' Mrs Lamb retorted sharply: 'he simply brought a friend home from a party – in this case an Earl's daughter – and she was just like anybody else. There-was-not-the smallest difference. Of course she was very young; Gavin put her in the lounge and she slept on the settee with her parrot.'

There was another, short, silence, then Marge, looking anxiously at Muriel, said: 'Well I never!'

Muriel, who had just discovered that she had eight damson stones on her plate (Gavin knew this because he had quietly counted them too), said: 'You can get a nasty disease from parrots: I'm surprised Lady What's-her-name's family allow that sort of goings-on. It sounds distinctly funny to me, don't you think so, Marge?'

'Of course her family have a deer park and estates to keep up, and naturally they're finding that things are not what they used to be.'

'You don't catch me having trouble with my deer park.'

Marge cast a look at her husband that was a marital compound of telegram and gramophone record. Gavin translated it roughly as: 'Watch out! You know you've always promised to shut up about politics with Mum and Dad. It's only once a fortnight, after all. You can't expect them to change their ways at their age . . . *Please*, Ken . . .'

'Anyway, speak as you find and *I* found her a nice, natural, young lady – just like anybody else.'

Ken winked at his wife so *that* part of it was going to be all right, but Mr Lamb, who was nettled at being made to change the subject, said: '*You* don't like everyone. I've known you be quite sharp with some people I could mention – ' but Judy interrupted with:

'Does she live in a castle, Gran?'

'I don't know, dear, I didn't think to ask her. I expect she does.'

Muriel, in whom a variety of emotions had been raging, said:

'Well, Gavin, I think you're a very dark horse – I really do. No *wonder* you said you weren't free. We had a little plan,' she explained to the table, 'we were going to go to the pictures and have a little supper afterwards, but I quite see now why it all fell through.'

Gavin was so incensed by this version of his arrangements that all pity for Muriel deserted him and he said: 'I had a previous engagement. A party with my friend Harry in London. I just happened to meet this girl at it – '

'Mrs Wilkinson at number 92. I've never heard you say a good word about *her*.'

This deflected Mrs Lamb, which was both a good and a bad thing. She would not in the least mind Mrs Wilkinson only she was common, fed her family on tins and dyed her hair. *And* she had gone to Majorca leaving Ginger to fend for himself – not at all a nice thing to do. Marge went to make coffee and tea; the children got down and mercifully Mrs Lamb remembered the bear in the lounge. Gavin decided to go and help Marge as a way of escaping from Muriel, who had begun to stack plates. Mr Lamb and Ken were left. Gavin heard his father say 'Women!' as he left the room.

Marge was putting cups and saucers on a tray. 'You're not going to *marry* this girl, are you?'

'Of course not! I only met her last night. All this fuss!'

'I thought not.' She looked relieved. 'I could see that Muriel was ever so upset.'

'Look, Marge, I'm not going to marry *her* either. I wish you'd stop trying to make something out of her and me. It's a non-starter.'

'She said you were wonderful to her when you did her hair.'

'It's my job to be wonderful. With hair, I mean. I don't want to marry anyone.'

'Oh well – ' She gave way so easily that he had a nasty feeling that they were back to square one (in this case Muriel) and he was right, because almost immediately she went on: 'I mean – if you don't particularly fancy anyone in particular, you might as well consider Muriel. I mean, Gav dear, you *can't* spend all your life living with Mum and Dad. It's not as though you're a homosexual.'

'If I was, I'd be out on my own in a flat, you bet.'

'A home – kids, surely you'd like all that. It would make all the difference to you.'

'I don't want all the difference made to me. I'm happy as I am. Just because married life suits you so well, you think everyone ought to have it.'

'Of course it isn't always easy.'

'It isn't a question of ease,' he said, and immediately started wondering whether perhaps it wasn't – just that. He watched her pouring boiling water on to instant coffee and a pot of tea and thought: 'Perhaps I haven't got the energy to be bothered enough with people'; the other idea of being too easily bothered by them instantly redressed the balance. It was as though everything about him was designed to keep him inanimate – poised for ever up a tree, on the brink . . . 'I don't find things particularly easy,' he said to Marge, 'but I just don't feel like marrying anyone. And of course,' he finished shrewdly, 'I can't marry someone if I don't love them.'

Her face cleared. Marge believed in love quite as much as she believed in marriage . . . 'I've told her she should cut down on her starches,' she remarked with apparent irrelevance . . . She gave him a quick little pat on the shoulder. 'Anyway, I don't know what Ken would do without you on these Sunday jamborees. He does find it difficult to associate with people who are politically unaware; and it's too early for him to show Dad his vegetables.'

He picked up the now heavily laden tray for her and carried it into the lounge; a scene packed with the familiar discomforts. Mr Lamb and Stephen were crouched before the television which contained its usual quota of steaming men trotting about and periodically hugging one another; Mrs Lamb was sulking because the chocolates had taken precedence over the bear. 'Poor Teddy, then,' she was saying. 'Who doesn't love you then?' 'Oh, turn that thing down, Fred, for goodness' sake!' Marge began pouring tea and coffee on these troubled waters, and her sheer good nature prevailed. Presently she sent Gavin in search of Ken whom he found in his workshop repairing a portable radio.

'Hullo, mate.'

'She told me to bring you some coffee. Are those your new speakers?'

'Yup. Like to hear them?'

'I would.' They settled down to a delightful demonstration of Ken's equipment.

Going home was not as usual because they had to give Muriel a lift. Mrs Lamb, who was wound up by the excitements of the day, seemed to have taken against Muriel, who was, or seemed to be, quite unaware of this. Her jealousy took a masochistic form: she plied Mrs Lamb with questions about her aristocratic guest. Gavin, like his father, remained safely silent.

'If she stayed the night suddenly without any warning I suppose she was still in her party clothes? She must have felt ever so funny at breakfast.'

'She was not funny at breakfast. Naturally she brought a change of clothing with her. What an idea!' she added.

'Which earl did you say she was the daughter of?'

'I didn't say.'

'I expect Gavin knows, don't you, Gavin?'

'Naturally, Gavin wouldn't go about asking her!'

'On the skinny side – she seemed to me.'

Nobody had expected Mr Lamb to speak and at first nobody answered him. Then Muriel remarked: 'Oh well, these very young girls think it's fashionable to be skinny, don't they? For some reason they seem to think it makes them attractive.'

Gavin, who was driving, thanked God she wasn't in front with him, and as an afterthought thanked Him even more fervently for not making him have to drive her home alone. If he'd been driving her home *alone* . . .

At peace, at last, in his room, he cast himself on his bed and allowed depression – like a sea fog – to approach and envelop him. He was absolutely no good at life: either he was scared stiff, or he was depressed. Or else he was just chugging along, doing what was expected of him – like at work. Other people were always urging him to change – to do something different. Instinct and behaviour patterns were what people admired in other forms of life – in their own, it seemed, that instinct was minimal, and you were supposed to discover your own behaviour patterns simply in order to change them. He remembered Evelyn Waugh in a television interview saying that he preferred people he knew well – they were totally predictable and therefore boring, but it meant that he didn't have to listen to them. Then he thought of Sartre saying, 'Hell is other people.' Amazing: he remembered that he had thought at the time that Sartre should have said, 'Hell *could* be other people.' But of course, as a remark, that didn't sound anything like so interesting: it hadn't got that sweeping, devastating neatness about it that would catch people who would then feel it must be true because they could remember it. It occurred to him that other people urged him to change in *their* direction whatever that might be: Marge's was marriage and a family, Harry's was queerdom and a steady alliance with another chap. 'Be like me so that I can understand you better' stuff. Or perhaps it was in order that he should understand *them* better? He started thinking about Minnie – wondering about her, where on earth she had driven off to. She had written his number on the bonnet of her car – it would have to rain an awful lot for that to be erased. Anyway, she knew where he lived; she could find him if she wanted to, whether *he* wanted her to or not.

He thought he wanted to sleep, but as soon as he had drawn some curtains, pulled his pillow out from under the Persian coverlet and shut his eyes he realized that he hadn't taken out his lenses; then, having removed them, he had the nasty feeling that his mind's eye was simply lying in wait with a whole lot of pictures to unnerve him. He'd have to go through the awful scene in the bathroom, and then the row with Spiro in Joan's flat – then Joan finding her bed in disarray . . . In view of how her party had ended, he decided that he wanted to write to Joan. He sat up, put his lenses back and started

hunting through his pack of picture postcards for the ingeni-
ously appropriate one. He realized that, away from her, her
physical appearance predominated. The cards kept being
cruelly wrong. The Duke of Urbino, Soutine at his most
freakishly grotesque, Lautrec, and somehow worse – Renoir,
Ramsay, Gainsborough, all depicting their fashionable
norm . . . He selected a Vuillard interior – a pot of primula
poised or posed by Vuillard in what looked like his studio. It
was one of those pictures where the composition was so
pleasing that you didn't bother to dissect it. 'Dear Joan,' he
wrote: then he paused for a long time – selecting and discarding
things he wanted to say to her. In the end he wrote: 'Thank
you for the party. Meeting you was far the best bit.' Then he
had to think about whether he had ever told her his name –
decided that she knew it anyway, and, if she did not, she would
still know that it was him writing to her, and signed the
postcard, Gavin. His writing was small and very neat and clear
but the lines always sloped downwards however hard he tried
to keep them level. While he was writing the card, he knew
that he would like to see her again, but he didn't feel he could
possibly put his address or telephone number on it as that
would look as though he wanted to see her again. He would
have to get the address from Harry, but he didn't feel like
ringing Harry up, in case Winthrop had walked out and Harry
would want him to go round to hear about it. Because then,
of course, he'd have to go. If you spent most of your life on
other people's terms, naturally you had to cut down on the
life, or too many things would happen to you that you didn't
want. He decided to play the Somervell 'Maud' cycle; then,
after one side, he decided to read Tennyson at the same time;
then he couldn't find his Tennyson. This led him to the
beginning of a vast new rearrangement of his books, and then
it was time for cold tongue and salad and 'Mastermind'. By
eleven o'clock, the books looked as though they were in a
worse muddle than ever – partly because it was impossible to

move them around as much as he'd decided to do without reading any of them. He popped down to the kitchen and made himself a cup of verbena and peppermint tea (somebody had told him that it helped clear the blood).

He had a bath; all through it he was looking forward to being in bed: in a bout of delicious fantasy where everything happened as he chose, before he lapsed into unconsciousness. But when he finally settled himself between the sheets and put out his lamp things simply wouldn't go right, as they usually did. It was as though he was trapped in some awful maze: he could hear her voice, a little, unknown way ahead of him – sometimes even catch a glimpse of her bare ankle, some gossamer shreds of her pre-raphaelite dress vanishing round a corner ahead of him, but round the corner turned into a dead end, and behind him scuttled Minnie or pounded Muriel – he was always having to double back faster to new turnings in order to lose them. Then, in a silence that several times he thought was perhaps the beginning of the real dream he sought, he would hear her distant laugh and in the (more magic) silence afterwards would imagine her chiselled mouth curving in secret, benign amusement – would hear birds calling in the high dark hedges, but he could not tell her name. If only he could see over the hedges, he would find her, and so with each step he took he began to leave the ground – with each leaping movement he began to fly a little and, in the middle of each flight, he could see over the hedge – once, look down upon her gold red hair streaming out behind her as she ran, and then to see the centre of the maze – a fountain with a marble seat round it. She was there, tall and quite still and holding out her small, white hand – as smooth and as cool as marble to his lips. 'I am not seventeen,' she said sedately.

He took her hand again and she glided a little ahead of him in the dissolving dusk until, together with her, he was no more.

CHAPTER SIX

ONDAY was usually a quiet day in the salon: a quick glance at the appointments book showed him that Daphne had arranged his clients so that he had a really decent lunch hour for once. He decided to buy sandwiches and eat them in St James's Park as it was a mild and sunny day . . . Mr Adrian did not always come in on Mondays and Sharon had returned. The atmosphere in the salon was friendly and light-hearted. They asked one another if they had had a nice weekend; this had become a habit from asking clients – a kind of courteous, acceptable curiosity (like the clients asking them if they had had their holiday yet), and everybody said that they had, because nobody expected a serious answer. Peter's general plea to him to come to supper – to see the flat and persuade Hazel not to get pregnant – had narrowed, or hardened, to something like a command: 'Hazel says you're to come on Friday. Right?' And before Gavin could answer he said: 'That's fine. She also said, do bring someone with you – we've got four of everything.' Then he dashed away to a client and Gavin felt he was committed. Iris, who had been standing by, said: 'He's a nice boy. He asked me and Alfred, but it's a top floor and Alfred couldn't manage.'

She sounded almost wistful, and this made Gavin feel that he ought to want to go far more than he did (which was hardly at all). Why didn't he want to do things more? Well – not exactly that – he *did* want to do some things: why didn't he want to do *more* things more? As he queued at the Italian sandwich shop that gave you the most *inside* the ready sliced bread, he started making a list of what he did want to do. There was work. Well, he wanted to do that; enjoyed it really; at least, he couldn't imagine what he would do without some such huge, regular commitment; also it was probably the only thing he was any good at, but after that . . . Oh well, no shortage of *things* – music – especially going to the opera when he could afford it, but also especially playing his records in the comfortable, secret familiarity of his room; going off on his bike on Sundays and looking at some great house (sometimes he and Harry had taken a weekend to do that), going to exhibitions; browsing through all kinds of travel brochures choosing holidays that he usually never went on; swimming, reading – especially re-reading, but also finding a new, riveting writer; reading poetry aloud to himself, going to films but not as much as he used to. Here he had to choose his sandwiches – cream cheese and cucumber on brown bread.

As he walked down St James's Street to the Park, thinking as he always did how sad it was that the Palace no longer had its own piece of sky round its roofs and clock tower, he realized that, except for Harry, he didn't really much like doing any of the things he liked *with* anybody. Often, when he was doing them alone, he had fleeting dreams of doing them with the ideal person, someone so beautiful that she invariably took his breath away and he had to dismiss her because what would he be doing with somebody like that? Anyway – people *weren't* ideal. Look at the girl at the cash desk where he had bought his sandwiches: dark with a greasy skin and an expression of passive hostility – it would be no good embarking upon anything with her. One couldn't go through all the agonies of approach, discovery, exposure, the trying to keep things perfect with a perfect stranger – not even knowing whether they would join in the conspiracy for perfection if they did not at least *appear* to have those attributes that could inspire *him* to believe in it. But then, if there was such a person, what would they think of him? They would have, he reflected hopelessly, to see below the surface – past his acne, and froggy eyes, somehow through all that, into what he was – or could be. He started counting up the things he didn't like doing. There were two categories here: things he didn't much care for, and things he hated. (There were, of course, things like family lunch with Marge; that was a bit more like work, in that he didn't especially choose it, it wasn't frightening, and he was so used to it that it had become structural. If he lived at home, it was part of that.) Well – things he didn't much care for . . . Going to supper with Peter and Hazel was a perfect example. Going to a disco with Harry and Winthrop; he wasn't at all sure that this didn't come into the hate category. The noise level, the psychedelic lights, the sweating, jammed couples of men dancing, everybody hunting, dressing younger, coming out with who they wanted to be with in the erratic and strident, dark half-light – it all seemed to make being a homosexual have only to do with sex.

He turned left when he reached the Park, as the two things he liked best were the Palace of Whitehall and the pelicans. It was sunny, with little warm breezes, and hardy couples were lying on the fresh green grass with their faces turned to the sky. He walked slowly past the Palace: it was the stone and its bleached bone colour that pleased him most – that and the fact that because of its open forecourt it could be seen entire – from skyline to Charles I's execution ground. He thought about that for a bit: how bitterly cold it had been, and the King asking for a second shirt to stop him shivering from the cold which his subjects might mistake for fear. When he tried to imagine the sort of courage required for walking up to the block, kneeling down and allowing them to cut off his head – he couldn't – at all. At least that sort of thing didn't happen any more – at least not here, where he was . . . He turned away from the Palace towards the lake. A girl in a white mac was feeding ducks from a paper bag. She was some distance away, but he realized that if he kept his course he would come up with her. Supposing he was the bold, adventurous type, he could keep on walking, reach the girl, and if she was beautiful (most unlikely) he could get into conversation with her – pick her up. The chances of her being *that* beautiful were very small indeed, and there was no *need* for him to say a word; the Park was a public place and he could walk anywhere – same as anybody else. If the world *were* full of beautiful girls, he would have had more practice – as it wasn't, he hadn't. So, naturally, the whole thing made him nervous. By now his path had reached a point where there were no more turn-offs: he had either to keep on till he reached her, or he could turn round and walk back the way he had come, but he didn't want anyone to think he was that frightened of them thank you very much. So he had no choice but to keep on. It was just the way that people met each other in books, he reflected, as his heart began to thud out of sync with his footsteps. In novels they could plunge into God-knew-what intimacies in a matter of pages. If she wasn't pretty he needn't do anything at all – plod on without a word. If she was pretty – he didn't *have* to talk to her – after all, think how awful it must be to be one of the few really beautiful girls in the world: *everybody* must be stopping to talk to them whatever they were doing, they must have to put up with being accosted from morning till night. She'd probably like him far better if he *didn't* talk to her (if she was really pretty): he'd probably get off to a much better start with her if he just walked on without saying a word, hardly even seeming to look . . . She'd be tremendously grateful to him and realize how nice he was. Would she? He had slowed down considerably to give the appearance of being plunged in thought – not a random collection of panic-stricken rumina-tions – but *thought* – take politics – sometimes he really wondered whether the present Government knew what they were doing; or even if their knowing – given the power of the unions – could any longer make much difference. Democracy atomized power to the point where the individual had none at all in fact. Take this poor girl – supposing she was beautiful – she had no power at all to stop him talking to her – it would be entirely up to his sense of decency. And if, which was most unlikely, she was ordinarily plain, well, she couldn't *make* him talk to her however much she might want him to. Could she? He had been studiously looking at the path and his own feet; now he glanced up for a second. She had her back to him: she had thin, girlish-looking legs and was wearing cork-wedged shoes or sandals he didn't have time to notice which – he didn't want to embarrass her . . . He was about ten yards off now, and decided to have a good sweeping, casual but intent look at the ducks she was feeding, ending up by having a (perfectly natural, surely?) look at whoever might be feeding them. He took a deeper breath, raised his head with such a sudden jerk that for a moment he saw nothing but bits of cloudy sky and the tops of trees – down to the greenish water spattered with waterfowl and then up a bit and straight into the girl's eyes. The girl was Jenny. Relief/disappointment surged – all that fuss about nothing. Of course if she had been beautiful he would have spoken to her – had geared himself up to do just that, and here was his junior, looking as much like a young owl as ever – hair en brosse and large gold-rimmed spectacles.

'Hullo,' she said.

'Hullo,' he said. He couldn't not speak to his junior, just because they met off duty: she might be hurt, anyway he liked her, but it *would* turn out to be her.

'That's the lot.' She turned the bag upside down, and a few crumbs fell out of it.

'Do you often feed them?'

'When the weather's okay and we get enough of a lunch hour. Not very often in fact.' She began a smile but, meeting his eye, it faded, and she turned back rather hurriedly to the ducks most of whom seemed not to have realized that the source of provender had ceased, and were swimming about in a greedy and expectant manner.

Gavin remembered that he hadn't eaten his sandwiches and got one out of his bag. 'They can have half my bread,' he said, 'there's always too much of it.'

'A lot of different kinds,' he remarked a few moments later as he embarked upon round two. 'Which do you like best?'

'The Carolinas.'

'Which are they? That one?'

'That's a Mandarin. They used to be my favourites, but now I've gone on to them. Over there.' She pointed out a wonderfully-marked bird in green and reddish brown with black and white delineations. 'But I like the diving ducks too. That cheeky little tuft on their heads that stays upright however much they dive. You can read what they are from boards on another bit of the lake. That's how I know.' She took an apple out of her mac pocket and started to eat it.

'Do the pelicans ever come?'

'No. They eat fish. It wouldn't be worth their while. They get specially fed.'

They stood there in silence for a bit while Gavin finished his second sandwich – there was nothing in them, really – and threw the last bit of crust into the water. The silence, which had been easy at first, became heavier with length, and Gavin started to feel uncomfortably responsible for it. Jenny finished her apple and chucked the core into the water. Most of the ducks seemed to know at once that they wouldn't want it and almost swam out of their way to make the point.

Jenny turned away from them and started to walk away just as he thought of something.

'Where are you going for your holidays this year?' he asked, walking with her.

'I don't know. I can't really go far because of the boy.' And, before he could wonder what on earth she meant, she added: 'My son . . . He's only three and a half. I took him to the seaside last year and he hated it. Although that may have been because they said there'd be sand and there wasn't. Not so's you'd notice . . . And we had shocking weather.'

'I didn't know you'd been married, Jenny.'

'Haven't bin.'

'Sorry.'

'You couldn't know. I met this bloke when I was on a camping holiday in France. You know – you can go diving and you live in a kind of club. It was the most exciting thing I'd ever done in my life . . . He was Norwegian – a student . . . He was much older than me. Afterwards, I wrote to him to tell him I was having a baby, but he never answered. I wondered for a bit whether I hadn't got his address right. Anyway, I never heard. So there it was.'

'You just went ahead and had the baby.'

'I had him all right. Everyone kept telling me I ought to get him adopted, but I couldn't see the sense in that. He might have had *any* sort of life if I'd done that. At least if he's with me I know . . .'

'And he's fine, is he?'

'He's a *terror*,' she said in a very warm voice.

They were standing, waiting to cross the road outside the Park: he glanced at her, and saw that she was smiling. She really didn't look at all old.

'How *old* were you?' he found he couldn't help saying.

'Seventeen. Well – nearly.' Then she added quickly: 'I haven't told any of the others, because I didn't want it to get to Mr Adrian. I had a job getting taken on as it was, and if he'd known *that* you wouldn't have seen me for dust.'

'I won't tell anyone. Thanks for telling *me*.'

'It just came up,' she said, 'because of the holidays.'

They walked in silence until they reached the bottom of St James's Street while he made timid generalizations about other people's courage, and how amazing people were when you got to know anything at all about them, and until he felt the pricking in his eyes subside.

'Who looks after him?'

'You sound a bit croaky! You haven't got that bug that's going round, have you?' She sounded genuinely concerned.

'I'm fine, thanks.'

'My mum. She's been lovely to us. I could never even have started my training if it hadn't been for her. That's why I always take Andrew out at weekends and away for my holiday – to give her a rest . . .'

'That's his name, then?' he said trying to sound jollier than he felt.

'I wouldn't have called him Andrew if his name wasn't Andrew,' she said with recognizable forbearance. (God – he sounded just like his father! Something he liked to think he never did!) He turned to her, blushing. 'That was silly of me.'

'Okay. Actually, it's nice to have been able to tell you. I feel a bit of a Charlie when the other juniors are talking about their boy friends and getting engaged and all that. Course, I'm older than them, but that makes them think it's even funnier. It's funny, isn't it, how everybody expects you to be just like them.'

'Feelings,' he agreed, 'they do expect you to feel the same.'

'Yes, but you couldn't feel the same if the same things hadn't happened to you, could you?'

'I don't know. You might imagine whatever it was a bit.' After a pause, he added: 'There's art, too, of course. You can't leave that out.' He felt shy about saying that, but he couldn't leave it out.

'What's that for?'

'Recognizing things, I think. I think it's for showing people that there is a lot more to them than usually meets their eye.'

'Oh. *That's* what it's for!'

'Well – only a bit. *I* don't know all of what it's for. Every time I think about that I think something else. Don't take what I say about it for gospel.' He was backing off; the whole subject was something he only discussed – and he didn't say all he thought to *him* – with Harry.

'When you say art, you don't just mean pictures and that, do you?'

'No – I mean the whole lot.'

'Music and reading and acting?' she persisted: she sounded childishly dogged, almost as though she was trying to catch him out.

'All that. And architecture, and opera and poetry. And gardens, sculpture. Films,' he added after a pause.

'Gardens!' she scoffed. 'I can't see that! I can't see the art in gardens!'

'I don't mean that every garden is a work of art: of course not. Not anything's that. I only meant it could be.'

They had nearly reached the top of the street, she nudged his arm and said: 'There's always old men reading newspapers in those windows.'

'It's a club. Called White's.'

'What do they do?'

'I don't know. They have drinks and food and things and just be there.' Winthrop had worked as a waiter in the R.A.C. very temporarily indeed, and what Gavin knew about Clubs was gleaned from his invective-studded account. 'Fuck all,' he had added absently.

'Perhaps they just want to get away from their wives.'

'Could be. They're the sort of men who went to schools without girls, so probably they aren't very used to them.'

'They have waitresses, though,' she said. 'I know that because a friend of mine did it for a summer.'

'They wouldn't have to talk to them.' Briefly, he wondered

whether that, in fact, was what Clubs were for: an escape; to provide an escape from the Ladder of Fear. In which case, he could absolutely see the point of them.

The afternoon would have been quiet had it not been for a telephone call from Minerva.

'Hullo,' she said. She sounded rather breathless.

'Hullo.' It was the most cautious thing he could think of to say.

'I'm somewhere terrifically boring, so I thought I'd ring you up.'

'I'm at work, really.'

'I know. I wondered what time you finished. Or – tell you what – I could come round and have my hair done . . .'

This stymied him. He only had two clients between now (three o'clock) and closing time.

'What do you want done to your hair?'

'That's up to you, isn't it? Okay, I'll come round.' She rang off before he could say anything. Then she rang back again to say what was the address, so of course he had to tell her.

She turned up about an hour later wearing green stretch pants, boots and what looked like a man's golfing jacket; it was about eight sizes too big for her. He happened to be combing out his client and it was Jenny who divested her of the jacket and put the nylon jacket round her. That looked too big for her as well: she seemed to have shrunk since Gavin had last seen her. Jenny gave her a magazine to read and she settled down quietly to wait. So perhaps she was going to behave herself, he thought, and not be a nuisance. He finished off Mrs Atkinson who slipped him his usual 50p, and then walked over to Minerva who had been watching him.

'How much did she give you?' she asked audibly.

'I don't know.' Mrs Atkinson had not yet left the desk where she was paying her bill.

'Don't you want to look? *I* would.'

'No. What do you want me to do with your hair?'

'Bet it wasn't any more than 50p.'

Out of the corner of his eye he saw Mrs Atkinson registering this . . . 'Would you mind just shutting up about that?' he said as quietly and as forcibly – a very nice adjustment that – as possible.

'Sorry.' She hunched down in the chair, and looking at her in the mirror he noticed that she had grey purple smudges under her eyes. She looked, in fact, rather ill. Her hair was in rotten condition too as though she was eating the wrong food or, come to think of it, not enough food.

'We'll give it a shampoo and a good conditioner, and then I'll cut it. If you want it cut.'

'Yes please, Gavin.'

He got Jenny over and sent them off together. Then he went out to the back to get himself a coffee. Peter was there.

'Is she your bird?'

'No.' He had to think what Peter meant for a second: he never thought of himself as a person who had them.

'Well – she seems to know *you*.' He swilled his coffee in the cup for a moment and then said: 'I mean – if you want to ask her on Friday – you're welcome. We're broad-minded, you know.' Then he went, before Gavin could work out what he could possibly have meant by *that*. Gavin, who felt often that his mind was like a small and partially disused branch railway line, had a natural and, he felt, well-founded terror of those who claimed the broader highways: it was either a way of telling you that they could put up with however silly you were, or it was a way of warning you that they couldn't put up with anything. Perhaps, he thought, it was Peter's way of telling him that he, Peter, could put up with Minnie because he, Peter, liked Gavin. That was all very well, but could *he* put up with her? He didn't have to; he advised himself to wait, not to hurry things, or rush into anything. Then he started wondering morosely when he had last ever rushed – you couldn't count being propelled – into anything, and decided that it was when he'd bought William, his white rat, from Mr Dean in New Barnet when he'd been thirteen.

'Mr Gavin. Client's ready.' It was Jenny, behaving as though they hadn't met in the Park, and had not, ever, talked about anything other than their clients. Following Jenny into the salon, he wondered how on earth somebody so slight could ever have produced a three-and-a-half-year-old son. She must have looked extraordinary when pregnant – like a very young tree with one enormous pear . . . with this he suddenly realized that he found pregnant women sexually attractive. By the time he reached Minerva, whose peaky face was surmounted by a white towel twisted like a turban round her head, he was blushing – thank goodness his mother couldn't read his mind – she would be even more shocked than he was . . . she called a pregnancy a condition – implying that it was not a very nice one at that.

Jenny unwound the turban and gave a final expert drying little rub. 'Shall I comb out, Mr Gavin, or will you?'

'I'll do it. You nip off for a coffee. Next client's not due till a quarter-to.'

He combed out in silence, aware of Minnie watching him intently. He *was* intent; the first time he cut any client's hair he had to get the feel of it: look at their face, see how to make the most of any good feature, how to soften any short-coming. She had a high and wide forehead – a double crown set rather far back. The hair itself was medium coarse, very much split at the ends. Her ears stuck out a little too much for beauty, but she had a long neck. It would be best cut just to the bottom of the ear lobe – a little longer at the back: he'd feather it to three inches all over the head. That would give the hair a better chance to recover. He began feeling for her natural parting – no, in view of the double crown better perhaps without one. He'd cut the hair short across the forehead on a slant. He felt in his pocket for his scissors, which weren't there.

'I'll have to fetch my scissors.' He'd left them in an overall pocket – extremely careless of him.

'There are some.' She pointed to the glass-topped table in front of them.

'I use my own.'

When he came back with them, she said: 'What's so special about your scissors?'

'They're Japanese. They're mine. Nobody else uses them.'

'How do you know?'

'I'd know if anybody else *had* used them. We all have our own scissors.'

'Does the man who owns the shop dole them out to you?'

'Oh, no. We buy our own.' The idea of Mr Adrian forking out sixty-five quid for a pair of scissors amused him mildly.

He told Minnie what he was going to do; she said, 'Okay – go ahead,' – and sat remarkably still for a while. Then, suddenly, she said: 'Lucky you!'

He met her eye in the mirror for a moment, but didn't reply, so she had to go on: 'To like doing something you're good at.'

'I don't think I'd be much good at it if I hated it.'

'You probably wouldn't be doing it then.' After a pause, she said: 'That's why I don't do anything. I don't know what I like.'

'Have you tried to find out?'

'Of course not! I'm waiting for it to happen.' And, seeing that he didn't think much of that, she went on: 'I've had to spend so much time being against things, you see. Can you imagine? They tried to make me do a secretarial course after school. They've given *that* up. Now they just hope I'll get married. Like my boring sister.'

'I didn't know you had a sister.'

'She's older. She's only a half-sister. She's called Sheila. I'm staying with her: she's awful.'

'You told me you were a model.'

'I told you I'd done some modelling. I've given it up: it's boring.'

'So now what are you going to do?'

'I told you: I'm waiting for something to happen.'

'I can't spell, you see,' she said after he hadn't answered. 'So it would be no good my trying to be a secretary. I don't want to do anything unless I'm terrifically good at it.'

'People don't just *start* good at anything.'

'Some people do. Still, I can't be one of them, I suppose, or I'd be doing whatever it was. I'd quite like to read the News. Or do some singing with a Group.' She yawned. 'Things are so dull when you get close to them. And difficult! Oh boy! When I was little, I wanted to be a conjuror. Surprise people with quite ordinary things. The trouble is I don't know how to find out what is interesting.'

'What about your friends?'

'Friends? Oh – you mean, people I knew at school. I don't see them. I don't much care for people of my own age . . . It's one of the reasons why I like you.'

He was combing her strands of front hair over her face and remembering the careers lecturer who'd come to his school. If he hadn't come, perhaps he, Gavin, would never have gone into hairdressing. Not that the man had suggested hairdressing: it was simply that all the careers he'd suggested seemed to Gavin so awful that he'd gone home and decided first that he couldn't go in for any of them, and then his sister had had a dud perm and she'd asked him to cut it off before their mother saw it. And that had made him think of going into hairdressing as a career. Perhaps Minnie hadn't had that sort of talk at her school. Perhaps girls didn't get the same opportunities. Then he remembered something else.

'You told me you were an actress.'

'Did I? Well I used to be. I mean I tried it for a bit. I went to a drama school but the trouble is getting work after you leave. And you're supposed to get an Equity ticket. You have to work to get one, and it's quite difficult to get work without one. Anyway, it wasn't a bit like I thought it would be – I say, Gavin, I think I'm going to be sick – ' She shook her hair back from her face and he saw that she looked really frightened. The nearest lavatory was outside the salon and up half a flight of stairs.

'Come on. I'll take you.'

He helped her to her feet: she crammed her hands against her mouth and he practically lifted her up the stairs.

'In there.' He moved down the stairs out of earshot – he loathed people being sick – and waited. It really was a good thing that it was Mr Adrian's day at home or wherever he spent his days not in the salon.

She seemed to be a very long time. Why did he feel so *sorry* for her? He really didn't like her much: she wasn't at all interesting. Then he realized that he didn't feel frightened of her – frightened, sometimes, of things she did, or might do, but not exactly of *her*. She didn't seem to fit anywhere much on the Ladder of Fear. He wondered whether this was a good or a bad sign. It was obviously good in a way, but on the other hand if he was only to feel unafraid of girls who he felt sorry for and who also showed every sign of being boring that seemed merely to leave the Ladder intact with him somehow beside it.

She emerged at last, shivering.

'Do you want to lie down for a bit?'

She shook her head. 'No – I'm okay now. I just feel cold.'

'Well, you'll feel warmer when your hair is dry. I've just about finished the cutting. Like a cup of tea?'

'No, yes, I would.'

He put her back in the chair and went to find Jenny.

'I'll start the blow dry but, as soon as my next client's come in and you've washed her, you'll take over.'

Jenny rolled her eyes and stumped off to get the tea.

'Feeling better?'

169

She nodded.

'I expect it was something you've eaten. What did you have for lunch?'

'Pea soup, steak and kidney pudding and treacle tart.'

'Whew!'

'Actually, I had a Mars bar and a Coke. It was all my fault. I'll know better next time, won't I.'

'I expect so.' He clipped some of her hair aside, picked up the hand dryer and set to work.

Jenny brought the tea and a plate with two biscuits on it.

'I don't want them,' she said: she sounded peevish.

'You could have said no, thank you.'

'I could have. I didn't though, did I?'

'No. You've got rotten manners for a Lady.'

'Who said I was one?'

'You did.'

'That was to please your mother.'

'You said it to me. At the party.'

'I *am* a lady,' she said instantly. 'And don't tell me how ladies behave because they behave any old way – like everyone else.'

Gavin said nothing. His next client had arrived and Jenny was helping her out of her cape.

'If you're nasty to me, I shan't tip you.'

'Oh dear.'

'I *hate* sarcastic people. I *hate* them.'

'Okay. All right. I couldn't think of anything else to say.'

'You weren't meant to be able to think of anything to say.'

He decided to say nothing at all – just concentrate upon her hair until Jenny arrived to relieve him.

'I *was* going to ask you a favour,' she said, as though it was the other way round.

'Two favours, really,' she said some time later. 'Although one of them oughtn't to be.

'All right, I'll tell you . . . One is, would you mind awfully if I don't pay for this hair do? The thing is, I've got a little cash, but I bet it's not enough, and there isn't any money in my bank at the moment, until my father antes up, so if I wrote a cheque it would simply bounce, and you wouldn't like that, would you? I've got enough to pay you a tip,' she added.

'Fabulous,' Gavin thought. 'She comes in without an appointment, gets me to do her hair, and then she tells me.' For the third time he thanked God that Mr Adrian wasn't in today.

'I'll do it this time for free,' he said. 'But I can't do it again. You were lucky today. Usually, I wouldn't have had time if you hadn't made an appointment. And the owner doesn't care for us doing people's hair for free.'

'It won't be quite for free, because I can give you a pound as a tip.'

'Never mind the tip. That's not the point.'

'Surely it's the point for you.'

'No. It isn't.'

'Okay,' she sounded sulky – almost as though *she* was the one who was making the concession. 'Well, the next thing is – '

'Mr Gavin. Client's ready.' It was Jenny again.

'Right. There's just this side to finish off. And maybe round the back again, Jenny.' He moved thankfully over to Lady Birdseye, who normally bored him with a whole load of social moralizing about the young: however, anything would be better than that girl. Today she was on about music. Pop, rock, folk (although he doubted whether she knew the difference), it was all degenerate stuff and only went to show something or other. He switched to his bland, neutral, apparently listening personality which simply meant worthless ruminations in the wake of her indignation: 'you wouldn't think so, would you?' and 'I don't know what they get out of it', stuff like that. Lady Birdseye often told her friends what an intelligent young man he was, after she had made clear how good she was at talking to people who worked for her. Once upon a time, Gavin would have made the mistake of trying to talk to her about Steptoe and Cage – of actually assuming that she was interested in real music, but he had learned better years ago. She only knew what she didn't like. While he put her hair into rollers he watched Jenny out of the corner of his eye. He could see reflections of both of their faces: he could see that his cut was turning out to be a minor triumph. From a distance, she looked – well, certainly striking: her pallor made her eyes look more interesting and the shortened hair emphasized the poise of her head on the slender neck. Jenny had her usual expression of wry amused acceptance as she listened to her client talking. In fact, Gavin realized, Jenny nearly always looked like that; it was only in the Park that she'd seemed different. In a way he knew her less well even than he knew Minnie. Which was funny when you thought how long Jenny had been in the salon – best part of three years, nearing the end of her apprenticeship . . .

'Run for miles if they're offered a proper job! Unlike you and me, Gavin, they've no idea what life is actually like – they expect everything to be handed to them on a golden platter!'

Gavin made sycophantic noises while he wondered how near Lady Birdseye had ever got to a proper job, and what her notion of real life actually might be, and what modern, gold platters might look like supposing them to be in such common use as she said they were. Two a penny – no, nothing was that any more – two for one-fifty with special offers in the Sunday supplements . . . Fortunately, Lady Birdseye didn't have very much hair, which made dressing her a tricky business, involving a lot of back combing, but it also meant the minimum number of rollers. Two ticks more and they'd be done; he'd have her safely under the dryer so that she would be unable to hear any more bricks that Minnie dropped. He'd remembered the other favour, as yet unasked for, with a sinking heart.

Just as he wanted her, Jenny was at his side with a clean net and ear pads. Sharon was sweeping up the hair from round

Minnie's chair when he got back to her. Minnie was staring at herself with an expression of critical complacency that he associated with any client who had her hair drastically cut.

'It looks – funny – to me,' she said.

'It'll take a bit of getting used to,' he said, 'but I think it looks good on you.'

'Do you really think so, Gavin? You don't think it makes my face look fatter?'

'No. Your face isn't fat, anyway.'

'Oh. Isn't it?' She stared at it for a moment and then said: 'It feels fat, to me.' Then, as he began taking off the towel from her shoulders, she said: 'Are we going?'

'Well – you are: you're finished, I've still got work to do.'

'When do you stop work?'

'It depends on my clients,' he said evasively; he had the feeling of being propelled into some trap.

'I'll wait,' she said. 'It's quite all right; I can read something.'

'When I've finished work I've got to get back home.'

'Oh. Look here, that's my other favour!'

'What is?' He wasn't having her back to supper, if it was the last thing he did.

'I wanted to show you something. They're at my sister's. I want your advice – that's what.'

'Where does your sister live?'

'Oh – bang on the Northern Line. Near Chalk Farm. It's not in the least out of your way. Just half an hour, Gavin: I haven't got anyone to ask.'

In the end, he agreed: he felt furious with himself, but he agreed.

All the while that he was combing out and dressing Lady Birdseye's hair and agreeing to God-knew-what nonsense that she was talking, he castigated himself for being so weak, so feeble with someone who was well on the way to becoming a pest. She read quietly enough until he was escorting Lady

Birdseye to the desk, whereupon she leapt to her feet and thrust a pound note into his pocket, saying with penetrating clarity: 'Thank you *so* much, Gavin – it looks great.' She had not collected her golfing jacket, and her nipples showed through her thin and faded T shirt: he saw Lady Birdseye fasten upon them and felt his ears burning – other people seemed to afford him nothing but discomfort. But when, finally, he was out in the street with her, she hooked her arm through his and said: 'I *like* you so much, Gavin. I think you're the most nice, unusual person that I know.' He felt disarmed; touched – she couldn't know many people, could she, and he felt sorry for her all over again.

They got on to the Victoria Line at Green Park to Euston, and changed to the Northern Line. It was the rush hour: along the passages unkempt youths were strumming guitars ignored by almost all of the travellers. Minnie had no money for her fare: 'I gave you all I had, Gavin – as a tip.' This meant queuing at the ticket office although he had a Season. On the Victoria Line they had to stand; on the Northern there was one seat. 'Why don't you sit in it, and I'll sit on your knee?' He managed to get out of that one – stood half-turned away from her while she sat, pretending that he had to be in that position to hold the strap.

The sister lived in Chalcot Square – a very pretty place, he thought, with the houses all painted good, but different, colours and children playing on the small patch of green. Minerva pulled at a piece of string round her neck on which a latch-key was hanging and opened the door. The hall smelled of cooking, but not the kind that his mother did, and on the right there was a door to a dining room, an oval, dark, polished table with silver candlesticks and a flat bowl of camellias and white, lacey mats. It all looked very grand, and for a moment he wondered whether all those tales of the deer park were, in fact, true.

'Is that you?'

'Yes.'

The voice came from above and they started to climb the stairs towards it.

'Where the hell have you *been*? Dr Rankin's secretary rang – she said you never turned up – again! And don't just sneak downstairs. I want to see you!'

The door to the room on the first floor was half-open and, motioning him to stay put, she went in.

'Good Lord! You've had it off at last! I must say it looks considerably better. Who did it for you?'

'A man called Gavin. He's marvellous.'

'I'm sure he is. Just so long as you don't drag him back here.'

'I did: that's exactly what I did.'

'Oh no! You are the limit: you know I've got a dinner party.'

In a slightly, but not much, lower tone she asked: 'Where is he?'

'Here. On the landing. He can hear every single word you're saying.'

There was the shortest possible silence and then Sheila stood in the doorway before him, saying: 'Sorry about that. My little sister up to her tricks again. I'm afraid we shall just have to pretend it never happened.' She was a tall, blonde woman, and while she spoke her eyes ran over him in an appraising and somehow offensively indifferent manner. Gavin felt that she did not think much of him and he began to feel responsible for not being someone she could think more of. She wore a navy silk dress with a frilly white collar and pearls and her gold hair was pleated neatly up the back of her head. She was not in the least like Minnie.

'I told her to be out tonight, you see. My husband asked some rather important people' – she turned to Minerva – 'the kind of people who would bore you anyway – as you well know.'

'Gavin and I are going out to dinner, thanks. We just dropped in for a drink.'

'Oh well.' Sheila seemed relieved. She looked at her watch. 'Well, you'd better go down and get some ice and some glasses. If you want a drink, that is.'

'Yup.' Minnie ran off.

'Come in, Mr . . .'

'Lamb.'

'Lamb.'

The sitting room was all done up in biscuit and white with hessian walls and bowls of white lilac.

'Do sit down, Mr Lamb.' She said it as though it was the most she could say. Gavin decided to stand, and then thought he couldn't stand all through a drink, so he sat down. Sheila walked over to a shelf where there seemed to be a lot of bottles.

'I'm sure you realize that my sister is a bit mad. My half-sister. Don't believe a single word she says. I only put up with her because my father has asked me to. She's in London to see a psychiatrist. So, for goodness sake, don't get involved with her. Nobody will help you if you do. Right?'

Gavin thought: 'I don't *like* her. I wonder what she means by mad? Poor Minnie – she probably can't help whatever it is: I don't want to be involved with her.' Then he thought that probably Minnie was the kind of person whom nobody wanted to be involved with and that perhaps this meant that he ought to be the exception. Then he thought: 'Responsibility again!' And then she said:

'You're very silent. Where do you come in? By the way, don't think for one moment that she's an heiress, or anything like that: she hasn't got a bean except the allowance her father gives her.'

Gavin said: 'I met her at a party. She came into the place today where I work and asked me to cut her hair. That's all.' He was acutely aware of his voice as he said this; knowing that she would think he was common, and feeling he wasn't, and *minding* her thinking that, and then hating himself for minding what someone whom he didn't like thought.

Sheila returned from the bottle shelf with a bowl of peanuts which she now offered him. Gavin who didn't want them, but would ordinarily have taken one out of weakness/courtesy, refused – the largest gesture of disaffection that seemed to him available. There wasn't a single decent picture in the room.

'Well – I'm sure you understand that, as her family, we get a bit steamed up about her. No offence and all that, but she does get involved with some pretty queer types.' She looked quickly at Gavin again – to see whether he was *queer*, he realized, but was unable to determine her conclusions on that front. She was one of the most insensitive people he'd ever met, he thought, with a small flush of experience.

'She asked me to come back here to show me something.' The moment he'd said that, he felt disloyal – to Minnie.

'Have you the remotest idea what?'

He shook his head; really it had been a stupid thing to say.

'Her room's always in a ghastly state. I've given up trying to have it cleaned. Patrick my husband's read the Riot Act several times now, but that only lasts about two days. She's *adolescent*.' She made it sound like a nasty disease. 'However, we've put her in the basement this time. Nobody goes down there, so it doesn't matter so much.' Gavin suddenly thought of Mrs Elton's offer of a piano to play on to Jane Fairfax – vulgarity went arm in arm with insensitivity, ha ha. In a way, he was almost enjoying how much he disliked her.

'Well – don't get any ideas about me,' he said. 'I'm just a casual friend – acquaintance more.'

Then Minnie returned with a tray on which there were glasses and a bowl of ice.

'Couldn't get the ice out,' she said. She had taken off the golf jacket and tripped across the room to the bottle shelf on little spidery, shining legs. The stretch pants were bottle green.

'Shall I pour?'

Sheila, who had been standing by one of the long windows, moved swiftly to the drinks. 'I'll do it.'

'Gin and tonic suit you?' she demanded a moment later.

'Thanks.' Minnie had joined him on the white sofa, but Sheila wasn't having that, either. 'Here's your friend's drink.' So she had to get up and fetch it. As she handed the glass to Gavin, she made her funny hideous face and used the two fingers of her left hand to screw her sister: he noticed again her bitten nails. He also wondered what on earth they would talk about when they'd all got their drinks. He need not have worried about that, however, because the telephone rang, and Sheila, motioning to her sister not to answer it, settled herself in a large white leather swivel chair before she picked up the receiver. There ensued one of those one-sided conversations as interminable as they are mysterious; it was impossible not to listen and impossible to discover what was actually being talked about . . . 'Did you?' Sheila was saying. 'That must have made the whole situation much trickier . . . Oh no, my dear, I don't think anyone in their senses would think that!' And so on.

After a bit, Gavin suggested – he thought, very quietly – to Minnie that she might get on with showing him whatever it was she wanted to show him, but Sheila made large negative gestures with her left hand. 'Do you mind? I really can't hear – ' and then to the receiver, 'Sorry, darling: some people were talking and I didn't hear all of that. You got there half an hour late and *what*?' She waited a moment and then said, 'But he must have realized! I mean, even Lionel isn't actually as tactless as that!'

Minnie picked the ice out of her glass and put it in her mouth. Gavin heard her crunching it up. Then she reached for the bowl of peanuts, perched it between her silken knees and started eating them one at a time very fast. Sheila, who did a lot of the talking considering she wasn't the person telling the story, said: 'Of course you couldn't. Nobody could after that!

What on earth did they *think* you were made of, for Pete's sake?'

Gavin suddenly decided he'd had enough. He put down his half-finished drink and got to his feet. Minnie looked up at him, crammed the rest of the peanuts into her mouth with both hands, and followed him out of the room.

Half-way downstairs, he said: 'Look – I've got to get back now.'

'You haven't seen them! You promised!'

Afraid that she would start wailing, he said: 'Well, just five minutes then. What are they, anyway?'

She led the way to the door leading down to the basement and said: 'Something very important. Something I want your advice about.'

The basement seemed very dark. 'The passage light bulbs have gone,' she said; she was ahead of him – opening a door.

Her room was quite large and looked out on to an area. The windows were barred; there was an unmade bed in one corner and clothes nearly all over the floor. Her parrot sat on a bar in his cage by the window. He started making surreptitious movements as soon as they came in.

'Isn't she *foul?*'

'I didn't take to her.'

'And my father thinks she's marvellous . . . Sit down, Gavin, I want you to sit here.' And she pulled what might have been a kimono or some sort of Japanese curtain off a chair, which turned out to be a kitchen one with a wobbly leg. As he sat, he noticed a glass case on the wall with bells inside and black and gold lettering saying dining room, morning room – the kind of thing you saw in TV plays about Victorian life. The walls themselves were painted yellowish green and looked dirty.

'Actually,' she said, 'she took the light bulbs out in the passage, because she said I left them on.' She was kneeling on the floor in a particularly dark corner of the room burrowing in some kind of trunk . . . From this she dragged out an immensely large portfolio: 'She's going to show me pictures of herself modelling,' he thought, 'then she'll ask me if I think she's attractive.' He thought of the casual offer of a friendly little screw and began to feel uncomfortable. This feeling was not soothed by Minnie suddenly dropping the portfolio and darting across the room to turn the key in the lock.

'She never comes down. But I suppose, since she knows you're here, she might.' Then she went back to her task of undoing the black tapes.

'Shut your eyes while I put one on the floor to show you.'

He shut his eyes. 'She keeps *making* me do things,' he thought. 'I've got to put a stop to it.'

'You can look now.'

He opened his eyes and looked. It was not a photograph at all – it was a very large oil painting which, in turn, was divided up into twelve small paintings, four across and three deep. They were divided from one another by thick black lines and were largely painted in crude primary colours. It was hard to say what they were about. At first, he had simply an impression of chaos; then he saw that an attempt had been made to depict things – a wood, a field with a birthday cake in it; some birds flying into a sunset or bonfire, the head of a girl with huge, dark Coptic eyes (he guessed that was a self-portrait), the sea (or a lake?) with an island and a tiny little pin figure upon it; then he began to see the pin figure everywhere, even on the ones that she had messed up so much that they just seemed to be a tangle of paint – someone, for instance, seemed to be stamping upon the birthday cake. She could not draw at all, and she had no idea of what could be done with paint – she had used white a bit to soften some of the primaries but she had not tried at all to make any other colours. The whole thing was like an older child's picture, but on a much larger and more intricate scale than most children had the patience to do. He looked at it for what seemed to him quite a long time –

trying to make it out – trying to think what to say about it.
Eventually, he turned to her. She was sitting cross-legged on
the floor staring at the paintings with an expression of rapt
complacency. When she caught him looking at her she said:
'Isn't it amazing? All done by me.'

'What else have you done?'

'What else? Why should I have done anything else? I just
did this! I wanted you to see it, to tell me if it's worth my
doing more.'

He thought for a moment, and then said, 'Do you *want* to
do any more?'

'If it's worth my while.'

'You're the only person who can tell that.'

'No – no. *You* can! I mean – would you go to an exhibition
to see it? Would you buy it – if you had enough money of
course – I don't suppose you have. But I mean, if you had,
would you? It would be framed, of course,' she added.

'No,' he said. 'I wouldn't. If that's what you want to know.'

'Why not?'

'It just isn't my kind of picture.'

'Is it anyone's kind of picture?'

'That's what I meant,' he said. 'Is it your kind of picture?
The kind you like, I mean?'

'I'm not interested in pictures.'

'Well, there you have it.'

'I didn't paint it for me. I painted it for other people. To
show them. I told you, I don't want to do anything unless I'm
terrifically good at it.'

'I don't think painting is a thing that you start terrifically
good at. It's pretty hard work . . .'

'Well – you know – does it show promise? If I went on at
it, that is.'

'I'm not the person to ask.'

'You mean, it doesn't. Why can't you say what you mean?'

'One of the ways to find out whether you are any good, is

to go on doing it, I suppose.' Then he thought of all the painters who'd gone on doing it all their lives without ever finding that out. Still, they must have wanted to. If a thing was worth doing, it was worth doing badly, as he'd read somewhere. He really must be going.

'Well – it's quite clear that you don't think I'm going to be a famous painter.' She was trying to be sarcastic, but just sounded sulky.

'I shouldn't think so. But why don't you go and get some lessons? Probably the people who teach you could tell you more about it than I could.'

'I'm never going to any sort of school in my life again. Ever.'

'That's that, then. Look, I really have to go now.'

'Aren't we having dinner together? You said – '

'No – *you* said that. To your sister.'

'She's turning me out. She doesn't want me at her beastly dinner party.'

'Well – you don't want to go, do you?'

'It's pretty awful not being allowed even to do things you don't want to do.'

'It can't be as bad as not being allowed to do things you *do* want to do.'

'What I *do* want to do, is have dinner with you.' She got up off the floor and came towards him giving the picture a vicious little kick as she passed it . . .

'We could go to Marine Ices. Not even have dinner. Just coffee and masses of ice cream.'

'Look, I can't do any of that, because I've got other arrangements.' He reached the door and unlocked it before she could stop him.

'I'll come with you.'

Outside, they walked for a few minutes in silence. Then, he said: 'I warn you, Minnie, I am going home, and you're not coming with me.'

'Okay.' In a muffled voice, she added: 'Your mother liked me, anyway.' As they crossed the railway bridge, she said: 'Don't you *ever* do anything without a plan?'

'Sometimes. Look – if you're at a loose end, there must be a friend you could ring up?'

'I've got hundreds of friends. The thing is, I don't like them very much. And, if you ask me, you're getting a bit like them.' She wiped her nose with her knuckles and then said: 'Tell you what. If you'll lend me a fiver – I'll be off . . . I swear I'll pay you back . . . I get my allowance on Monday. Those bloody paints cost so much, you see.'

Gavin only had three pounds on him. He gave her that, standing outside the tube. It felt treacherous, giving her the money, rather than kind. She took it expressionlessly, with her eyes on his face.

'What are you going to do?' he asked. He badly wanted to feel better about her.

'I'll go to a supermarket.' She started a little smile, which went suddenly out, leaving her face quite bland. 'Okay then. Thanks. I'm off.' She turned on her heel, and walked, very fast, away – back across the bridge.

In the train, he felt very tired, and dropped off, but just before that he recalled her voice saying: 'Don't you *ever* do anything without a plan?' and remembered that it had actually made him very angry, and he'd lied to her. He always made plans.

CHAPTER SEVEN

SOMETIMES, however, plans branched out into other things that hadn't been planned. Gavin had got seats for Harry and himself to go to Covent Garden the following Wednesday evening. The opera was *Traviata*, 'good old *Traviata*' Harry called it: he shared with Gavin a predilection for Verdi. Gavin loved going with Harry, because they both wept copiously at all the desperate and sad moments (often, indeed, at any moment at all) and Harry was the only person with whom Gavin felt comfortable at such times. They usually met in the Circle Bar with time for a drink, and ate in a Chinese restaurant off Shaftesbury Avenue afterwards. They always got good seats, and had Pekin Duck with all the trimmings afterwards; 'you're only young once,' Harry would say, and Gavin, while he did not particularly associate youth with pleasure, felt that a treat was not a treat unless they were doing everything they could to make it one. He looked forward to Wednesday to brighten an uneventful and slogging week at the salon.

On Wednesday morning, Harry rang up to say that Winthrop had hit him so hard with yet another ashtray (not the Pisa one) that he had a huge great black eye and wasn't at all sure that his nose wasn't broken. Anyway, he felt dreadful, and Gavin would see that he couldn't go out like that. Also, he needed to have a serious chat with Winthrop who was clearly not himself. 'See if you can sell my seat,' Harry said, 'and if you can't, well, never mind.' He went on to give Gavin a blow by blow description of Winthrop's blow by blow behaviour until his voice broke . . . Gavin said he'd ring on Saturday and come round if wanted, and that was that.

Gavin did actually think for a bit about whether there was anyone at all that he would like to ask instead of Harry, but there wasn't. Domingo was singing, and he sold the seat quite easily and then wandered up to the bar to get himself a drink. He had arrived early, because of selling the ticket, but part of the treat was simply being in such a beautiful building – surely the most beautiful and suitable in the world? Only the people, he thought, as he caught sight of himself in the enormous mirror half-way up the main staircase – only the people let the place down in their boring clothes. Still, *he* couldn't talk; he was simply wearing the better of his two suits. It was amazing, really, the way the opera house went on being so majestically festive in spite of its drab occupants: if he had any choice in the matter, he'd make everybody have to have special clothes just for going to the opera in . . . He, for instance, would have a velvet suit and an enormous cloak lined with red – no, not red with *his* complexion – with pearl-grey satin. And of course, in this case, he would be accompanied by the most stunning, fabulous amazing girl the place had ever been graced by – in a long yellow silk dress with a little crown of diamonds: a kind of Violetta, really, only without anything wrong with her chest . . . Here he remembered Garbo in the famous film and the wonderful way that her eyes had flickered upwards as she died . . . That was another thing that he and Harry enjoyed together, 'the golden oldies' as Harry said . . . Briefly, he wondered whether it was better to die in the full flood of an undying passion – rather than hang on and get hit by ashtrays – it might depend a bit upon whether you were the one who died and/or the one who got hit. He had a feeling that that was the one he'd be: the usual, no win situation. Then he thought that, as he certainly didn't want to go to the Chinese restaurant by himself, he'd better have a sandwich. They were expensive, and very good: he decided that, if he had one now, he'd want another in the first interval and then, probably, another in the second. He'd put it off and save some money. He'd have another drink, instead.

The place was filling up, and he had to wait. He waited while someone who looked startlingly like Professor Moriarty collected three glasses of white wine and turned to donate two of them to – this was really too much – two people who could easily have been Dr and Mrs Watson . . . What on earth would Holmes have thought of that? Impossible to accuse Watson of treachery; he probably thought that, by having a straight talk with Moriarty, he was calming everything down between them, and getting everything above board. He was probably the only person in the world who could believe for an instant that Moriarty would connive at anything above board . . . But then he realized that, of course, Moriarty was simply Holmes in disguise; any minute now, he'd pull off his wig, grow about two feet in stature and have Watson laughing heartily at having been so taken in.

He paid for his drink and wandered off with it. He was beginning to wish that he had someone to talk to: it would be all right once the opera started . . . he certainly didn't want anyone *new* to talk to . . . he had collided with a girl who smiled at him almost as though she *liked* people running into her and spilling her drink . . . good God, she might have thought he'd done it on purpose! As he apologized, backing off and feeling the sweat prickling his skin, he wondered with angry terror whether she simply came to the opera by herself for the sole purpose of making it seem as though people bumped into her with a view to getting off with them. It was quite possible; anything was possible. But she wouldn't catch *him* like that – he knew a thing or two. It was exactly the sort of way that Minnie would behave. Thank goodness *she* wasn't here. He went and bought a programme (he collected them) and thence to his seat (in the Amphitheatre), well chosen in the middle of the front row. The occupant of Harry's seat was

a very small, old man with gold-rimmed glasses and a ragged
white moustache, who turned out – they spoke because Gavin
tripped over his feet – to have heard every Violetta Gavin had
ever heard of and some that he hadn't, and the ones he had
heard of he only knew through his seventy-eights – like Rosa
Ponselle – he had a recording of her with Martinelli doing two
arias from *Aida* . . . But he didn't need to do much talking;
the old man produced an uneven flow of happy reminiscences,
with great names periodically exploding like rockets in the hazy
dark of his memory. By the time he got to Caniglia whom
Gavin knew only through the Rome Opera Company recording of Verdi's Requiem, the house lights were dimming, the
conductor had arrived, and they were off.

In the interval, rather to his relief, the old man elected to
stay put, drawing magically from some pocket a jar of Brand's
Essence which he proceeded to eat with a plastic spoon. Gavin,
who did not want to hear the present performances unfavour-
ably compared with the past, decided to go in search of his
sandwich. Then, in view of the crowds round the refreshment
bars, he decided to give that up in favour of the Gents, and it
was coming out of there that he met Joan; almost, in fact, ran
into her, since she was emerging from a box.

'Well, Gavin, how *are* you?' she immediately said.

'Fine.'

'Well, come and have a drink with me. I'm on my own –
like you.'

She strode purposefully ahead. She was wearing a dress
with a lot of black sequins on it, and two black sequin
butterflies in her orange hair. How did she know he was alone,
he wondered, but he felt quite simply glad to see her; glad,
and a bit excited.

She had reserved a little table on which stood a bottle of
wine in a bucket and two glasses.

'I have it out here, because I like to smoke,' she said. 'You
pour the wine.'

The wine was white, cold, and with a delicate flinty taste.

'How did you know I was alone?' he asked after a short, easy silence.

'I saw you come in . . . I watched that old man talking to you. I have some very powerful opera glasses. Also, it didn't surprise me.' Her spectacles were black diamanté this time and the plate-glass lenses seemed to be tinted.

'Did you get my card?'

'I did. Meeting *you* was the best part for me, too. Although, when you come to think about it, it's a pretty guarded compliment. It was a pretty terrible party.'

'Why did you have it?'

'I had it for Dmitri. He said he'd be home by then. And he gets into a frenzy of boredom if I don't arrange things like that for him.'

'Would he have enjoyed it?'

'Would he? I don't know. Because, you see, if he'd been *there* it would have been a different kind of party.'

'Is he – has he got a very strong personality, then?'

'He's certainly a personality. He's got a wonderful side to him,' she added, which to Gavin opened up vistas of terrifying other sides, but he nodded.

'What's with you? What happened to you after the party? If you feel like telling me, that is.'

'That thin girl – in a red dress – she offered me a lift to get my bike, and then it turned out that she had nowhere to sleep, and she sort of chased me back to my parents' house and in the end she slept there. On the settee,' he added defensively . . . Her large orange, painted-on mouth smiled, and he wondered what her real mouth inside it was like. She asked him to pour more wine.

'Do you often come alone to the opera?'

'Yes,' she said. 'Often. Most of the people I know either don't care for it, or they regard it as a luxury. That's the last thing that it is. For me it's like being a fish put back into water.'

'You mean – because it's larger than life?'

'It's exactly the *size* of life. There are just a lot of under-sized people about.'

'I don't suppose Alfredo's father would mind anything like as much today about who his son went about with, though.'

'He wouldn't mind for the same reasons. Anyway, that's just plot. Themes don't change: they're elemental.'

'Morality changes, though.'

'Not as much as you might think. Most fathers would worry about their only son marrying a renowned prostitute; they'd find different reasons for it, but they'd mind.'

'You mean if Graham Greene, for instance, was writing about Violetta, she'd only have to be a married Catholic and Bob's your uncle.'

'Alfredo would be the married Catholic: she'd have leukaemia.'

'But if it wasn't a Catholic writer – '

'Oh, then Alfredo's wife would have to be brought into it. After God, you get Freud and guilt. I bet you Freud's inhibited far more people than he's liberated.'

This was a new idea to Gavin and he digested it in silence. Then he said: 'You mean, hell has simply changed into being other people – like Sartre said?'

'Yes. I don't care for it much, do you? It still smacks of us all being victims. Smarter, and more knowing, but still victims. I really prefer the happiness is energy notion.'

'Who said that?'

'I think,' she said, after a pause, 'I think it was Balzac.'

'I haven't read much of him.'

The first bell went, and she said: 'Make with the wine . . . Listen: would you like to sit with me? I've got a box – all to myself . . . It's the kind of box for four where two people can see properly.'

'Thanks very much. I would.' He had never been in a box. He poured the rest of the wine, feeling exhilarated.

Following her back into the auditorium, he wondered how much playing that curious game with her had to do with this absence of any discomfort that he felt in her company. Something, surely – there was a feeling of intimacy, and dishonest intimacy was not, he thought, possible. But he wasn't much of an authority upon intimacy really.

The box was just what he hoped it would be: glamorous, cosy, and dark red. It also gave him a kind of Lautrec view of the audience which somehow made being there doubly exciting. Then the curtain rose on the second Act idyll, and he became lost in Alfredo's rapture.

Once or twice during the Act, he glanced at his companion, who sat motionless, turned away from him, her face resting upon one hand. Silhouetted thus, she had at once a vulnerable and a mysterious air: her absorption enhanced his own; each time he looked back to the stage with another dimension to his pleasure.

In the second interval she proposed that they go out 'for our drinks' and which this time proved to be two large brandies waiting on the same table.

'I suppose one thing that would have to be different, *morally* speaking, would be Alfredo's sister's future in-laws. They'd have to be real Washington bourgeoisie to refuse to let her marry their son because of what her brother was up to. So you may be right about morality changing.'

'It doesn't really need that bit, though, does it? I mean, the father not wanting them to marry would be enough.'

She lit another cigarette and gave him an absent little smile, but he could not really tell what her expression was, because of the tinted glasses. He wanted to ask her to take them off, but decided that it would be forward of him to ask that.

'Do you understand Italian?' she asked after quite a long pause.

'Good Lord, no! I'm hopeless at languages. Tried to learn one once, but I didn't make much headway.'

'Which one?'

'Latin, actually . . .'

'What made you choose Latin?'

'Well – feeling I stopped my schooling a bit young. And they didn't teach Latin where I went, anyway. I was reading a lot, and I kept not understanding words, and I know at the posh places where you really get an education they seemed to go in for Latin so I thought that was the ticket.'

'Did you want to be thoroughly educated, then? Go to university, and all that?'

'Me? I never really thought. I mean it didn't come out like that. I wanted to *know* things, you know, but they mostly seemed to be things they didn't go in for much in my school. I just took to reading really, because the teaching was so dull.'

'You must have had *one* good teacher though.'

'Funny you should say that. I don't know if he was much cop at teaching, but he knew a lot. He taught arts and crafts where I was, and he loathed it. And he knew I loathed it. We used to talk about books and things . . .' His voice tailed off. Whenever he read anything that really touched him, or made him laugh, he thought of Mr Allsop, who had a bald patch on the top of his head that went shiny when he got excited . . . Aloud, he said: '*He* knew Latin. I think I sort of thought I'd like to be a bit like him, and that's what started me on the Latin.'

They finished their drinks, and he said:

'How did you know to get two glasses of brandy?'

'I always order two of things to be on the safe side . . .'

'Do you often meet people here, then?'

'No.' She said nothing more, and he felt he'd stumbled, as it were, into being forward. Then, for the millionth time since he'd met her this evening, he remembered the Secrets game and said: 'If you don't like me asking you questions, you've only to say.'

'Would you stop then?'

'Yes.' Then he added: 'I might go on wanting to know, but I'd shut up.'

'That's very sweet. Thank you.'

The bell rang. She got to her feet before he did; the black dress was another tube – like the silver one in which he had first seen her and, as he got up, he realized again how very tall she was, taller than he by about three inches. He also noticed that people were looking at her – with the kind of glancing stares that denoted curiosity more than anything else. This made him feel angry for her, because *he* would have hated being stared at in that way, and, on impulse, he took her arm and marched back to her box beside her. When they were back, and seated, she said:

'It was nice that we didn't spend the interval having little judgemental comparisons of performances. A look-what-a-lot-I-know-about-opera-conversation.'

Gavin agreed, and then, as the house lights went, he remembered that, in a way, that *was* the sort of conversation he often had with Harry. This lent a discomforting dishonesty to his agreement, and then the beautiful prelude to Act Three began – one of his favourite bits of the whole work and he remembered nothing but that Violetta was to die and that not even love could save her.

From then until the end – 'Oh God, to die so young!' – he was transported past the physical confusions of impending grief – thorn in throat, hammer on heart, icy fingers, scorching eyes, until he had given himself, soul and body, to the sad magic.

Applause always came too soon for him and he resented it: it was like being shaken awake on the instant of a dream and he sat plummeting helplessly back into himself until the (infinitely) milder sensations of gratitude and admiration took over . . .

When the last call had been taken, she said:

'Would you like some dinner?' And, not needing to think about it, he said that he would.

In the taxi they talked a bit about opera, but not much. He asked her whether she thought that in real life people did actually die for love. She said she thought that people would do anything for it, and for some that would include dying. 'Harder to live for it, though,' she said. 'It goes on so much longer.'

Later she remarked that beauty was useful stuff.

'Why do you say that?'

'Well, it enables us to accept so much truth that we would otherwise find unbearable.

'What I find so awful, Gavin,' she said, 'such a dirty trick, is our life span. That was the wicked fairy at the christening all right. We shan't live long enough to make the best use of our experience . . .'

'Really? Do you think that?' Redoubtable old geniuses like Bach and Einstein were in his mind backing disbelief.

'But of course!' she said impatiently. 'We spend the first quarter of our lives like good, innocent little slates on which any old graffiti get written; we can't choose anything much. Then there is the heady time when we *can* make choices, but by then they're going to be conditioned by the graffiti, you bet. And then, when a little wisdom starts creeping in, we start breaking up physically, so that we have less and less power to use what we know. And practically the only weapon we have against all that is art. I think that was the late fairy's attempt to give us a chance, at least. Let there be condensed experience available.'

'What about the great people? What about genius?'

'The point about them is that they're the exceptions, aren't they? They've slipped through the net: lonely, privileged bastards.' She laughed then, and added: 'I can combine being envious of them with not in the least wanting to be one of them. I'm simply full of *human* nature.'

Gavin said nothing: he was thinking – testing himself to find out how much, if at all, he agreed with her. She was talking about too many things at once, he decided, or else he was lacking in any overall philosophy (most likely, that), and for a moment he wished he was at the Chinese with Harry – a relatively familiar and undemanding situation. Then, as though she knew something of his mind, she said: 'Look here. Let's have a simple, merry time. To hell with it: you're only whatever you are, once.'

And that was how it turned out, or certainly began to turn out. She took him back to her flat, now seeming even larger without all the party in it. It was completely silent up there, and although lights were on – in the hall, in the large sitting room with its open doors – it seemed a rich and desolate place. She went away to take off her coat and he stood uncertainly, beginning to wish that he wasn't there, with small nagging thoughts about the last train back to Barnet, and wondering how he could mention that without being rude. She was away a long time. He stared at a Rouault over the hall table (by now he had come to accept that there would be no doubt of its being a Rouault – whom he didn't care for anyway), confidence ebbing: if happiness *was* energy, he was fast approaching a limbo of paralysis where he could feel nothing at all.

She returned through an unexpected door in the passage – not the way she had gone, and she had not only taken off her coat, she had removed the sequin tube dress and was now clothed in a kind of housecoat, or wrap – voluminous, but somehow not shapeless and of a strikingly beautiful colour that was neither grey nor green.

'Now,' she said, 'we're going to move to another part of the forest. Follow me.' They went back through the unexpected door, into another, much smaller passage that seemed to lead nowhere. Her skirts trailed at the back, and he was reminded of Callas in *Norma*. At the end of the passage was a fitted bookcase which swung open at some touch of hers to reveal a narrow staircase. 'You go up first, because of my skirts,' she said.

There was a final door at the top: he opened it and stepped into a place so different from the rest of the flat at first he could hardly believe it. It was a room, a studio, an attic with an enormous skylight revealing the reddish glow of a London sky faintly peppered with stars. The floor was painted yellow, the walls white, and at the far end of the room was an open fireplace with long, large logs burning in it, and a large multi-coloured rug of a kind he had never seen before. It was so surprising, so different from the rest of her flat, that he simply stood trying to take it all in. There was very little furniture, but it seemed furnished; there was a feeling of space, but also of intimacy. It was the most beautiful comfortable room he had ever encountered. He said so.

'It's my one private place,' she said. 'I spend a lot of time here. When Dmitri is away. Which is quite often. Go and sit by the fire, while I get our food.'

He went and sat on a small stool on the multi-coloured rug which turned out to be made of rags. The logs that were burning made a fragrant fruity smell. It was wonderfully silent; he could hear nothing but the sounds of the fire.

When she returned to him with a tray of food and drink which she put on the rug between them, he said: 'It's a bit magic, isn't it? Isn't that what you mean it to be?'

'That's right. It isn't meant to be like the rest of life at all. Now, let's eat and drink.' She poured some wine, handed him a glass and said: 'Help yourself to food.'

There was some kind of fish pâté and dark bread, and, the moment he started, Gavin realized that he was very hungry. There was also a dish of cold meats and a salad full of delicious and unexpected things, followed by cherries in a very beautiful white bowl . . . She sat opposite him, on the rug, with her back resting against an enormous cushion, and with her feet tucked up under her – he had noticed earlier that they were bare. They talked: indeed, Gavin realized, by the time they got to the cherries, that he had been doing most of the talking. 'I'm curious about you,' she had said, as they spread the pâté on their bread, 'start by telling me three things about yourself that you know I don't know. Unless you absolutely don't want to, of course.' He had been momentarily confounded: she already knew some things about him that nobody else knew; what could she want to know? What *was* there about him that could possibly interest her? He began to feel frightened – both of her, and of boring her. 'I'm not playing any games,' she said, 'just being personal.' So he told her that he lived with his parents in a house that his father had built, and that he, too, had one room that was really his own. And that he cut people's hair. 'I knew that,' she said. 'Somebody at the party told me that.' There was a short silence while he tried to think of something else. Then she said: 'Tell me about your room.'

'It's not as good as yours, not by a long chalk. But it's got something about it that I like.'

'Describe it to me.'

So he told her about the faded red sofa, and his mirror with gilded birds and roses on it, and the second-hand flowered carpet, and his old Persian silk rug with its faintly musty smell and the white walls and his books and records and plants by the dormer windows . . . 'It's far too crowded, really,' he said, 'but I have to keep everything I want in there.'

'Does anybody else ever go into it?'

'My mother – to clean once a week. But you can't count her.'

'Why not?'

'Because she doesn't really *see* it. She's not aware of it at all, except as rather a difficult place to clean. I'd rather she didn't, but it would hurt her feelings if I asked her not to.'

'Nobody else?'

'Only Harry sometimes. He's the friend I was meant to be going to the opera with tonight.

'Why?' he said, a moment later. 'Don't people come up here?'

She shook her head. 'You are the second person who has ever been here.'

'Oh,' he said. 'Oh.' He felt a bit shy of her when she said that; it seemed like a great compliment, but he wasn't sure that it was and anyway, if it was, he didn't know what she expected him to say back. Instead he asked: 'Why is the rest of your flat so very different? I mean if this is what you like, you could have it everywhere, couldn't you?'

'The rest of the flat has been entirely designed by Dmitri. He did it for me, so I wouldn't want to change any of it.' There was a pause then she added: 'He's a designer, you see.'

This made Gavin remember the conversation in the car going to the party; when people called Joan and Dmitri had been mentioned; it seemed a hundred years ago; what was it Noel, the Australian, had said, that Joan had started Dmitri on interior design in an effort to keep him at home, but it hadn't worked because he kept going away and designing the interiors of yachts. Something about her marrying him with her eyes open, and the other one saying that she'd had to keep them shut ever since . . . That made him think of something else, but he didn't know how to ask her that . . .

'Is Dmitri away designing something now, then?' he asked.

'That's what he says he's doing . . .' She said it without emphasis. 'I'll make some coffee.'

He got to his feet. 'Let me help.'

'You can bring the tray. But first, if you're going to walk about, I'd rather you took your shoes off. My yellow floor doesn't respond well to shoes.'

He took off his shoes, and then, on second thoughts, his jacket, since the room was very warm.

She had a sort of kitchenette in a cupboard, and there was a hatch into which she told him to put the tray. 'It goes down in a lift.' They were standing side by side, and without her high heels she was only an inch or so taller than he. She was pouring water from a kettle into a coffee machine: the wide sleeve fell back as she poured and he saw her strong, white, rather muscular arm that ended in an unexpectedly delicate wrist and narrow hand. She reached with her left arm for a bottle on the shelf before her, and without thinking and before he could stop himself he said: 'Why do you wear those stupid glasses? They really don't suit you at all!'

Then immediately he said, 'I'm sorry; can't think why on earth I said that. It must be ever so late; I've got to go soon anyhow.' She laughed then, and said: 'Oh, Gavin! What do you mean "anyhow"?' – and took off her glasses. Then, he was hardly aware of how it happened, she put her hands round the back of his neck and kissed him, or rather simply put her mouth gently against his. The most extraordinary thing about this was that while it was happening he didn't feel anything – except her mouth – anything at all: no thoughts, no time, nothing, as though the whole of him was holding its breath.

She withdrew and, at arm's length, she looked at him. Her eyes were a dark brown that was almost black, so that the pupils were almost lost in the iris. Being able to see her eyes changed her whole face for him, or, it occurred to him, it had changed anyway. Now, the orange hair and orange-painted mouth seemed no more than clownish trappings – clapped on to conceal some reality – a sense of sadness so private that he could only receive it in silence.

Without taking her eyes from his face, she moved one hand from his neck, lifted the orange wig from her head and let it drop to the ground behind her. Her own hair, dark brown and perfectly straight, sprang to life from a deep and irregular peak on her broad forehead; he could see, now, her real mouth curving to a smile inside the painted paeony, and he put his finger on that to rub it out. She pulled out a handkerchief then, from the grey and green robe, and scrubbed until the paint, still perceptible, was almost gone. There was a new and separate silence.

'Here I am,' she said.

There ensued, for Gavin, a time so far exceeding his dreams of what might ever occur that he could never go back to what for ever after seemed to him mawkish invention; nor could he dream at all of any woman without this one lending something of herself. There were moments that he could afterwards clearly recapture – when he pulled the robe from her shoulders, apart from her breasts, wide of her belly and across one thigh until she was lying, like some beautiful sprawled painting to be seen and touched and stirred to life. There was the moment when she set him free within her, and there was a hush even to sensuality; they remained locked, motionless, eye drinking eye, until he moved in her and the trance was broken by a shock of ecstasy – of feeling so deep, so sharp, so near, so new and so shared that he was engulfed. And, after that, a kind of adoring sadness when he knew they were again separate – the magic fusion gone – that, in touching her, he was touching someone else. He would always remember her face then, ageless, pagan, washed of thoughts, with a beauty that was at once hers and belonging to the whole world.

And that was just the beginning: there was, there turned out to be, the whole night. There was a bed behind the Chinese screen and at some point they repaired to that. 'Let's move it by the fire,' she said. The bed was on castors, and moved at a touch; it seemed all part of the dream-like ease – only it wasn't a dream, it was reality. All through the night, he kept rediscovering that: the third time that he wanted her, and she said, 'It doesn't all have to be Wagner; we could be at home with Mozart,' and there began to be an element of lightness, of playful gaiety that in no way diminished passion. Her body bore no resemblance to those bodies of his dreams;

it was heavier, fuller, older, and, released from the tube dresses, deeply curved. Her skin smelled of some fruit or fruits, sometimes sweet like melon, sometimes sharper, like strawberries. He had not imagined that skin smelled of anything. When he told her, she said, 'I know,' and a look of child-like complacency flitted across her face that made him want to laugh, it was so endearing. Once, he said: 'Tell me what you like,' and, without saying anything, she showed him and he could watch her face change. But perhaps the most amazing discovery that he made was that responsibility for what happened was no more his than hers. One of the things that had frightened him all his life was the idea that he would have this responsibility alone; that the other person expected him to take entire charge; they would simply lie there and judge him afterwards . . . When he told her this, she simply said that it would be a lonely way of going about it. There was a wonderful time when she found out what *he* liked, which turned out to be practically everything. At some point he fell into a deep and dreamless sleep and when he woke the stars had gone from the sky which was now the colour of grey pearls and the room was filled with a discreet early light. She was not there, and for a moment the night did seem like a dream and he felt panic and fear that it should come to so arbitrary an end. But, 'I'm making tea,' she said, and he saw her, wearing the robe again, pouring real water into a real teapot.

'You shouldn't have let me go to sleep.'

She brought the tea over to the bed. 'We both slept. In any case I don't think I could have stopped you. You went out like a light.' She sipped her tea, and then said: 'The fire's hopelessly dead, because there aren't any more logs up here. I've just had a hot shower to warm me up.'

'I could have warmed you up.'

She smiled and touched his face with the tips of her fingers: 'I know.'

There was something vaguely maternal in her voice and the

gesture that he did not much like, and this feeling was accompanied by a wave of anxiety – general in nature, but prepared to attach itself to almost anything. Was he in love with her? Did she love him? What was going to happen next? What about Dmitri? Did she do this sort of thing with anyone who turned up? What did she, or *would* she, expect of him? How did he *feel* about her?

He looked up to find her steadily regarding him. After a pause, she said: 'You know when we played the Secrets game, I said that there was a law about not having post mortems? Well, I don't think they're ever any good. But there are one or two things I should like to tell you. You are a lovely person to go to bed with. I'm married to Dmitri, and that's what I want. I'm going away today for a week or so. You don't need to feel in the least responsible for me, and I shan't for you.'

Perversely, because a part of him felt relief, he heard himself saying: 'What about Dmitri, then?'

'He's still in France, so I'm going to join him. For a bit.'

'Do you love him?'

'I love him.' There was a silence while he searched for the way to ask what he discovered he really wanted to know. Before he found the way, she said: 'He doesn't love me, you see. He doesn't – *love* – anyone.'

'Do you – sort of – hope he might?'

'That's it. That's what I hope. So long as he doesn't love anyone, he might love me. He has affairs with people, of course.'

Before he could stop himself, he said: 'You mean, like you've had an affair with me?'

He felt she was angry then, as she answered coolly: 'I haven't the slightest idea.' Then she added more gently: 'There's no need, you know, to compare you and me with anybody else in the world. One of the best things about us is the impossibility of doing that. But I will tell you something about you, if you'd like me to.'

'I think I would.'

'You need to trust yourself more. You don't need reflections of yourself from other people. You're the original. There is no one in the world exactly like you. Enjoy that. It's not a question of good or bad, or better or worse. Your life is simply a question of you being faithful to you. Making the most of what you are. Everything else is one kind of Jellabyism or other. I take it you know about Mrs Jellaby?'

'The Africans, and her own curtains being held up by a fork?'

She laughed. 'I love you, Gavin. I really do. You know all the right things. But Dickens was writing about that syndrome on a fairly coarse level – as so often. It really applies in all kinds of ways he probably didn't think of at the time. That's one definition of genius. Only knowing part of what they do. Don't you think?'

'Could we get back into bed now?'

'I don't know. Could we? What time do you have to go to work?'

'Not now.'

This time was different; he *wanted* to be in charge – to please her, to make her remember him. Once, he whispered: 'I shall miss you,' and she whispered back: 'Don't miss me *now*, I'm here.' This time he was more conscious of her body than of his own; her few words about Dmitri had touched him past any kind of jealousy; he felt generous and tender towards her, and wanted to give her everything she could want. Afterwards, she lay with her face turned towards his, tears streaming out of her eyes without a sound. Then he felt so close to her that he knew it was not comfort she needed, or words of any kind, simply time and his being there.

When it was over, she picked up his hand and kissed it. Then she said:

'Would you like a shower while I get some breakfast?'

The remaining time seemed both rapid and vague: afterwards he had very little recollection of it, and could remember only things like the coffee scalding his tongue, that a button must have come off his shirt when he had torn it off the previous evening, that the razor she lent him was a kind he'd never seen before. He asked her when she was leaving for France because he wanted to be able to think of her then. He also asked her why she bothered with the red chrysanthemum wig and all that. Dmitri preferred her like that. This silenced him. She came down the stairs with him, but left him to find his way out from the false bookcase door. 'Don't let's say good-bye,' she said. 'You simply go.'

So he did. Out of the flat door, down in the lift and out into the unreality of the street.

CHAPTER EIGHT

'**G**AVIN?'

'Yes, Mum?'

'Is that you?'

Of course it's me, he thought irritably, whoever that may be. 'Yes, Mum.'

'Your father has been wondering where on earth you've been. Haven't you, Fred?'

'No, I haven't . . .' Gavin had reached the doorway to the lounge, just in time for one of his father's inexpert winks that implied unspeakable complicity. 'Bin out on the tiles enjoying himself,' he suggested unhelpfully. This, as Gavin knew it wouldn't, didn't go down at all well.

'Who asked you for your opinion? He's old enough to please himself, isn't he? It's none of your business *what* he does. He can stay out all night and it's nothing to do with you! Nasty ideas!' she added. She was stirring something on the stove with furious energy. Mr Lamb raised his paper again to within eighteen inches of the eye he chiefly used for reading, winked at Gavin with the other eye and made a movement with his shoulders that indicated he was opting out.

'I got the brochures for your holiday, Mum.'

'You weren't getting *them* all night.'

'I went to the opera, Mum, and met – some friends – and had dinner and it got too late to come back. I didn't have my bike with me, you see.'

'There's no call to tell me you didn't have your bike with you. I've got perfectly good eyes: I could see you hadn't got your bike with you. What's your *bike* got to do with it?'

'I meant, I missed the last train.'

'None of these opera dinner places had phones, you'll tell me next.'

'By the time I thought of phoning, it was too late.' As he said this, he wondered if it was in the least true: he hadn't thought of it at all until going to work in the morning which was clearly so much too late that it couldn't count. This made him wonder, fleetingly, how often people told *him* that sort of lie. 'What's for supper?'

'It's Chicken Mole. It's a Mexican dish out of one of my papers. And it'll be ready very soon,' she threatened, as he showed signs of escaping.

'I'll go and wash.'

As he entered his room, he remembered – or rather he suddenly heard himself – describing it to Joan, and this rush of memory was accompanied by a longing for her so violent that for moments he leant against the door, made dizzy by the unexpected – and, to him, quite new and strange assault. He walked unsteadily to his red sofa and sat upon it. This was, he realized, the first time in the day since he had left her that he was really alone. There had been the walk to the train, in the morning, which must have seemed so unreal, he felt, because in spirit he had not really left her. Then the train – jammed with people, none of whom seemed to have noticed what had happened to him – then the salon where he had worked so continuously that he hadn't even got his lunch hour. Two o'clock, even, had passed before he remembered that that was the time that her plane had taken off for France. He hadn't even remembered her *then*, as he had planned to do. And, in the train home, he had fallen asleep – passed out – it was a guard who shook him awake at Barnet. Then, walking back home, his thoughts had been full of what Mum would be like about his having stayed out all night, and how he was going to deal with her. He'd try and get dinner over as quickly as possible – have some time to himself.

This resolution proved to be impossible to carry out. Chicken Mole, or Underground Chicken as Gavin privately called it, proved, gastronomically speaking, to be a hurdle that not even the combined efforts of his father and himself were able either to circumnavigate or to overcome ... Mrs Lamb was in a fine state of nerves about it; partly because she had never cooked it before, and partly (or also) because, being a foreign dish, her confidence in the recipe had proved to be less even than usual ... Mr Lamb had tried an unwise joke about Moles, and not being too sure whether he would fancy them, and been crushed.

'Mole is Mexican for chocolate. Moles are vermin. You wouldn't catch me serving *them*,' she declared as she ladled huge steaming portions on to their plates ...

'What's this, Mum?' Gavin had unearthed what looked like a hippo's tooth.

'That? That is a Brazil nut, I should imagine. The recipe said to use that nasty, unsweetened chocolate, but I paid no regard to *that*; there's half a pound of Cadbury's Fruit and Nut in there.' She picked up her crochet, which experience had taught her family in no way detracted from her being able to watch their every mouthful.

Mr Lamb made the first attempt and, eyeing his expression-less face as he slowly shifted the food from one side of his face to the other, Gavin knew that the situation was pretty bad, but even then, he was unprepared for exactly how terrible the stuff was going to taste until his own first cautious forkful. Then he knew that nothing – no amount of concern for his mother's feelings, no stringent desire for a quiet life, no strength of aversion to family scenes – was going to coerce him into swallowing this lot.

'I'm sorry, Mum. I can't take this.'

'You can't – *what*?'

'This food. It doesn't taste very nice.'

'A lot of Mexicans would be ever so grateful for it.'

'Well, I'm not Mexican. It tastes queer to me.'

'Chicken's off?' suggested Mr Lamb with uncharacteristic brilliance. Mrs Lamb had a horror of things going off. It was also recognized as the one way out. If you ate off food, you could drop dead, according to Mrs Lamb.

'Could be,' Gavin took this up at once. 'Now you come to mention it, I expect that's what it is. It does taste distinctly queer. Try it, Mum.'

'I had my tea over an hour ago, thank you. In any case if it's off I have no more wish to be poisoned than I have the wish to poison you. Either of you,' she added. She had put aside her crochet and was now poking vigorously at the casserole which still contained a frightening quantity of stew. 'It smells perfectly all right to me. Foreign, of course, but that's only to be expected. I'll give that butcher a piece of my mind tomorrow. You'll have to make do with beans on toast.'

She had given way with surprising ease, Gavin thought. Then he wondered whether this was because he had said outright what he felt about the food, instead of trying to find ways of getting out of eating it. As soon as Mrs Lamb was in the kitchen heating the beans and making toast, Mr Lamb rolled his eyes at Gavin and flapped his hand in front of his face, indicating a narrow escape.

'Although, I expect you've been eating all kinds of foreign stuff in your opera dinner place. Upset yourself as likely as not . . . And dear knows when you got to bed?' This last turned into a kind of ambushing question. He felt himself going red. 'Late, Mum. Too late, I know . . .'

'You're only young once.' Mr Lamb was always in danger of pouring oil on to banked-up fires. She turned on him.

'Gavin's not all that young. Old enough to know better. Better to be safe than sorry. He knows an ill wind blows nobody any good. If he doesn't, he ought to,' she ended rather breathlessly, dumping the baked beans on the table. 'All I can say is I hope you're not going to make a habit of it.'

'Of what?' The back of his neck prickled, as it occurred to him that she somehow *knew* what he had been up to.

'Staying out all night without a word.' It was general scolding: she didn't really know – how could she?

'Don't you want to go through the holiday brochures?'

'I'm upset. If I read when I'm upset, I get a migraine.'

'I'll read them to you, Mum.' The moment he said that, he wished that he hadn't: he wanted time to himself, and offering to discuss her holiday with her was no way to get it . . . He was really only cravenly levering himself back into her good books. This, he discovered, had to be done the hard way. When the baked beans were finished, and she had made tea for his father and coffee for himself and they were settled at the otherwise empty table with the brochures in front of him, she started in again.

'You look tired, Gavin.'

'I'm not tired.'

'You look as though you've been up all night.'

'Well, I haven't.'

'You don't look as though you want to do a whole lot of reading.'

'I feel fine.'

Reassured by this small pack of lies, she sat down, pulling her chair round so that she was close beside him and he could hear her breathing.

'Start with the top one,' she said, which meant, he knew, that she expected to go through the whole lot.

'Every amenity – miles of unspoilt beaches in the Mediterranean sun,' he began, and as he did so remembered that last year he'd had a terrible cold when he was reading to her, and that she'd caught it.

Mrs Lamb's holiday plans were a prolonged and complex affair. Roughly speaking, they entailed her announcing that this year she had it in mind to go abroad for her holiday (the subject nearly always came up on Sunday lunches with Marge), and every year Mr Lamb telling her she didn't want to do that (his opinion of abroad was a. that it was a dangerous place to go – he'd served in Normandy and Belgium at the end of the war – and b. that it wasn't a respectable place for a family holiday – his pre-marital sex had taken place there and so far as Gavin could make out still filled him with a kind of gloomy underhand triumph). His views, however, only hardened Mrs Lamb's resolution and her senses of justice and adventure. *He* had been there, so why shouldn't she? Also, the magazines that she read were full of stories about foreign holidays; advice to people having them and advertisements telling her how cheap and easy they were. But she also collected information of a more anxious kind: she had, for instance, ruled out the whole of Spain last year because there had been some incident of food poisoning in an hotel on the Costa Brava, and France had been knocked out because of a forest fire near Ste Maxime. She did not wish to go to Italy because of the danger of being kidnapped. But these embargoes did not prevent her wanting Gavin to read about the no-go areas: 'We might as well hear what they have to say for themselves.'

Mr Lamb, who from long practice had found it wiser to dissociate himself from his wife's early ruminations, said he was going to pop over to Friern Barnet to see a lady about a job. His departure caused a halt in the reading, and after it Mrs Lamb reverted to personal matters that very quickly boiled down to her intense curiosity about Minnie. 'Lady Minerva likes the opera then, does she?' was her opening shot. Gavin said he didn't know. As he said this, he realized that Minnie simply hadn't even crossed his mind since he'd parted from her in Chalk Farm. This made him feel guilty, and his mother misinterpreted the guilt.

'No need for you to be shy about her with me. You know what I thought about her. I thought she was a thoroughly nice girl. Just like anybody else.' This last Gavin privately thought was one of the things that she wasn't.

'I didn't go to the opera with her.'

'I've no wish to pry,' she answered stiffly. 'How can I know anything about your friends? You never tell me.'

'I've told you about the people at work.'

'That's not what I mean at all. Work!' she said witheringly. 'They sound a funny lot to me. You could have been a teacher!'

'Oh, Mum – don't let's go into that.' He could see that she was working herself up, and a fresh wave of tiredness assailed him. He yawned – covertly – and then decided to make a performance of it and yawned again – this time with sound effects. She pretended not to notice, but it deflected her. 'Marge said that Portugal was nice. Read me something about there.'

So he read about the Algarve with its miles of beaches (they always went on about beaches), its magnificent seafood, its superb hotels with swimming pools and buffet luncheons, its quaint old villages, its friendly simple peasants, its night life, wines, pottery and proximity to an airport . . .

After a bit, she said: 'They sound much the same to me. What's so special about Portugal? It's just that Ken likes to go to a different country every year. "You'll run out soon," I told Marge. Course, I suppose the languages are different. There's bound to be a difference somewhere. I should really like to go to the Caribbean on one of those islands with palm trees. *They* look different, but of course they're much dearer – I'm not sure Fred would stand for one of *them*. But at least on an island you'd know where you *were*.'

Gavin said that he hadn't got any brochures on the West Indies and how about Norway? But he must have said it in the wrong tone of voice, because she retorted:

'Gavin, you look tired to death. Whatever you may say, I know when you've been overdoing it and we all know what happens then.'

He was able to escape. Before he went upstairs, and when they were both standing by the table, he gave her a hug, stooping a little – she only came up to his shoulder. A flush, starting at the bottom of her neck, spread upwards rapidly. 'Don't be silly,' she said.

But, alone at last, he did not know what to do with the privacy: wandered round his room – pulled out a record with the last duet of *Traviata* on it, remembered her sitting in the box, absorbed, with her face resting on one hand, and felt no need to play the music, and then heard her laugh and her husky voice when she said: 'Oh, Gavin! What do you mean "anyhow"?' and then – slowly – relived her stripping herself down to her own self until he was hard with lust, painfully imprisoned by his clothes. Which he had no sooner got rid of when there was a knock on the door.

'Gavin?'

'Yes, Mum – what is it?'

'Are you asleep?'

He seized his dressing gown. 'No, Mum.'

She came into the room. 'I didn't want to wake you up.' She was carrying the painted cat tray upon which was a steaming mug of Horlicks and a plate with custard creams.

'This is to settle your stomach,' she said.

Feeling guilty, irritated, and slightly ridiculous, he walked away from her towards the window. 'You needn't have bothered.'

'I know that. I also know what happens if I *don't* bother. You remember that time when you were doing your A levels? When Marge couldn't go for that job in London because she got glandular fever? That time that Fred had all that trouble with the dry rot up on Hadley Common? When there was that nasty murder, too, on the Green?'

He said he did remember – it was true about the A levels anyway, and he hadn't got his mother's multi-storey memory.

'You couldn't keep anything down then. You got overtired

overworking and then you couldn't digest your food properly. You were living on Horlicks then . . . I'm not having that again. I'll put it by your bed and you can have it nice and cosy.

'That was a terrible summer,' she added, as she prepared to go. 'I shan't forget *that* in a hurry.'

'Thanks, Mum,' he tried not to sound surly, but that was how it came out. When she had shut the door, and after he had listened to her going down the stairs, he kicked his trousers round the room as viciously as he could, but as they neither whimpered, nor fell into a thousand pieces, they were hardly a worthy target. 'She thinks she can come into my room *any* time she likes – *any* time – she doesn't even let me be private in my own room! For God's sake!' He went on in this vein for quite a bit, until he suddenly stopped wanting to, and collapsed on his red sofa, just as he had begun telling himself that, after all, he *chose* to live at home, had, in fact, begun to tell himself all the things other people might say . . . If he wanted freedom and privacy, he had only to go out and get them. The thought terrified him. Finding somewhere, getting all his stuff moved, getting kitchen stuff, and then just *being* there every evening after work; even Harry didn't have to do that – he had Winthrop. The particular and irremediable disadvantages of living with Winthrop only made him feel that this meant that everybody else would probably turn out to possess a different set. Like always being there when he wanted to be by himself; or *never* being there when he wanted them. He got into bed and decided that he might as well drink the Horlicks.

In bed, he wondered what Joan would actually be doing now. At a party probably, on some floodlit yacht that Dmitri had been decorating, dressed up in her wig and her spectacles so that nobody would know who she really was . . . This started him wondering about Dmitri, and he decided immediately that, whatever Dmitri was like, he wouldn't like him. How on earth could he be married to someone like Joan and keep on going away and leaving her alone? How dared he, in fact, collect and accept her love without returning it? He could not answer this question – nor did he very much want to. He had eaten the custard creams without realizing it, just because they were there, and all he wanted now was to put out the light, lie in the dark and go through all the amazing things that had happened to him with Joan. He put out the light and lay down, but he had hardly reached the first moments when she had stood in the kitchen saying, 'Oh, Gavin! What do you mean . . .?' when he fell suddenly and deeply asleep . . .

In the morning, he woke, wanting her, feeling, he thought, as though perhaps he was in love with her. How did one know that sort of thing? He thought that it was unlikely to be a state that the recipient was in doubt about: unless, of course, there were degrees of love as there seemed to be degrees of every-thing else. Degrees of fear, for instance – he was an authority, he felt, about *them*. But one of the things that she had done for him was to remove herself entirely off the Ladder of Fear. He couldn't think of any other woman who had done that; so perhaps this meant love? But you couldn't surely love some-body simply because they didn't frighten you. In the train going to work he counted up the other things he thought about her. She was intelligent: well, Harry was that, and he certainly wasn't in love with Harry. The idea made him smile, and he caught the eye of the girl sitting opposite and felt himself flushing. He hadn't *meant* to catch her eye. If he wasn't careful, she would think he was wanting to get off with her which of course he didn't. Joan enjoyed opera – Harry again. He'd really got to think of some things about her that couldn't possibly apply to Harry. She was marvellous to go to bed with, but this was a real sticking point. Since he hadn't been to bed with anyone else, how did he know that she was particularly marvellous in that respect? Well, she just was, that's all: if you lined up all the girls in this train, he betted she'd come out near the top. There was no way of proving this, thank God: he could hardly go up to each girl or woman and say, 'Would you mind going to bed with me so that I can see whether the person I have been to bed with is better than you?' She was easy, and interesting, and he just *liked* her very much; the charms and pleasures of her body had simply been a totally unexpected, almost a miraculous, bonus. In any case, he was beginning to see that love was not measurable stuff; approval might be, but he was considering much more than approval . . . He tried a few more tests: would he be excited if he was going to see her this evening, instead of going to dinner with Peter and Hazel? The answer to that was yes, but he wasn't at all sure how much not wanting to go to dinner with Peter and Hazel conditioned it. Did he wish that she was not married to Dmitri? Well, yes, in a way, since it made her unhappy, but on the other hand she *wanted* to be married to Dmitri. He recognized, then, that in an awful way he was quite glad that she was so tied – it left him free – he wasn't quite sure for what: but it gave him time to think, if thinking was the thing to do.

Walking from the train to the salon, he suddenly realized that the reason why he felt so confused – had descended to thoughts about feeling – was that Joan in no way conformed to his lifelong ideal of a possible love. She was not ethereal, not young, she had none of the enigmatic but total compliance with his requirements that he was familiar with. She was not, in those terms, a beauty; in no sense did she give him the impression that she had been waiting for him all her life; in many ways she seemed to him to be a remarkably self-contained woman. But, then, he had always discovered *his* girl in scenes of such shimmering romance, that talking to her had never really come into it, and in the end, whatever you felt about someone, you were reduced to talking to them: well, he hoped not 'reduced' – you *wanted* to talk to them. Otherwise, how could you *go on* with them after the first few magic encounters?

There was, there must be, ordinary life to be lived with whoever it might be somehow. He trudged up the stair to the salon to his own particular brand of regular and repeated doses of that.

'You got someone?'

Gavin simply looked at Peter: he couldn't think what he meant.

'For tonight. You remember I told you we'd got four of everything?'

'Oh – yes. No, I'm afraid I haven't.' He didn't feel up to telling Peter that it had totally slipped his mind . . .

'Well, can you ask someone this morning? Hazel's been getting everything ready for the last two evenings: I wouldn't like to disappoint her . . .' and he sped off from the coffee room to his first client.

It was all very well for Peter to say that, Gavin thought, as he sent Jenny off to wash his first client, but he hadn't *got* anyone he could ask . . . Gloomily, he reviewed the possibilities – such as they were. Harry, apart from the state of his eye, and any other state he might be in, would simply refuse to come. Newly married people were not his style, and although Gavin knew he would refuse as nicely as possible saying he didn't really feel up to it, or had planned a quiet evening with Winthrop – refuse he would: it was not even worth asking him. After that, the possibilities became bizarre. Minnie, who would be bound to make some kind of reckless scene; she could be relied upon to shock Peter and Hazel, no amount of briefing her beforehand could rule that out. He didn't really know the sort of girl that Peter and Hazel would expect him to know. Muriel Sutton, for example; when he thought of what she would read into such an invitation, he wanted to laugh aloud, or scream. He didn't have any girls about who were *friends*. Come to that, he had very few friends of any kind. The person who came nearest this category, really, was Joan. But taking Joan to such a thing would be a waste of her – anyway, she was miles away. Then he thought of his sister, Marge; *she* might be persuaded, if she was free. As soon as he'd got his client through the tricky part of timing the solution for her perm, he went and rang Marge. She was going to the pictures with Ken. She seemed surprised, to be asked. 'I always think of you as such a lone wolf, Gav,' she said. 'Well, I hope you find someone. Have a good time, anyway.' A few minutes later, she rang him back and asked him why he didn't take Muriel: 'She's almost sure to be free.' He didn't want to go into the reasons why he wouldn't ask Muriel on the salon phone, so he just said no to that. A few minutes later, Mr Adrian summoned him across to the desk in order to inform him that this *was* the salon phone. Over the years, Gavin had run his gamut of responses to this kind of remark, from apology, to excuses, to dumb insolence, to breezy dismissal to apology again. The best way to deal with Mr Adrian, he'd discovered, was to use words that couldn't be faulted but in the way most calculated to irritate the old bastard; an apology that sounded as though he was answering back. Now he said how tremendously sorry he was, and how much he hoped that Mr Adrian had not lost too much business in the minute that he had been on the phone and how he mustn't make matters even worse by keeping his present client waiting which he was sure Mr Adrian would understand. He could hear Mr Adrian's false teeth gnashing together, so he knew that he had scored – in a minor way.

Jenny unwound the white towel from Mrs Strathallan's head, and he ran his fingers through her new little snakey ringlets.

'Is it all right?'

He smiled at her in the mirror. 'Taken very nicely. I'll set it on fairly big rollers so that it won't come out too tight.'

'You didn't get your big rollers back from Mr Peter.'

'Oh. Well, get them for me, would you?'

Jenny stumped off, and Mrs Strathallan said, 'What a nice girl that is.'

He agreed absently; he would have appeared to agree even

if he didn't – one never knocked any of the staff to Clients. But Jenny *was* nice: he remembered the walk with her up St James's Street from the Park, and how he'd very nearly felt hardly nervous of her. An idea struck him; and when Mrs Strathallan was safely under the dryer, he said: 'Peter's asked me to bring someone to supper with him and his wife this evening. I wondered whether you'd like to come?'

'I know it's very short notice,' he added, as she didn't reply.

'I would like to,' she said. 'I'll have to phone my mother to see if it would be all right . . . I'll have to wait till my lunch hour, though.'

'All right.' He noticed that she had gone a very dark pink.

At two o'clock she told him that it *was* all right, but that she would have to go home first – to see Andrew into bed. He said he would pick her up if she liked, and if she didn't mind riding on the back of his bike.

'Oh, no,' she said, 'I'd like to.' He arranged to pick her up at seven. When, however, he told Peter that he was bringing Jenny, Peter did not seem particularly pleased. 'She's a junior!' he exclaimed. 'Oh well, if you're mad keen to have her, I suppose it's all right,' he said a moment later.

'I'm not mad keen to have her, but you said get someone, and she was the only person I could get at such short notice.'

'It wasn't short notice when I asked you.'

'Well, I forgot – I told you.'

'Okay then. Seven-fifteen to seven-thirty. Here's the address, and here's a sort of map I've made. It isn't very easy to find till you know it.

'Don't be late,' he said, as they were changing to go home. 'Hazel gets terribly worked up if people are late.'

'All right. I'll try not to be.'

He looked at Peter's map in the train going home. It was the kind of map that only included the streets that Peter felt were important and at the bottom of the map he remarked that there was a very complicated one-way system that he couldn't really explain. It wasn't much use, really – and he decided to use his 'A to Z' and trust to luck. He'd got to look up Jenny's address, anyway – she lived in Kilburn.

It was a beautiful evening: when the train emerged into daylight, the railway banks were full of buttercups and cow parsley, and the sky was blue, with large whitish clouds. He wondered what Joan was doing. His knowledge of the South of France was scanty; he had only been there once; hadn't enjoyed it much. It was the year of his acne being particularly virulent; he'd felt self-conscious in bathing shorts and it had been tremendously hot with mosquitoes who zoomed about biting him from dusk till dawn. It wasn't a very good place to be alone in; everybody else seemed to be with someone. He'd headed north after a few days, and spent a much happier time looking at châteaux on the Loire. But it was probably quite a good place to be if you were rich and had friends and there was nothing wrong with your body. But Joan was rich, and she seemed to know a lot of people – and she wasn't self-conscious about her body. Or was she, perhaps? The gear she wore was a fairly self-conscious business, and although she said she wore it because Dmitri liked it, a bit of her must surely *want* to look like that. He remembered in the Secrets game she had said that she was grotesque: well, he knew now that she wasn't. Did she *believe* that she was, or had Dmitri somehow got her to believe it?

Trains were not a good place to think about Joan's body, he discovered; if he thought about her for more than a second or two, he started wanting her. He started thinking resolutely about the evening ahead, and wondered what it was about him that allowed him to embark on things (like this evening) that he didn't really in the least want to do? But, come to think about it, he *never* wanted to embark upon any social do. He hadn't wanted to go to the party with Harry and Co. and, if he hadn't gone, he would never have met Joan. Or, come to that, Minnie. But, in a way, he *expected* such situations to yield a heavy crop of Minnies: he had never expected a Joan – or anyone like her. It was getting more and more difficult not to think about Joan: whatever else he thought about seemed to end up with his thinking about her. Did this mean love? He was really sick of asking himself this question, because he never seemed to get any nearer answering it.

He walked quickly back from the station to his home; the air felt both warm and fresh on his skin; swifts were wheeling and streaking after the tiny flies that milled about; snatches of the six o'clock news reached him from the open windows of various houses. The scene was so familiar that he could observe the smallest changes in it; buds on the roses starting to have colour, a garden gate painted since this morning; a large oak tree thicker with its sun-encrusted unfolding leaves.

Mrs Lamb was hovering about the hall, obviously waiting his return.

'Ah, there you are,' she said after he had kissed her hot and downy face. 'Somebody's been phoning you with a very nice invitation. So far as I know, I said to her, my son is free this weekend, but mark you, I'm only his mother, so I don't know anything for certain. She sounded ever so nice on the phone . . .'

Gavin, who for one glorious moment had envisaged Joan calling from the South of France and inviting him to join her, was brought up short by the sounding ever so nice on the phone bit. Before she said it, he knew who it was.

'Her Ladyship herself. Asking you for the weekend in the country. To meet her parents. I got that egg off your nice tie, and I've cleaned your dark shoes. Expect him back by six at the latest, Lady Munday, I said, because I happen to know he has an evening engagement. Would you like him to phone you as soon as he comes in, I said, but she said no, don't bother, she'll be giving you a call in the morning.'

'Thanks, Mum.' He started to move past her to get upstairs.

'Is that all you've got to say? There's no need to give

yourself airs with me, young man. I don't know what's come over you in the last few days! Suddenly you're out and about and everywhere and go on acting as though nothing is happening!'

'There's no need to get excited, Mum. I'm not going anywhere for the weekend.'

But he could hardly have said anything worse, and they embarked upon one of those altercations made more painfully indeterminate by the fact that she could not possibly admit to him that she was dying to know how Minnie's parents lived – let alone the more permanent ambition that she nursed about Minnie in what she thought was deadly secrecy. Gavin, who was dimly aware of both factors, refused to face her with them, and took refuge in sulking or seeming to be airily unconcerned. In the end, he shut her up by having a bath.

The prospect – even of the faintest kind – of spending the weekend with Minnie (and her parents) lowered the price of the forthcoming evening. Which was something: after all, he'd known Peter for years: he was not (presumably) going to have any kind of *tête-à-tête* with Hazel, and the presence of Jenny would preclude – he hoped – any embarrassing discussions about whether Hazel should embark upon motherhood or no. And one person he wasn't frightened of was Jenny; she was a quiet, nice, amiable girl – the antithesis of Minnie – or even of Joan – who, whatever else she was, could not be described as quiet. It was no good starting to think about Joan: he couldn't even afford a long bath – had to get changed and be off as soon as possible.

In his room, he put on some Wagner at maximum volume to discourage his mother from coming up and going on about the weekend. Then he had a good look at his 'A to Z', first for collecting Jenny, and then for finding Peter's flat.

He escaped his mother by literally running out of the house, shouting that he was late; then caught himself having to pretend he *was* late in order to circumnavigate dishonesty

. . . All the time he was fixing his pillion and strapping another helmet to it for Jenny, he ruminated about honesty – how everyone made aggrieved or bland assumptions about it and went to tortuous lengths to preserve their own image of themselves – why was he saying 'everyone'? He meant himself. He liked to think of himself as honest, but let there be any kind of confrontation with anyone, and he fell back upon twisting with the best of them. He wanted people – even those he didn't like, in fact often *especially* those he didn't like – to approve of him. On top of that, he would go to almost any lengths to give the impression that he was honest as well as likeable, when everything that he was now thinking showed only too clearly that he was neither . . . As he sped through the back streets up to the main road he wondered what would happen if he had a go at being honest for the evening. Nobody would notice probably. But *he* would notice, and he was the person he was going to go home with at the end of the evening. For some reason, he felt suddenly light-hearted about the prospect ahead; it was as if he'd decided to go with somebody whom he both liked and felt was something of a challenge: there were uncertainties attached to such an idea, but they were of a kind that he felt he might take charge of.

He found Jenny's street quite easily: she lived in a semi-detached Victorian house. The door was answered by Jenny's mother who looked rather young for the part – largely, he quickly realized, because she didn't look in the least like his own mother. She wore jeans and an Indian smock, but he knew that she *was* Jenny's mother because she had the same, rather round eyes and specs, but horn-rimmed, not gold like Jenny's specs.

'I'm Jenny's mother,' she said. 'Would you like to come in? She's nearly ready.'

He followed her along the passage to a room at the back which turned out to be a sitting room with the kitchen at one end of it. There was an ironing board out and a basket full of washing, but Gavin did not notice very much else, because sitting at the table wearing a pale blue T-shirt and eating a bowl of Puffed Wheat was Jenny's child. When he saw Gavin, he stopped eating with spoon in mid-air and favoured him with a stare of the most penetrating impartiality.

Jenny's mother said: 'That's Andrew. Put your spoon down, Andrew, and say hullo.'

Andrew shut his eyes very slowly and then lowered his head.

He was the most beautiful child – well, almost the most beautiful *person* – Gavin had ever seen in his life. His hair was a riot of silvery curls, his eyes, when open (and he opened them almost at once to continue his appraisal), were the colour of aquamarine, a wonderful greeny blue, and his skin was a faintly flushed, translucent white.

'He's inclined to be shy,' Jenny's mother said. 'Eat up your supper, Andrew. I'll go and tell Jenny!'

Andrew put down his spoon, seized his bowl with both hands and began drinking from it, making a surprising amount of noise and watching Gavin over the rim of the bowl – judging to a nicety when Gavin's attention would falter, as, the same second that it did, he blew an astonishing amount of milk and Puffed Wheat back from his mouth into the bowl . . . Then he put his hands over his face and shrieked with laughter. Then he upset the bowl, and Gavin who had been infected by the joke rushed to find a cloth to clear things up. He was in the middle of this when Jenny's mother returned.

'She won't be a minute – oh, Andrew! Don't you bother: I'll do it. You were showing off, weren't you? Don't take any notice of him: he's usually as good as gold . . .'

'He's a marvellous little boy, isn't he.' Even as he said this, it sounded a lame way of describing Andrew.

'He's marvellous, all right. Quite a handful. It's very nice that Jenny is getting a chance to get out. She hasn't been out in the evening for I don't know how long: must be before

Christmas – oh no, Andrew had a chill then, and at the last minute she didn't go. Anyway, it's nice for her.' By now she had mopped up the table, Andrew's face and most of his chair.

'Sorry to keep you waiting.' It was Jenny. She wore a bright blue cotton boiler suit and she looked excited. Andrew held out his arms to her and, in a wonderfully husky voice shouted, 'Cheese!'

'You can't have cheese at this time of night! I mashed him some banana, Mum, would you give him that? I'm off now, Andrew. Sleep well, see you in the morning.' She bent down to kiss him which ended in her hugging him. 'I'm coming back soon,' she said, almost as though she was reassuring herself. She gave Gavin a look which implied that she wanted to go at once.

'Thanks,' he said to Jenny's mother. 'Good-bye, Andrew.' Andrew, he could see, was working up to intense disapproval of the situation; his face was suffusing, his mouth becoming square. He rejected the plate of banana offered utterly and it fell to the floor. Jenny's mother said: 'Go on, love – I'll look after him. He knows me.' And Jenny, with one backward glance, as her son finally expelled his breath in a roar of despair, almost ran out of the room. In the passage she said:

'It's just that he's not used to me going out in the evening. I told him I was when I was bathing him, but I can see now he didn't believe me.'

She looked so worried, that Gavin said: 'Do you want to stay with him?'

'Oh no. I want to go. He'll be all right.'

By the time they reached his bike propped against the privet hedge, the wails had stopped. Gavin gave her the helmet. 'You been on a bike before?'

'Once. A long time ago.' She took off her specs and put them in her shoulder bag. The helmet made her look like a little Action Man.

'I won't go fast.'

'Is it all right if I put my arms round your waist?'

It seemed to be quite all right. In any case, Gavin reminded himself, if she had only been on a bike once before, there wasn't much else she could do . . . 'We may have a bit of a job finding Peter's flat,' he warned, and they set off.

Conversation was so difficult during the ride, that he didn't try to have any. After he'd asked her once if she was all right (he could feel she was nervous from the way she gripped him round the waist) and she'd said something that he'd not heard but taken for an assent, they concentrated upon getting to wherever it was Peter and Hazel lived. This proved to be not far, but after asking two Poles, one American and finally a policewoman, they discovered Greenwood Close, a gaunt block of flats set between a car park for a supermarket and a bus depot.

'Have you been here before?' Jenny asked in the lift.

'No. I've no idea what it will be like.'

'It's funny, isn't it? Meeting people you work with away from work. You expect them to be different in ways that they aren't.' She stopped at this, and Gavin noticed – or rather realized that he'd noticed before but not remarked on it – that away from work Jenny seemed to blush quite often. At work, she rolled her eyes and stumped about, but stayed the same colour. She had put on her specs again, and run her fingers through her hair – en brosse as usual. She had a very small pearl in each ear: at work she wore tiny little thin gold rings.

'Is it okay if I call you Gavin? I mean just this evening.'

'Course it is.' He felt both embarrassed and touched.

Peter met them at the door. 'I thought you were going to be late,' he said, looking at his watch. 'Hazel!' he called. 'It's all right; they've come!' He was wearing a scarf tucked into his neck – like Gavin, but there was nothing casual about his demeanour. He led the way along a passage that smelled very strongly of paint into a narrow room with picture windows at each end. Everything in it was various shades of brown: after

Gavin had been there for some hours, he could see that this was not entirely true, but the first, overall, impression was of brownness: biscuit, coffee, caramel, oatmeal, treacle, peat, chocolate, cow dung (and others) were all toning to such an effect that it was a bit like being inside a very old and heavily varnished picture – even the air felt thick and coloured. At first there was no sign of Hazel, and he wondered whether she was also in brown and therefore temporarily invisible until the eye could pick her out, but then he saw the top half of her through a hatch: her hair *was* brown and cut in a rather unadventurous fringe and she was putting peanuts into a brown pottery bowl. Peter said:

'That's Hazel. Hazel, this is Gavin. And Jenny.'

Everybody said hullo. Then there was a pause until Hazel left the hatch and came into the room. On a coffee-coloured coffee table stood a jug and four amber-tinted glasses. Peter said:

'Do you want us to have our drinks yet, Haze?'

'I think we should. Peter's made a special brew.' She indicated that they should all sit, and they did: Jenny and Gavin on the chesterfield upholstered in near-brown leather; she and Peter on severely architectural pine chairs. There was a short silence. Then Hazel said:

'What do you think of it? We only finished it last night.'

'Oh! Drinks!' Peter started to deal with that.

Jenny said: 'Did you do everything yourselves?'

'Oh – we had to. Couldn't afford anything else. But it does mean that in the end you get exactly what you wanted. It's the only room we have finished as a matter of fact. Do you know, that if you have paint mixed by those paint shops, they *charge* you for it? We found that out the hard way with the loo!'

While talking, he had poured out four drinks from the pottery jug, and now handed them round. Gavin sipped his: all he could say about it was that he hadn't the slightest idea what it was. He wanted to know, so he asked.

'Ah!' said Peter: 'It's a speciality of the house. What do you think of it?'

Hazel said: 'It's a bit sweeter than last time you made it, Peter.'

'Don't you like it then?'

'I didn't say that. I said it was a bit sweeter.'

'Oh well, I didn't have a measure: I just chucked things in.'

Jenny said: 'It's got lemonade in it, hasn't it? I mean that fizzy kind.'

'Right. What else?' He looked challengingly round. Gavin took another sip. As a drink, it wasn't growing on him. At random, he said 'Guinness? Red Cinzano? A dash of Angostura bitters?'

'You might have been *there*! When I was mixing it! You've left one or two things out, though.'

'I can't guess them.' He put his glass down and took a peanut.

Hazel said: 'Oh! I forgot the crisps.'

Peter called: 'What's the timing on dinner, Haze?'

'It'll be about half an hour; I think. The cooker's been a bit funny.'

'We got one of those re-conditioned ones. They have some bargains, if you're prepared to wait and keep going to look every week. The one we got would have cost a hundred and ninety-four pounds if we'd got it new. Hazel's parents said why didn't we get one on the H.P. I had to explain to them that that would have cost even more. Then I saw this place from the top of a bus. In the end we paid seventy-five, wasn't it, Haze?'

'Seventy-six fifty – including delivery and fixing.'

'That's right. She's amazing about figures: it must come from working for an accountant.'

Hazel re-appeared with another pottery bowl full of potato crisps.

'You'll have to eat all these, and the nuts,' she said, 'because we need the bowls for the sweet.' Everybody had some of both. There was a brief silence, during which Gavin could see Hazel sizing up Jenny, and, he thought, deciding to like her. Then Peter said: 'Tell you what. We'll do our tour of the flat now, Haze, while you're popping the first course under the grill.'

They toured the flat. It consisted of a bedroom in which Hazel and Peter slept, which was going to be done in shades of lilac, Peter explained, although at the moment it had bare plaster, what looked like a concrete floor and no curtains – in fact contained a double bed with bright brass rails each end, and a lilac candlewick coverlet and a fitted cupboard covered with primer that Peter said he'd made. When he had showed them everything about the cupboard and said that it had taken him four weekends and three weeks' worth of evenings to make, he told them that they had plumped for lilac because an Aunt of Hazel's had given them the bedcover. 'It meant changing duvet covers and pillowcases, but we thought it was worth it.' Then they saw the bathroom, that had a cork-tiled floor – a very recent piece of work – but not the tiles round the bath yet because they'd put them on with the wrong stuff and had to take the whole lot off, and in taking them off they'd broken some; 'and then when we went back to the place where we'd got them, they'd run out, so *then* we swopped what we'd got left (and I had an awful job getting the wrong glue off the backs), and what we got – well, I'll show you when we get to the spare room.'

In the passage, Jenny suddenly winked at him, and Gavin stopped minding about being shown everything so much, and winked back.

They stood in the doorway of the lavatory about which even Peter could not say very much since its size precluded it being anything more than strictly, not to say uncomfortably, functional.

'You mustn't mind the state of our spare room. We aren't

planning to have anyone to stay until the end of the year. We keep all our decorating gear in it.' He opened the door and they saw what could only be described as a very single room indeed filled with plastic buckets, and rollers and pots of paint. Peter edged his way round most of these and opened a cardboard box out of which he proceeded to take a succession of perfectly white tiles. 'The point is they're not all like this – ah, here we are!' And he held up a less white tile with the picture of a courgette on it. 'And each one is different, you see. It was Hazel's idea – she does have the odd brainwave – '

'Dinner's ready!'

A moment later, Hazel appeared at the spare room door; 'Dinner's ready,' she said more quietly but with greater urgency.

Peter bundled the tiles back into the box saying: 'Right; we're coming; we'll be right with you.'

At the car park end of the sitting room, a small, round table covered with brown formica was laid. There were brown paper napkins, brown candles in amber glass holders, brown pottery plates amorphously decorated in a paler brown, and cutlery with wooden handles. On the plates were four steaming grapefruit.

Everybody sat down, and Hazel explained that the grapefruit was hot.

'I put brown sugar on it,' she said, 'but there's more if anyone wants it.'

Peter, who had fetched their unfinished drinks from the coffee table, lifted his glass. 'This is our first sit-down meal here,' he said, 'quite an occasion, really.' And he smiled at his wife. He had an engaging smile which relieved his face of the stern anxiety that was his usual expression, Gavin thought, whether he was cutting someone's hair, or worrying about his home.

Jenny said: 'Goodness! You have done a lot. I don't think I'd have the patience.'

'You will when you get married. Hazel used to go out every night, before we got engaged, but now I only let her out for her lampshade classes. This is jolly good!' he prompted, and Gavin, honesty deserting him, murmured assent.

For the rest of the dinner, aubergines stuffed with something or other, Peter talked to Gavin about how terrible Mr Adrian was, and would he be likely to give them a rise in the autumn – not *he*, mean old ponce – and Hazel asked Jenny where she lived, and whether she liked working in the salon, and whether she worked for Peter much and what was *that* like? But after Jenny said that no, she worked nearly all the time for Gavin, Hazel said – confidentially, but Gavin, who only needed half an ear to listen to Peter heard her quite clearly: 'Are you walking out with him then?' And, even if he'd been in any doubt, the colour of Jenny's face – a very pale scarlet – would have left none. The colour of Jenny's face seemed a confirmation to Hazel too, but of a different sort. She said: 'Sorry, I didn't mean to pry. I think he's lovely,' and went to fetch their sweet – over which there was some delay as the crisp and nut bowls (not emptied) had to be cleaned out to make way for the crème caramel.

'To be quite frank with you,' Peter said as though this would be an innovation, 'this whole dinner's a kind of dry run for having Haze's parents. So what I thought we'd do, over coffee, is give everything *marks* – you know marks out of ten, and then add it all up and see whether we need to make any changes. We've got a week before they're coming, so Haze and I could test out any alternatives. You see, we don't want them to feel that we're laying on a particularly terrific feast; on the other hand we don't want them to think we haven't tried . . . Also, Haze gets so nervous cooking in front of her mother, who's pretty good at that sort of thing in an old-fashioned English way, that I want her to feel she can do her recipes blindfold.'

'I'm not sure that Dad's going to take to the aubergines much,' Hazel said, 'he really prefers plain food.'

'I dare say he does! But look at what it costs! On our budget, it's a roast once a week, and then there wouldn't be enough for outsiders!'

'The pudding's very good,' Jenny said. 'I love crème caramel.'

'It doesn't matter so much about the sweet,' Hazel said. 'Mum doesn't eat sweets because of her figure.'

'But there has to *be* a sweet,' Peter pointed out. 'We don't want them to think we didn't know there ought to be one.'

With any luck, Gavin hoped he could be deflected from the marking system, and it seemed to work out that way, because Peter offered to make the coffee, and suggested that Hazel move them back to the bus station end of the room. This meant moving two of the chairs, and Gavin did that. He watched Hazel and Jenny settle themselves on the chesterfield, which Hazel told Jenny had been a wedding present from Peter's parents – 'of course we chose it – really we did the whole room *round* it.' Gavin noticed that Hazel's face looked smudged with fatigue and it briefly occurred to him how tiring it must be being married to such a dedicated homemaker. He decided to leave the girls to talk and go and help Peter who was surreptitiously clearing up plates and things.

'Haze gets so worn out,' he confided to Gavin. 'I don't know what it is! It isn't as though we *go* anywhere or *do* anything.'

'Perhaps you do too much work on the flat?'

'Oh, she loves doing that! She's hell bent on getting everything done: even the spare room. She's even keener than I am on finishing that.'

He was rinsing plates and putting them into a plastic rack. 'She wants to do it all in pale pink with a frieze of bunnies all round. It seems extraordinary to me. She didn't even call them rabbits. Anyway, she's bought the frieze so now we're commit-ted. Where's the coffee now? It isn't in a tin yet, because we're buying one of them a month and we haven't got to one for coffee.' He felt his beard with his hand, a nervous gesture that Gavin recognized as the prelude to some more confiding confidence. 'I say – you remember what I talked to you about when I asked you if you'd come to dinner? You remember. It was something *she* suddenly wanted to do that isn't commer-cially feasible. *You* remember,' he urged, so urgently that Gavin had to say that he did.

'Well – she hasn't dropped it. Far from it. She brings it up every time we – well at night-time mostly. Do you think it would be all right if we had a frank talk about it in spite of – you know' – he dropped his voice even more – 'Jenny being here?'

'I don't honestly see that it would be much use. I mean – it's a private matter between you two, isn't it? Nothing to do with anyone else.'

Peter had measured the coffee and he now poured boiling water over it without replying. Then he said: 'She's not rational on the subject. So, when it's between the two of us, I don't feel she listens to my point of view at all. Last night, she accused me of not loving her. That shows she's mad.' He put the coffee on a black glass tray. 'Of course I love her,' he said, as though Gavin had asked him. 'She's the only girl I've ever felt like this about. I tell you what,' he decided suddenly, 'let's play it by ear.'

This was not a soothing suggestion to Gavin as he didn't feel very sure of Peter's ear, but there didn't seem much that he could do about it . . . Peter took the coffee tray into the part of the room where the girls were, and Hazel poured it out. Nobody said anything for a bit, and then Hazel asked Gavin where he was going for his holidays. Gavin said he'd been thinking of Greece, but, even as he said it, he suddenly felt sure he wasn't going to go there, nor did he *mind*, which was even more strange.

'How lovely for you,' Hazel said. 'We've had our holiday getting married. Not that we went for one.'

'We'll go one day though, won't we, Haze?'

'You always say that we're *going* to do things. I'd like something to be going to happen now! It's the same thing about a family,' she explained to the others. 'Peter wants to wait for years and years, but I think one should have one's family when one's young.'

'Hazel – we've been over and over – '

'No, you be quiet for a moment. I want to hear what the others think. Just talking to you about it makes me feel I'm *unusual* or something, and it's not true. *Most* girls get married to have babies. And, anyway, I don't think it's the sort of thing you ought to plan. I think it ought to just happen. What do *you* think?' It was a direct appeal to Gavin who muttered something about it being a joint decision, he supposed, but then, it wasn't the kind of thing he knew about – when Jenny interrupted him.

'Couldn't you sort of compromise?' Everybody looked at her, and she started blushing. 'I mean – get the flat straight, and then start one?'

'That's the whole *point*! We *can't* get the flat straight without Haze working, and obviously she can't work if she has a baby! You're not married, so you wouldn't have *thought* of all that,' he said as kindly as he could manage to Jenny, 'but babies have to be looked after, you know. You don't just have them, and that's that: with respect, Jenny, you don't know what you're talking about.'

Gavin saw Jenny open her mouth and shut it again. She wasn't going to tell them about Andrew, because of Mr Adrian ... The whole evening was becoming unenjoyable in a completely different way. Up till now, he'd been bored – really the whole time, except for that moment when Jenny had winked at him, now, he felt, anything might happen; well, not anything, but one of a large number of uncomfortable things, the most immediate of which was that Hazel was going to cry. And, whatever did happen, he and Jenny were only captive spectators: they weren't involved, and there was nothing they could do. All this time, Peter was holding forth – much in the vein that he had employed with Gavin in the salon (probably in his only vein), about money and time, and mortgages and hire purchase, and Hazel sat biting her finger and trembling and clearly about to explode in one way or another at any moment. Then he saw Jenny looking at him.

'My God!' he said. 'I've just noticed the time! I promised Jenny's mother to get her back. Afraid we'll have to go.'

Hazel burst into tears and ran out of the room.

Peter got to his feet with alacrity: 'Don't let us keep you. I'm afraid Hazel's a bit upset,' he explained. 'It'll take me hours to bring her round. Thank God it's Friday. Sorry about all that, but I warned you it was a problem.' He was conducting them to the door. Jenny said:

'Would you thank her for the nice dinner? And for having me – and everything?'

'I don't suppose it'll do much good, but I'll tell her, of course. So long, Gavin. Sorry about all that – but I did warn you.'

Gavin said good-bye, and the door was shut . . . Jenny and Gavin looked at each other and then made for the lift. In the lift, Jenny said: 'Cor!'

'I'm really sorry – ' Gavin began, but she interrupted him: 'Don't you be. It wasn't *your* fault. Not exactly fault, at all, really.'

'What I meant was, it was intended to be a nice evening out for you: your mother said you didn't go out much.'

'Well, you couldn't have known.' There was something both sturdy and forlorn about the way she said this that made him feel really sorry she'd had such a dud evening . . . They walked to the bike, and he almost wished they were going back by tube: at least they could have talked a bit. But, as they were putting on their helmets, she said: 'Would you like to come back and have a coffee or a tea?' And he said, yes he would.

Her mother had gone to bed, and the kitchen, without Andrew in it, was completely tidy . . . It had obviously been a back sitting room: there were french windows looking on to the back garden and there was an old marble fireplace behind the cooker . . . Jenny had filled a kettle and lit the gas. 'I got some biscuits,' she said. 'Have a chair.'

There were two kitchen chairs pushed against the table which was scrubbed wood and had a small standard lamp upon it – which reminded Gavin of a restaurant. 'Sorry if I wasn't good on the bike,' she said. 'It's exciting, isn't it? But I felt a bit nervous going round corners.'

'You were fine. It takes some getting used to '

She put some assorted biscuits on a plate and switched on the lamp. 'I'll turn off the other,' she said, 'we only use it for cooking.'

'Have you lived here long?'

'Ever since my Dad died. My Mum bought this with the insurance money, but we only live on two floors. She lets the rest. I sleep next door with Andrew. Do you mind if I go and see he's all right? He will be, of course, but I like to see.'

'Course not.'

While she was away, the kettle boiled, and seeing that she had decided they would have tea, he poured some into the pot to warm it.

She returned almost at once and said: 'I never asked you! Which you wanted.'

'Tea's fine.'

While she was making it she said: 'It's interesting how other people live, isn't it? I don't see much of that. It was a funny meal, wasn't it? I didn't care for that main course. They have a funny old time together, don't they? Like a couple of kids playing houses.'

'Pretty depressing.'

'I expect they like it really.'

'Why do you think that?'

'Well, he's always getting ready for occasions, isn't he, and she wants to have them.'

'You mean, he's a nest-maker, and she just wants to get on with laying eggs?'

She started to laugh, and clapped her hand over her mouth. 'I mustn't wake Andrew. But *he's* like that in the salon as well: I wasn't surprised.'

'How do you mean?'

'When he's cutting, he gets obsessional. Goes on and on and *on*. Getting slower and slower. Not like you at all.' There was a pause and then she said: 'You can learn a lot about people watching them cut hair.'

She sipped her tea, staring ahead of her over the cup. Then she asked: 'Do you think everyone who gets married is a bit like Peter and Hazel? Not entirely like them – but a bit?'

'You mean sort of enclosed?'

She nodded, and waited with an expression that looked as though she thought he was going to be very interesting about it all. 'I don't know,' he said and, as he heard himself saying it, he wondered how many times he'd said that just this evening. He always *felt* as though he didn't know about almost anything that came up. 'I don't see a lot of married couples.'

'Nor do I,' she said. 'In fact, outside the salon, I don't see people. Andrew and my Mum and that's it. I wanted to know, because I kept feeling like laughing tonight, and then I thought no, it's really sad. All the girls at the salon – well, you know, all the juniors, and I've been there longest so I've seen quite a few – all of them waiting to find the right chap and setting up house and that. If *that's* what it all adds up to – I mean is *all* it adds up to – it *is* sad, isn't it?'

236

'It would be if you're right. I don't think you are, though.'

'Tell me some people who aren't like that.'

'It wouldn't make any difference – you wouldn't know them.'

'It would help. I'd believe you,' she added.

'My sister. I don't think they're like that. They're very close, but I think they have a good life with their friends and their children. I think they enjoy themselves. Will that do?'

She shrugged. 'Have to. It doesn't sound – much like an adventure, though.'

'Is that what you think it ought to be?'

'You know what you said about art and that?'

As he just looked at her, trying to remember what exactly he had said about that, she went on: 'About art being for recognizing things. For showing people what a lot there is about life that they don't know?'

'I remember now.'

'Well, I feel all the time as though I'm living just *outside* everything. In a kind of backwater. All I ever do is work in the salon and look after Andrew . . . There doesn't seem *time* for anything else to happen. It's not that I don't want to work, or don't like looking after Andrew – ' she stopped suddenly. After a moment she said: 'I don't want to bore him, you see. End up being one of those Mums you can rely on if things are tough, but you don't want to be with them in between. I mean, when he goes to *school*. I did try one thing. Went to the library and asked them for a history book. But it was all about fighting and Acts of Parliament and I couldn't get into it. When you said that about art, I thought it might be a bit easier for me to take in.' She looked at him so earnestly that he felt completely stuck for an adequate response. He finished his tea to give himself time, and she immediately poured him some more, and then remained with her trusting owl eyes fixed upon his face. It shot through his mind that on the Ladder of Fear this was supposed by him to be pretty high up and *he didn't feel frightened* – a whole lot of things, but not that.

'I don't know what you like,' he said at last, 'I mean – it has to start with *you*. Well, you finding something interesting, or beautiful, or extraordinary.'

'Well, couldn't you tell me some things, and then I could see whether they seem like that to me?'

'I could. I could try. Tell you what. I'll make out a sort of list of different things and you could try some of them.'

'Okay.' She sounded defeated in some way, he didn't know why. There suddenly didn't seem to be anything to say, so he said he thought he ought to be going.

'Okay.'

As they walked down the passage to the door, he did think of something.

'What are you going to do when you finish your apprenticeship?'

'I don't know. Try and get a job nearer home. My mother wanted to sell this house and start a small business so that we could live where we work because of Andrew, but I don't think there'll be enough money. I'll have to get a job first, and save a bit before that.' She sounded dispirited at the prospect. 'I'm just tired,' she said. 'It'll all seem easier in the morning.'

'Good night, Jenny.'

'Good night, Gavin.'

She stood at the door while he put on his helmet and mounted his bike.

'Thanks for the evening,' she called.

'I'll try and make it a better one next time.'

She smiled then, and rolled her eyes like she did in the salon.

On the way home, he thought that it must be the night with Joan that had made so many things (with other people) seem so much easier.

CHAPTER NINE

SUNDAY morning found Gavin at Waterloo catching the 11.30 to Weybridge. It was a sparklingly beautiful day, but he felt gloomy. He was doing exactly what he had told his mother at breakfast, and then Minnie on the telephone, he would certainly not – not on your life – do. Go to Weybridge to have lunch with Minnie and her parents. Three telephone calls had spelled his defeat. They had begun during breakfast, which on Saturdays was a much more leisurely affair – with Minnie.

'Gavin?'

'Yes?'

'You can come, can't you?'

'I can't really, I – '

'But I've *told* them you're coming now. Your mother said last night that she was sure you'd be pleased to come. It would be extremely rude if you didn't.'

'My mother didn't know what I was doing this weekend when she said that.'

'What *are* you doing, then?'

'I've got a lot of things to do. Work to catch up on.'

'Work! You don't work on Saturdays. I know that.'

'I'm very sorry, Minnie, but I'm not coming for the weekend.'

'Why not?' She was wailing when he said: 'Because I'm not, that's all,' and put down the receiver.

He had hardly returned to his bacon and eggs, when the telephone rang again.

'Just come for one night. I've got a very special reason for asking you.'

'What?'

'I can't possibly tell you on the phone . . . Telephone. Oh, Gavin, do just for once do something for me when I need it so badly. *Please!*'

'Sorry. I told you. I can't come. I don't want to come,' he added to make weight . . . Again he put down the receiver. This time he left it off, but his mother, who did not like the milk to be left on the doorstep for a split second if she could help it in case it went bad, had heard the milkman, and, as usual, had scurried out down the path to meet him. When she came back, she said: 'The receiver was off. You naughty boy. I don't know where your manners have gone, I'm sure.' So of course it rang again.

'Look; if you'd just come for lunch. You needn't stay long. Just come. It's my parents, you see. I've told them you're coming. I'll meet you at the station. It's Weybridge. Catch the 11.30.' And then *she* rang off.

Anybody in their right mind, anybody with any gumption at all, would have just let her stew: meet the train and find him not on it. He hadn't turned out to be one of those people. He had used up all his gumption sulking with his mother at breakfast. After a brief, sharp interchange about why on earth he didn't want to go for a nice weekend when she'd cleaned his tie and spent the evening going through his socks, and he had said that he would manage his own affairs without any interference from her, and then, from the piercing glance she gave him, wondered whether he had chosen a rather unfortunate word, she had plonked his bacon and eggs back from the warmer and on to the table and gone into a general harangue about how he had changed lately – how he was secretive, always dashing about, never home till heaven knew when and what did he think his father thought of it all (this by now interspersed with the telephone calls to which he knew she listened with breathless interest), he had sulked: refused to say anything until her commentary on his life simply ran out. Mrs Lamb's sulking, however, was a very active affair; she trembled with repression, and emitted sounds – heavy sighs, sniffs, even grinding her real teeth against the false ones in a menacing manner that implied she might erupt into words again at any moment, and only the deadest of silences with his eyes on his plate prevented it (he thought). His tacit agreement to go for lunch which she interrogated out of him – 'So you've changed your mind again, have you? Well, thank someone for that!' 'Catching a train are you?' – and various other questions that he did not answer, or at least deny, had informed her that he must be going and had cleared the air from pitch-black ignorance to the twilight of bare knowledge. It was details that she liked and felt baulked of.

Sitting in the sullenly dirty little railway carriage, it occurred to him that his life *had* changed a good deal of late. He was not, at least not exactly, the same person that he had been a few weeks ago. Was it the night with Joan that had changed everything? He could no longer be sure: the episode, for lack of any follow up – he had not heard from her and did not even know exactly where she was – had resolved itself into legend. He sometimes was not absolutely sure that it had happened, or happened the way that he remembered it. He even felt spasms of resentment, since she, he felt, had annihilated those dreams of beautiful, compliant girls – his private company for so many years – and put only this single instance of herself in their place. Recapturing something – re-running that script – was proving less and less satisfactory. In exchange for that, he felt less apprehensive about things. The trouble was that he was so accustomed to apprehension he felt its loss – almost as though it had been a pleasure, rather than an acute discomfort. It was as though, in relation to people, he didn't have any other feeling – except those few idyllic hours with Joan. Take today, for instance. He wasn't *frightened* of what it would be like, while not having the least idea what it would be like. He didn't expect to enjoy it much: Minnie had a way of turning quite ordinary situations into something bizarre. Then he thought that probably the presence of her parents would inhibit her. He wondered briefly, and with such ignorance about them, that he soon gave it up. At least he would discover whether they did indeed live in a castle with a deer park, but at Weybridge this seemed unlikely. Her sister had the air and the voice of a lot of people who came to the salon and the likelihood was that the parents would be the same.

As the train trundled through south London past rows of little houses with well-tended back gardens he was reminded of Jenny and her request for some things that she could get into (that she might find interesting, or beautiful or extraordinary). Looking back, he realized that he had actually been touched by her asking him, in a way that had seized him up. He hadn't really been very understanding about that: he could *see* that she felt trapped in a backwater and she obviously wanted to try not to be. He'd just been rather matter of fact about it all – and vague. He *had* said he'd make out some kind of list for her. He got his battered leather loose-leaf notebook out of his pocket. Instantly his mind became a blank. The arts – all the branches of them and the enormous *amount* of everything – defied distinctions and choices. Anyway, how did he know what she knew, let alone might like? Supposing everything he thought of turned out to be like the history book that she couldn't get into? Well, it wouldn't, of course. He wrote down MUSIC in capitals at the head of a page. She must have heard *some* music, but probably didn't know what it was. Well, if she recognized anything he suggested, she'd get some confidence – people usually enjoyed recognition, something familiar cropping up – like tunes they had heard people whistling in the street turning up in the middle of an opera. But it wouldn't be much good suggesting operas to her. He had had the feeling that money was scarce, and he knew that juniors earned a very bare wage. She might be getting some State benefit for Andrew, and she might not. He guessed she wouldn't have any hi-fi and he had the impression that there wasn't even a telly. Well, they would have a radio, and if she looked in the paper, she would find things to listen to. Mozart, he wrote. Chopin, Beethoven, Tchaikovsky (always a good way in for beginners). She might take to Bach. Haydn; the B.B.C. were always making him Composer of the Week. Perhaps he'd better get her a copy of *Radio Times* and mark the evening music for a week: yes – that was a good idea. Really, of course, the best thing would be for him to play her carefully selected records so that he could *see* what she enjoyed, or didn't, as the case might be. But he'd never invited a girl to his room before – at any time, for anything – and he had a fair idea of the effect that doing so would have upon his mother. He moved on to PICTURES. Andrew seemed a bit young to take to public galleries; not that they wouldn't let him in, but trundling him about and worrying whether he was bored or wanted to go to the lavatory would take her mind off what she'd come to see. She needed someone to *do* that with. He thought the Tate was a better introduction than the National Gallery, but the great thing about taking people for the first time to galleries was not to take them for too long. He supposed she could go to some of the galleries near where they worked in her lunch hour. He'd have to choose those for her. Really, one way of starting to look at pictures was to look at them in books: he'd got a fair number at home, but there was the Mrs Lamb problem again. (It crossed his mind then, in a sneaky kind of way, that his parents would be going on holiday, and that possibly Jenny and Andrew could come over in their absence.) They could go for a picnic in Hadley Woods, and then he could take them home for tea and really show her things . . . He thought about that for a bit, and it seemed a thoroughly good idea. It would save her from getting depressed from trying composers or painters who meant nothing to her. It was very important to start right; acquire the muscles for appreciation slowly. Take poetry, for instance. It would be no good getting her books to struggle through – at least not until she had heard some poetry that moved her – once she had found something and been caught by it, more of the same could follow, and she could be left to herself. People unaccustomed to reading poetry had awful trouble with the rhythms, and often thereby lost the sense. He had never tried educating anybody before, and the thought excited him. He turned over a new page and wrote LITERATURE at the top. Perhaps the best way to start her off on that would be to choose a first-class short story and read it aloud to her. A ghost story perhaps; or one of de Maupassant's little slivers of life, or Kipling – but not Saki. He was just settling down to considering the merits of 'The Rocking Horse Winner' and 'The Maltese Cat', when he realized, with a shock, that the train was reaching Weybridge.

She was there to meet him, of course: she could be relied upon to be reliable when he didn't want her to be. If she hadn't been there, he reflected morosely, he could have gone straight back to London as he hadn't the faintest idea where her parents lived. But she was there, wearing a pair of faded and insultingly patched jeans and a T-shirt that had been put in the washing machine with some other wrong colour.

'Hullo,' she said, as though she was surprised and not particularly pleased to see him.

'Hullo.'

They walked out of the station where her battered little car was parked. Her hair looked dirty to him, and she seemed even paler than he remembered.

'I gave up the painting kick,' she said as they got into the car. 'You were right about *that*. Too much hassle.'

'Why were you so keen to get me to come today?'

'Oh!' There was a long pause. 'If you must know, my father's furious with me. He's threatening to stop my allowance completely. Goes on and on about my not working enough (what *at*, for God's sake?) and says I have disreputable friends. So I told him a reputable friend was coming all the way from London to see me. Got it?'

'There's a swimming pool,' she said as he didn't reply. 'And a tennis court, but I don't suppose you play tennis.'

'No, I don't. I can swim though – learned in the public baths.'

'I've made you cross now, haven't I? Honestly. I don't mean to. I love you really. I think you're marvellous. And, if you think it's unfair of me to make you meet my horrible parents, just think what I did for you about your Mum.'

'What did you do for me?'

'All that pretending to be grand to please her. *You* remember!'

He thought of pointing out that he had not in the least wanted her to meet his mother, and then decided that a first-class row just before his lunch would be too much. Of course, if it was a bad enough row, perhaps he needn't go to the lunch at all? He had to face (for the hundredth time) what a lot he would go through to avoid rows.

'Just for the record,' he said. 'What is your father called?'

'He's called Sir Gordon Munday. My mother's called Stella, but she won't notice what you call her. She doesn't notice much at all.'

He looked at her in some surprise when she said this, wondering what she meant, and noticed that her profile was almost beautiful if her skin hadn't been so stretched over her bones, like silk on a model aeroplane.

'It's a hideous house, you'll find.'

'You do make it sound attractive.'

'But there'll be a huge lunch,' she said, as though he hadn't spoken.

They were driving through quiet suburban roads spasmodically edged by white gates, wrought-iron gates and sometimes just openings to the sort of drives that curved simply for the

245

hell of it. Glimpses of mansions could be seen and the odd, huge aimless dog. Wing mirrors of motor cars glinted through privet or leylandii hedging. Just as he was wondering whether you could tell more about the architecture behind the hedge – or the class of people living there by what sort of a hedge it was – it became clear that they were arriving.

The gates had a pair of wrought-iron lanterns attached to their linch-posts; the drive was tarmac, edged with green, well-cut lawns. It curved, and a flurry of evergreens hid the house temporarily from view. When exposed it proved to be a sprawling, Tudor-type mansion on two floors, networked by silvery bleached beams and with a quantity of mean little leaded windows. Scarlet geraniums, butcher-blue lobelia and white alyssum were planted in white-painted tubs at very regular intervals. They had the sort of rigid gaiety that he associated with groups of people having their photograph taken. The front door, heavily studded with iron nails, looked like something from the set of *Fidelio*. It was shut. Minnie brought the car to a sputtering halt immediately in front of it.

'Remember – I'm mad about you,' she rather strangely (he thought) said.

He followed her through a dark hall with a tremendously loud grandfather clock in it into an enormous half-panelled room, with a stone and brick open fireplace, and a highly polished oak floor with shaggy off-white rugs on it that looked like the cast-offs from several classy polar bears. There were a number of squat sofas and armchairs – all upholstered in powder-blue Dralon – and the curtains round the formidable bay window were of the same material.

Minnie led him to a powder-blue window seat. 'If you sit down, I'll find them.' And she disappeared through an oak door opposite the fireplace. He didn't sit, but prowled cautiously. The walls were regularly hung with large oil paintings in the genre of 'The Hay Wain', 'Fishing Boats off the Dutch Coast' variety. There were one or two extremely still lives of unlikely combinations of fruit and game juxtaposed. There was a coffee table with neatly stacked magazines and newspapers and a brass bowl full of scarlet carnations. He returned to the window seat in case Minnie came back with one or more parents. The room looked out on to a garden with a lot more neat lawns, beds of standard roses and a rock garden yelping with aubretia and something that looked like mustard, but couldn't have been ... He'd just got as far as noticing the large Monkey Puzzle and some more wrought-iron gates when he heard sounds of people arriving – footsteps and subdued voices – and hastily sat down.

Sir Gordon and Lady Munday, followed by Minnie, processed into the room. Sir Gordon had Lady Munday by the arm and without taking the slightest notice of Gavin steered her slowly to the largest Dralon armchair into which she subsided – considering her measured approach – rather suddenly. Minnie stood on one leg with her other foot hooked round the ankle. She had taken off her shoes. Gavin rose to his feet and waited.

'There we are, then,' said Sir Gordon to his wife. The remark, though not the accent, reminded Gavin of his own father. Sir Gordon straightened up and stood looking straight in front of him. His hair was white and copious, and he had a military moustache.

'Well, Minerva, you'd better introduce your young friend,' he said.

'This is Gavin Lamb – I told you his name, Daddy, come on, Gavin.'

Gavin advanced and, at some point, Sir Gordon held out his hand with a gesture just short of warding him off that turned into a handshake. He wore a blazer with a great many gleaming brass buttons and a tie with sailing yachts on it. 'Find your way here all right?' he said. Gavin said that he'd come by train and that Minnie had met him. (Of course he'd found his way; otherwise he wouldn't be here, would he?)

'And that's my mother.'

Lady Munday, on closer inspection, looked rather like a raddled version of Claudette Colbert, with a wispy fringe, pencilled eyebrows, a mouth the colour of the carnations beside her, smudged, but liberal mascara and a chalky face. She was dressed entirely in beige with a double string of pearls. She looked at Gavin without interest and said: 'What about a drink, Gordon?' Sir Gordon turned towards an enormous oak cupboard carved with monks praying. They had pained expressions, probably, Gavin thought, because they had stiff necks as their bodies were in profile and their heads were facing. The open cupboard doors revealed a battery of bottles and glasses.

'I'd like my usual, Gordon.'

Sir Gordon took a tumbler which he filled in turns with Rose's Lime Juice and Gordon's gin. He gave this mixture a perfunctory stir and then moved slowly towards the armchair. 'Get your mother a table. Go on, girl, make yourself useful, for once.'

Minnie pulled out the smallest of a nest of tables and carried it over to her mother. The drink was placed on it. Sir Gordon surveyed it for a moment and then turned back to the cupboard. His movements were measured and ponderous – rather like an elephant's: it would be a mistake to get in his way once he had embarked upon going anywhere.

'Now then. Let me see. I suppose you drink, young man?'

'I do sometimes.'

'You do sometimes. And I take it that this is one of those times. Eh?'

'Yes, thank you.'

'I don't imagine you expect us to have got the champagne out for you.'

'Oh no. A gin and tonic would do nicely.'

'A gin and tonic would do nicely.' He unscrewed a bottle of tonic with which he three-quarters filled a tumbler and then added a dash of gin. After contemplating the glass for a moment, he added another, equal, dash of gin. 'Minerva! You can give your young friend his drink.'

'And what can I do for you?' he went on after she had given Gavin his tumbler.

'A Coke. I'd like a Coke.'

'Disgusting stuff.' He produced a tin and a tumbler and handed them to her. Gavin sipped his drink. It tasted as though it had spent the night in the linen cupboard.

Nobody said anything for quite a long time. Lady Munday got a rather long cigarette holder out of her beige bag, fitted a Silk Cut into it, and made several ineffectual attempts to light it with a gold lighter. Sir Gordon, who had poured himself a half-tumbler of Scotch to which he had added two dashes of water, turned to observe her efforts.

'Your mother needs a light,' he said.

Minerva went to the stone fireplace and collected a box of matches which she gave to her mother.

Gavin now noticed that there was not a single book in the room.

Lady Munday, who seemed to have drunk a surprising amount of her drink, said: 'When's Sheila coming?'

'Sheila,' pronounced Sir Gordon, 'is in London. She will not be coming to lunch. She is entertaining for her husband. It was not convenient for her.'

'I didn't say I *wanted* her to come to lunch. I simply asked. *I* think she's stuffy. Do you know what I mean by stuffy?' She turned to Gavin.

'Pompous?' he suggested. 'Boring?'

'There, you see. I'm not the only one!'

Gavin realized the trap he had fallen into just as he fell into it. Lady Munday drank deeply, put down her empty glass with a flourish and said: '*Other* people find Sheila stuffy. If it was just poor old me, we might take no notice, but it isn't, is it?'

Gavin said: 'Um – what I meant, Lady Munday, was that I thought I knew what you meant by stuffy. I – I didn't mean that your daughter – '

'She's not *my* daughter . . .' She pointed to Minnie who throughout this time, Gavin noticed, had sat on the arm of a chair scuffing the polar bear rug with her foot. 'That's my daughter. She's pretty awful, but it's a different kind of awful to Sheila. She may not be spotless as the driven snow, but she isn't smug. Or bossy,' she added after thinking about it and holding out her glass for another drink.

Sir Gordon moved over to take the glass. 'There is nothing wrong with Sheila,' he pronounced. 'Sheila is a wonderful girl. Our young friend has not come here to talk about Sheila. I should prefer the subject of Sheila to be closed . . .'

It was. But no alternative subject was opened up. Gavin tried to catch Minnie's eye, but she remained wilfully apathetic – staring at her foot. So he took refuge in some futile remark about the nice garden.

'And where do you hail from – Mr – Lamb, is it?'

'Yes. And I live in New Barnet.'

'*New* Barnet. And do you propose to continue there?'

'I think so, yes.'

Sir Gordon occupied the next minute by returning a full glass to his wife. 'I see,' he finally said, as though Gavin had fallen into some other trap. It was a relief when a subdued man in a white coat announced that luncheon was served.

It turned out to be impossible to shift Lady Munday until she had finished her second drink. Sir Gordon bent down and got hold of her upper arm, but she twitched him away and settled further into the armchair, the drink slopping danger-ously in her hand.

'You wish to finish your drink,' he pronounced.

For an answer, she tipped the glass to her mouth and drank in steady gulps with her eyes fixed upon him like a child drinking milk. They all stood about – waiting, while she did this. Gavin moved over to the uncharacteristically silent Minnie, who met his eye blankly.

'All gone!' Lady Munday announced in nursery tones, whereupon Sir Gordon renewed his attack upon her upper arm and they all processed slowly through yet another door hardly observable because of the panelling.

The dining room was very full of beams and black, glistening oak. There was a huge silver épergne with carnations and smilax in it, and the chairs were upholstered in tapestry that reminded Gavin of the Battle of Hastings, since armoured men seemed to be staggering about bristling with arrows, and the chap on his chair actually had one in the eye. The table was long and rectangular, and their four places were set like points of the compass. They were going to have to shout at one another, Gavin thought, which would make conversation (if there was any) pretty difficult. Minnie's parents sat at either end, and he and she faced each other. After a pause, the man in the white coat brought in four plates which he set in front of each of them. There was a longish pause, and then he returned with a silver dish with what looked like a green and pink blancmange on it. He served Lady Munday and her daughter, and by the time it got to Gavin he could see it was some kind of mousse. He waited for the others to start eating, which was just as well because they didn't, just sat in silence until the man re-appeared with a silver tray and sauce-boat – also handed round. Gavin then picked up his fork and realized too late that he was still premature. The white-coated man went away and returned with a flagon of what turned out to be a rather nasty white wine. When everybody had been given some of that, he went away again (he must walk *miles*, Gavin thought, like a postman) and they all began to eat. When this had gone on for a bit, Sir Gordon cleared his throat in a way that made it clear that he was going to speak:

'My daughter tells me that you er – well, not to put too fine a point on it, that you mess about with people's hair.'

'I'm a hairdresser, yes.'

'Do you own an establishment, or do you merely work in one?'

'I work in one.'

'I'm forced to commend your frankness.'

'There was a gel,' announced Lady Munday, 'who went orf with a hairdresser. Once. It was in the papers.'

'Quite right, Stella. There was. Turned out badly, of course. But what would you expect?'

He turned his pale blue marble eyes on each of them in turn; when they got to Gavin, he said: 'I don't know what I'd expect.'

'You don't know what you would expect.'

'Well, not really, no.'

'We know what *you* mean, Gordon. You mean you think hairdressers are a poovy lot. That's what *he* thinks,' she told Gavin.

Minnie suddenly said: 'But you'd have to go *miles* for a gay seat belt manufacturer. Daddy's a seat belt manufacturer,' she explained – started to giggle – and choked.

Both parents looked at her without expression, which, as she went on choking, congealed to a lack of concern that Gavin found rather horrible. He got up and walked round the table to Minnie, to bang her on the back and get her some water if she wanted any.

There didn't seem to be any water in sight, so after a few thumps he offered her her wine. When she seemed to be through the worst of it, he went back to his place. The silence round the table was oppressive, and he realized that the Mundays were both waiting for him to finish what had turned out to be fish mousse. Although she hadn't said anything, Minnie's eyes had brimmed with tears when she nodded to accept the wine. She left her fish.

The second that Gavin put down his fork, Sir Gordon reached under the table and rang a bell. The white-coated man appeared and cleared their plates one by one. He then set fresh ones before them. During all the time – and there seemed to Gavin to be a hell of a lot of it – that it took him to serve them with a dish of sliced roast lamb, peas, carrots and new potatoes, mint sauce and redcurrant jelly, and finally red wine in a second glass, silence prevailed. After positively his last appearance, however, everybody started to eat what Gavin recognized as very good food, although he no longer felt hungry.

'You must tell us more about yourself,' Sir Gordon announced, after he had loaded his fork with some of every-thing on his plate. His tone was not inviting, and it was difficult to know precisely what he meant.

'There's not much to tell, really.'

'Are your parents living?'

'Yes.'

'Both of them?'

'Yes.'

'Are you the only child?'

'Oh, Gordon, what difference could *that* make?'

Sir Gordon waved his heavily laden fork dismissively at her and a pea fell on to the table. 'Please don't interrupt, Stella. I am talking to Mr Lane.'

'Lamb.'

'I am talking to Mr Lamb.'

'I have a sister. She's married.' Lady Munday, he noticed, had different eating habits. She had speared up all her peas and was now popping bits of carrot into her scarlet mouth. He glanced at Minnie who seemed simply to be re-arranging the food on her plate.

'And what does your father do? Is he also concerned with hair?'

'According to *you*, Gordon, he couldn't be. Poovy people don't have kiddies, do they? According to *you*.'

'He has his own business. He's a builder.'

'His own business.'

'I can't see what difference it would make anyway. I mean,' she explained to nobody in particular, 'he might be a poove and working for someone else. *Or* he might be poovy and have his own business. Or normal and not. My husband's idea of normal is another matter; no more of that. I'm sick of that subject. Do you go to the theatre, Mr Lamb?'

Relieved that the subject looked like changing, Gavin said that he did.

'And what do you think of it? Nowadays?'

This gave him a fair idea of what *she* thought of it, but he said mildly: 'Well, we've always had marvellous actors, haven't we? But we seem to be a bit short on playwrights.'

'I used to be in the theatre and I couldn't agree with you more . . . No *spectacle*. No tunes you can sing in the bath.'

'If he has his own business, why did you not go into it?'

'I didn't want to.'

'Seven thousand sequins sewn on to my dress for one little number! I sang it on a swing: the ropes were made of ostrich feathers. The whole thing only took four minutes. That was the sort of trouble they took. Now everything's as drab as can be.'

'Am I to assume that you are one of those people who believe in pleasing themselves?'

Gavin looked desperately at Minnie, but she, most surprisingly, was positively gobbling her meal; eyes fixed on plate, and shovelling the stuff in as hard as she could go . . .

'I believe in *trying* to,' he said; 'but it's not all that easy, is it? I mean, there are so many other things you find you're doing instead.' (Like having this amazingly boring lunch with you. *Why* had Minnie asked him?)

'The old-fashioned virtues such as duty to others, a sense of responsibility and unselfishness mean absolutely nothing to you?'

'I can't imagine what on earth they mean to you, Gordon.

I've never known you to do the teeniest thing for anybody else in your life. You always used to tell me how you knew how to look after Number One. And I soon found out who that was.'

'Stella, I am trying to hold a conversation with Mr Ram.'

'I don't call cross-examining someone a conversation. We don't usually *have* conversations at meals . . . We usually eat them in silence. It isn't a question of "pas devant les domestiques" it's pas devant any bloody body. I married beneath me,' she explained more directly to Gavin, 'and that's saying something, if you saw where I came from.'

And, before the silence could become ungovernably awful, she went on: 'He's a self-made man, and quite frankly I don't think he's made a very good job of it. I think anyone else would have done better.'

Minnie quite suddenly slid off her chair and almost ran out of the room.

'You will observe, Stella, that your thoughtless rambling has upset the girl.'

'I expect she just wanted to go to the lavatory. And by the way, *his*,' she pointed a scarlet-tipped finger at Gavin, 'name is not Mr Lane. We all know that.'

'I am perfectly aware of Mr Ram's name,' said Sir Gordon heavily. His face which had suffused to the colour of a ripening plum during the last few minutes was now draining to the mauve twilit dusk of far-off hills. Unexpectedly (to Gavin) he offered his wife another gin, and unsurprisingly she accepted. When he had gone to get it, Lady Munday threw back her head and made a little rocketing raucous noise that Gavin recognized as being her way of laughing. He had been feeling as though he was in some vehicle whose brakes had failed careering downhill towards some – as yet unseen – dangerous corner: he felt frightened and irresponsible. He looked at his companion warily. He was beginning to see where Minnie got her capacity for embarrassing people from.

She said: 'Don't mind *me*. I must have a little fun sometimes. I am so hellishly bored. If it wasn't for that wretched
girl I wouldn't *be* here – would never have married him.'

In spite of not wanting to, he went on looking at her: she
was looking straight at him in just the way that Minnie did
when she was telling him something unlikely – except that
these same round eyes were spikey with blue mascara. Also, he
had the feeling that she was not lying.

'For goodness' sake, don't marry her whatever you do.
You'd have an awful time.'

Before he could say anything to this, Minnie came back
into the room. Her face was chalky, but she looked relieved –
even managed a little smile at him as she slid back into her
seat. She was immediately followed by her father, whose
measured tread and concentration upon the tumbler that he
held precluded anything else happening while he was walking
about with a drink. Then, when he had set it before his wife,
he went to his seat and rang the bell, so conversation was
further suspended.

By the time their meat plates had been cleared and they
had all been served with apple pie and a choice of cream or
custard, Lady Munday had practically finished her new drink,
but Gavin realized that it had had the effect of shutting her up,
since, when conversation was again due to break out she
remained silent, picking pieces of apple out of her pastry with
her fork. It was Sir Gordon who returned to the charge.

'And what are your ambitions? If you have any.'

Gavin, after thinking for a moment, said that he thought
he'd like to travel more.

'You would like to travel more. And what do you intend to
do on your travels?'

'Well – just see things. Look at things.'

'*See* things? See things,' he repeated heavily. After – presumably – further thought, he said: 'I fail to see what looking
at things can have to do with *hair* . . .'

Gavin, who failed to see that too, remained silent.

'I was, after all, inquiring about your ambitions.'

'I thought you were asking me what I was interested in. I don't think I've got any ambition in the way you mean.'

'No ambition,' reported Sir Gordon in a tone that balanced incredulity with disapproval. He looked round the table in a chairman-like manner to gain backing for this decree, but his wife and daughter were engaged upon eating and not eating their apple pie. 'I think we will adjourn this discussion until after lunch. We can resume it in my study.'

Which is what happened. Sir Gordon dispatched the women – Lady Munday to a sitting room where she could watch the tennis on television, and Minnie to the swimming pool by herself, after she had said that she was going to take Gavin for a swim. He then conducted Gavin to a smaller, and intensely dark, room whose walls were upholstered in what looked like dark brown leather. There was a stupendous desk and Sir Gordon seated himself behind it with his back to the small leaded window. Gavin, who he indicated should sit in an extremely uncomfortable chair facing him, could see Minnie's diminishing figure as she wandered aimlessly across the lawn towards the Monkey Puzzle and the wrought-iron gates.

There was a silence, during which Gavin wondered why Sir Gordon, who did not seem to like him, should want to go on talking to him, and secondly, why he, Gavin, who did not even want to be here at all, was putting up with it.

'Well, young man. Now we are alone, what have you to say for yourself?'

'I don't know what you mean.'

'Don't come *that* one on me. I wasn't born yesterday.' He gave a rather nasty smile, as though there was something obscene in the notion that he might have been, waited, and as Gavin said nothing – simply stared at him – leaned forward, put his elbows on the desk. 'I'm waiting,' he said. The brass buttons on his cuffs were angled and winking like a flarepath.

Then he said: 'I can understand your not wanting to bring up the subject in front of the women. But we're alone now!'

'Bring up what subject?' In spite of himself, Gavin began to feel vaguely frightened. Here he was, miles from anywhere, shut up with this ghastly old tyrant –

'It's no use trying to brazen it out. I have information. I am perfectly aware of what you have been up to.'

This made Gavin feel momentarily better: so far as he knew or could think, he hadn't been up to anything – didn't lead that sort of life . . .

'I happen to know that you have designs on my daughter. Have actually, in fact, the confounded cheek to get engaged to her without my permission, and we all know what getting engaged means in these modern times. Don't interrupt me. I also know the motives you must have for such behaviour. You think you're on to a good thing. You think Daddy will pay anything to get you safely married and you'll live the life of Riley ever after. Don't interrupt me. But you've made one serious mistake. My daughter hasn't a penny of her own. Not – one – single – penny.' Here he leaned back in his chair again and folded his arms. 'And finally,' he announced, 'if you were thinking of running away with her or anything silly of the sort, let me tell you it won't make a blind bit of difference. *Now* you may speak. If you can find anything to say.'

It ought to have been easy, but it wasn't. Really, he didn't know where to begin, and almost before the words were out of his mouth he realized that he'd begun in the wrong place.

'I don't want to marry her at all,' he said . . .

'You don't want to marry her! Well, you young hound, you may have to! I'm not having my daughter interfered with for nothing.'

'I haven't done anything to her! I don't know what she's told you, but I'm just a sort of friend. I hardly know her!'

With some trepidation, he noticed that Sir Gordon's face was slowly suffusing again to plum, but he felt pretty hot

himself. He remembered Minnie's voice on the telephone –
'I've got a very special reason for asking you' – and felt himself
blushing with rage. This, he soon realized, was misinterpreted
by Minnie's father who leaned forward suddenly and stabbing
a podgy finger at him said: 'You can't quite bring yourself to
say *that* without shame, can you? When you know all the time
the girl's pregnant. I suppose you'll tell me next that you had
nothing to do with that?'

'Yes. I *will* be telling you that. I mean I *am* telling you.
But I don't believe that either. She tells *lies*. She's always told
them,' he added, discovering this clearly for the first time. 'You
must know that. She's neurotic, or something.'

'Oh – we've spent a fortune on that nonsense. If we find
someone for her to go to, she doesn't stay with them. No
expense has been spared, believe me. But the fact remains, that
she *is* pregnant; can't keep her food down, been fainting, all
that sort of thing; dammit, she must be pregnant!'

'She might just be ill. I don't mean "just",' he amended
hastily, 'but if she's told you she's pregnant and it's me, ten to
one she's making it all up.'

'You've had nothing like that to do with her?'

'Nothing like that – no.'

Sir Gordon was palpably taken aback. 'I stopped her
allowance,' he said at last. 'To try and flush out whoever it was.
I thought it had worked because she asked if you could come
down, and I said why, and then she told me. All that. Naturally,
I thought you were after her money.'

'How could I be when she hasn't got any?'

'You must have known I was well-heeled. Don't tell me
you didn't know that.'

'She told me you were a lord and lived in a castle with a
deer park.' As he said this, he was conscious of treachery to the
wretched Minnie. *She* had said all that to please his mother;
she *was* maddening, of course, but she looked ill and was
probably off her rocker, and here he was almost colluding with

this awful man – getting himself off the hook by vilifying her. 'It was just a harmless joke,' he said weakly.

'I don't know about that – course, she was exaggerating a bit. After all, I've a title, and this isn't the only property I own, you know – not by a long chalk.'

It was almost as though he'd *tried* to be appeasing – as though the mention of the deer park was a kind of sucking up.

'Well – it would seem that you're *not* after my money, and that's one up to you. I'll make you a proposition. If you marry her and make a success of it, I'll give you a real job with prospects. Meanwhile, I'll pay you a lump sum (to be decided at some later date) to get out of this hairdressing caper on condition that you put the money down for a house – or a flat if that's what you turn out to afford. I've given up any hopes of her turning out like my Sheila: she's not going to better herself and I'm no snob. Mind you, there's nothing like a wife and child to give a chap a nudge up the ladder. And, if you feel discouraged at times, 'cos mind you, I'll work you *hard*, make no mistake about that, remember *I* did it. Think of me. Left school when I was fifteen and worked my way up from making the tea.' Self-satisfaction was making him sweat, and he pulled out a huge silk handkerchief with bull terriers on it to wipe his face. 'I've her interests at heart,' he finished, 'and there's no more I can do for her. Won't be sorry to have her off my hands!' He smiled as though this was a little joke that he knew Gavin would understand.

The enormity of this suggestion left Gavin momentarily speechless. Then he thought, of course, it was all quite simple – all he had to do was to say that he wanted no part of it, backing up this general statement with the salient point of not wanting to marry Minnie: that would do it. But it didn't. To his horror, Sir Gordon simply raised the price of the bribe: he'd buy them a house. Gavin explained all over again how much he didn't want any of it. Sir Gordon congratulated him on his shrewdness. 'We'll make a business man of you yet,' and added more financial inducements. At the end of what seemed to Gavin like about half an hour, but was probably only a few minutes, his future – married to Minnie – contained two houses, a three months' honeymoon in the West Indies, a directorship of one of Sir Gordon's subsidiary companies and an account of up to £500 a month at Harrods. 'My word, you're a sharp operator.' As the price went up, so did Sir Gordon's estimation of him: he seemed to admire greed almost as much as he admired dishonesty.

At his wits' end, Gavin said he would have to think it all over: he felt craven saying it, but it seemed to be, and in fact was, a possible way out.

'Take your time, my boy!' he cried. (He had completely stopped repeating Gavin's words after him: Gavin thought that that must be because he had – most unfortunately – stopped disapproving of him.) It also became clear to Gavin that his saying that he wanted to think it over was regarded as merely a form: he felt the tentacles of bonhomie closing in when Sir Gordon clapped him painfully on the back. 'One little point,' he said, lowering his voice. 'I shouldn't pass on any of this to the girl: not now, anyway. Savvy?' Gavin, who'd thought people only said that in books, said he wouldn't dream of it and he must be going.

'Enjoy your swim. We can have another talk before dinner.' Just then, the telephone rang, he walked with ponderous speed back to his desk, and his attention was deflected. He picked up the receiver and then made elaborate mime to Gavin about having to talk on it. Gavin escaped.

Into the hall. The front door was before him at the other end. He wasn't going swimming; not he – not on your life. He opened the door, shut it as softly as he could behind him and ran lightly down the drive. Reaching the road, he turned left and continued running. He had the fear – possibly irrational – that Minnie would discover he was no longer with her father and that then she would give chase in her car, and he simply did not feel equal to her tenacity. Twice he hid behind hedges when he heard a car but neither of them was hers. His luck held when he got to the station too; there was a train drawing in as he arrived and in spite of the crabbed and slow-motion efforts of the man in the ticket office he managed to catch it. He flung himself in an empty second-class compartment just as the train moved off. His heart was pounding from running. He was pouring with sweat and he was almost sobbing with the effort to get his breath back – and from relief.

CHAPTER TEN

AT Waterloo station, he went to a call box and rang Harry. The one thing he didn't want to do was to go home, in case she started ringing him, since he neither felt equal to dealing with her, nor with his mother *about* her. Harry was in. No, he wasn't doing anything that night, because he'd got a case of mangoes from a street market and was in the middle of making chutney. 'And Winthrop, of *course*, is going to Heaven, but I've told him I'm damned if I'm going with him. I can't stand the noise. You come round when you like, dear boy.'

The moment that he had settled this, he felt safer, and the situation he had escaped from seemed even more unreal than it had begun to feel in the train. On his way to Harry, he even started to try to imagine what life as Sir Gordon's son-in-law could possibly be like. A mixture of being bullied and being bored. In a way it would add up to an endless life round tables; tables with food on them, and tables with papers on them. There would also, of course, be Minnie, who presumably was well on her way to becoming as hellishly bored as her mother had said she was. But, when he thought of Minnie, he knew that there was something much wronger with her than that . . . It was easy to say that she was off her head; but that, too, seemed now to be a rather callous way of simply writing her off. It was in the train on his way to Harry that he began to feel bad about her, which irritated and unnerved him. What on earth could *he* do about it, after all? He hoped that there was absolutely nothing, but his uncertainty about this nagged at him. It opened up the whole question of how responsible was he meant to be for other people? And, if at all, to whom, and how much? He hadn't *invited* Minnie into his life; she had occurred and then clung like a little limpet. But then he hadn't invited Joan, either: it was she who had done the inviting, he had simply – thank God – gone along with her. He suddenly wondered whether he was one of those craven, passive people who hung about all their lives waiting for things to happen to them – merely reserving the right to complain if they weren't the right things.

If Harry hadn't made him go to that party, he wouldn't have met either Minnie or Joan. He certainly wouldn't have gone to it without being pushed. And, if he hadn't gone, he would have been at the opera the same night as Joan, but he wouldn't have known her so nothing would have happened. But if he was a different sort of person not knowing her would have made no difference. He made the resolution that, when Joan returned to London, it would be *he* who did the inviting and felt his body give a little lurch of assent. Certainly that party had changed his life; so how many parties had he *not* gone to that might have done the same thing? It had altered the Ladder of Fear: once he *knew* people, they were off it, whereas before, everybody had some sort of position on it. Excepting Harry. He was really looking forward to seeing Harry, to having a good long talk with him about – things.

He could smell the chutney on the stairs, and when Harry opened the door he released a great blast of it – so strong it brought tears to the eyes.

'You'll have to *bear* with me because we are nearing the potting stage and it keeps sticking.'

The glass coffee table was covered with the remains of lunch for two. Harry had darted straight back into the kitchen, so Gavin followed him.

'Winthrop's taken some Black Magic to his mother. He's lost interest in the culinary arts.' He was vigorously stirring a huge cauldron from which steam was rising; the odour of boiling vinegar and spices was overpowering.

'I know – if it was alcohol I should definitely be unable to walk straight,' Harry said cheerfully.

Gavin went to look at the blackish-brown mixture that bubbled and periodically spat at them.

'Put a kettle on, dear child. As soon as I've potted it, we can have some tea.'

Gavin put on the kettle and then went to the lavatory which was in the bathroom. The towel rail was hung with T-shirts inscribed with cheery/belligerent messages – Winthrop's, no doubt. This reminded him that he hadn't seen Winthrop since the night of the party, and that Winthrop had shown unmistakable signs of not liking him then. He remembered the powerful ease with which he handled people he didn't care for – like Spiro, for instance – and began to worry about what he would be like if he came back from visiting his mother in a bad temper.

'How *is* Winthrop?' he asked when he returned to the kitchen.

'Well, he's all right in him*self*, but he's restless. He's working for a mini-cab company now, because he wants to save enough to go to America when I get my holiday . . . I'm glad he's dropped the modelling because I don't think it brought out the best in him. We're going to San Francisco in the autumn. It's given him some kind of goal, but on the other hand he spends a fortune on these discos, and of course he meets all kinds of people there. You have to be very patient, but I expect one day he'll grow up and settle down. But if you're . . . fond of someone, you have to take the rough with the smooth.' He lifted a small amount of chutney out of the pan and put it on a saucer. 'Just want to see if it looks done when it's cooler. It's not as critical as jam, but on the other hand you don't want it slopping about in the jars.'

His eye, Gavin noticed, had faded to a livid yellow with

tinges of green. 'You'd better not buy any ashtrays when you're in San Francisco.'

'We always buy ashtrays, dear boy; for our collection.' Then he got the point and, feeling the wounded side of his face, he said: 'But, even if we didn't, *he'd* find something else. Winthrop's very resourceful when he's angry.'

'I got the impression he was angry with me last time I saw him.'

'When was that?'

'At the party. The famous party.'

'Oh – that! It was that wretched little quean Spiro he was angry with. He likes Joan, and he can't stand dishonesty.' He inspected his saucer. 'Right: I think we can go ahead.' He turned off the gas under the chutney and opened the oven door. A batch of Kilner jars filled the small oven.

'Why do you keep them in there?'

'They have to be hot when the chutney goes in, or they'd crack. Winthrop's fond of you. He's just a bit nervous of people who've been educated. Well, we all are, aren't we really? I mean, if education is relative, I suppose there's always one lot somewhere that we're afraid of. Winthrop really slipped through the net as far as formal education was concerned. His mother's working hours meant she was always asleep during the hours of education, and no one else seems to have bothered about seeing what he got up to during them. It has left him at something of a disadvantage . . .' He was pouring the chutney into the jars from a steaming jug; and standing too close to him (there wasn't much room) Gavin jolted his arm so that some of it spilled – down the side of a jar and on to the tray.

'Sorry!'

'Look – you go next door; I shan't be long. Put on a record if you like.'

He went, but he didn't put on a record. He didn't want to: he didn't *want* to do anything, he felt suddenly and completely fed up. He'd had a really awful day so far, and he'd come all this way to see what amounted to his only friend and all *he* did was make chutney and talk about his boy friend. It was no use his going home, because his mother would go on and *on* at him, and even if he escaped to his own room she would bring him angry trays. He had no privacy; he didn't even have his own place – like Harry – where he could do what he liked. And what did the rest of his life amount to? He worked for a man he loathed, but who would one day retire or die, and then where would he be? Come to that, his *parents* would die eventually, and *then* where would he be? Supposing Harry stayed in San Francisco, what would he do then? By now, having deprived himself of home, job and friends, he felt considerably more than fed up – he felt frightened. This was *his* life, but was anybody else faring much better? Could he, if it came to it, think of *anybody* who would claim to be, if not happy, at least content? Obviously the Munday family weren't; Joan, for all the marvellous things about her, could not be described as *happy*; his attitude to his mother, made up as it was of so much side-stepping, evasion and conciliatory gestures, was really based upon his certain, unspoken knowledge of how disappointing she had found her life; Harry was nearly always on the rack about Winthrop whose compensating features seemed to Gavin to be sketchy and unreliable – to say the least. Even his clients in the salon – God, think of them! – poor little Miss Wilming with her appalling stutter and her blatant loneliness; Mrs Blake, the one who'd been nearly, or quite, in tears all through her perm; even Mrs Courcel (what kind of life could be hers if she had nothing better to do than to come in nearly every day to have her hair fiddled about with?). And Muriel Sutton; *there* was somebody who wasn't getting anything they wanted out of life! And of his colleagues Iris had her terribly ill husband to worry about; she must spend all her spare time warding off his inevitable death which would leave her with nothing to worry about but being alone. Even Peter and Hazel, he reflected morosely, were probably heading for the rocks of strife and unhappiness: either Hazel wouldn't have a baby to please Peter and would secretly blame him for it, or she *would* have one, and Peter would drive her mad by replanning their economics. And so on. And what was he supposed to do with his life? Here he was, at thirty-one, tooling on in a job with no prospects, consoling himself with day-dreams that he could now see had no bearing at all upon reality, stuffing himself up with reading and record-playing (and he hadn't done much of either lately). In any case, the Arts were probably mere palliatives: a series of tricks that enabled people to get through their dreary lives. Without reason, he suddenly thought of the succession of his annual holidays; times when he had gone to places to look at them; the endless meals in small pensions or big package tour hotels – reading, a book propped up against his carafe of wine; spending God knew how much energy on not meeting people; trying, even abroad, to evade the unknown; to remain intact – and lonely – waiting for that wonderful girl who never turned up. People *had* made advances to him of course, but he had become expert at choking them off. Once, though, he now remembered, he had had to go to the lengths of pretending to be ill for a whole three days – until her package tour came to an end and she was safely gone. A very ordinary girl with sunburned shoulders – nowhere near the kind of girl he had in mind . . . But then Joan was nowhere near her either. Before that party, he *had* been content, in a way. He'd even been smug, congratulating himself upon all his interests, his nice home, his steady job. That had been when he was getting ready to go to the party, he remembered. And that was – good lord! – only a week ago! In one week he had changed from being somebody to whom hardly anything happened, into someone to whom things never seemed to *stop* happening.

So why was he so fed up? Because – apart from the night with Joan – it had been seriously suggested (by Marge) that he should consider marrying Muriel Sutton. It had been more pressingly suggested (by Sir Gordon) that he should marry Minnie and become an industrial stooge. *That* was what the week had consisted of (apart from the night with Joan). And it was typical of Life that *she* had immediately gone off to another country. He might never hear from her again, and if one sexual (and romantic) encounter in thirty-one years was his ration, he was just about due for one more night before he dropped dead . . .

'Sorry to be so long – one of the jars cracked – made a terrible mess – hey, what's up?'

He took his head out of his hands: 'Nothing much.'

Harry put the tea tray on the floor and started to clear off the lunch plates. 'I know what that means.'

'What does it mean?'

'It means, "I'm not going to tell you unless you take me seriously."' He took the dirty plates into the kitchen, and came back with a J-cloth. 'Can't have all these crumbs. Winthrop will make crumbs of *anything*.'

'Oh, do *shut up* about Winthrop!'

'Okay,' said Harry equably. 'Let's have a serious conversation about Gavin.' He poured tea into two mugs that Gavin noted irritably as being highbrow pottery, and started opening a packet of biscuits.

'Now you're probably having a panic about how much to tell me,' he observed. 'Well, I'll tell you one thing. Everything you say here to me will be strictly private. I'm very discreet. And you'd be surprised at what people do tell me.'

Gavin felt himself blushing: Harry was dead right; he *had* been trying to decide whether to tell him or not about Joan, and had just about decided not to. 'I'm not sure where to begin,' he said. 'It's not exactly just what's been happening – it's how what's been happening has made me feel. I've been thinking about it, while you were in the kitchen, and I suppose it all started with that party. It seems ages ago, but it was only last week. You know I'm not much good at parties.' Then he remembered how Harry had been feeling by the end of it. 'Perhaps you don't want to think about the party,' he said.

'I don't mind. It had its awkward moments, I admit, but otherwise it seemed to me more or less what they're usually like.'

'You mean Joan's parties?'

'I mean large unknown parties. They're always a bit of a risk. That's what most people like about them.'

'Oh.'

'Not you – I can see that. You're not one of the world's risk-takers, are you?' He said it so nicely, that Gavin found that he didn't mind someone else knowing that about him.

'I suppose not.'

'Anyway – you were at the party.'

'Yes. Well, I don't know whether you remember but when we went down in the lift there was a girl with me? She was wearing a red dress.'

'Oh yes.'

'Well, I could *not* get rid of her! She gave me a lift in her car – I thought she was just taking me to the station, but she took me all the way to here – where I'd left my bike – and *then* she followed me all the way home. Said she had nowhere to sleep.'

'Your mother must have had something to say about that.'

'She didn't know till next morning.' He could tell Harry this bit; Harry understood about mothers. 'At breakfast she pretended to be the daughter of an earl or a duke or something and Mum enjoyed that. Anyway, after breakfast I got rid of her, and I thought, "That's that." Not a bit of it. She turned up at the salon . . .' And he told Harry all about *that* bit: the basement flat in Chalk Farm and the silly picture she'd made. 'But that's not the worst of it.' And he told Harry all about going to Weybridge and the awful house – Harry was fascinated by that and kept asking for more detail – and the lunch and then Sir Gordon's duologue with him in his study (which also didn't have a single book in it, he remembered, except for the telephone directories in mock leather folders), and finally about his running away. When he had finished, he waited for Harry to say something. Eventually, Harry said: 'And then what?'

'That's all.'

'What's worrying you then, Gavin?'

'Well – ' he felt himself beginning to flounder. 'I mean, there's obviously something wrong with her; I mean, look at all those lies! Telling her father we were engaged without even mentioning it to me!'

'She sounds demented. So what's your problem?'

'You sound as though you think I haven't got one.'

'No, I don't. I just sound as though I want to know what it is.'

'Well – apart from the fact that I bet that's not the last of her, I feel – sort of – well, responsible in a way.'

'What way?'

'Well, she's sick, isn't she? I mean, it's not only the lies – she looks ill. And she never seems to eat anything. And she's always trying to shock people.'

'Trying to get attention, I expect. Wouldn't you, with parents like that?'

'Yes, but so what? Those are the parents she's got. I can't help feeling she needs help.'

'Do you want to help her?'

'I've told you, I don't want anything to do with her . . .'

'Well, there you are then.'

'No – I'm *not*! I'm sure there isn't anybody else to help her, and she needs help.'

'But you wouldn't be any good at it, if you really don't want anything to do with her. You can't help people you don't like. It doesn't work.'

'I can't just abandon her. One reason I'm feeling so bad now is because I ran away from her this afternoon. Just left her to it.'

'Listen, Gavin, I won't pry, but you sound as though you've been to bed with this girl and that's made you feel guilty about her.'

'Oh no! Nothing like that!'

'All right. If you're really feeling bad about her, you'd better see her when she's in London. Tell her it's no go with you – absolutely nix – but tell her she ought to get some help because she's screwed up, and after meeting her parents you don't blame her. She might take that from you.'

'And she might not.'

'Well, that's up to her, isn't it? You'll have done your bit.'

'It seems a pretty feeble bit.'

'Well, your feelings for her are on the frail side, aren't they? For God's sake, Gavin, you're not Jesus Christ. It's difficult enough to give the right things to one person if you *love* them; don't think you can do the right thing by anyone you meet. You live in a dream world, dear boy.'

'I don't think waiting for the right person to turn up is living in a dream world.'

'How *right* they are is relative, isn't it? You think someone completely *perfect* will one day put in an appearance and that'll be it. They won't. And it wouldn't be if they did. Because they wouldn't stay like that. Nobody ever stays like anything. The most you can hope for is that with any luck you'll both want to move in approximately the same direction.'

There was a short silence. Harry drank tea.

'But, on your basis, how do you ever find anyone? I mean, why would one person be any better than another?'

Harry gave his sly smile. 'Chemistry, dear child. That's always working for you – you just have to keep tuned.' He tried the teapot but it was empty. 'I expect you're still suffering the after-effects of her father's proposition.'

'I don't think so. I mean, I didn't have any doubts about turning that down.'

'No – but it's always a trifle unsettling to be presented with an entirely different way of life. It presents one with a choice which one would like to think one didn't have.'

'Why wouldn't one like having a choice?'

'One might *like* having one from time to time, I suppose, but broadly speaking one likes to feel that one enjoys one's work, or that one *has* to do it. In the latter respect, a choice is rather undermining. Mark you. I'm speaking from Number One the groove.'

'You mean, however awful an alternative seems you go on feeling that it might have been better than you thought it would be when you turned it down.'

'Right. Want more tea?'

Gavin shook his head. 'I think being offered something like that does make me look at how things are,' he said. 'I mean, things like my still living at home.'

'Ah! I agree with you there. I think that is something you should possibly review . . .'

He was interrupted by hearing the key in the door, and a moment later Winthrop appeared.

'Oh hullo, Gavin,' he said, amiably enough. 'Just the person I wanted to see.' He unzipped his windcheater on the black leather chesterfield. 'There's a fair pong in here.'

'I told you, I was making the chutney. He wants you to cut his hair,' Harry added, as Winthrop went into the kitchen.

'I haven't got my scissors.'

'We've got some.'

People never understood, Gavin thought, resigned to it, that you didn't cut hair with any old scissors. Still . . .

'How was your mother?' Harry called to the kitchen.

'She was very low.' Winthrop appeared at the door; he was stirring Nescafé and milk together in a mug. 'That place gets worse and worse, and none of the old bags in it dares to complain. I saw the supper trays as I was leaving. I had to ask one of the staff what the hell it was. And do you know what it *was?*'

'What was it then?'

'A *nut* cutlet! And some tinned Russian salad. "You've got a nerve giving them that," I told them. Full of nourishment, they said. My Mum's not interested in nourishment, she wants something she can fancy. But I didn't like to make too much trouble.' He disappeared as the kettle whistled and returned with a steaming mug. 'Those places would get anyone down. The television's lousy – always going off and it's not even colour. She liked the Black Magic. Scoffed the lot. Said she didn't want to hand them round. I took her a miniature Drambuie as well. She liked that all right. She says they can't even make a decent cup of tea. She asked me to take her to the pub.' He looked really sad, Gavin realized. 'I couldn't,' he said. 'She's still got that ulcer on her leg and she's on antibiotics. "I've had more men than I've had hot dinners in this place," she said; she couldn't keep off the food and how awful it was – nothing else to think about, and she says all the others do is talk about all the things they used to do in their past lives. *She* can't do that. "You should have sold your story to a Sunday newspaper," I told her – that made her smile, but she said she has her pride.'

'I expect she was very pleased to see you,' Harry said gently.

'It's not much, though, is it? An hour or so once a fortnight.' He yawned. 'Christ! It's no good being old. I'm just not going in for it.'

'You'll have me.'

'*You!* You'll be old too! Even older!' Gavin didn't know whether Winthrop noticed the look on Harry's face or not because he was on his way to the kitchen again. 'Chutney's good – fucking hot, though.' He came back sucking his finger. Then, with unexpected, and therefore even more charming, charm, he asked Gavin if he would give his hair a bit of a tidy-up, and Gavin, more to please Harry than anything else, said that he would. It was agreed that it should be cut wet, and

Winthrop retired to have a bath. He was a long time having it, and Gavin helped Harry wash up the chutney-making apparatus; they talked about music and everything got calmer.

Winthrop finally emerged with a scarlet towel wrapped round his waist, his auburn curls standing out all over his head in glistening corkscrews. Harry fetched a dustsheet, and the scissors, which were not good, but not impossible, and Gavin seated his client on a kitchen stool which was just about the right height.

'Don't want too much off, but it's too long at the back.' His shoulders were milk white, and smooth as silk.

'I need a comb.'

'Fetch him a comb.'

'You two going to have a nice highbrow evening?' he inquired when Harry came back with it.

'We hadn't made any particular plan. Why don't you change your mind and join us? We could find a good movie. Have some curry at the Standard.'

'I told you – I'm off to Heaven.'

'I know you told me – I just thought you might change your mind.'

'Well, you just thought – wrong. I'm off for a little bleeding *fun*.'

'Okay, Winthrop – I only asked.'

'It's when you *only* do things that you get on my wick.'

'What's Heaven like?' Gavin asked, to fill a rather black silence.

'It's just a disco.' Gavin had realized that. After a pause, Winthrop added: 'It's where you meet people; it's very good for that – isn't it, Harry?'

'If you *want* to meet people, yes, it is. Some of us do, some of us don't.'

'Oh – fascinating! The trouble with you is you're jealous!'

Harry said steadily: 'That's what it is.'

Winthrop seemed slightly taken aback at this because he

was silent for a bit before repeating, more or less to himself: 'That's it. You're jealous.'

It was almost, Gavin thought, as though they had found a solution. The atmosphere lightened; Harry said he was going to write the chutney labels and went to find them in the kitchen. Winthrop in tones of affection said: 'He's never liked cruising – I can't think why not. After all, that's how he met me.'

Gavin said: 'He's very fond of you.' He had wanted to say 'loves you' but felt a bit shy.

'I'm fond of him. He knows that, really. But Harry believes in love, you know – it makes him narrow-minded. He has fixed ideas.'

'I think that's the lot.' He brushed the loose hair from Winthrop's shoulders. He didn't want to go on talking about Harry when he was only in the kitchen.

Winthrop went to get dressed and Harry painstakingly wrote out Mango Chutney on twelve labels. Gavin had a look at *Time Out* to see whether there were any enticing films, but he couldn't find one that they both wanted to see. When Winthrop emerged in his white jeans and a black T-shirt, Harry started talking about Truffaut to Gavin while Winthrop got into his windcheater, and in the end it was he who went over to Harry and kissed him. 'I'm off,' he said. 'Thanks for doing my barnet, Gavin. Have a highbrow old time. Don't do anything I wouldn't do.' And he went.

Harry's narrow nose was quivering slightly. Gavin said: 'Shall we have a beer?'

'Yes, let's.'

Gavin got his Wilhelm IIs out of his pocket. 'Like one of these?'

'No thanks – yes, I will.'

Gavin said: 'We could go and get an Indian take-away and play records?'

'Yes. Right. We'll do that.'

After a minute, he said: 'We could play something now. Something heartening.'

So they played Mozart's clarinet quintet, and that did the trick, as always, Gavin thought afterwards.

'It's very marvellous, isn't it?' Harry said, and Gavin felt a surge of comfort about them feeling the same.

They went together to the Indian, and got dhal, and chicken biriani and okra in a dry sauce and some plain parathas. When they got back, Harry put it all in the oven while they sliced an onion, and put the smallest new pot of chutney on the tray with two more cans of beer.

'We were talking about you setting up on your own.'

'We'd begun to talk about it. The thing is, I know in some ways it would be a good thing, but I feel rather daunted about how to start.' (I might as well *talk* about it, he thought; just to feel what it feels like to take it seriously.)

Harry fetched the food and set it on the table. They were both hungry, and concentrated for a while on eating. Then Harry said:

'I have the feeling that you've only told me the tip of the iceberg. Your week, I mean.'

Gavin had a moment's panic. Did Harry know, or guess about Joan? What nonsense, how could he? To gain time, and because he felt he should have said it before, he said: 'Chutney's marvellous.' Then he thought, 'Harry's my friend: he won't let me down.' So he told Harry about meeting Joan at the opera, and said that he had had dinner with her, and added, rather lamely, that he had liked her very much.

'Yes: she's an unusual type of person. Winthrop says she would be very powerful if she wasn't so hooked on that layabout.'

'Does Winthrop know her well, then?'

'He *knows* her.' He finished his beer. 'Winthrop has instinct about people. He's hardly ever wrong. Of course it makes him rather dashing. And, of course, he's quite different when you're alone with him.'

Why 'of course', Gavin wondered? But then he thought that, in some senses, most people *were*. Before he could reply, Harry said:

'People confide in him. She told him that her father was homo – but he never came out with it.'

'Joan did?'

'We were talking about her,' Harry pointed out. 'Have you met Dmitri?'

'No. Have you?'

'Briefly.'

'What's he like?'

Harry thought for a bit. 'Stunning to look at,' he said at last. 'And full of charm. You know, the kind you like to think you're impervious to until you actually meet it face to face – and then you find you're just like everyone else. He's perfectly conscious of it, of course – uses it all the time to get what he wants. He's like a very *experienced* ruthless child.'

'Does he love Joan?'

'You must be joking. He loves Dmitri; that's who he loves.'

'But she loves him?'

'She's mad about him,' Harry said absently. 'Like some coffee?'

'I would.'

While they were clearing things up and Harry was making coffee, he said: 'I have a feeling that a certain party has rather cleverly *sidestepped* the main issue. We were talking about you – remember?'

'I thought we'd finished that.'

'Just as you like. But I wouldn't have thought that your little excursion to darkest Weybridge was entirely responsible for how you were feeling when you arrived.'

He thought back to how he had been feeling when he

arrived. Guilty about the present, and hopeless about the future; or something like that. He'd got over the salient feature of the Joan bit without telling Harry about it, but in any case that hadn't been what had been making him feel awful. It was much more to do with seeing people in traps – Minnie's awful mother and Minnie herself, and Peter and Hazel in a different sort of trap, and even Jenny, he supposed, and then realizing that he felt trapped himself – by Mr Adrian and Mum. He tried to explain some of this to Harry.

'Well, you have remedies there, haven't you?' Harry remarked. 'I mean you could leave the salon and work for someone else, and you could leave home and set up on your own.'

'But how do I know that the someone else wouldn't turn out to be just like Mr Adrian?'

'You don't, but you could take some steps to avoid it. I mean, you are, or you ought to be, an expert on Mr Adrian, so you ought to recognize any likeness to him in anyone else who interviewed you. You could give that a try. After all, you've got a lot of experience, and anybody would take notice of you if you'd been in the same place so long.' Then he added rather irritatingly: 'That's what Winthrop's so good at. Spotting bastards.'

'He was wrong about Spiro,' Gavin pointed out.

'I grant you he got a bit carried away by Spiro . . . Sex does rather go to his head from time to time.'

It seemed to Gavin to go to everywhere where Winthrop was concerned, but he didn't want to hurt Harry's feelings, so he picked up the coffee tray and carried it back to the living room.

Then he said: 'It's all very well to talk about me getting out, but where to? I've managed to save five thousand, but that's the lot. That's not going to get me very far with a flat.'

'It would. You could get a mortgage with that much to put down.'

'Then I'd have to be in a good job and not leave Adrian and wander about unemployed.'

'Who said you'd be unemployed? You're just the right age with the right experience to get another job. Probably pick and choose one.'

'In my work, you have to be able to say roughly how many clients you'll bring to the new place. I mean how many from the old one who'll follow you.'

'Well?'

'*I* don't know. I haven't thought about it. There's nothing very special about me.'

'Well, you'd start by counting up how many clients always ask for you – won't have anyone else, wouldn't you? It's probably a percentage of them.'

It all seemed to make sense, and Gavin began to feel quite frightened.

'I'll have to think about it.'

'You do that. I agree you'd be better off tackling one problem at a time. But nothing venture, nothing win as the saying goes.'

Gavin recognized that the cliché – or maddeningly right old saying – was one of Harry's ways of closing conversations. After it, they played a Lipatti record of Bach and Scarlatti, and then Gavin said that, as he hadn't got his bike, he'd better be getting home.

On the train back to Barnet he started worrying about whether Minnie would have called, and what his mother would be like about all that, or as much of all that as she knew. This relieved him from worrying about his conversation with Harry, but he knew that that, too, was lying in wait for him. He told himself he was extremely tired, and by the time he got out at Barnet and started to walk down Meadway he had the beginnings of a headache and was longing to take his lenses out.

The moment that he was in the house he knew that something was wrong. There were sounds of tremendous activity coming from the kitchen and the television was switched off.

'Is that you, Gavin?'

'Yes, Mum.'

He went into the kitchen, where she was mashing an enormous quantity of potato.

'I've had some very bad news,' she said; she stopped mashing and looked straight at him. 'It's your Aunty Sylvia. She's been in a terrible accident! Terrible,' she repeated, her voice shaking. Gavin went and put his arm round her. In spite of seldom seeing her, she was devoted to this sister.

'Oh, Gavin!' she cried and began to weep. 'She might never have taken that bus! She usually caught the earlier one. It was Timmie's music lesson!'

'Timmie was with her?'

'Oh, Gavin – he's dead! He didn't live a minute. They found him with his little arms round his violin. She's in hospital. She hasn't come round – in a coma – of course she doesn't know. I'm going down first thing in the morning. To see to the other children – and sit with Sylve a bit. Phil wants me to tell her. If she does come round.'

He hugged her – she was rocking herself against him in his arms.

'Come and sit down, Mum: it's all right, I'll come with you.'

He led her to the battered chair in which his father watched telly and felt for and found his handkerchief. He sat on the arm of the chair while she wiped her eyes and furiously blew her nose.

'Where's Dad?'

'He's off to see Lennie to tell him to look after the business. He's coming with me. That poor little boy! What did he ever do to deserve that!'

'Is she hurt very badly?'

'She's got concussion and her leg's broken, but there's

something wrong with her back – that's the worst of it – she's in intensive care, Phil says they don't say – oh, Gavin – he was her only son!' She clutched him. 'I know what I would feel like if – '

'It's all right, Mum, I'm here. Would you like me to make you a nice cup of tea?'

'I would, dear. I must get on with my pies.'

'You're not taking pies with you?'

'Of course not! They're for you. I don't know when I'll be back, but it won't be for at least a week, I shouldn't wonder, so I'm making you six pies for the freezer; three fish and three shepherds.'

'You really needn't bother. It'll do me good to fend for myself.'

'Since when have you done any cooking? I don't want to come back and find you laid low with food poisoning. They'll all be in the freezer and all you'll have to do is take them out and put them in the oven and warm them up . . . I must do something,' she added, and he saw the point of that.

So he made the tea and she topped her pies, and quite soon his father came in.

'Terrible business,' he said to Gavin.

'How did it happen, do you know?'

He shook his head. 'It was a lorry jack-knifed at a round-about – *I* don't know. First Phil knew about it was when they rang him to go to the hospital. The little boy died at once. Terrible thing. Tell your mother you want biscuits: she hasn't eaten anything for her tea.'

They had the tea – and biscuits – although she only started one, put it down, forgot about it, telling Gavin to be sure to take the milk in in the mornings and to lock up properly before he went to work, and to ring Marge from his work in the morning to tell her what had happened – 'I daresay she'd give you a nice meal one evening, only mind you put the lights on before you go out' – and that she'd put clean sheets on his bed that ought to last him, but if they didn't, he was to take the bottom left hand pair from the pile in the linen cupboard. She would ring him tomorrow evening to tell him how poor Sylvia was. After a good deal of this, she ran out of injunctions and things to say generally, and began to look very unhappy again.

Gavin said: 'Perhaps you ought to go to bed, Mum. Get a good night's rest before the journey.'

'I shan't be able to sleep for thinking of that poor little boy – and my own sister!' Her tears began again, but she took out Gavin's handkerchief and blew her nose with repressive violence. 'You're quite right, dear. I shan't be any use to them if I keep breaking down. I'll just lay up for breakfast, and then I'll be off.'

'I'll do that, Mum. I'd like to,' he added.

For once, she let him. He gave her a good-night hug and a kiss, and she didn't tell him not to be silly. Mr Lamb gave Gavin a lugubrious wink before departing: he had a remarkable range of winks.

When he had finished downstairs and was in his room, the shock of what had happened impinged. Timmie was his youngest cousin: he had hardly known him – in fact had only met him twice when Sylvia had brought her children up to London. Sylvia was very much younger than his mother, and she, unlike her sister, had married late; his cousins had not been contemporaries, and the last time he had seen Timmie had been two years ago, when he had been nine. Now he was eleven – and dead. No life at all; a young child. The fearful impartiality of life appalled him. He remembered, that, egged on by his mother, Timmie had said that he wanted to be a violinist when he grew up, if he was good enough, he had added. Then his mother's phrase about little arms round the violin recurred, and he remembered that when he was a boy – not so very much older than Timmie – he had heard of the French violinist, Ginette Neveu, dying in an air crash. It had struck him at the time, because he had just bought a record of hers. She, too, had died cradling her instrument, in a vain effort to protect it. This made him cry – for both of them.

Afterwards, when he lay in bed with hot eyes and a much lighter feeling in his chest, he thought of Timmie's sisters, Molly and Barbara, having lost their brother, and wondering whether their mother was going to recover: or not. He felt he ought to send up some sort of prayer that she should, but he hadn't much hope of God (if He was there) taking much notice of somebody who didn't pray the rest of the time. 'I just hope she gets better,' he said – whispered – in the dark. As he was falling asleep he remembered that tomorrow he was going to be on his own here; funny – after that talk with Harry about leaving and setting up somewhere. Well, he could look on the next week as a sort of practice. No dreams: he couldn't take anything more in, but as though his subconscious was some kind of salesman, it produced a flickering catalogue of what was in stock: lunch with the Mundays but he was the only one without clothes; himself running – *from* something *to* Joan; riding his bike and trying to explain how wonderful Mozart was to an owl who could not fly fast enough to keep up; standing on the edge of a cliff and having to jump because there was someone lying hurt on the roundabout below; standing in a pool of water, unable to move because all the people round him couldn't decide what he was, 'Hello, Froggy; we're not glad to see you're back'; swimming with his feet horribly tangled in all the red hair, and it was raining, each drop slamming on the water making such a noise he couldn't hear himself speak until he was on a small, round island where he couldn't hear Harry warning him – he couldn't hear anyone if he didn't want to . . .

CHAPTER ELEVEN

H E was amazed at how he became used to being in the house without his parents. The first morning had felt a bit odd; Mrs Lamb had washed up their breakfasts – eaten at God-knew-what hour – and left him a final note about locking up carefully – even if he just went out to buy a paper. He had felt guilty at not being up to see them off, however it had not occurred to him that they could possibly be going earlier than himself. But his mother got extremely nervous about trains – not trusting them in the least not to leave twenty minutes earlier than they had promised to, and she was determined not to give any train the chance of doing that to her. So, to catch say a ten o'clock from Paddington, she would probably have left the house at seven. He had washed up his own breakfast, and then left in a hurry because he hadn't allowed time in his morning schedule for even such a small addition. He had arrived in time for Mr Adrian to notice that he was late: to look at his watch, click his teeth and say that there was something he wanted a few words about whenever Gavin could spare the time. Gavin succeeded in not sparing it all the morning which was a busy one.

Jenny had stumped up to him wearing her cork wedge sandals and said:

'Have you done the list?'

'What list? Oh – no – no, I haven't. I've been thinking about it though,' he added, partly because it was true, but chiefly because she had looked so transparently disappointed. They had worked hard together all the morning, which included Mrs Wagstaffe and her dog, Mrs Courcel, and an elderly lady who wanted her long, dank grown-out perm cut off. At one point, he had nipped out to the back for a quick cup of coffee and was shortly joined by Peter.

Gavin said: 'Thanks very much for Friday evening. Hope Hazel's okay.'

'She came round in the end. I did all the washing up – I think that made a difference to her. Women are quite tricky when you're married to them,' he explained.

'I suppose they would be.'

'What we never got around to asking you was, what did you think about the dinner?'

'Oh – fine.'

'I expect you to be perfectly frank.'

'I enjoyed it.'

'You didn't think the main course was just a touch way out?'

'Um – no. How do you mean exactly?'

'For Hazel's parents, I mean. They live in West Byfleet.'

'I suppose it depends if you like aubergine.'

'But it didn't taste of *them*! I quite agree if it had *tasted* of them, they might find it a bit much. But with all that miso and bean curd I don't think the average person would guess.'

Gavin tried to finish his coffee, but it was too hot.

'Still, I asked you, and if that's what you think, we must take it into account . . .'

'Mr Gavin! Client's ready.'

'Thank you, Jenny. I enjoyed it,' he lied again and saw Peter's stern missionary face relax a little. On his way through to the salon, he remembered that he hadn't rung Marge. In the end, he had had to leave that until his lunch hour (which was very late). He couldn't risk using the salon's telephone unless Mr Adrian went out, which he didn't.

Marge hadn't answered, so he hadn't got hold of her until after work.

'Poor Mum,' she said. 'She's very close to Sylvia. And the little boy! Oh dear! How long is she going to stay in Swansea? Well, if you ever feel lonely, pop over to us, but I expect it's a chance for you to whoop it up a bit there all on your own. Don't worry, I'll ring Mum at Uncle Phil's.'

That first evening, he had gone home, realized he'd forgotten to take in the milk and walked into the empty house. It did not smell of washing as usual – just rather fusty. He had opened some windows, got one of the pies out of the freezer and put it in the oven. Then he had looked in the paper to see if there was anything he wanted to watch on television, but there wasn't. He had looked round the room; it was spotlessly neat with absolutely nothing in it that was not functional, and it had seemed smaller without his parents there.

It wasn't really the kind of room he liked, at all. He had decided then that he did not want to spend the evening in it. So he had made himself a supper tray, turned the oven to low and had had a bath – longer even than the ones his mother countenanced on a Sunday morning: only now he was able to have it with the doors wide open to his room as well as the bathroom, and his gramophone as loud as he liked. Also, when he had eventually finished his bath, he had realized that there was absolutely no need to put all his clothes on again. That first evening he had spent in his pyjamas and dressing gown, but he had felt vaguely uncomfortable in them – a bit like a convalescent. People who went about in their dressing gowns probably had special ones made . . . After that, he settled for jeans and a shirt too old to wear with a tie. He ate his pie and played the B flat posthumous sonata – one of his favourite works of Schubert and absolutely his favourite piano sonata. Then he had looked at a book on Greek islands that was overdue back at the library because he'd never got down to it. For some reason that he wasn't at all clear about, he couldn't summon the enthusiasm for his holiday that he usually had. Did he really want to go to Greece entirely by himself? And how did one – come to that – go on a holiday partly with someone? Even if he found somebody who said that that was what they wanted, how could he know whether their partly was the same as his? He shut up the book. His holiday wasn't until September, so he had plenty of time to think about it. That first evening, he had decided that he wouldn't wash up his supper; he'd leave the tray and do it when he had more to wash up. He'd watered his plants and cleaned his shoes and listened to more music. Minnie, and what was becoming of her, had crossed his mind: surprisingly, she hadn't bombarded him with telephone calls. The family situation in Swansea had recurred, several times, but his mother hadn't rung him. Somehow it all seemed rather distant. He had ended by going to bed earlier than usual with a novel by Paul Scott that had won some literary prize and also seemed to him to be a very good read.

The next day it had suddenly struck him at work that he didn't particularly want to go home, get out another pie and do generally what he had done the previous evening. He rang Harry, but Harry was going to a party with Noel and Winthrop. He was invited, but declined . . . It was a bad day at work: everything seemed to go – not wrong, exactly – but not quite right. Jenny seemed uncharacteristically absent-minded, and apathetic when he reminded her. In the end – when she had let him run completely out of papers during a tricky perm – he snapped at her. She looked at him for a moment with her eyes filling with tears and then she simply ran out of the salon – to the back . . . She returned in time to wash the client – very pale and refusing to meet his eye. He managed to catch her during the lunch hour – outside on the stairs.

'Hey – what's the matter, Jenny?'

'Nothing.' She continued walking down the stairs below him.

'Look. Something is. I've never known you wash hair

leaving conditioner in, *or* forget things all the time. Something must be wrong. Is it Andrew?'

'He's all right.'

This only made it clear that something else wasn't. He suddenly wondered whether she was sulking about the list that he still hadn't made for her.

'I've started the list for you.'

She said nothing for a bit, and then – and he could hardly hear her – thanked him. 'But it doesn't matter, really,' she said.

'Like a sandwich?'

She shook her head.

They had reached the passage on the ground floor. She said: 'I'm going for a walk, and I'll pull myself together.' She said it as though he had told her she must. She walked quickly away from him out into the street.

In the sandwich bar he met Iris drinking Espresso. He had a coffee with her and told her that he was worried about Jenny.

'I expect she's just a bit out of sorts today,' Iris said with a delicate emphasis.

'It's not like her.'

She looked at him kindly: 'We can't always be like ourselves all the time. She's nearing the end of her apprenticeship, isn't she? I expect she went for a job and didn't get it . . .'

It seemed a reasonable and likely answer . . .

In the afternoon he was caught by Mr Adrian who gave him a long and reasoned discourse on the results of everybody getting to work later and later which culminated in he, Mr Adrian, being clean out of business. Just as he reached this interesting – and to Gavin quite delightful – conclusion, Daphne phoned through from reception to ask Gavin to come and look at the book with a view to fitting someone in. When he got there, Daphne looked at him with a wealth of no expression and said: 'I'm afraid they've rung off now.' The most uniting thing about the salon, he thought, was the way in which everybody hated Mr Adrian.

His afternoon consisted of a succession of routine washes and sets; Jenny had returned punctually and he felt her making an effort to do what was required of her. They both behaved as if nothing had happened until, about half an hour before they closed, she said: 'I'm sorry I was so scatty this morning.' He realized that she found saying that an effort, since she started to blush, and with no thought at all he heard himself suggesting that she should come over to his place to hear some records, and even while he was wondering why the *hell* he'd said that, he heard her saying that she would like to . . .

'Do you mean this evening?'

'No – no, I don't. I didn't mention any particular evening, actually.'

'Well, that's good, because I couldn't have come tonight; my mother's going out.' There was a pause, and then she said: 'But I could tomorrow.'

Then she said: 'And if you could find me a book – a good one, I mean, but one I could get into, I'd be able to read it on the train, you see.'

'Yes. Okay, I'll find you one.' He turned to go, but she said:

'Look. I don't know where you live. Your address.'

'I live in Barnet, New Barnet, to be exact.'

'Oh. How do I get there?'

He thought rapidly. If she came back with him, he'd have no time to get anything ready. On the other hand, it was a hell of a journey from Kilburn. 'I'll fetch you on the bike,' he said.

'Right. Thanks.'

So here he was, on evening number two, having eaten pie number two (fish this time) in the kitchen, because he'd done some shopping on his way home and had to arrange the food in the fridge and see that he hadn't forgotten anything. He was no cook. After much thought, and resisting asking Harry's expert advice, he had gone to the best grocer in Barnet and bought a tin of expensive lobster soup, a small carton of single cream, and half a pound of ham cut from the bone. Then he'd had to go to another shop to buy a lettuce and tomatoes and a pineapple. He'd have to buy the bread tomorrow. He washed up yesterday's and that evening's pie suppers and laid a tray for himself and Jenny. Then he went up to tackle his room. During these activities he was conscious of feeling excited at the prospect of entertaining someone, and apprehensive about entertaining Jenny (though there were, of course, a good many girls or women about whom he'd have felt a good deal worse). After all, he'd known her – in a way – for a long time. He was – in a way – doing her a favour. The prospect of actually imparting knowledge to someone else made him feel responsible but it was also rather exciting. He looked carefully round his room trying to imagine how it would seem to someone coming into it for the first time. The first thing that he supposed they would notice was that it was indubitably a bedroom. There was his rather large bed. Supposing she thought he'd asked her – especially when his parents were away – to come over and spend the evening in his *bedroom* and merely pretended about the records? After all, there was the whole house they could be in. But the gramophone was in his room; parts of it were delicate and some parts were rather on their last legs – it was out of the question to move it. Could he move the bed? Of course he couldn't. It had had to be dismantled to get it up the narrow stairs – a task that would be quite beyond him. Perhaps he could make it look less like a bed? Make it seem it was a sort of sitting room he sometimes slept in? He tried putting the cushions from his red velvet chaise-longue on to the bed, but this made it look wantonly voluptuous as though it was *asking* for people to sprawl on it. He tried surrounding the open side of it with his larger potted plants: but this made it look like a secret den in a jungle, him Gavin her Jenny stuff, and drew attention to it more than ever.

In the end, he settled for laying out an unnecessarily large quantity of records all over it in neat rows as though for inspection. That certainly made the room look as though it was one in which one played records rather than . . . anything else. At this point the telephone rang, and he went down to the hall to answer it.

'Gavin?'

'Yes, Mum.'

'Is that you?'

'Yes, Mum.'

'She's come round, but she's still very weak. She's going to pull through, they say; but they don't want her told about Timmie till she's recovered more from the shock. I'll be staying a while longer, because Phil needs help with the girls. Are you all right, Gavin?'

'I'm fine.'

'Is the house all right?'

'Yes. How's Dad?'

'Nothing's the matter with *him*. He's in the garden all day: just comes in for his meals.' She said this in the tone of voice that made him sound like a cat. 'Gavin!' she added.

'Yes, Mum?'

'When you've got through the pies you'd better go to Sainsbury's and buy yourself a nice pork pie. That should last you a day or two. But whatever you do, don't you go eating food out of tins. Mind you don't do that.'

'No, Mum.'

'I can't be in two places at once. All right, Gavin. I'd better be ringing off, we're not millionaires.'

'No. I see that. Good-bye then, Mum.'

'Good-bye, Gavin. I'll let you know if there's any change – either way.' She rang off.

The telephone reminded him of Minnie. It was strange that she hadn't rung at all. No, it wasn't really. Any ordinary person who'd been ditched as he'd ditched her on Sunday would feel that that was that. They might be angry about it, but pride would prevent most people from any further efforts to get in touch. But Minnie was not an ordinary person – in that sense: she was a bit mad or something. Well, Harry had said that if he really felt bad about her, he ought to go and see her and tell her she needed help. That's what he'd better do. Upstairs again, he realized that all the records would have to come off the bed so that he could sleep in it, and put back tomorrow preferably before he went to work. In his bath he thought that Chopin and Degas might be a good double to start Jenny with, but he lay until the water was cold, unable to think which book would catch her.

'I didn't know you had a car.'

'It's my father's. He doesn't mind me using it now and then. I thought it would be warmer than my bike.'

'It's quieter too. For talking, I mean.'

A moment later, she said: 'If I had known, I wouldn't have worn my track suit.'

He didn't know what to say to that. Why wouldn't she, he wondered? It was a beautiful evening; a bright, light blue sky and a tranquil golden light on the fields and trees; chestnuts were flowering, their candles tipped with light; the young leaves on the oaks were livid and molten from the sun. They passed two donkeys in a field who stood motionless with their heads lowered.

'They look as though they're waiting for something awful to happen,' Jenny said.

'They always look like that.'

'It's like the country!' she exclaimed a few moments later.

'Well, we are in Hertfordshire.'

'It must be very nice to come back to in the evenings.'

'I usually come by train, and that isn't as nice as this, but it's still good when the train comes above ground.'

She didn't say anything, and he glanced at her to see if she was all right. Her small useful-looking hands rested on what would have been her lap if she had not been wearing trousers, and she was gazing contentedly out of the window.

'It's nice in a car, isn't it?' she said a while later. 'You see more than in a bus somehow.'

'More than on a bike, anyway.'

'If I had a little car,' she said, 'I'd take Andrew for picnics in the country. I didn't realize it was so near.'

'I missed Andrew tonight.'

'I'd settled him down. My Mum wanted a quiet evening: she's got a friend coming to see her . . . Oh yes, you saw him, didn't you; coming up the street just as we left. The bloke I said, "Hullo" to.'

'The army bloke?'

'He's a sergeant major or something.'

'You sound as though you don't like him.'

'I don't have any feelings about him at all!' she retorted, so Gavin knew that she didn't like him, but was certainly not going to ask why she didn't.

They drove in silence until he had crossed the main road into Barnet and he turned left into Potter's Lane.

'This looks as though it is going to be country, but it isn't,' he warned her. 'It suddenly breaks out into suburbia.'

'Gavin! You don't mind me calling you Gavin?'

'No, I don't at all.'

'Do you mind me asking you something?'

'No,' he said, but more warily.

'Do your parents know about Andrew?'

'No. No. I haven't told anyone. I thought you didn't want me to.'

'I didn't really. I just wanted to know.'

'Anyway, my parents are away.'

'Are they?'

'My aunt was in a road accident. My mother's gone to

see her and look after her children. My father's gone with her.'

'Oh. I'm sorry about your aunt,' she added. After that she was silent.

She remained silent, after they had arrived, and he had unlocked the front door and gone ahead to the kitchen to open windows. She was still standing in the hall, when he came back to find her.

'Just got to heat up some soup,' he said. 'Come in here, I've got some wine.'

She followed him into the kitchen. He'd mixed the cream with the soup and had got it in a saucepan. He felt exhilarated to be organizing everything.

'I'm not much of a cook,' he said. 'It's just soup and ham and salad.'

He saw her looking at the empty table through the alcove to the living room. 'We're eating upstairs in my room. I've taken the main tray up. There's just the soup.' He poured two glasses of wine and handed her one. She looked frightened, and did not take it. 'You can have a soft drink if you like,' he said. 'Hey. What's the matter?'

'I just have to tell you something.'

He waited – he was beginning to feel nervous.

'I hope you don't think . . . I'm not the sort of girl that – I mean just because I've had Andrew doesn't mean that – ' she'd gone her usual, but unusual shade of pale scarlet. 'I mean – I may have got it all wrong. I didn't think you were that kind of person. If you are I mean.'

He looked at her in amazement. She was not only scarlet, she was trembling. She was afraid of him! She was probably the first person in his life who'd been afraid of him. He felt confounded; then touched; poor little thing, to be afraid of *him*! She must have had some pretty terrifying experiences to make her feel that. He knew what it felt like to be afraid of people. It must be much worse for a girl.

'Listen,' he said, talking very quietly in case noise made things worse, 'I just thought you'd like to come and have a meal and we could talk about the list, and perhaps I'd play you a record, or read you something; to show you how marvellous some things can be. I asked you when my parents were away because it isn't their sort of thing, you see. They'd think it funny. That's why we're going to my room – because everything like that's up there. I certainly wouldn't dream of' – he was blushing now – 'well – taking advantage of you or anything like that.'

'Oh,' she said. 'Well – that's all right then. Fine. I'm sorry I brought it up.' Then, looking down at herself rather disparagingly, he felt, she added: 'I hope you don't think that I think that everybody – ' but she didn't finish because, just then, the soup boiled over. It made a bit of a mess. 'Oh, sorry! It's my fault,' she said; 'let me help.' So they cleaned it up together, and there seemed to be quite a lot of soup left in the pan. It was a relief to have something to do for both of them.

'Would you like wine? Or, if not, there's some Express Dairy orange juice?'

'Oh, I'd like wine, please. Nicer than those funny drinks they gave us the other night,' she said after tasting it. He'd chosen a white wine – he didn't know that much about wine, but he thought that girls preferred white. He liked red, himself. It was rather sweet.

'It's lovely,' she said.

'If I take the soup and the glasses, could you bring the bottle?'

She nodded.

He'd arranged the records on the bed as previously planned, and he'd turned his chest of drawers into a sort of side-table with the ham and salad on it. He'd bought a bunch of wallflowers and the room smelled sweetly of them. He'd put his low table, and two chairs that were too high for it but it couldn't be helped, a nice long way from the bed.

'Here we are,' he said – just like his father, he immediately thought.

She stood in the doorway. For a moment he thought she was scared again, but she was just looking all round at the room – taking it in.

'It's lovely up here,' she said. 'I like your mirror with the birds and roses and things. It's beautiful. And your lovely sofa thing. Is that what it's called?'

'It's a chaise-longue,' he said, and nearly told her about Mrs Patrick Campbell and the deep, deep peace of the double bed after the hurly burly of the chaise-longue, but double beds seemed quite the wrong subject just then.

'A chaise – longue,' she said thoughtfully. 'You've got a terrific vocabulary, haven't you? I mean you say more words than most people do.'

'I read quite a bit.' He was secretly flattered that she'd noticed.

He poured the soup into Mrs Lamb's soup plates with ferns round them.

'Come and have the soup before it gets cold.' (A bit like Mum, he thought.)

They both sat down and started to have it.

'It's very nice,' she said, 'what is it?'

'Lobster. I'm afraid it's only out of a tin . . . I put cream in it.'

'You can taste the cream.' She licked her spoon and said: 'But if, when you're reading, you come across a word that you don't know what it means, what do you do?'

'Look it up. In a dictionary.'

'So you need one of those, then.'

'It's fun having one.'

'Are they expensive?'

'They come in different sizes and prices. I can lend you a little one if you like.'

'Thanks. Do you have a lot of them, then?'

'I happen to have two. A pocket dictionary I've had since I was at school, and then I bought the Shorter Oxford a couple of years ago.' He took the soup plates away and put the dish of ham on the table. He had made a French dressing for his salad which he now poured on to it, and mixed it thoroughly. 'Help yourself,' he said.

'Why do you want the shorter one? 'Cos you know the longer one?'

'No, the shorter one's longer than the one I had to begin with. It has more words in it. There's the complete one, but that's too expensive for me. Have to save up for it.'

'I see. It's a lovely meal, Gavin.' She smiled at him. 'Nicer than the meal we had the other night.' Her smile was quite new to him; he could not remember her smiling at work.

They had some more wine, and he started telling her about Chopin. He explained that he was going to play her the music as orchestrated for the ballet *Les Sylphides*.

'I've seen some ballet dancing,' she said. 'It's when people go on their toes, isn't it? Very pretty. I wouldn't have seen that one, would I? It was in a Variety Performance, on television.'

'You might have seen a bit of it.'

'It was about swans,' she said. 'But they didn't have a swan. It was just two people.'

'That's another one. This is a ballet that Fokine did for Diaghilev. I'll tell you about them later.'

'Gavin! Could I just go to the toilet first?'

'Of course. It's down the stairs and the first on the right.'

He had the record ready on his machine, and waited in a fever of impatience. He desperately wanted her to fall in love with Chopin, and Chopin was only the first step: they wouldn't have time for much more in one evening. If she didn't like Chopin, she mightn't be prepared to have a second go. When she returned, he said:

'You could lie on the chaise-longue, if you like. It's very comfortable for listening to music; I often do.'

She sat rather primly at one end of it, bolt upright, hands clasped together. 'It's just as you like, of course, but I should lie on it. Far more comfortable.'

'I'd have to take my shoes off. Don't want to dirty it.'

'Do.'

He waited while she did this, and lay cautiously back with one of his orange cushions behind her head.

'Right. Chopin.'

She was very quiet all through the record, quiet and quite still. He tried not to watch her too obviously – sat well away from her, but her feathery head with its upright, honey-coloured hair was in view and sometimes, when she moved her head, an ear with a gold ring glinting in it. When it was over, he took the record off and put it carefully back into its sleeve, before he came over to her end of the room.

'Did you like it?'

'It was *pretty*,' she said, 'really nice! I could imagine them dancing. You know, wide dresses with sequins on them – really romantic.'

For a moment, he was outfaced; the words seemed faint and cosy for someone he revered; then he thought, 'What the hell; she enjoyed it, that's the point,' because, looking at her, it was clear that she had. She had that small glow about her that he recognized came from and followed enjoyment. 'Stage Two,' he said to himself.

'I've got some pictures to show you. They show you what that sort of dancer looked like. I think I'll put the book on the table as it's quite large, and then we can both look at it.'

He put the Degas book on the table and they sat on the floor and he showed her some of it. She didn't take much notice of the drawings, but the paintings enthralled her. 'Look at *her*! She's just whizzing across the floor – you feel you'll have to catch her! Oh – aren't they *pretty*! I wish I could dance like that with a little black ribbon round my throat!'

When he closed the book, she said: 'And did you find me a book?'

He hadn't, but he didn't want to tell her that. 'Tell me what kind of book you think you'd like.'

She sat back on her heels, considering. 'Well – I like things to *happen*, and I don't like the people just to talk all the time, but the books I read at school used to have very long descriptions in them. And I don't want to read about people falling in love and all that. I don't know, really.' She looked hopefully at him.

'Well – ' he was thinking hard, and quite suddenly, from nowhere, he had an idea. He remembered that, last Christmas, he'd bought a copy of *The Secret Garden* for Judy, and then Marge said she'd read it. So he'd read it himself, and simply kept it.

'Don't mind the inscription,' he said when he'd found it. 'I bought it for my niece, but she'd read it.'

She took it. 'How old is your niece?' she asked.

'She's nine.' Then he saw her face and said: 'Okay, it's a children's book, but *I* enjoyed it. When books are really good, it doesn't matter – anybody can enjoy them.'

'I see. What's it about?'

'What it says. A secret garden. Some children discover it, and bring it to life.'

'I'll try it then,' she said, but a trifle sulkily.

'I think I'd better take you home, now. We've both got to work in the morning.'

'Shall I help you with the supper things?'

'Don't bother.'

She was very quiet in the car, and he began to wonder whether the whole thing had been a failure, but it hadn't seemed to be that at the time. Perhaps she was still sulking over being given a children's book? Well, the only way to find out was to ask her.

'Jenny! About that book – '

'Actually, I like children's books. I get them from the library for Andrew, but . . . but sometimes I get one that's too grown up for him and just read it. I felt funny when you said it was a book you'd got for your niece; as though you'd found me out. Felt on my dignity a bit.' She gave a husky little chuckle. 'Not that I've got much of that. Andrew's the one with dignity in our family.' Then she fell silent again for such a long time that, while still thinking about whether to do it, he heard himself asking: 'Jenny! Is something worrying you?'

After a bit, she said: 'Something's worrying me all right.'

A minute later, she said: 'I suppose that's another thing about Art. It takes your mind off your troubles. I didn't think about . . . anything this evening till now.'

'Is it something you want to talk about?'

'I don't know. Yes, of course I *do* want to – but it seems . . . kind of disloyal.'

'Well – I'll have to leave that to you. But if it's about a new job I might be able to help a bit.'

'It isn't about a new job in the way *you* might think it would be. It's more about everything. I think something awful is happening, and if it is, everything would be different.'

He waited, realizing she was going to tell him.

'I think my Mum is falling in love.'

'With that soldier?'

'How did you know?'

'I just guessed. Why is that awful?'

'He doesn't live in London. He doesn't live anywhere; he's in the Army. She'd – well, she might go off with him!'

'And you'd miss her,' he said. He still didn't see why the idea upset her so much.

'I'd miss her all right! My whole life would change! There

wouldn't be anyone to mind Andrew while I was at work. I'd have to stop – stay home, at least until he starts going to school and even then I'd never get a part-time job in hairdressing. I'd just have to do anything I could. I'd probably have to live on Assistance,' she finished miserably. 'One thing I said I'd never do.

'And don't think I don't mind about my Mum because I do. I love her. She's been wonderful to me all through everything. I don't suppose it's been much of a life for her this last four years – my Dad dying so suddenly, and having to look after me. And then Andrew. Of course she loves him. *He'll* miss her something awful.'

She was crying now – discreetly, snuffling, wiping her face with her hand. He slowed down. He was appalled for her.

'Look,' he said 'you might be wrong. Perhaps she's just having a bit of a walk-out, and his leave will be up and he'll be off. You don't *know*!'

'I've got a good idea, though.'

'Couldn't you talk to her about it? Ask her?'

'He's there all the time! He's living with us. Got the rooms the lodger had. What with Andrew and work and him being there, I never see her alone.'

He did not know what to say. It was a problem of a kind and size that had never come his way.

'Does the house belong to your mother?'

'Yes. She sold the one we had when Dad was alive and bought this one. *She* wouldn't turn me out, or anything. Would she?'

'Of course she wouldn't. Look, Jenny, you don't even know for certain that she's going. I still think you should talk to her and find out.'

'I think *she* should be the one to do the talking.'

'Well, maybe she should, but if she isn't, then you'll have to do it.'

'You're probably right,' she said, in the tone of voice that showed she clearly didn't want him to be.

'It's not that I don't sympathize with you; I just don't know what else to say.'

'There's nothing *to* say, really. I didn't mean to spoil the evening, Gavin. I truly enjoyed it, Chopin and Dig – what was his name?'

'Degas.'

'Him. Did Chopin do a lot more music?'

'Oh, yes. A lot more. What you heard tonight was music he wrote for the piano. It was orchestrated for the ballet . . . I'll play you the piano music next time, if you like. And, when the ballet is on, I'll take you to it.'

'Will you really?'

'Yes. It might not be on for some time, though,' he added truthfully. He was also faintly worried by the glib way he was making these promises.

'Oh. Oh well.'

'But we might go to another ballet.' (There he went *again*.)

When they arrived at her home, the hall light was on, but the rest of the windows were dark.

'It must be late!' she said; 'I'll just go in quietly. Thanks again for the evening. It was great.' She put out her hand, so he shook it. He watched her into the house, she turned and waved at the open doorway. Then he drove home.

By the time he got back to his room and started to clear it up, he'd given up trying to solve her problem. Some problems – even other people's – were quite simply insoluble, in the sense that whatever was done about them, or happened if nothing was done, the status quo dissolved into something else. In fact, perhaps a great many problems consisted of people trying to hang on to the status quo, whatever it was like, and in spite of it having had its natural life.

He took all the supper things down to the kitchen, put the food away and decided to do the washing up tomorrow evening. He had a lot on his mind. His mother would have a fit if she knew, but she couldn't know, so *that* was all right. None the less, some household habits prevailed, and he laid his breakfast.

Clearing up the records from his bed, he reflected that perhaps next time Jenny came, he needn't bother to lay them all out. After all, they had sort of cleared up Jenny's anxiety about his being the sort of person who asked girls into his bedroom in order to take advantage of them. 'Take advantage'! What an awful phrase! It was the kind of thing his mother would say: it implied that there was not the slightest chance of Jenny enjoying his making love to her. Which was a bit unfair, because if he *did* make love to her – or anyone, of course, it didn't have to be Jenny – obviously he wouldn't do it, if they didn't want to. It probably wouldn't even be possible, if you come to think of it. He thought about it for a bit – drawing heavily upon his recent experience with Joan – and decided that whereas with Joan it *wouldn't* be, or have been, possible, with Jenny, who was physically completely the opposite – a tiny little creature in comparison – things might be different. She might start by resisting him, but probably, if he went the right way about it, she could be got to change her mind. The moment when she might stop wanting him not to and start wanting him *to* would actually be rather wonderful. In a way, it would be more wonderful than if she started by feeling exactly the same as he did. It would be amazing in a quite different way to the way that Joan had been amazing. It was fairly exciting even thinking about it. It would, of course, be exciting with any girl; he was only using Jenny as an example because she happened to have been here – but *any* girl, provided she moved him in the first place, would do. But when he said 'any girl' he was back to the now oddly anonymous girls of his dreams: who never seemed to materialize in real life and who also maintained a kind of passive serenity that no longer seemed to him to be ideal. And, as he had always made them perfect to start with, there was no way of affecting them deeply – or even at all. Anyway, he'd never actually *fucked* any of them – never even got their Rossetti-like garments off – never *even* kissed them. There was the girl on the beach, of course; the one with streaming red hair and only half her bikini, but he'd never actually reached her; by the time he took the plunge over the cliff the sun had set and it was dark, or else she had gone back into the sea – out of his depth. The only reason that Jenny came into this picture was because he had been so struck by *her* being afraid of him.

Perhaps that was the reason why she didn't go out with people; she was too scared of them. After all, when he came to think of it, it must be pretty staggering if you went together one time, as Jenny had said, and got Andrew out of it. However much she loved Andrew – and there was no doubt about that, her voice changed whenever she even mentioned him – it would be likely that she would feel pretty wary of men. It was up to him to show her she needn't be afraid of that sort of thing – as *well* as showing her about Art.

By this time he was ready for bed and very tired. Just before he fell heavily to sleep, the thought drifted into his mind that he hadn't made it very clear to himself whether it was up to him to show her that she needn't be afraid of that sort of thing by that sort of thing not happening – or not . . .

He felt faintly embarrassed meeting Jenny at work the next morning in case she thought that something was going on between them and would behave differently towards him because of getting such an idea into her head. But she stomped about on her cork wedge sandals, doing what she was told, occasionally rolling her eyes whenever there were awkward moments – her customary way of saying that things were awful, but there you were . . . They were bad that morning. Daphne had double-booked him, and Mr Adrian emerged from his racing paper to tell all of them just what a mistake this was and how easy it was not to make such a mistake if one took any trouble at all. Gavin could not stay for the whole homily – he had two clients waiting for him, but Daphne was nearly in tears. Mrs Wagstaffe's dog managed to nip him: 'It's amazing, Gavin, how he *always* remembers you!' And Miss Wilming told him, at painful stuttering length, so much about the *Raj Quartet* that he wasn't sure he would ever be able to face reading it. Mrs Silkin ran out of nearly everything for the clients' sandwiches, and Sharon had to be dispatched to go and buy salami and cheese from the nearest sandwich bar, and this, as it was Mandy's day at college, meant that they were short of juniors for shampooing. The day, which had started bright, darkened, and by mid-morning it had begun to rain quite heavily and they had to put all the lights on in the salon. That would put paid to a peaceful sandwich in St James's Park. The only piece of luck he had was that Harry rang him five minutes *after* Mr Adrian had gone to his lunch.

'Have you settled your little problem?'

'What?'

'That girl you were so worried about.'

'Oh, her. No, I haven't.' Something craven in him made him add: 'I'm going to see her this evening, as a matter of fact.'

'Ah. I was going to ask you if you felt like a movie. Winthrop's going out.'

'I could manage the second show. Well, it depends where it is, but if it's not too far from Chalk Farm, I could.'

'I haven't decided on a movie, I just thought I'd like to go to one.'

He then agreed, most obligingly, to meet Gavin at Marine Ices.

After he had rung off, Gavin thought what a shallow and

heartless person he must be. He hadn't even *thought* of Minnie since Sunday with Harry. He'd given Harry the impression that he was really anxious about her; indeed, he had *felt* anxiety for her on Sunday. Where had it all gone to? Or hadn't he really been feeling it at the time?

At least he'd do what he had said he would do. Tell her she needed help and encourage her to get it. The thought of going to see her and saying that sort of thing to her was depressing. And she might not even *be* in her sister's basement. She might still be in Weybridge with her awful parents. Somehow this didn't seem very likely; he was pretty sure that, because he was dreading the visit, she would be there to receive it.

She was. The shutters were shielding the ground floor windows, but he could see a light on in the basement. There was only one bell at the front door and after he had rung it twice – with a longish wait in between – it occurred to him that the basement might have a separate entrance. So he went down the steps: it was still raining and the area had an enormous puddle as though a drain was blocked and the water had nowhere to run to. Facing him was a dingy black door. There were bars on the basement window, and a pair of thin red curtains were drawn across it but there was certainly a light on inside. He pressed a rusty bell that looked as though it was never used, and heard it ringing shrilly. After a moment or two, the light went out. That was somehow just like her; to try and pretend that she wasn't there when it was much too late. He rang again, tapped on the window and said: 'It's me – Gavin. You might as well let me in; I know you're there.'

There was another pause, and then he heard some shuffling sounds; by now, he was listening intently; had a faint prickling at the back of his neck, warning him – of something. He knocked again on the window and called to her. 'What's the matter? Are you ill? Let me in, Minnie, it's raining and I've come a long way to see you.'

With startling suddenness and without a sound, the door

swung open: she must have been the other side of it, listening to him, but he could not see her. He stepped inside, took a couple of uncertain steps in the gloom – aware of a sour and very unpleasant smell. Before he could say or do anything, the lights came on, and he swung round, aware that she was standing at the door behind him. Seeing her, he got his first shock. She was wearing the red cheesecloth dress in which he had first seen her, now filthy with what looked like food stains, but, what was somehow more frightening, her belly was strained against the dirty thin cotton like a football. Her legs were bare except for a pair of thick, dirty woollen socks; her hair was matted, her face puffy and like pale, sweating cheese. She was holding a half-empty packet of Jaffa cakes which she was eating continuously, without a single pause, her fingers pulling the next one out while she was swallowing the one before – as though it was a mechanical process. For a second he stared at her, then she moved past him into the room, still eating, but moving this time to a carton in which he saw there were dozens of packets like the one she had in her hand. She reeked of the sour smell – vomit, he recognized, as he retched himself.

She dropped the empty packet on the floor and picked up another one – tearing it open with practised speed, and cramming the first cake into her mouth almost whole as though to catch up on the split second pause that the change from one packet to the next involved.

Eventually he managed to say something. 'Minnie what's the matter? Why are you doing this?'

With her mouth full she answered: 'Having a binge.' She sniggered, retched, put her hand over her mouth and swallowed several times; she was swaying slightly. Then she dropped the new packet of cakes and reeled over to where there was a tin of Coke with a straw standing in it. She drank until the tin was empty, whereupon she chucked it on the floor, and then kicked the tin with her foot. The room was littered with cartons and packets of food; with waste paper and empty Coke tins. By the unmade bed was a bucket and a filthy towel. She saw him looking round, and said: 'Too far to the lavatory when I throw up.'

A part of him wanted to turn round, and rush for the door to flee the scene for ever. But he couldn't do that. He'd come to help her; he'd got to try and help her.

'Listen; stop that for a minute.' She had resumed eating. 'Stop that and talk to me.'

'Oh no!' she said. She shook her head slowly several times. 'No – I won't do that because I don't want to. That's why not.'

'All right, go on eating and talk to me.'

There was no response to this; she simply went on eating.

'Where's your sister?' he asked as conversationally as he was able.

'She's away. For a week . . . That's how I got the Coke. And some other things. On her account. Much less to carry . . . I said – a children's party.' She sniggered again and bit into another cake.

'Minnie, I came to say that I'm sorry I ran out on you on Sunday.'

She looked confused, and then said: 'Why are you here? I don't want anyone here. I don't like you.' She tore at the cake packet and a cake rolled out of it on to the floor. She tried to bend down to pick it up, but lost her balance and ended up on her knees. She whimpered, grabbed the cake and pushed it against her mouth with the palms of her hands: the whimpering was suddenly cut off. She stayed for a minute with her hands against her mouth, rocking slightly. Then in a quite different voice she said: 'I've got *such* a pain.' Before, she had been watching him; now, she looked straight ahead – at nothing.

Compassion seared him. 'Have you?'

'Mm.' It was scarcely audible. Then she gave an odd little laugh, not at all like her previous noises. 'It *never* – goes. It doesn't matter what I do.'

He knelt in front of her.

'Minnie, it could matter, honestly. You need some help.'

She looked at him with such pure hatred that again he felt scorched. 'Oh no, I don't. You mean pass the buck and have someone paid to treat me like a looney. Don't think I haven't been through all that. People trying to get me to be like them.'

'They wouldn't do that. They'd want to help *you*.'

'You know what people are like? They're like *you*. You just want *someone else* to help me. To get me off your back. Like she wanted to get me out of her stomach. I thought you were different.' She groped about on the floor and found the half-eaten packet of Jaffa cakes, and bit into one. 'I've given up all that. Now I just put things on top of it. Have a binge.' She filled her mouth and then mumbled: 'You just piss off.' She started retching – tried to get up, failed, and began crawling towards the bucket. Struggling with his revulsion, he fetched the bucket over to her – the stench was dreadful and his stomach heaved. He left her hardly knowing what he was doing – just had to get out; shut the basement door, ran up the steps, held on to the area railings and was reluctantly, agonizingly sick.

It was raining, but not so hard. He lifted his face up to the sky to get some of the cool, fine rain on his skin: then he realized that his teeth were chattering and that his body was beset by a spasmodic shuddering. He knew he'd got to do something about her, but his mind seemed to have seized up; if he tried to think at all about it, he started feeling that he might vomit again.

After a bit he walked slowly away from the house – aimlessly: he didn't know the district, but somewhere in the back of his mind he knew that he'd better find a telephone box. Who should he ring up? A doctor – but how did one find a doctor to ring. Nine nine nine; then he'd have to ask for an ambulance, and they'd ask him what was wrong; how did one explain what was wrong? 'This girl's on an eating jag; I can't stop her – I think she's been doing it for at least two days – possibly more.' Did people die of what Minnie was doing? He didn't know. He hadn't the slightest idea. And how was anyone who *did* go to rescue her to get in? He very much doubted that she'd open the door to anyone a second time, and there were bars on the windows. Then he thought of her parents. He didn't know their number, but he ought to be able to get it.

He found a telephone box, got through to Directory Enquiries, explained that he only knew the name and not the address in Weybridge, and managed to get the girl batting enough for him to look for it. But she came back with the news that the number was ex-directory. Oh Christ! 'Well, could you get through to them and ask them if they would be prepared to speak to me? It's about their daughter: she's very ill. Please do – I don't know what else to do.'

'Have you rung for an ambulance?'

'It's not quite like that, but it really is serious – I'm not making it up. Would you just *ask* them?'

There was a pause, and then the operator in a resigned voice said: 'Hold on.'

Eventually, he got through to what he recognized at once to be Sir Gordon, and explained as quickly and simply as he could what was happening to his daughter. Sir Gordon listened, interposing a few grunts that gave no indication of his feelings. 'Have you rung her doctor?' was all he said.

'No – I don't know her doctor.'

'Suppose I'd better ring him. Can't come up myself, I'm expecting a call from Chicago. Can't you stop her?'

'No – no, I can't. I can't do anything with her.'

ELIZABETH JANE HOWARD

'You could take the drink away, couldn't you?'

'It isn't drink – it's food. I think she's been eating non-stop for days.'

'Only left here on Sunday evening.'

'For God's sake, it's Thursday now!'

'Don't you take that tone with me, young man!'

'I'm not taking any tone with you. I'm just warning you that your daughter's in a seriously bad way, so that you can do something about it. And you'd better do something about it.' He had a brainwave. 'She might do anything. Set fire to Sheila's house – or anything.' That was a stroke of genius. The idea of family property being at risk clearly shook the old monster.

'I'll get on to her doctor right away,' he said at once, and in a far more anxious tone of voice.

'Right. Well, I'm also telling you that *I* can't do any more about her: I'm handing her back over to you. Good-bye.' And he rang off.

That was that. His knees were shaking and his head throbbed. He also felt near to tears – a concomitant for him with being sick – something that hardly ever happened to him and filled him with retrospective revulsion. He looked at his watch. It was time to walk over the railway bridge and meet Harry in Marine Ices. But he didn't want coffee – however good – he wanted a brandy and ginger ale – the drink he kept for dire emergencies . . . And he wanted a Wilhelm II like he had hardly ever wanted one in his life before.

The telephone box was immediately outside a pub. He hesitated – then decided that he'd better fetch Harry first.

Harry was waiting for him.

'We're going to a pub.'

Harry looked up from his coffee and at once got to his feet.

He paid for his coffee as they walked out. He didn't say

anything until Gavin had ordered his drink – and Harry's, a small sherry and they had carried them to a quiet corner. Gavin got out his cigars and began lighting one. His hands were shaking.

When he had lit it, he looked at his friend and tried to speak, but felt his eyes simply filling with tears. Harry said:

'You knock that back and I'll get you another one. Plenty of time.'

He finished his drink, and by the time Harry returned with a refill he felt steadier, and told him.

'And of course I don't *know* that her father *will* actually do anything. When I was talking to him on the phone, I sort of assumed he would, but once I'd rung off I began to feel bad about him not.'

'I don't see how you could have done more.'

'Well, I could go and stand outside the house now, couldn't I, and see if somebody does come to look after her.'

'You could, I suppose, but what are you going to do if they don't?'

'I – don't know. I thought of ringing nine nine nine, but then I didn't know whether to ask for the police or an ambulance. I don't see how the ambulance people could get in if she didn't want them to. And the police don't go breaking into people's houses because they're *eating* – I mean they can't be expected to assume she's eating herself to death, can they? Or can they?'

'I don't suppose she'll do that. It all sounds a bit to me as though she's done this kind of thing before. She sounds as though she's anorexic.'

'She may be – whatever that is. But I feel *responsible*, Harry – that's what I mean.'

'You may *feel* responsible, but you aren't. And as you aren't you've got to recognize that she's a neurotic and get on with your own life. Neurotics are always trying to make other people feel responsible for them. They're often very good at that. It's often their only idea of a relationship. Don't you start letting it be *your* only idea of one.'

He sounded so steady and certain that Gavin felt a mixture of relief and irritation.

'Don't you ever feel responsible for Winthrop?'

'Of course I do, sometimes. I feel everything about him. Sometimes one of the hardest things is standing back and letting them get on with whatever it is they want to get on with – even if you think you can see it's going to spell disaster.'

'I mean,' Gavin persisted, 'you have terrible rows, don't you?'

'We have *shattering* rows. I used to think I wouldn't be able to stand them.'

'Well, *I* couldn't. I mean, I couldn't live with somebody if that was always liable to happen.'

'If you counted up all the things you don't think you could stand before you started living with anybody, there wouldn't *be* anyone for you to live with. You can't take out a kind of emotional insurance policy with people. You can't love some-body by a process of elimination.'

'But on your basis – any of us could live with anybody.'

'You get little internal messages about *which* people that are quite sound if you listen to them. But not if you smother them with judgements and things like social approval and them *not* being a whole lot of things that you're afraid of. The trouble with you, dear child, is that you're a judger. You judge everyone from morning till night, starting with Gavin Lamb . . . I have the impression that you're always lying in wait for yourself – waiting to pounce. And, if you're so hard on yourself, you're bound to be a bit hard on other people.' He looked into the bottom of his very small sherry glass and said: 'I think a certain party has had enough of my moralizing. Shall we go and find some food?'

Which they did, and Gavin was grateful to Harry both for

what he had said and for his not going on saying it – as many people might have done. They ate a large curry, and it was not until they were almost finished and had ordered lychees that Harry said:

'By the way, what with all the *drama* of this evening, I nearly forgot to tell you: Dmitri's left Joan.'

'Oh!' Gavin stared at him in dismay. 'Really left?' He could imagine someone like Dmitri doing a good deal of blackmailing about going or staying.

'Yes. He's gone off with some Greek millionaire he's been seeing in France. Doing up their yacht or something. No – he's gone, all right.'

'Where's Joan?'

'She's back. I gather she's pretty shattered. She's always been afraid it would happen, but she's always thought it wouldn't actually *happen*.'

'Have you got her telephone number? She's not in the book.'

'I haven't. Winthrop may have. I'll ask him, if you like.'

'Yes,' Gavin said. 'I would.'

CHAPTER TWELVE

'**G**AVIN!'

'Hullo, Mum.'

'Is that you?'

'Yes, Mum – it's really me.'

'Don't you be cheeky – this is the expensive time for phoning but I never seem to get you in the evenings.'

'I've been out.'

'Oh – so that's what it was. Are you all right?'

'Yes. I'm fine. How's Aunty Sylvia?'

'As well as can be expected . . . I didn't have to tell her about Timmie, Gavin – she knew. That's why she never asked about him – she knew all the time . . . The hospital says they may let her out at the weekend . . . If they do, we shall be coming back on Monday. If they don't – we shall have to see . . . It's the funeral tomorrow. I'll send a wreath from you; I thought you'd like me to.'

'Yes, Mum, do.'

'Is the house all right?'

'Yes – everything's all right. Don't hurry back because of me, Mum, I'm perfectly okay.'

'You're not warming up any of those pies twice, are you?'

'No.'

'Because you know what'll happen if you do a thing like that?'

'It's okay, Mum. How's Dad?'

'He's laying a floor in their sun lounge. Under my feet all day. If it's not one thing, it's something else. Well, I'll be saying goodbye to you now, Gavin – we're not millionaires.'

317

This conversation meant that he couldn't finish the washing up (from the night before last) without risking being late again. He put everything to soak in the sink, shoved the empty milk bottle outside the front door and set off. If she *was* coming home on Monday, it meant cleaning up the house a bit; it was beginning to look dusty – not a question of specks, to each one of which she paid furious and daily attention, it was more a miasma; he had a feeling that he could write his name with his finger on the top of the telly – something that would not go down at all well.

There was another aspect to her coming home that he thought about in the train the whole way to London, which was that her return put paid to Jenny's cultural visits. There was no *way* that he was going to be able to persuade his mother that having a girl in his bedroom to listen to records was because they wanted to listen to records . . . She would take an instant dislike to whoever he invited upstairs. Poor Jenny wouldn't stand a chance. Even if he was *engaged* to somebody, she wouldn't countenance it. If he *did* try it, she would probably keep coming up with cups of tea, but really to see how they were getting on. If she happened to come up when they weren't actually listening to records, were perhaps simply talking, she would instantly believe the worst. And if she found out that Jenny had had an illegitimate child – well, he'd never hear the end of it. The possibilities seemed many, likely and awful. This led him to experimenting with the idea of moving out; getting a place of his own: 'Thought I'd move out – get myself some sort of flat,' he said to himself – as though he was telling someone about it. It sounded all right. It *sounded* all right, but what would it be like actually to do? He hadn't got enough money to buy anywhere; he'd have to get a mortgage. Would that mean that he was laying cork tiles every night and having five-year plans like Peter and Hazel? No, it bloody well wouldn't. All he wanted was one room – quite simple – and a bathroom – and, he supposed, somewhere

to cook: Harry might have ideas about where to look for that
– supposing that he should ever want such a thing. Anyway,
he'd only been casually wondering about it: it wasn't the kind
of thing he would decide in a hurry.

Walking from the tube to work, he thought about Joan.
Last night, he'd considered writing to her, but almost immediately had felt defeated about what to say. Better to ring her
and sort of see how things were. An irrepressible part of him
began to wonder whether things would be at all as they were
last time, but he squashed that part as selfish, unpleasant,
arrogant, shameful and heartless, and altogether like *him*. Even
saying he was surprised at himself didn't carry conviction but,
once having said it, he was well away.

By the time he reached the salon, the Courts had had a
field day with Gavin Lamb, who had been tried, and found
wanting or guilty about practically everything. The worst thing
about him was his shallowness: the moment something wasn't
in front of his nose, he stopped caring about it. Take Minnie,
for instance. He'd been in a fair old state about her last night,
and look at him now! A clear case of out of sight, out of mind!
And his only reaction to his mother's news had been to worry
about not having the house to himself. It hadn't occurred to
him to send a wreath for Timmie. *She'd* had to think of that:
even to send a wreath on his own seemed beyond him. And
yet, when he'd heard about Timmie, he had felt deeply sad –
or so it had seemed at the time. And Joan: sacrilegious to be
thinking about sex when she'd just been left by the person she
adored. (Here there was a vestige of stuttering defence: she
had, after all, spent the night with him while she was in love
with someone else. He didn't understand why – but the fact
remained that she had done so.) The summing up was that he
simply didn't seem to have enough concern to go round –
even for the sort of ordinary life *he* led. He wished a few things
would happen that he didn't have to care about: Mr Adrian
breaking a leg, for instance – both legs . . . By the time he was

walking up the stairs to the salon, Mr Adrian had been in a really quite serious accident: broken his jaw (so he couldn't speak), and got two black eyes, a broken nose and a fractured right arm as well as his legs. He was going to recover, but it was going to take a very, very long time, and suffering would radically change his nasty nature into something quite different – humility and gratitude would be to the fore. 'I can't thank you all enough for the loyal way in which you have kept my business going, but the least I can do is to make all four of you partners . . .'

'Better wipe that smile off your face – the boiler went out in the night, the water's stone cold and his lordship's on the warpath.' Iris made a small throat-cutting gesture.

Daphne said: 'He's sending the juniors down to the basement to get buckets of hot water off the caretaker.'

Just then, the salon door was kicked open and Jenny staggered in with two brimming buckets. Gavin took one look at her: her arms – like little sticks – looked as though they would break; she was breathless and she looked more than usually like a disgruntled owl.

He relieved her of the buckets; took them over to the basins, and then – his heart hammering with rage – went to beard Mr Adrian.

He found him with his feet up in his cubicle, telephoning on his private line, '. . . and finally, at fifty to one, twenty each way on Nepalese Boy,' he was saying.

'And what can I do for you?' he said when he had replaced the receiver. His tone implied that there couldn't be anything.

'I understand that the boiler went out.'

'You understand correctly.'

'Well, if water has to be carried up from the basement – we should be doing it – not the juniors. It's too much for them.'

'And who is we?'

'The men. Me, Peter, Hugo – and you.'

There was – what was meant to be, Gavin recognized – a dangerous and frightening silence. But he was too angry, fed up, to be frightened.

'Are you suggesting that these young people are utterly unable to do any physical work at *all*? Are you suggesting that someone with a heart like mine should jeopardize it, solely because young people whom I am *paying* to train should not soil their hands with any menial job whatsoever? Is *that* your case?'

'I'm just saying that I don't think young girls should be made to carry weights like that when there are people who are physically stronger and perfectly able to do it. That's all. And I'm also saying that I won't have *my* junior made to do it. That's final.'

And he swept out before Mr Adrian could retaliate.

He heard Mr Adrian calling him back, but luckily for him Lady Blackwater had come in and Daphne was loyally claiming his attention at the desk. This time, though, she really wanted him.

'A friend, calling you,' she said.

It was Harry. 'You wanted Joan's telephone number. Got something to write with?'

Daphne gave him a pen and he wrote it down.

'Thanks, Harry. No more for now.'

Jenny was washing Lady Blackwater, so he went to Peter and said what he thought about the buckets. Peter agreed, but said that Hugo had varicose veins and he didn't think carrying heavy buckets would do them much good. 'The water should be hot in about an hour and a half: or hot enough. Iris needs water too, for washing the tints off,' he added. 'So I'll do Hugo's water, if you'll do Iris's.'

Mandy came through the door with steaming buckets. She was flushed, and said that the caretaker was a dirty old man and he'd pinched her bottom and she didn't fancy going down there again.

'Isn't Sharon in yet?' she said. 'Trust her to get out of anything.'

'You won't have to do any more. Take a bucket through to Iris – she's been asking for you.'

Gavin set Lady Blackwater, with Jenny handing him the rollers and pins. Lady Blackwater said how tiresome it must be for them having no hot water, and wasn't it interesting how one took things for granted until one was without them, but that she supposed that that was simply human nature, something that she, personally, had never got to the bottom of . . .

Gavin, glancing in the mirror as he finished the last roller, saw that Jenny was looking at him. When she caught his eye, she grinned faintly and rolled her eyes. The message was something like, 'Cor! How boring!' and her expression so quickly reassumed its look of choirboy innocence that he wanted to laugh.

'A net on Lady Blackwater, and put her under the dryer,' he said, and went to collect a couple of empty buckets.

It was a hard morning – Fridays were usually busy, and the water wasn't hot enough to use before noon. Gavin tried ringing Joan in his – rather late – coffee break, but there was no reply.

He tried again in his lunch hour and got what he presumed was one of the Filipinos, as a voice answered and said: 'Madam out – no answer.'

'Is she in this evening?'

'Madam *en*gaged this evening – no answer.'

'Thank you.' He rang off. Afterwards he thought it had been silly of him not to leave his name; next time he rang, he would.

At some point in the afternoon, Jenny said: 'I've read that book.' She paused expectantly.

'Did you like it?'

'I loved it! It was just what I'd like Andrew to have.'

'How do you mean?'

'You know: a secret garden that he could do wonderful things in. I thought it was going to be sad – about Colin, you know, but it wasn't. If you ask me, they were very silly about him in the first place. I loved Dickon best. I had a bacon sandwich for supper last night – just like him . . . It was a *lovely* book. As soon as Andrew's old enough, I'm going to get a copy and read it to him.' She paused again – expectantly. And when he didn't immediately say something she said: 'When will you give me another one?'

'Tonight, if you like,' he found himself saying. 'I'll play you some Mozart and find you another book. You could come back with me, if you like. We'd have more time that way.'

'I'd have to see whether my Mum could put Andrew to bed. If she'd mind, and if she thinks he'd mind.'

She rang from the station after work and he stood outside the box. After a minute, she opened the door and said: 'She thinks it'd be all right. She doesn't mind at all, but she thinks she'd better have your telephone number in case Andrew starts to kick up.'

It was rather enjoyable travelling on the tube with a girl. They had to stand the first bit and he put her in a corner and stood in front of her so that she didn't get bashed by other people. Then when they got seats – opposite each other – he played the game of pretending that he didn't know Jenny, that she was simply a girl sitting opposite him. He decided to look at her quite dispassionately, and see whether, if he didn't know her, he would think she was an interesting girl to know. This wasn't as easy as it would have been if he *hadn't* known her, because she kept meeting his eye, and when she did gave him one of her little grins before she resolutely read the advertisements above his head.

He started with her hair. It looked more like curly and silky fur than hair. It was the colour of darkish honey, and he thought might be much improved by adding some red highlights – Iris would do it beautifully. He tried to imagine it longer because, cut like that, her hair and her round specs dominated her appearance – had been the reasons why ages ago he had dubbed her a cross between an owl and a young choirboy and thought no more of it. He looked at the rest of her face: she certainly had a marvellous complexion – fine and fresh, she wore no make-up and there was not a blemish in sight – her best feature, really; the only other noticeable thing about her was her mouth, which turned up at the corners when she smiled – which she was doing again to him – only this time he realized that she smiled because she was excited – she was looking forward to her evening. There was something child-like in her lack of concealment about this that touched him: the reason why he'd added the choirboy to the owl; she was a very, if not completely, *un*sexy person who happened to be a girl. Ever since he'd reassured her that he wasn't the dread kind of person she had worried about his possibly being, she had seemed utterly trusting: she must like him, if she could trust him as much and as easily as that. The thoughts he had had about her after the first evening dimly recurred – enough to make him feel uncomfortable, but after all he had only *thought* them – had no intentions: there was no law about what you thought about anyone, and in a way they had been pretty general ideas and not *particularly* connected with Jenny. He wondered whether she had found anything more out about her mother – to change the subject.

He asked her this as they were walking from the station.

'I haven't said anything to her. But he's gone: went yesterday evening and she didn't mention it, so I think I was imagining things.' She sounded almost carefree about it.

When they got home – having bought some bananas and some cream to have after Mrs Lamb's pies – he warned her that the kitchen would be in a bit of a mess. 'That's something I *can* do,' she said. 'I'm always clearing up after Andrew: he can make a room look as though he's been in it for *weeks* in about half an hour.'

In the narrow, stuffy little hall, she said: 'Would you mind if I used your phone? I'd just like to make sure that Andrew has settled down all right.'

Of course he didn't mind. While she was doing it, he got two pies out of the freezer, put them in the oven and started clearing the table. He felt light-hearted.

She helped him do the washing up, and then they tried the remains of the wine from Wednesday. It was not bad, but not so good as it had been: still, there wasn't anything else to drink and they agreed that it was nice to have a drink.

'It's lovely to go out, really,' she said. 'I haven't been out since Andrew. I mean of course I go to the shops and things, and once I went to the pictures on a Saturday afternoon, but I didn't enjoy it by myself, and my Mum couldn't come because of Andrew.'

'You've given up a lot for him, haven't you?'

'Well, he has to be looked after, doesn't he? And I've had ever such a lot from *him*. I look at him sometimes and I think: "You wouldn't be here, my boy, if it wasn't for me," and I feel so proud I want to laugh and find someone to tell.'

'He is a beautiful child.'

'I can't see anything wrong with him,' she said.

'What do you do in the evenings then?' he asked casually, while he was looking to see how the pies were doing.

'Oh, there's always plenty to *do* – sometimes I have a job to get through it all. I do all the ironing, you see, and most of the washing, and I make a lot of Andrew's clothes. At weekends I do the cooking to give my Mum a let up, and on Saturday mornings I do the big shop at Sainsbury's. But evenings . . . I go to bed quite early. When I started as a junior I thought my feet would never hold out. I did used to find books to read, I told you, but I never found anything as good as the one you gave me.'

'Pies not ready,' he reported. He had been going to ask her about her friends, but now he had the feeling that there were none, and thought it better not to ask. He would hate people asking him about his friends, if it weren't for Harry.

'Mrs Hodgson-whatever-her-name-is has written other books, I saw. Are they all good too? She's got a name like a client, hasn't she? You know, double-barrelled, they call it.'

'Hodgson-Burnett. Her best-known book is called *Little Lord Fauntleroy*.'

'Go on! What a name! Is it as good?'

'Not to me. It's a sob story. Sugary. Sentimental,' he added.

'All right. Perhaps I'd better read another author.'

'There's plenty to choose from. Tell you what. We'll go and listen to some Mozart while the pies are getting ready.'

'All right.'

She stumped upstairs after him. At least he'd made his bed, he remembered, although this time there were no records on it.

But she didn't seem to mind about the records. She sat on the chaise-longue while he went through his catalogue, trying to find the right piece to start her with. In the end he selected a horn concerto – with Tuckwell playing. She listened very quietly and, when it was over said: 'He's posh, isn't he? Compared to the other man. Chopin. I like the main person playing.'

'That was a French horn. It was a concerto.'

'What's that?'

'Well – it's a piece of music usually written in three movements, for a solo instrument, with an orchestra.'

'And French horns do the solo part?'

'No: a concerto can be written for all kinds of instruments. Mozart wrote a lot of piano concertos, and some for the violin as well. But you can have them with almost any instrument: harps, trumpets, oboes, clarinets, violas, 'cellos and so on.'

'If I went to a concert, I'd see what the instruments were,

wouldn't I? I'm not fishing to get you to take me to one,' she said starting to blush, 'but I'd really like to know.'

'We will go to a concert, but I'd like you to hear more music first. Concerts go on for rather a long time, and I don't want you to get bored.'

He put the record away and suggested that they go and eat their pies.

Eating them brought up the subject of his mother, and he felt he had to warn Jenny that, once his mother was back, there couldn't be any more evenings like this one.

'Doesn't she let you have people then?'

'It's not exactly a question of let.'

'What is it, then?' She had her elbows on the table, her chin propped in her hands; he saw that she was asking with genuine concern rather than curiosity – none the less he felt obscurely irritated.

'Oh it's all kinds of things. I don't think mothers are particularly quick at recognizing that one wants to lead some sort of independent life. She'd fuss a lot – it wouldn't be the same.'

'And I suppose *you* want to get out, but like most people, you can't find anywhere to go. Prices are terrible nowadays, and people expect you to buy places, don't they?'

'That's it. I'd go if I could find the right place.'

'That *is* bad luck.'

They had their bananas and cream. 'Andrew's *mad* about bananas. Sardines and bananas – he'd live on them if I let him.'

Later, she said: 'I should thank my lucky stars, shouldn't I, having a place like I have to live. I don't know what I would have done if it hadn't been for my Mum.'

'Would she mind you having people to supper?'

'She wouldn't mind. I just haven't done it. I sort of kept away from the people I'd known at school and that, when I had Andrew. Some people said some horrible things. I went

327

off people rather and Andrew takes up so much of my time that what with work and him I don't seem to have any over. I've told you all that, though, haven't I? But I *want* to have more things in my life now, because if I don't, I'll be a terrible bore for Andrew, and when he's older he won't have any time for me.'

'You mustn't do everything you do only for Andrew,' he said gently. 'You must do some things for yourself, as well. Like some coffee?'

'Please. I'll do the washing up while you make it.'

As she was drying their plates, she said: 'Do you only like highbrow things?'

'No. And it's difficult to say what is highbrow really.'

'How do you mean?'

'I mean that what's highbrow for one person may not be that at all for someone else.'

'Oh,' she said politely. Then she said: 'Is Fred Astaire highbrow?'

'What made you think of him?'

'Well, I thought that, as his movies are all old ones and they keep on happening, he might be. I think he's marvellous.'

'So do I.'

'There was a film club I belonged to when I was seventeen. They showed a whole lot of his films. I loved the songs too. You could remember them easily afterwards. But perhaps,' she said, after thinking about it, 'perhaps Art isn't meant to be easy. Perhaps it's meant to be hard to understand. Like Shakespeare. We did him in school and I didn't understand him at all. Well – not much. We did a play called *Julius Caesar*. I couldn't get the point at all.' She looked at him challengingly: 'But I expect you'd say it was good.'

'I think you might feel differently about some of the other plays. I don't think that was a very good one to start with.'

'Do you know them all, then?'

'I've read them all. I've hardly seen any of them.' Harry

didn't care so much for the theatre, and he didn't enjoy going by himself, so much.

They went back upstairs and she asked if she could look at his books while he was choosing a record. He had just decided that it had better be more Mozart – one composer per evening seemed enough – when the telephone rang. He shut the door of his room after him, because he thought it would probably be his mother, and he didn't want Jenny to hear him talking to her.

It was Harry. 'I just wondered whether you were at all at a loose end.'

'Sorry, I've got someone here.'

'Oh. Well, the best of luck to you. Winthrop's spending the evening with Joan, so I just wondered.'

'Wondered, what?'

'Whether you would be free. Never mind. See you soon.' He rang off.

Gavin stood in the hall a moment, wondering why Winthrop should be doing that, when he, Gavin, had not even managed to speak to Joan. It seemed odd, to him, odd, and vaguely humiliating.

Jenny was sitting on the floor by the bookcase.

'I've found a book called *Jane Eyre* that looks quite interesting. I picked it because it was a girl's name, but the beginning seems good. Shall I read that?'

'Why not? Jolly good choice,' he added absently. He was trying to remember how well Winthrop *knew* Joan, but he couldn't get any further than supposing that it was because he *did* know her that they'd all gone to the party in the first place.

He'd decided to play Jenny part of a piano concerto, and had picked the first movement of K.491. He explained what it was. She got up from the floor and went at once to the chaise-longue, took off her sandals and lay down, as though this was the agreed way to listen to music. Not a bad idea, either, he thought, and cast himself on his bed.

He came to with a start – sat up to realize that the music had stopped, which must mean that they'd had the whole concerto, two and a bit movements of which he hadn't heard. He looked across to the chaise-longue. Jenny lay motionless, and when he went over to her he saw that she, too, had fallen fast asleep. Quite funny, really: if it had been just her, he honestly recognized, he would have written her off as not interested, but he couldn't, could he, because he knew *he* was interested, and yet he'd fallen asleep. He looked at her again. She looked rather waif-like; very small and vulnerable, even younger. She had taken off her specs and she lay with one side of her face resting in the palm of her hand, her breathing light, and even. His heart lurched; he wanted to pick her up and hold her in his arms; he felt extraordinary. The feeling went; he couldn't possibly do that anyway. How would he feel if he was asleep and someone suddenly grabbed him? And she was frightened of people, and he knew what *that* was like, he had no intention of frightening her. The feeling had completely gone now, leaving him with a sense of unreality – it occurred to him that he'd just imagined feeling it. He walked away from her and called her name while he was taking the record off the turntable.

She was apologetic and embarrassed at having slept. 'I'm not used to staying up so late,' she said. He told her that he'd dropped off as well.

In the car, she said: 'We haven't done poetry.'

'No. Well, we'll have to do something about that. But we haven't *done* anybody really. I'm just introducing you – starting you off. Poor old Mozart didn't have a fair chance this evening. Mozart wrote over six hundred works – all kinds of things – including opera. You haven't heard any opera yet.'

'When is your mother coming back?'

'She may come on Monday.'

'Oh, I see.'

He glanced at her; she was staring straight ahead, but he had the impression of overwhelming disappointment. He said:

'Tell you what. We'll have an intensive course till then. I'm free except for probably going to see someone one evening. And, when she does come back, we'll think of some other way.' He couldn't think how, but he couldn't bear for her to feel let down.

As she got out of the car, she said: 'Gavin, I really appreciate all the trouble you're taking. All this driving and giving me meals and not laughing at me because I don't know things. I really appreciate it.' And, before he could say anything back, she had slipped out and was running up the path to her house. He watched her in, waited for her to turn and wave as she had done before, and then waited for the door to shut. 'Just seeing her safely in,' he said to himself. He drove home with the windows down: the damp night air was amazingly exhilarating.

In many, if not all, ways, that Saturday morning was like any old weekday. He worked hard at the salon: the boiler was back in business but, on the other hand, it was a particularly busy Saturday. He made several attempts to ring Joan and got put off by the Filipinos; although one of them once admitted that Madam *in*. He told Jenny that he would be free in the evening, and she said that she'd told her mother that they only had a few more days before *his* mother returned, and that her Mum had said, 'Make the most of them.' He had faint feelings of discomfort at the idea of Jenny discussing his relationship with his mother: it would almost certainly show him up, he felt, in a rather weak and unfavourable light. Most people would think it a bit odd, surely, if, at the age of thirty-one, one's social life was circumscribed by one's mother? He tried taking refuge in the fact that she couldn't know the whole story, but then honesty shoved the knife in: the whole story would simply show him up in a worse light than ever. Mrs Lamb had never *tried* to keep him at home, he had just gone on being there;

laziness and fear of the unknown had combined to keep him a comfortable prisoner of her régime. Of course, she *liked* having him, but he could not recall a single thing that she had ever said or done which could be interpreted as pressure to make him stay. Which was not at all to say that she wouldn't kick up now if, after thirty-one years, he said he was going. She was used to him being there, and she had a profound distrust of all change. But he really couldn't stay in a place where he couldn't even have the odd girl in to supper and to play his gramophone. Supposing he didn't leave – simply said that that was what (from time to time) he was going to do? This was when the first of many imaginary conversations with his mother began.

He: Oh – by the way. Mum, I'm having the odd girl in to supper from time to time . . .

Mum: (interrupting – you bet) You're what? What girl? What do you mean 'odd girl'? Is there something funny about her? It doesn't sound very nice to me. However did you meet someone like that?

He: I didn't mean that I *was* going to do that, Mum. I simply meant that, *if* I meet a girl, that's what I might want to do.

Mum: If every single time you met somebody you brought them back here the place would be like Piccadilly Circus.

He: It wouldn't, Mum, I'd never bring them all back at once.

Mum: There you go. One minute it's one girl, and the next it's dear knows how many. What do you want to bring them back for?

He: We want to play the gramophone, Mum.

Mum: Play the gramophone? That's your *room* the gramophone's in. That sort of girl who'll go rampaging up there in that room with your bed in it will not be at all a nice type of girl, I can tell you . . .

Even this first conversation showed him that he was much better at putting his mother's point of view than he was at putting his own; however, there it was. One of the things about his mother's points of view upon anything was that they were definitely not subject to change. He walked out of the pub where he had been having a sandwich, and then rather aimlessly down the street to nowhere in particular. What he was actually thinking about, he discovered, was *how* he was going to introduce Jenny to poetry – so that she would think it neither soppy, nor incomprehensible, nor dull. 'We haven't *done* poetry indeed!' He must also disabuse her of the idea that he knew everything: although he had to admit that, being the person in the know, relatively speaking, was an intoxicating change. He probably liked having her for these evenings for reasons of vanity.

He tested to see whether it was vanity that was conditioning his idea that, to get Jenny on to or into poetry, he would need to read some aloud to her, and decided that it wasn't. He always found that he had to read a poem aloud, as well as just reading it: at some point he needed to hear it coming from outside himself. However, if that part of it wasn't vanity, it was extremely probable that everything else about it was. He had caught himself smiling at her in a superior way – about the words she used to express her feelings or views about the composers: Mozart being posh, for instance. Then he thought: no, posh was her word for grand, and grand in one sense was next door to noble – and there was certainly a nobility about Mozart's music.

He realized that he'd got to get back to the salon; he'd walked some way without thinking where he was going. Perhaps he stuck to worrying about what poetry he would read to Jenny that evening because it was a more superable problem than others. Joan, for instance. Was he worrying enough about Joan? Perhaps she was utterly prostrated by Dmitri's departure: perhaps he ought to stop trying to telephone her and simply go and see her? He felt he owed her a great deal, and he wanted her to know that he cared about her. Perhaps she didn't want to talk on the telephone. Perhaps Winthrop had known this, and had simply gone to see her and she was so lonely that she was so glad of anyone. Winthrop didn't strike him as at all the person one would *choose* to see for comfort. He could ring Harry and find out how she was and, on the strength of what Harry said, he could make some move. Right: that was that ... Why didn't he feel better? Because the *real* problem – whether he was going to go on living at home or not – was nowhere *near* solved. He thought about it in little nervous spurts – for long enough in fact to feel panicky, and then of course he stopped thinking about it – until the next time.

That evening, when he fetched her from Barnet station, Jenny said:

'My Mum was wondering whether you would like to come to lunch on Sunday. She wants to cook you a meal because of all the ones you've given me, and you could see Andrew properly.'

He said he'd like to, and to thank her.

'She would've made it today but she's got to go and see a friend in the country,' she added, as though there was still some doubt about his acceptance.

'She hasn't said anything more about the soldier?'

'Not a word. I think I was just tired and imagining things.'

They had decided to have bacon and eggs as a change from the pies, and Jenny cooked them while he laid the table. He asked her how she was getting on with *Jane Eyre*.

'I've only just started it: in the bus this morning. She's in an awful school. They've all got chilblains from being half-starved and given all the wrong food as well, I shouldn't wonder. You feel that things like that must have happened to her – the author, I mean – or how would she know to write about them?'

'I think things a bit like that did happen.' He told her about the Brontës and their austere and tubercular-ridden life in Yorkshire, and she listened round-eyed.

'Didn't they know it was catching?'

'No, they didn't know about that then. Charlotte didn't catch it though.'

'What happened to her?'

'She married her father's curate and was very happy with him. Then she died in childbirth.'

'They didn't have any luck, did they? How do you know so much about everything? I hope you don't mind me asking,' she added.

'I *don't* know so much. I know it looks as though I do. But, you see, I'm only telling you about the things I *do* know – there's tons of stuff I don't.'

'Well, even if that's true, how do you know what you *do* know? Who told you?'

'Just reading, really. One thing leads to another.'

'Nobody taught you?'

'Well, there was a teacher at my school. He used to talk to me about books. I suppose they started it.'

'A bit like you're doing for me?'

'Yes.' Then he said: 'You mustn't ever pretend to like things, Jenny. And the other thing is that you can't expect to like everything straight off – at first go. Some things take a bit of getting used to.'

'Like people,' she said unexpectedly, and started to go her amazing colour.

'What's up?' He couldn't resist asking.

'I was just thinking how you first seemed to me. It was so different.'

'You'll have to tell me, now, won't you?'

'I can't do that. I really can't!'

'All right.' Probably better not to know, but his curiosity had been thoroughly aroused and he felt frustrated. There was some constraint between them after that.

In his room, he started looking through his catalogue for some music that he thought she might be taken by, and then he suddenly thought of that splendid piece of birthday music, 'Zadok the Priest': Handel at his best.

That went down a treat. She had started by lying on the chaise-longue which had become the routine, but when the singing began, she sat bolt upright, hands clutching her knees, shot him one look of amazement, and then remained motion-less until the end, when she said it was the best piece of music she had ever heard in her life. 'It made my hair stand on end.'

'It *is* on end,' he said, and found himself wanting to touch it.

'Could we play it again?'

'If you like.'

This time he lit a Wilhelm II: he wanted something to do with his hands. For one insane moment he thought of telling her that he was turning into the kind of person that she had hoped he wasn't. *Was* he, though? Bloody good thing he hadn't said that if he wasn't even sure! 'I like her enthusiasm,' he said to himself. And that was not a lie – it was merely one of those ingenious half-truths that he knew he went in for.

After they had had the Handel again, he said it was time to go home.

'No poetry, tonight?'

'It's too late.' Reading aloud a poem that he loved struck him now as about the second most intimate thing he could do with her. He didn't feel equal to it.

'. . . you mean to tell me you're thinking of going off with a girl you've only known for a week!'

'For nearly three years, Mum, actually.'

'For only three years!'

'It is rather a difference.'

'You'll find things are different! Plunging headlong into dear-knows-what! I expect she's trapped you. A lot of young girls will stop at nothing. Gavin, you haven't done . . . anything silly . . . have you?'

'Not yet, Mum.'

'Don't you be cheeky. I've never known you be like this. You've never done anything like this before! . . .'

It could go on for ever. The trouble about these conversations was that while they made it clearer and clearer that – sooner or later – he'd *have* to leave home, and that whenever he did she would be very upset, they did not at all clear up his feelings about Jenny. In fact they seemed to make the whole thing more complicated: he had the feeling that his mother's reaction to his association – of any kind with any girl – would be calculated to push him further with whoever she might be than he necessarily wanted to go. Just because Jenny enjoyed him showing her things didn't mean that he wanted to be with her all the time. He was only spending so much time with her *now* because his mother was away. And, if you spent a lot of time with one girl, she would have to be pretty hideous for you never to want to touch her – or anything like that. Wouldn't she? His mother was someone calculated to blow up molehills into mountains . . . By now he was in bed and too tired to think straight about anything. 'I'm fed up,' he said to himself but, because he was in the dark and nobody could see him, he smiled.

He had one more go at telephoning Joan, with the same result. By now, he was beginning to feel obscurely angry with her. He asked if the Filipino had taken his last message and was told yes. Nothing more. If that was how she felt, to hell with it.

Monday was The Hon. Mrs Shack's morning and he had telephoned while she was under the hair dryer (Mr Adrian never came in as early as that). A few minutes later, while he was getting a quick cup of coffee, Daphne called that he was wanted on the phone. Joan calling him back! He was surprised at how excited this made him feel.

It wasn't Joan; it was Harry.

'I wondered whether you were by any chance free this evening?'

Gavin hesitated. He could tell from Harry's voice that something was wrong; on the other hand it was one of Jenny's last evenings . . . While he was hesitating, Harry said:

'Do be free. If you possibly can.'

'Yes, I can be. Shall I come to you?'

'Thanks, Gavin. Yes, do.'

'I'll go home and fetch my bike.'

'What time will you get to me?'

'Half-past seven?'

'Right.' He rang off.

He sounded *awful*: much worse than an ashtray-bashing. But it must be something to do with Winthrop; nothing else would make him sound so shaky and tense.

He didn't get a chance to tell Jenny that their evening was off until the lunch hour, and even then he had to be quick about it, as Jenny's lunch wasn't coinciding with his. Her face clouded, but she listened quietly and then said, 'Never mind,' in tones that were admonishing her not to.

Once or twice, during the afternoon, when he was cutting, he looked up to the mirror to see a client's head, and caught her watching him: juniors were supposed to watch the hair-dressers when they cut, it was one of the ways that they learned, but she wasn't watching the cut he was doing, she was watching *him*. Each time he caught her eye, she gave him a little fleeting smile and hurriedly looked away.

It felt quite funny, walking to the station without her: she went home by bus, and they parted in Piccadilly. He turned back to see her joining a large bus queue – she was wearing the white mac that she'd worn in the Park, the day she'd been feeding ducks and he'd talked to her for the first time. It had taken him nearly three years to talk to her. And then he'd only done it because, in the distance, he had thought that there was the faintest chance that she might turn out to be the girl of his dreams. Which of course she wasn't. She just somehow seemed to have got into his ordinary life.

Harry's Entryphone was working for once but, even though he ran up the flights of stairs, Harry was waiting for him at the top. He wore his tartan pullover over a dirty white shirt, and he looked as though he hadn't shaved. Gavin followed him in silence into the lounge which was littered with dirty coffee cups.

'Do you want some coffee?'

'Not unless you want some.'

'Might as well.' He went into the kitchen, and Gavin wasn't sure whether to follow him. Then Harry said, 'I'll just put the kettle on,' so Gavin sat down and waited.

Harry came back: he seemed unable to meet Gavin's eye, but wandered about, began stacking some cups and saucers which he picked off the coffee table and put on to a bookcase, and then abandoned. He seemed unable to keep still. Finally, with his back to Gavin, he said: 'You might as well know. Winthrop's gone. Went last night. Left – no warning – just said he was going, and went.' His voice seemed to give out then, and there was a silence.

Then Gavin said: 'But he'll be back, won't he, Harry? You know he'll be back.'

Harry turned round: he was hugging his elbows. He was trembling and his eyes were bright. 'No. He's gone off with Joan. They're going to America. He won't be back.'

'With *Joan*?' He couldn't believe it. '*With – Joan?*'

Harry nodded. Then he tried to say something, but he couldn't.

Gavin said desperately: 'There must be some mistake. She wouldn't – ' but he couldn't go on because Harry made an awful dry sobbing sound and then seemed to lose his breath altogether; stood, frowning, shutting and opening his eyes, wrenching his arms round himself, seized up with agony. For a moment Gavin was paralysed with the shock of it. Then he went to Harry, put his arms round his rigid body and led him to a seat. With his arms still round Harry, he knelt by him until tears streamed from his friend's eyes and he was able to weep.

After an unknown amount of time, Harry said: 'I thought I'd got through that bit.' His voice was husky. 'It was telling you. It was like telling myself again.'

'Yes.'

'When he went – I looked at the time. I sort of collapsed for a bit. When I came to – he'd been gone half an hour. I thought, "That's not much: you've spent a lot of half-hours in your life without him – whole evenings often." But they came to an end; he'd come back. This half-hour's just the beginning of forever.' He looked at Gavin. 'I loved him. He can't have *known*, can he?'

'I don't know.' He felt he knew nothing.

Harry said: 'He's been going out every night this week. He told me he was going to see her one evening. I thought he was just sorry for her; he said she'd had a bad shock. Everybody knew she cared about Dmitri. I said: "Give her my love." I wish I hadn't said that now.'

'It doesn't matter.'

'You know what I think? I think she's *bought* him. He's very impressionable and he always was attracted to excitement and high life. She bought Dmitri really.'

'Perhaps she'll get tired of him.'

'It won't make any difference. He won't come back.' There was a short silence, and then he said, 'They must have been planning it all this week. When I got back from work last night, he was all packed up – waiting. "I'm off," he said. I thought it was a joke at first – no, I didn't – it never really felt like one – I sort of knew it was true, but I couldn't take it *in*.'

Fragments of post mortem, attempts at analysis, pieces of anecdote, fresh, but more articulate outbursts of grief; his distress, like water, found any way that it could to pour out of

340

him, and Gavin, who began by feeling helpless in the face of such misery, ended by recognizing that all he could do was to be there. He discovered, bit by bit, that Harry had not slept, nor gone to work, nor eaten since Winthrop had left, although he seemed very unclear about how he had spent the time. He had had coffee, he said; he had sat on the balcony for a while; he had got terribly cold; he hadn't been able to face the bedroom; Winthrop had left one of his records on the turntable, he had played that; he thought he had played it several times – he'd never liked that sort of music, but he hadn't been able to bring himself to put it away; he thought he'd leave the flat because they'd always been in it together; he'd run a bath at some time or other, but there hadn't seemed to be any point in having it – it must be stone cold by now . . .

Gavin made him some tea, and ran him another bath, and, by saying he was hungry himself, persuaded Harry to consider some food. He found the remains of a stew in a pudding basin in the fridge, but decided that even that might have unhappy associations, so he scrambled some eggs for them both, and Harry ate some of that. But, during all this, he was wondering what on earth to do next: he couldn't leave Harry like this; should he take him back to Barnet for the night? And then what about tomorrow? He couldn't take him to lunch with Jenny's family. At least, perhaps he could from their point of view, but he didn't think Harry would be able to cope. This problem was solved for him most unexpectedly, by Stephen ringing up: he'd heard the news and was deeply concerned. He and Noel would come and fetch Harry in the morning and take him away for the weekend. He seemed to have the right touch, because Harry agreed to go: it would get him out of the flat, he said, and he thought he'd be better out of the flat. Gavin offered to stay the night with him, but Harry, who seemed stronger for the hot bath and the food, said that he could manage. 'I've got to start some time. And if I know they're coming in the morning, I'll be all right.' He still wouldn't go into the bedroom, so Gavin fetched a couple of blankets off the bed and made him comfortable on the chesterfield. He could see that he was worn out. He made him a hot drink and gave him a couple of aspirin.

'I'll stay with you until you're asleep.'

Harry agreed to this; he was past arguing about anything; he tried to thank Gavin, but this made him cry. Gavin said he was his friend, and gratitude wasn't in order, and Harry, recognizing his own phraseology, actually smiled. Then he lay down – passed out, more like, Gavin thought, watching his poor ravaged face stilled in sleep. He waited until he felt sure that it *was* sleep, then he wrote a note saying: 'Gone home; ring if you want me *any* time of night,' put the note on the floor where Harry would be sure to see it, and left.

It wasn't until he'd got home, and he realized that he, too, was exhausted, that anger with Joan manifested. He felt so angry that, briefly, the idea of killing her occurred – and went. He was too tired to think about it then, but he knew that he couldn't leave it at that: he had got to do something.

He had gone to bed with his door open in case Harry rang, and, in fact, was woken up by him next morning. His watch said quarter-past nine: he'd overslept. Harry said he was all right: Stephen and Noel had come for him and he was going off to have breakfast with them. 'In view of your very kind note, I thought I'd just tell you I was off. In case you rang me.'

'I was going to. Afraid I overslept.'

'You deserved it. Thanks, Gavin. I don't know what I would have done without you, last night.'

'Think nothing of it. Take care of yourself. Ring me when you get back.'

He had a bath and made himself some coffee: the feeling that he'd had last night about having to do something about

Joan hadn't changed, in fact he felt clearer about it. It occurred to him now that perhaps Joan didn't know what she was doing in taking Winthrop away from Harry. He felt that, if this was true, and he told her, there was a fair chance that she would desist. He went out to the hall to the telephone – noticing that the table on which it stood was now very dusty. He'd have to spend at least one evening cleaning things up.

All that week he tried to ring Joan, but the line was either engaged or the bell simply rang unanswered. But on the morning of his lunch with Jenny he struck lucky. He got through, as usual, to a Filipino, but this time he simply said, 'Get Madam. You just go and get her. Important. Danger,' he added for good measure. That worked. After a pause, there she was; sounding rather guarded, but there.

'This is Gavin. It's very important that I see you.'

'Oh – Gavin,' she said: she did not sound enthusiastic. 'I'm afraid I'm going abroad.'

'Well then, I'll come round this evening. At six o'clock.' He rang off before she could reply. Of course, she *might* just not be there but somehow he felt she would. She would want to know what he thought was so important. Years of working with women had taught him some things about them.

The following Sunday was like early summer: sunny and windless. People were wearing summer clothes; dogs basked on doorsteps, and cats crouched prosperously on garden walls. He'd taken the car, in case Andrew and Jenny wanted to go to a park after lunch. He drove slowly through the back streets – the way he had come that evening – which seemed such a long time ago now – when Minnie had chased him in her car. An awful lot seemed to have been happening lately: not only things outside him – but events within. He didn't *feel* the same. He didn't feel up to analysing the difference, but he knew it was there. For instance, he was looking forward to this lunch, which was managing to be a new experience without being nerve-wracking. He saw a barrow at a street corner, and

343

stopped to buy two bunches of pink and white striped tulips for Jenny's mother. There was a newsagent's shop just behind the barrow, and he went in to see if he could find something for Andrew. There was a large card with little toy cars attached to it, and he chose a fire engine because that was what he would himself once have liked best from the selection. Then he felt bad about having nothing for Jenny. It was the kind of shop that had a little of everything, and he found a Penguin copy of Laurie Lee's *Cider with Rosie*. The front of the book had faded a bit from being displayed in the sun, but it was far the best choice. In the car, he got out his pen and wrote 'To Jenny'. Then he thought for a bit and put 'from Gavin'. It didn't seem quite right, but he couldn't think of anything righter. Then he bought two packets of Wilhelm II for himself.

Jenny opened the door to him, wearing an apron over a sleeveless yellow dress. She had the pearl studs in her ears and looked excited. 'We thought we could have lunch in the garden,' she said, 'if you could help get the table out.'

He put his presents on the draining board and helped her with the table. Andrew was sitting in the middle of a very small sandpit. He wore a pair of scarlet shorts and a toy wrist watch strapped sloppily round his wrist. Jenny's mother was picking him dandelions which he was planting on a turned-out sand-castle. Gavin said: 'I've got something for him.' He wanted to give the flowers and everything at once – when he met them. Jenny followed him back to the kitchen, so he gave her her book. 'I'm sorry it's faded a bit,' he said, 'but it is a lovely book: the next one for you to read. The flowers are for your mother.' The fire engine was in a weak paper bag, and the ladder had already punctured it, so he took it out. 'I'll just give it to him like this.'

'Thank you very much,' Jenny said. She had read the inscription, and for the second time he felt that it wasn't quite right, but it was too late now. 'You go and give them their presents,' Jenny said. 'I'll just have a look at the meat.'

In the distance, Jenny's mother looked extraordinarily like Jenny. She wore a blue denim skirt and paler blue shirt – sleeveless, like Jenny's dress. They had the same arms, long, and thin, and capable. Her hair was darker, brindled with grey and tied back in a pony tail. She was delighted with the tulips. 'How lovely,' she said. 'I don't know when I was last given flowers. Is that for Andrew? He'll like that. He loves fire engines. We go on a walk to look at them: it's his favourite walk.'

Andrew received the fire engine with majestic gravity – it was rather like bringing tribute to a king, Gavin thought. He grasped it and put it very close to his face – almost as though he was smelling the colour – and then, holding it with both hands, he perched it on top of his silvery head. Jenny's mother said: 'Say thank you, Andrew,' but he merely looked at her sorrowfully – as though she had committed a grave breach of etiquette. The engine fell off his head, and he gathered it up, muttering: 'enchin enchin enchin'. Gavin felt he could take it that the gift had been well received.

Before lunch, a brand new half-bottle of gin was produced together with tonic water. They all had a gin. Gavin and Jenny's mother smoked, and when Gavin lit her cigarette for her, she asked him to call her Anne, as people calling her Mrs Fisher made her feel over a hundred.

For lunch they had roast stuffed breast of lamb with spring greens and carrots and very good roast potatoes. Andrew was strapped into his high chair and given a bowl of chopped-up food which he ate with his fore-finger and thumb. He spent a lot of time staring at Gavin in a penetrating but impassive manner, but except for putting all his carrots in his mug of water, he was unobtrusive. The sun was quite hot: Jenny produced some cider to drink with the lamb, and Gavin began to feel pleasantly relaxed if not sleepy.

When they were eating apple pie with custard, Jenny's mother, or Anne, said: 'Jenny tells me you're finding it very difficult to get yourself a place to live. We've got two rooms on the top floor here that our last lodger has just left. I wondered if you'd like to see them after the meal?'

A quantity of conflicting feelings hit him. The first was that it served him right for telling Jenny that glib lie about leaving home if only he could find somewhere to live. Then he thought that something that he had thought very difficult was turning out to be easy – or perhaps difficult in a different way. Then he wondered what Jenny thought, or felt, but she was eating with her eyes fixed on her plate. He couldn't refuse to see the rooms. At least he had to do that. He said he'd like to see them.

'Don't feel that you've got to take them because you know us. Just have a look at them and think about it.'

Jenny said: 'We've only got one bathroom.' But he couldn't tell from the way she said it whether she meant, 'Don't come,' or, 'Sorry about one bathroom.'

Anne said: 'That's one reason why we have to choose our lodger pretty carefully. There is a little kitchenette up there though. Anyway, you can have a look.'

So, after mugs of coffee and Andrew going back to his sandpit, Anne said she would do the washing up while Jenny showed him.

There was a large front room with a fireplace and two windows, and a smaller back one with a basin in it, that looked on to the garden. On the landing there was a small sink, and cooker. The rooms were very barely furnished with linoleum on the floors, but the large one had a real fireplace with cupboards each side of it. Jenny showed them to him in a silence that became oppressive . . . He said they were nice, and when she didn't say anything, he asked her how she would feel supposing that he did come and live there.

'You must please yourself,' she said in a colourless voice.

'You don't sound as though you think it is a very good idea.'

'I haven't thought about it at all!'

He gave up: he didn't believe her, which also meant that he didn't at all understand her. He felt piqued by her lack of enthusiasm for the enterprise. In the kitchen he told Anne that he would think it over. 'Did Jenny tell you the rent?'

'No – no, she didn't.'

'It used to be fifteen, but I've had to put it up to seventeen fifty. We let them to cover the rates, you see. I know there's not much furniture up there, but Jenny said you had some lovely things. Of course you could bring anything you like. I have to let them as furnished in case I ever have to get anybody out.'

It all seemed very simple and straightforward, but it wasn't. He didn't feel he knew Anne well enough to mention Jenny's reluctance, and anyway, it was a big decision, and he needed time to think about it. He said again that he would think it over. Jenny had gone straight into the garden and was playing with Andrew.

'Are you taking Jenny out tonight?'

'I can't, tonight. I've got to see a friend.'

'Oh. Well, I think she thinks . . .'

'I'll go and tell her.'

Jenny had made a house for Andrew out of two chairs and the tablecloth. Andrew was inside it, and Jenny was ringing the bell and asking if Andrew was at home. She stopped when Gavin approached, and he saw her face close up in the same way that it had when they'd been upstairs . . .

'I'm sorry Jenny, that I didn't tell you before, but I can't manage this evening. I've got to go and see someone. To do with the friend I saw last night,' he added.

'That's all right. You never said we were doing anything this evening, anyway.'

'Would you like to come tomorrow?'

'All right: yes.'

'I've got to clean the house up a bit before my parents get back. Shall I ring you up when I've done that?'

'If you like.'

Andrew had come out of his house and was now clinging to her dress.

'Jenny, is something the matter?'

But she answered violently: '*Nothing's* the matter.' She picked Andrew up in her arms and gave him a fierce hug. 'Come on, Andrew. Let's see Gavin off, shall we?'

He said good-bye to Anne who was arranging his tulips in a jar and Jenny walked to the door with him with Andrew. He picked up Andrew's hand and gave it a little, friendly shake, whereupon Andrew shut his eyes and buried his face in Jenny's neck. 'Thank you for lunch,' he said, 'it was great.'

'It was nothing.' She sounded a shade – but not very much – more friendly.

In the car, he realized that it was only just after four: he had nearly two hours before his appointment with Joan. So he drove across Hyde Park, stopped the car by the Serpentine and went and sat in the sun for a bit. What *was* the matter with Jenny? It was irritating of her to keep saying nothing, when there clearly *was* something. The lunch had been thoroughly enjoyable; they'd talked about all sorts of things; he'd learned quite a bit about Jenny's childhood – in Buckinghamshire when her father had been alive. They'd talked about different parts of the country, the animals that Jenny used to have – she took after her father, Anne had said: good with animals and children. He'd liked her mother: she seemed very young to be a widow, and he gathered obliquely that the last few years had been far from easy. Everything had been fine until when? When Anne had mentioned the *rooms* to let – that was it. Jenny had changed then, and she certainly hadn't changed back. Perhaps she really didn't want him to have them, but felt she couldn't say so. That might be it. But, since he was far from sure himself whether he did want them, he felt that she was coming on rather strong too soon about that. And perhaps she'd been more upset than she'd let on at his not seeing her for the second night running. She probably *had* been banking on tonight. This made him think of Harry, and wonder how he was getting through the day. Then he started worrying about the meeting with Joan, and whether he would handle it right, and get her to *see* about Harry. Well, all he could do was try, and he was glad that he hadn't told Harry he was going to, because it would then be doubly awful if he failed.

He was shown into the library by a Filipino who invited him to sit down and then vanished. He didn't sit: by now his mouth was dry and he felt extremely nervous. He looked round the room, which looked exactly the same as it had when he had played the Secrets game with her such a long time ago. He wandered about: the picture of Dmitri was still on the vast desk. This was also the room where Winthrop had beaten up Spiro and there was the painful piece of the mantelpiece that had nearly knocked him out. The artificial logs were back in their studiedly casual positions. And that was the door through to her bedroom. As he recognized this, it opened and Joan came through it. She was in full regalia; orange wig, a white face, a dark green satin tube dress with dark green satin sandals, and a brighter, dark green nail varnish.

'Why – hullo,' she said, as though he wasn't the person she expected to see but never mind – a kind of genial indifference that he found chilling.

'Hullo, Joan.'

'Yes: well, we'd better have a drink. Whatever you've come about, it's bound to make things easier.' She went over to the drinks table and picked up the brandy bottle. 'I'm having my usual. Will that do you?'

He thought he'd said yes, but she couldn't have heard him, because she turned round holding the bottle as a query: he nodded. She gave him his glass and, taking her own, sat in a large, high-backed chair, indicating that he should sit on the sofa . . . 'Well, cheers,' she said. 'You've been calling me up quite a bit, haven't you?'

'Yes. I was worried.'

'What was worrying you?'

'I heard about Dmitri.'

'Oh, yes. Everyone seems to have heard about that.'

There was a silence. Then he said: 'I wanted to tell you that I knew that was very important to you and I was sorry.'

'It *was* bad luck, wasn't it? I thought he'd stay because of my money, but he managed to find someone even richer than me. I hadn't bargained on that.'

'Is that really what you thought?'

'It is really what I thought. But it's not all that I really thought.' A spasm of what he guessed might be pain crossed her face, leaving it hard and bland. Then she said: 'But I don't think that's all you wanted to see me about. I have a feeling you may have come to see if the coast was clear?'

He opened his mouth to say, 'No,' but then he remembered that it had crossed his mind that comfort might have taken the form of another extraordinary night with her, and felt trapped.

'I have to tell you that it isn't,' she said – she had been watching him – 'or perhaps it would be more true to say that there is no coast.'

He waited, and she went on:

'You would be surprised at the number of people who have wanted to take Dmitri's place. I had to leave France to escape some of them, and I'm leaving England to escape a whole lot more.'

'I'm not one of those people,' he said, surprised at discovering this, and certainty about it making him suddenly very clear.

350

'I thought that. But then you are somebody who'd make the stakes so high, you'd never play.'

'What do you mean? What are you talking about?'

'Love. You're all for love, aren't you? And that's so difficult and precious and important, that it lets you out of being *for* anything.' The way in which she said it made it unpainfully acceptable – simply true.

'Yes,' he said, and found he was smiling at her. 'I hadn't thought of that.'

'Time for another drink.'

But, while she was getting them, he remembered what he was really here *for*, and the feeling of ease which he associated with any length of time spent with her began to evaporate.

The moment she gave him his drink, he knew he had to plunge in.

'I have come about something else.'

'Right.' She sat down again, crossing her long legs.

'I've come about Winthrop.'

'Oh yes?' She seemed mildly surprised.

'The chap he was living with happens to be my best friend: Harry.'

'Yes, I know. You all came to the party together, didn't you?'

'You *know* about Harry? Well then, why are you taking Winthrop away?' As she sat motionless, regarding him but not saying, he plunged on: 'Harry *loves* Winthrop. He really loves him! It's breaking his heart. Perhaps you didn't know that. I expect Winthrop played that part of it down. I expect he's just so keen on the excitement and living it up with you – America and all that – he didn't bother to tell you about Harry.'

'Of course I know that he's left Harry. That's nothing to do with me.'

'It *is*! Of course it is! He wouldn't have gone if it wasn't for you!'

351

'Did Harry send you to see me?'

'No. He doesn't know anything about it.'

'Then, what's your point?'

'My point is,' he was beginning to feel angry, 'that surely, once you know that you're breaking up somebody else's life like this, you surely won't go on with it. *You* aren't in love with Winthrop, are you?'

She said, 'I'm in love with Dmitri.' She said it without any expression.

'Well then, you must have some idea of what Harry is feeling like.'

'I'm sorry for him,' she said, after a pause. 'Of course.'

'Is that all you can say?'

'What else is there? What else could *you* find to say to *me*? And what difference would it make anyway, whatever you said? As a matter of fact,' she went on, 'I'm not particularly keen on pity. Pity takes something away from grief. People think they're sharing it, but really they're just taking some. I prefer to keep my grief intact.'

'Look,' he said, 'you said that Dmitri had managed to find someone even richer than you. That's what you said.' He felt uncomfortable about repeating it, it sounded so hard on her. 'Well, don't you see that you're doing exactly the same thing to Winthrop? Providing him with someone much richer than Harry who can give him a more exciting time?'

'Yes – that's perfectly true. But you seem to have forgotten one very important thing.'

'What's that?' He didn't know, and he didn't want to know, because already he had the sense that it would be annihilating.

'You've left Winthrop out of it. You haven't counted him at all. You haven't, for instance, considered that he must want to go. That if it wasn't me, it would be somebody else. The result would be the same for Harry. People usually find what they seek, if they really search for it. But they also often start by knowing what they *don't* want. Dmitri didn't want me.

352

Winthrop doesn't want Harry. You see? It's quite simple, really
– devastating but simple.'

There was a long silence. Then, he said hesitantly: 'But is it
going to make *you* happier to take Winthrop away with you?'

'I shouldn't think so, for a moment. He's a companion;
and a ranger.'

She had been staring into her empty glass. Now, without
lifting her eyes she said:

> 'They flee from me, that sometime did me seek
> With naked foot, stalking in my chamber.
> I have seen them gentle, tame, and meek,
> That now are wild, and do not remember
> That sometime they put themselves in danger
> To take bread at my hand; and now they range
> Busily seeking with a continual change.'

'Do you know that?' Her voice was husky, so low he could
hardly hear her.

'It's a poem of Wyatt's, isn't it? I don't know it well.'

'I can't get it out of my mind. That's just the first verse. I
don't think I shall be *happy* with Winthrop, but I think that
with him, or perhaps through him, I shall know a little of what
it feels like to be Dmitri. That's as near as I can get now, you
see.'

She was looking at him and, although nothing about her
seemed in the least like him, he was reminded of Harry.

'I think I'd better go now.'

She got to her feet at once. 'Yes.'

She went with him through the large hall to the door. At
the door, she said: 'I admire you for coming. I hadn't forgotten
you. Read the second verse of that poem sometime.'

He pressed her hand, and, on second thoughts, kissed it.
'Good luck,' he said. It seemed a hopeless, but the only, thing
to say.

In a second, the door was shut gently between them, and he turned to walk slowly down the stairs.

He sat in the car for some time without thinking of anything very much at all. Feelings for Joan – of nearly every possible kind – were uppermost, but they were in such confusion that he could not use them with his mind. Most of all, he felt that he was not going to see her again, and knowing that something was over was different to discovering later that it had ended. He had only met her three times, but each time she had affected him deeply. He felt a kind of love for her for that.

He started to drive northwards. Coming out of the Park he thought that he would like to go and see Jenny: he now had the evening free, and he wanted to get things right with her, or, at least, find out what was wrong. Then he thought, no, they might think that he wanted supper when he'd already had lunch with them, and he didn't want an evening with Jenny's mother as well. He began aiming for home; then he thought that perhaps he'd better pass by Harry's, in case he was back and by himself. He was aware of half-hoping that Harry wouldn't be there, but when, in fact, he stopped outside Havergal Heights and saw that all Harry's windows had no lights, he felt both relieved – and depressed.

The house *was* getting rather dirty – even he could see that. He didn't feel hungry, so he made himself a cup of coffee and went upstairs to find Joan's poem. Wyatt – he knew he had it in an anthology somewhere. He found it and read the second verse aloud to himself.

> 'Thanked be fortune it hath been otherwise
> Twenty times better; but once, in special,
> In thin array, after a pleasant guise,
> When her loose gown from her shoulders did fall,

And she caught me in her arms both long and small,
Therewith all sweetly did me kiss
And softly said, "Dear heart how like you this?" '

He was back in the firelit room with her in her loose, grey-green robe. She hadn't forgotten him. He felt tears come to his eyes, and he read the verse again. The poem was called 'Remembrance'. He had to read the rest of it.

'It was no dream; I lay broad waking:
But all is turned, through my gentleness,
Into a strange fashion of forsaking;
And I have leave to go of her goodness,
And she also to use newfangleness.
But since that I so kindly am served,
I would fain know what she hath deserved.'

She had said nothing about the last verse.

It was odd, he thought, how moved he could be by something that he did not thoroughly understand: for the end of it seemed to him almost deliberately enigmatic – could be taken as profound bitterness, or as some kind of fatal resignation. All he could be sure of was that it touched him; conjured the mystery and passion of a long dead poet's long dead love.

He shut the book and, as he did so, it occurred to him that he would one day read that poem to Jenny. Then, without any warning, and almost reluctantly, he supposed that he must love Jenny. He stopped at this: in some ways the idea was not credible; he had none of the feelings about her that he had read about or imagined having; she was quite an ordinary person really, not particularly anything; in fact he couldn't think of anybody who was *so* not particularly anything as she.

When he arrived at her house and rang the bell, he had

made up his mind to say that he wanted to take her out – to dinner, or to a pub, or somewhere. He'd manage to sweep her off somehow.

The door was opened by Anne, or Jenny's mother.

'Oh, it's you,' she said. 'Come in. I'm afraid Jenny's out,' she said as they went into the kitchen.

'Out?'

'Yes; it is funny, isn't it? But she said she wanted to see a French film. She hardly ever does that kind of thing, but I wanted to be in anyway because of a telephone call so it didn't matter.'

They sat down each side of the kitchen table which he now remembered he hadn't offered to help carry back into the house.

'I'm just heating up some baked beans. Would you like some?'

'Thank you.'

She pulled a cigarette out of a battered packet and lit it from her last one.

'I know: I'm chain-smoking. It's very bad. Shall we finish the gin? There's not much left, and we don't usually drink it, but one way and another I feel like one tonight.'

'A small one for me.'

'It'll be a small one for both of us: never mind.' She found the bottle and poured them drinks. As a matter of fact, Gavin, there's so little left because I don't mind telling you I've had one already. I'm trying to make up my mind about something – and it's impossible: I don't seem to . . . be able to.'

He realized that she was very near tears: 'Oh, God,' he thought, 'this is all I need,' and then felt ashamed.

'Are you serious about Jenny?'

'Serious?'

'You know what I mean. You may think it's none of my business to ask you, but I've a very good reason.'

'I – I care about her – what happens to her, I mean. I'm sort of getting to know her – finding out – '

'Oh!' she said. 'You are alike!'

For some reason, this annoyed him. 'What's your reason?'

Instantly, she became more serious, as he noticed people usually did about their own affairs. 'Someone's asked me to marry them. Chap I used to know when we were in Wendover. He was a policeman then: now he's in the Army. That means living wherever he happens to be stationed.' There was a pause, and then she added: 'He's given me a month to make up my mind.'

'And, if you go, you'll feel you're letting Jenny down?'

She nodded miserably. 'I *know* I will be. She can't bring up Andrew and get a decent job; at least not until he's older. She can't come with me. And I don't think she'd hear of my taking Andrew, even supposing George was willing.'

'But, you want to go, don't you?'

She said: 'I never thought I'd want anything as much again.' She took off her glasses and fumbled for a handkerchief.

'She's had such a hard time! We shouldn't ever have let her go off on that holiday so young! But I thought it was a kind of school thing. Of course it wasn't. And then she got knocked up in one go! She only went with him the once. "You don't want to have it," I said, "not at your age," but she wouldn't budge. I thought she'd get him adopted, but not she! And of course, once he was there, we wouldn't either of us have parted with him . . . She's had no youth, really. When we moved to London, it meant she lost all her friends, and anyway she's never had the time for herself; it's been nothing but work and looking after the boy . . .' She blew her nose furiously several times and groped for her cigarettes.

When he had lit one for her, he said: 'Is that why you offered me the rooms? So that there would be someone around?'

'Well, it did seem an idea. But it's upset her; I don't know why. That's why she's gone out actually; we nearly had a row about it.'

'Because she doesn't want me to have them.'

'I can't make her out. She thinks the world of you. I don't know what's got into her. Of course, she's very nervous about men. I expect you knew that.'

He thought about that; yes, he did know, but he didn't say anything.

'Well, I can't take the rooms if she doesn't want me to, can I?'

She looked at him and then, with a mixture of defeat and exasperation in her voice, said: 'I really don't know.'

She got up then, and started slicing bread and opening a tin of beans which she put into a saucepan.

He sat and watched her. He had the sense that events, other people, life generally were all combining to corral him into a decision, that, whatever else it might turn out to be, should surely initially be a matter of private free will . . .

'Jenny would have the house,' she was now saying, 'and there's a little money that her father left me. I could let her have that; or at least the income from it till Andrew's older. With the rooms let, she should just about manage.'

'You've made up your mind to go, haven't you really? You really know you're going to go.'

'I know I want to. I'll have to talk to Jenny about it.'

'She knows. She told me about it several days ago, when your chap was staying here. But then she thought you didn't mean it, because you didn't say anything after he left.'

She put his plate of baked beans in front of him and sat down with hers. 'Why didn't *she* say something?'

'I expect she was waiting for you. When you mentioned the rooms at lunch, she guessed you were thinking of going after all.'

'Oh dear.' But she went on eyeing him; as though she was willing him to find a solution.

He didn't want to eat: he'd come to see Jenny; now he wasn't sure that he could face her – not tonight, anyway, he decided; he felt confused, obstinate, and out of sorts; he was sorry for Jenny's mother and he wanted to blame her for everything going wrong . . . He said that he thought he'd go, and added that he would ring Jenny in the morning. 'Sorry about the baked beans,' he said, 'but I'm not hungry.'

She came to the door with him, apologizing in a general sort of way, and, now he was leaving her, he felt able to be more generous.

'It's not *your* fault,' he said, 'I see you have a difficult decision to make . . . Don't worry: something will work out.'

He drove a little way down the street towards the main road, and then stopped. He couldn't leave things like this. He stopped the car and waited for Jenny to return.

He had nearly fallen asleep, and had just got out a cigar to keep him awake when he saw her, walking quickly on the opposite side of the road towards him. He honked the horn, once, gently; saw her look towards him, square her shoulders and walk faster. He wound down his window and called her.

'Goodness! I didn't think it was you.'

'Get in for a moment, will you, Jenny? There's something I want to say to you.'

He opened the door for her and she slipped into the front seat beside him. She was wearing a heavy knitted jacket over her dress, and her hands were plunged in its pockets.

'I know why you were upset today. You thought your mother had decided to go, and was trying to get me to rent the rooms so that she would feel all right about going. Right?'

'Right.'

'Well, now – listen. What I'm going to say is a bit difficult, but I want to tell you exactly what I mean, and I really want you to hear what I say. *Exactly* what I say,' he repeated. She looked at him then, her eyes solemn and attentive.

'All right. I hope I can,' she said, 'understand you, I mean.'

'And you won't interrupt me.'

'I won't.'

'I care about you very much, I think I've fallen in love with you. But I wanted more time to be sure. I feel we're sort of being pushed into things, and that makes me unsure about whether I'll ever be able to find out. Also, I've no idea how *you* feel about me. I know you like me and we get on well when I'm showing you things – and working together, but I don't mean just that. What I feel is – if we sort of knew how each other felt, we could sort out the rest; or even if we knew how each other didn't feel,' he added, and then he couldn't think of any more to say. There was a silence.

Jenny said: 'You finished?'

'For the moment, yes.'

Then she said: 'I feel a bit like you. Well, really, quite like. And I thought that about Mum and the rooms. I felt she was pushing us and it made me feel so angry – and sad. I mean, how can we know?'

'We haven't known each other for very long.'

'Three years,' she reminded him, 'but I suppose you can't really count most of that.'

'No. I didn't meet you properly until that day when you were talking to the ducks.'

'And you were wearing your olive green sweater.'

'Was I? You were in your white mac: I remember that. In some ways we've only known each other about a week.'

'I suppose so.'

'I mean – deciding who you're going to spend your life with is a terrible decision.'

'You never said anything about *that*!' she said.

'Oh – well, I sort of took that for granted. *If* we found we liked each other – got on generally – it might lead to that. It might. Probably take a long time though,' he added: he wished she'd say something *positive*.

'I suppose so.' She didn't sound very enthusiastic – rather forlorn.

'You see – it's not just a question of liking – it's far more than that in the long run.'

'What more is it?'

'It's a question of love,' he said cautiously, 'total commitment – of one kind or another.'

She said, 'I don't believe in people being unfaithful to each other. If that's what you mean,' and started blushing.

'I don't believe in that, either. But ideally, of course, one shouldn't even *want* to look at anyone else. And people seem to find that quite difficult. The other thing, of course, is that the love should be mutual – '

'Why do you keep saying "of course"? Is it because you think I won't agree with you, or aren't you sure whether you mean whatever you're saying?'

'It's because I want us both to agree with me,' he said, and suddenly felt – a fraction more – light-hearted.

That didn't last. She turned to him, and laid a hand on his sleeve. 'Listen, Gavin. I'm not at all sure that I'm up to it: your idea of love, I mean. After all you've been saying, I still don't know how you feel about *me* – so I sort of feel I don't know where I am. It all sounds a bit calculating to me.'

'Yes, but what I'm doing is trying to cut down on the risk.'

'That's it,' she said. She spoke slowly, as though she was trying herself to find out what she meant. 'But I don't think loving somebody works like that. I only know about Andrew. But I couldn't plan how marvellous he was going to be before I had him. I just had to take the risk. And that really meant loving him whatever he was.'

As always, when she spoke of Andrew, her maturity struck him, in this case to silence. She knew far more about love than he did. Perhaps she loved Andrew so much that she didn't need anybody else.

'What do you think we ought to do?' he asked.

'It sounds as though we shouldn't do anything. Until you've made up your mind.'

'Till *I've* made up my mind – what about you?'

She said: 'Do you know what you sound like? You sound like Peter – with Hazel. A Five-Year Plan for everything. Plan, plan, plan and never leave anything to chance. They made us both laugh – do you remember? If we never take a chance, we'll never know, will we?'

'I only asked you how you felt. Jenny, *do* help me: I really want to know.'

She turned deliberately to face him, took off her glasses and rolled her eyes, shrugging with the mock-comic gesture he knew so well. Then she put her thin arms round his neck and gave him two kisses – a short firm one, and a much longer one. She drew a little away; her eyes, luminous and warm, looking into his, and the rest of her trembling. 'How did you like that, then?' she said.

It was no dream.